"You spend the ni[...] [...]ol as you please to a da[...] [...]'re still married to th[...] [...]leave him? I can assure you that from where I was standing the two of you looked awfully cozy."

"What on earth are you talking about?"

"I happened to walk into the Palace Hotel at lunchtime today. Unless I'm much mistaken, you were on a sofa by the window of the lounge smiling at someone who was kissing your hand. You didn't seem too upset about it."

She drew back, shocked at just how angry he was. "Harlan came here to try and persuade me to return to Savannah—he's worried that my absence makes him look bad. I told him that wasn't an option right now. We had lunch and now he's leaving again."

"Do I look stupid, I wonder?" Johnny asked conversationally, hands stuffed in the pockets of his corduroys.

"No, you look jealous," she retorted, matching his tone. "And with no reason to be."

"Jealous? Ha! That's a good one. Why on earth would I be jealous? After all, we're just having a holiday fling, aren't we?"

"Yes. I suppose we are," she replied quietly, looking him straight in the eyes.

"If that's what you really feel, then I agree wholeheartedly," he responded stiffly.

FIONA
HOOD-STEWART

Southern Belle

MIRA®

ISBN 0-7783-2078-2

SOUTHERN BELLE

Copyright © 2003 by Fiona Hood-Stewart.

www.MIRABooks.com

Printed in U.S.A.

To Carter Parsley,
the other Southern Belle
With love

ACKNOWLEDGMENTS

Many thanks to all those who have helped me while writing this book. To Remer and Susan Lane, Howard and Mary Morrison, Remer and Christina Lane and Fran Garfunkel of Savannah, Georgia, for their generous hospitality and helpful input. To Bill Riley for the reference to the Samovar, which he told me over dinner at a castle in Switzerland, and last but not least to those whom I share my life with and who patiently bear with my writing every day: John, Sergio and Diego. As always my thanks to my editor Miranda Stecyk and the team: Dianne Moggy, Amy Moore-Benson and Donna Hayes.

Part I

1

The much awaited rain—the rain everyone had been praying for, because the drought had been so bad—poured heavily down in doleful drops, battering the roof, dripping from the tiles and the gutters, past the windows of the wide, netted porch, before streaming relentlessly onto the grass. Within a few hours the yellowing lawn was nothing but a broad, soggy puddle stretching down to the Ogeechee River, giving the plantation's freshly planted gardens an abandoned, almost forlorn look.

Curled in the rocker in the enclosed section of the porch that had once served as the nursery, Elm MacBride stared blindly out the window, her fingers tweaking the tiny red shutters of the well-worn dollhouse that dated back to the turn of the century. Only a week earlier she'd sat in this very spot, begging for rain. Old Ely—whose great-granddaddy was the trusted slave who'd helped her ancestors save the Hathaway family fortunes by stashing gold in the plantation's well—had talked about it day after day for a month, how the land was too dry, how the garden so desperately needed it. Yet now, as she stared at the rivulets tracing irregular patterns down the windowpanes, her mind overflowing with the bewildering events of the past few days, the rain seemed strangely irrelevant.

What did seem relevant was just how blind she'd been—

how profoundly dim-witted and completely oblivious to the affair her husband had apparently carried on right under her nose. She shifted restlessly, still trying to assimilate Harlan's betrayal—and the fact that he'd had the gall and total lack of sensitivity to drag her through the humiliation of adultery within their own circle. She swallowed a suffocating rush of shame and frustration and brutally reminded herself that she'd needed a snide remark from the woman her husband was sleeping with before she'd realized what was going on.

The corner of the tiny shutter dug into her palm and she drew her tense hand quickly away from the miniature house and its many memories. In her anger, she'd almost crushed it. Taking a deep breath, she straightened her stiff shoulders and blinked. That Harlan had taken a mistress was inexcusable. But worse, she reflected, cringing, was learning that he didn't care that she knew.

At first, just thinking of him in bed with Jennifer Ball, her all-time nemesis since play school, had left her feeling physically sick. Then, once she'd mastered the nausea that rose in her throat after hearing Jennifer mention blithely at the tennis club that Harlan was "a great fuck," she'd carefully finished her lunch, signed the club voucher and driven back to their town house, determined to confront him.

She'd found Harlan in the bedroom, straightening his tie in the gilt mirror above the mantelpiece. Their eyes met in it before he turned, checked his cuff links and prepared to leave for his congressional office.

"Hey," he'd murmured noncommittally, the practiced smile not reaching his eyes.

"Hey." Elm had felt strangely nervous, as though the man before her was a stranger and not her husband of twelve years. She'd watched, disbelieving, as he'd stood, arrogantly at ease by the pocket windows, and chitchatted as if nothing were amiss, when surely Jennifer had called him, crowing about her run-in with his stupid wife. He'd even remarked that they were expected for dinner at the Thomas-Leighton house that evening, to please not forget to send flowers; the same things he always remarked upon in that slightly cynical, somewhat patronizing tone she'd become used to.

Elm had watched as he'd picked up his briefcase, bereft of speech, desperately trying to summon up the feverish flood of abuse—so alien to her nature it frightened her—that she'd prepared on the drive home, and been ready to hurl at him.

But the words just wouldn't come.

Then, before she could gather herself, he'd flashed her a calculated smirk—one that said he knew she knew, but also that he doubted she had the guts to do anything about it—and left the room before she could find the language to hold him back, to ask him why. But the message couldn't have been clearer: he expected her to ignore what had happened and get back to being a dutiful wife.

And there was the crux of the matter, she realized bitterly, gripping the well-worn arms of the old chair and rocking rhythmically. It wasn't so much Harlan going to bed with another woman—though that had hurt dreadfully—particularly as it was only six weeks since she'd subjected herself to one last, unsuccessful in vitro fertilization treatment. Or that their sex life—the one area of her tottering marriage she'd desperately wanted to believe had remained intact—was clearly a sham. It was the knowledge, the glaring recognition, that the man she'd known for as long as she could remember had little or no respect for her.

And so she'd run to the plantation, to the welcoming safety of Oleander Creek, to hide from the harsh new truths about her marriage. It was what she always did, she reflected, angrily pitching a faded, flowered cotton cushion across the room. And worse, in the five days she'd been here, she'd solved nothing. All she'd done was ask herself repeatedly why her husband was risking their marriage—and his political career—for the sake of a white-hot affair, right here in Savannah, the community that had twice elected him to Congress.

Elm's hand dropped in her lap and the chair stopped rocking. What had she expected from him? Embarrassment? Defensiveness? Shame? That she would have understood, could have tried to deal with—might even have made an attempt to bridge the gap and mend the rift.

But he'd demonstrated neither. She'd reviewed the scene repeatedly since that awful morning, and realized that his complete lack of emotion or contrition had turned the ache in her heart numb.

It had also cast a healthy damper over her prickly rage.

Nothing seemed important any longer, neither the facts nor the words nor her stunned feelings. In fact, she'd spent the better part of the week in a haze.

Then, finally, this morning she'd woken with a new focus for her fury: herself. Elm Hathaway MacBride, who at thirty-four years old should know a damn sight better, still hadn't taken any action, had done nothing to alter the status quo, she reflected with disgust. It was especially galling to know that was exactly what Harlan was counting on.

It was as though she'd been fast asleep and someone had abruptly drawn back the drapes, exposing her to harsh, glaring light. At first she'd blinked, then all at once she'd seen clearly, realized that it wasn't only Harlan she despised, but herself for having lived for twelve long years like a myopic mouse, making pathetic excuses for his absences, justifying his late nights at committee meetings, applauding his campaign-planning reunions, in a desperate desire to pretend everything was fine. Now, as she sat swaying in the rocker, arms hugging her slim, T-shirted torso, she felt more than just hurt or betrayed; she felt foolish.

For a few moments Elm tried to clear her mind by listening to the rhythmic sound of pattering rain, that relentless, decadent, passionate Southern rain that could rant and rave like a banshee, weep till it tore out your soul, make you yearn as it dripped sensually from trailing Spanish moss perched on the ancient branches of the live oaks that bordered the house and the lawn, and stretched on and on, all the way down to the river. Turning, she gazed out across the property toward the Ogeechee, aware that it was in the same state she was: bursting and about to overflow. Yet even as she whipped up her anger again it felt suddenly remote, as though in the past few hours she'd distanced herself mentally and physically from what, only yesterday, had represented a major disaster. Perhaps, she considered thoughtfully, it wasn't quite as catastrophic as she'd first imagined.

She glanced at her watch. It was nearly 2:00 p.m. Tracing a pattern on the faded carpet with the toe of her loafer, Elm faced the truth: her well-ordered world had been turned upside down, and the protective barriers she'd so carefully built around herself had collapsed as thoroughly and dramatically as an imploded building. Worse, this dreadful lack of inner peace she was experiencing would continue to haunt her until she took action.

Shoving her fingers through her straight, blond shoulder-length hair, aware now that she hadn't washed it in two days, Elm took a long, stark look at the wreckage. It was time, she realized with a jolt, to pull herself together and get a grip, instead of hiding out at Oleander Creek.

Usually her family's centuries-old plantation afforded immediate comfort in times of distress. But not this time. Neither had immersing herself in her painting, the one area of her life that Harlan hadn't taken over and that afforded her not only pleasure, but the beginnings of success, as her landscapes and portraits—usually Southern scenes and people that she captured with a bold, distinctive brush stroke—became increasingly known throughout the country.

But this time, nothing seemed to help.

As suddenly as it had started, the torrential rain slowed abruptly to a trickle, its intense fury spent. Rising quickly from the wicker rocker, Elm knew an urgent need to get outside, to wander around the plantation's grounds, desperate to rediscover the sense of serenity that the place had always brought her in the past. She longed to be enveloped in that hazy, magical soothing cloak of oblivion that always caught her unawares the minute she stepped past the ancient wrought-iron gates of the property.

Moving through the dining room, Elm automatically straightened the Hepplewhite chairs surrounding the wide mahogany table and reflected that since Harlan's betrayal she had experienced no delight at the ancient wisteria covering the Oleander's trellised walls, nor captured that wistful touch of recognition when she'd stepped—as she always made herself—in the crack in the river-mud brick steps where some careless Yankee soldier had smashed his rifle butt almost a century and a half before. Nothing.

Not even a gentle sigh escaped her as she stepped onto the wide porch, home to the balmy breezes that blew softly in from the river, where she'd spent so many dreamy nights of her girlhood, gazing at the full moon shining bright and clear, while moonbeams played a stealthy game of hide-and-seek over the river and the ever-present scent of lavender and thyme seeped gently past the oleander trees and the camellias. Not even the sight of the old canvas hammock, strung up between the two live oaks a few paces from the hunting lodge, had helped one iota. And reluctantly Elm realized that for the first time in memory Oleander Creek had failed her.

Even as this occurred to her, she wondered if it wasn't she who had failed Oleander Creek. The plantation had long been home to people of great courage and initiative, rare individuals who'd faced stark, seemingly insurmountable obstacles with decisiveness and grace. Maybe it withheld its pleasures from those who didn't deserve her.

At the thought, she ran from the dining room, through the study—an addition built in the 1920s by her grandmother—into the hall, and grabbed her jacket, confused. She felt irritable, antsy, shaken and desperate, as though the needle of her compass was suddenly spinning. Opening the front door, she headed quickly down the steps to the old Jeep Cherokee parked on the gravel and shells, unwilling to admit that her safe haven wasn't safe anymore; that the long hours spent churning up trowel-loads of earth in the gardens had resulted in nothing; that slashing swabs of thick, rich, brightly colored oil paint on endless canvases had in no way assuaged her feelings. And that, like it or not, she was going to have to delve inside the closed Pandora's box deep within herself to find the answers.

Letting out something between a huff and a groan, Elm turned the key in the ignition, drove around the flower bed and down the bumpy drive that stretched for two miles before it reached Ogeechee Road, knowing definitively that her world had changed and was engulfed by a wave of nostalgia. Nothing would ever be the same again. She'd only felt this way once before, when her mother had died—robbed, defiled and defrauded. But back then she'd been too little to understand, with no one to blame except cruel fate and the cancer that had taken her mother, two bewildering forces that had seemed too huge to counter.

But this was different.

Now, she acknowledged, veering past the gate and waiting for a break in the oncoming traffic, she had a say in the matter and knew where the blame lay. It was her own damn fault for choosing to remain oblivious, aloof, content to sail blithely along, pretending—to herself and others—that everything in her marriage was just dandy, never once admitting that her life was not quite the picture-perfect postcard she'd tried so hard to project.

Elm shifted gears, sat straighter and peered to her left before turning onto I-16 and heading toward Savannah, reflecting as she gripped the wheel tighter that perhaps if she'd done something about the situation sooner, she might have—

The harsh, urgent honking of an oncoming car made her sit up and swallow as she wrenched the Cherokee back apologetically into her own lane. She must stop being so distraught and take action. After all, things weren't going to fall conveniently back into place simply because she wanted them to. It was too late for that.

A clear stretch in traffic allowed her to put her foot on the accelerator. Glancing down, she glimpsed her old beige Gucci loafers and her smooth feet—still tanned, even though it was early December. That she should notice something as trivial and insignificant as a tan when her life was spinning out of control seemed almost funny. It was also superficial

and ridiculous, she reflected, pinning her attention back on
the road, a knot in her throat. Typical of the person she'd
allowed herself to become.

She let out a small sound of repressed frustration. She
didn't smoke, drank only moderately and didn't chew
gum—that was unladylike. But right now, Elm felt like driving straight to the beautiful mansion featured in *Southern
Living* that she'd shared so dutifully with Harlan for the past
twelve goddamn years and getting rip-roaring drunk.

Instead, habit won and she drove carefully into town and
made her way sedately through the squares and streets she'd
frequented all her life. Waving her manicured hand at Mrs.
Finchely on the corner of Abercorn, she parked neatly in
front of her own garage, turned off the ignition and took a
quick peek in the rearview mirror.

What she saw was a brutal reminder of all that had
changed since she'd last been home. Her dark eyes, such a
contrast with her hair, had rings under them; her usually
healthy skin looked dull. For once she actually looked her
age, she reflected, making a feeble attempt to right the of-
fending hair that fell lank on her shoulders. Not that it mattered, she argued, glancing at her hands—well tended despite the daily contact with the earth and all her work
gardening. Sliding them over the thighs of her beige chinos,
she tried to think. She must talk to someone or she'd go
crazy.

But whom?

Aunt Frances, her mother's sister and her lifelong confi-
dante, was out of town. Anyway, she was an elderly lady
and shouldn't be worried by her niece's problems.

Elm alighted absently from the car, but instead of entering
the house began walking. A passing acquaintance nodded,
and automatically she plastered on the practiced, obligatory
smile of a senator's daughter and congressman's wife, still
wondering who, in the whole of Savannah, she could talk
to.

Really talk to.

Of course there was Meredith, but Elm recalled her friend

mentioning that she was working on a big case, so she'd be too busy right now. But after several steps and a quick review of her long list of acquaintances, she realized, shocked, that there was no one else, simply no one, whom she trusted enough not to broadcast her private hurt, her status as betrayed wife, to the world.

Crossing the road into Forsythe Park, Elm shuddered at the spectacle she would afford. The mere thought of her private life being relayed in murmured confidential whispers at the gym or over chardonnay-drenched lunches at the tennis league was too appalling to contemplate.

Oh, God. Down the street, approaching rapidly, was General Mortimer. He would want to stop for a chat, tell her the weather forecast. Usually she listened, smiled, nodded at the same remarks she'd heard, day in, day out, for years. But not today. Right now she simply couldn't face it. Dipping her chin, Elm hid behind the curtain of long hair, hoping her black designer shades would disguise her sufficiently, and swerved up the nearest path, realizing as she did so that she'd instinctively walked in the direction of Meredith's law offices. For a moment she hesitated, then stopped on the curb and closed her eyes tight shut. She simply had to let loose or she'd explode. However busy Meredith might be, she was the one and only person Elm needed right now.

Opening her eyes once more, she stared past the old-fashioned street trolley packed with eager tourists, necks craning as they hung on to their guide's practiced description of precise locations where *Midnight in the Garden of Good and Evil* was filmed, and walked determinedly across the street. She'd witnessed this scene countless times, typically with good humor, sometimes laced with a mild flash of irritation for the notoriety Savannah had achieved.

But not today.

Today she couldn't have cared less how many tourists invaded the city. She felt strangely detached from her surroundings, could visualize herself—tall, well dressed despite the casual nature of her clothes, waiting to cross the street—like an out-of-body experience.

How many affairs had Harlan had, she wondered suddenly, stepping absently into the street. It was as though, all at once, so much of what she hadn't understood—hadn't wanted to see—made perfect sense. It must have been obvious to all those surrounding her. Yet she'd refused to get the message, refused to face reality inching its way insidiously into her world, had remained trapped like a rabbit in headlights, dazed by Harlan's charisma, her father's ambitious plans for his son-in-law, and her own dogged determination that the marriage shouldn't fail, couldn't fail.

The panicked blast of a horn and the screeching of tires made her jerk up, aghast. She'd wandered into the street and hadn't noticed.

Sending the outraged driver of the enormous SUV an apologetic smile, she hurried to the opposite pavement. *Shit.* That was the second time in under an hour she'd lost all sense of reality. But the pang of—not pain—that was something you endured, something you went through for a worthy cause, and this certainly didn't qualify—but the strange, angry torment she was experiencing, directed as much at her own obtuse need to go on believing in the dream she'd so carefully constructed as at Harlan, wasn't allowing her to think straight. Perhaps she was being ridiculous and this happened to most marriages at some point. But deep inside she knew that, too, was a lie.

By the time she took stock of her whereabouts, Elm realized she was opposite the Oglethorpe Club and Meredith's office. Rollins, Hunter & Mills, attorneys at law, practiced in the magnificent mansion standing on the corner. She crossed the road, carefully this time, and rang the buzzer at the ornate wrought-iron gate, feeling as though someone had pressed the button on a stopwatch and put her life on hold.

2

The buzzer buzzed.

Elm pushed the gate open and walked up the shallow steps to the law office's imposing front door.

As soon as she stepped inside, she was plunged into the high-powered, hectic world of Savannah's most prominent law firm, of successful attorneys barking sharp orders to Mylanta-popping paralegals in high heels and T.J. Maxx power suits. She stood for a moment and studied the pleasant face of the pregnant receptionist sitting unfazed in a bright pink smock behind a large antique desk as wide as she, trilling out the firm's well-established name every few seconds, juggling calls, while anxious, six-hundred-dollar-an-hour clients were put on hold, waiting impatiently to be connected.

"Mrs. MacBride?" Ally, Meredith's rake-thin secretary, halted her sprint down the hallway and stopped, surprise evident on her pallid face. "Were we expecting you?" she asked, an anxious frown appearing as she mentally reviewed the day's agenda.

"No. I don't have an appointment," Elm replied. And for the first time in memory she did not apologize or add *if it's not convenient I'll return another time,* or *don't bother Meredith if she's in an important meeting.* Right now—to use Meredith's language, rather than her own—she didn't give a flying fuck how busy her friend was, she needed to speak with her. Now.

"Right." Ally, immediately businesslike, took charge. "If you'll wait here just one second, Mrs. MacBride, I'll check if she can see you right away. Why don't you take a seat?" She indicated the group of studded leather sofas and armchairs strategically placed in the inner alcove, overshadowed by a gigantic Christmas tree, that looked out over the secluded garden and served as a waiting room.

"Thanks. But I'll just wait here." Elm smiled politely in the poised manner that was a part of her nature, and stayed put.

"Sure. I'll—" Ally smiled nervously, indicated Meredith's door, and after the briefest of knocks disappeared.

"Elm!" A booming baritone echoed behind her and a large palm clapped her on the shoulder. "What are you doing here, young lady?" Ross Rollins, senior partner, ex-state supreme court judge, and intimate friend of her father, Senator George Hathaway, shook her hand with delight. "Well, if this isn't a wonderful surprise. Best get one of those gals in there to find us some coffee." He gestured to the hall at large.

"Actually, I just popped in to see Meredith."

"Sure. Now, tell me, Elm—" Ross slipped a broad arm about her slim shoulders "—how's that handsome husband of yours doing, eh? Getting ready to win another term, I'll bet. A little bird whispered to me that he has some pretty ambitious aspirations this time round. Particularly now that Jeff Anderson's gone," he added, lowering his voice. "Sad he went so young, very sad indeed," the older man muttered, donning a suitably concerned frown for the recently deceased house minority leader. "Still, might just be Harlan's lucky break, mightn't it?"

She was saved from answering by Meredith, who appeared, beige-skirted and white-shirted, on the threshold of her own little empire.

"Hey. This is a surprise." Meredith pecked Elm on the cheek, registering her friend's pale, set face. With a quick word she dismissed Ross, linking her arm with Elm's and sweeping her toward the open office door. "What brought you in here?" she asked, mentally filing the municipal-trash case—it would just have to wait—her bright eyes studying Elm's fixed smile and controlled posture.

Something was obviously wrong, she reflected uneasily. In all the years they'd been friends—and that went back longer than she cared to remember—and not once since she'd begun practicing law, had Elm ever appeared unannounced. She invariably called first, making sure in that soft, elegant, well-mannered way of hers that it was convenient. "Come in. It's good to see you." She smiled more brightly than she felt.

"Sorry not to have called," Elm murmured, following Meredith into her large, square, high-ceilinged room, a maze of stacked legal files, cardboard boxes with their contents labeled in thick black marker, and piles of miscellaneous documents waiting to be filed and delivered to the document bank. The desk was the one orderly area in the entire room.

"What's wrong?" Meredith said as soon as the door closed. She pointed authoritatively at a new gray chair bought last week to replace the sagging green one that had finally collapsed. "You look as if you've seen a ghost."

Elm stared straight at her and remained standing. "Mer, did you know?"

"Know what?" Meredith's brows met in a dark ridge over the bridge of her straight, thin nose.

"That Harlan was having an affair with Jennifer Ball?" Elm's voice sounded almost casual, as though the discovery of her husband's affair with one of Savannah's most notorious divorcées was an everyday occurrence.

"Oh, Jesus!" Meredith sank behind her desk and pushed her glasses back into position. The day she'd long been dreading had arrived. The shit had finally hit the fan.

"Well? Did you?" Elm's black shades stared blankly at her.

"I—look…kind of, okay?" She let out a sigh and again gestured for Elm to take a seat.

"And you never said a word." Elm gripped the back of the chair.

"Look, sit down and I'll explain." She'd always known that one day Elm would suffer a rude awakening from the daydream she'd been living for more than a decade. Just hadn't expected it would happen today.

"Why didn't you tell me?" Elm asked tightly. She sat on the edge of the gray chair and removed her shades. "Why didn't you warn me, Mer? And by the way," she added, her tone bitter, "just who else knows that my husband is fucking Jennifer? Everyone except me, I suppose?"

"Pretty much," Meredith muttered, suddenly wary. Elm never used bad language.

"I repeat, why didn't you tell me?" Elm pinned her mercilessly, her eyes two huge chestnut pools of pain, anger and crushed pride.

"Hell, Elm, how could I?" Meredith burst out, cringing inwardly. Should she have told her? Would it have been fairer?

"You're my friend," Elm bit back, "the only friend I trust in this damn cesspool. But you didn't see fit to warn me. I don't understand."

"Hold it. It's not quite that simple," Meredith countered, leaning forward and reverting to the measured tone she used to announce a lost case to a client. "How could I tell you," she queried deliberately, "what you didn't want to know?"

"Of course I would have wanted to know," Elm countered with a scathing laugh. "That's ridiculous."

"I hate to burst your bubble, hon, but that's not strictly true." Meredith leaned farther forward, elbows posed on the desk. "For twelve years—make it thirteen, if you include your engagement—you've stuck Harlan so high upon a pedestal that you made sure he was unreachable. Even by you."

"That's absurd," Elm spluttered.

"Oh, yeah? Well, why is it, then, that during the entire course of your marriage I have never once heard you criticize him, or even say a single negative word about him?" Meredith asked, eyes narrowed.

"I don't approve of criticizing one's spouse." She grimaced at her prissy words.

"Right." Meredith sucked in her cheeks and nodded. "Very laudable, I'm sure, but at times I have to say I found it hard to swallow. Hell, I love my Tom but I'm always bitching about him."

"That's different."

"In what way?" Meredith quirked an interested brow.

"I don't know—" Elm gestured nervously "—it just is."

"Bullshit. You made up your mind Harlan was going to be Mr. Perfect, then you stuck to that notion through hell and high water, even though I reckon you knew it wasn't working out right from the start," she said shrewdly. "Look, I'm sorry it's happened this way, Elm, but maybe it's time to wake up and smell a megadose of double espresso?"

"It would certainly seem so," Elm murmured dryly, nervously fiddling with the sunglasses on her lap, the bitter truths she'd denied for the better part of her adult life rising in her throat. "I guess I must be plain stupid not to have seen this coming," she said finally. "I must need fucking bifocals," she added, her mouth set in a tight line Meredith had never seen before.

"Don't beat up on yourself." She reached across the desk and touched Elm's icy fingers. "You did it because of the way you are. I've never known you to take on a cause and do a half-assed job. Take the garden project you're working on right now. I'll bet nobody shovels more damn earth than you do, nobody plants more seedlings. Or your exhibitions." She shrugged and smiled. "It's all the same, Elm. You throw yourself into everything you do, give every ounce of your being. Only, sometimes others don't meet your expectations and you're bitterly disappointed. Problem is," she added, picking up a pen and doodling speculatively, "not everyone—and that includes your hubby—has your high standards or is as dedicated and sincere as you."

"Gee, thanks! Knowing I'm an obsessive perfectionist who's blind to the world makes me feel a hell of a lot better."

"Rubbish. You know that isn't so."

"Really? Then how do you explain that Harlan's gotten away with this affair? And I suppose there must have been others. It's only that Jennifer is the first one who couldn't resist the temptation of telling me Harlan's a great fuck! I suppose I should be grateful to her," she added grimly, knuckles strained and white from gripping the glasses, as though crushing them might relieve some of her bewildered anger.

"Not so fast," Meredith countered. "Let's go back and review the circumstances. Right from the start, long before you married Harlan, you'd convinced yourself that he was Mr. Right."

"He was. At least he seemed—right." Elm bit her lip and glanced at the porcelain ashtray on the desk, wishing she smoked.

"For whom?" Meredith's eyes narrowed thoughtfully. "You or Uncle George?"

Elm's head flew up, then she hesitated. She'd been about to protest vehemently, but her friend's words made her stop. She glanced toward the window. Was it true? Had she wanted Harlan to be perfect because her father was so enchanted with the idea of his prospective son-in-law's glittering political future? She let out a long sigh, then met Meredith's eyes straight on. "Both, I guess."

"Exactly." Meredith nodded, satisfied. "Harlan had all the prerequisites of the successful politician—handsome, great charisma, old family. Poor as church mice, of course, but hey, who gives a damn since he's in some way related to Oglethorpe and the founding of Savannah, right?" She enumerated the qualities, ticking them off one by one. "A truly great candidate. Your father's dream boy. The son he never had."

"There was nothing wrong with that," Elm replied defensively.

"No, except that somewhere along the line, having Harlan in the family became more important to him than your own happiness."

"That's not true," Elm lied. "I truly believed I'd be happy with Harlan, and there was never any question of Daddy—"

"I know, I know," Meredith soothed, "he's the other Mr. Perfect in your life. But let's face it, Elm, I remember talking when you got engaged. Christ, you had so many dreams, such focused expectations. Remember all the idealism? How convinced you were that being his wife would be a fulfilling path? That together you would achieve all sorts of worthy objectives?"

"You make it sound all trite and stupid and it wasn't. I really did believe it."

"I know, and I'm sorry." Meredith smiled apologetically. "I didn't mean to diminish your dreams. They were very worthwhile. It's just a pity Harlan never believed in them. Let's face it, babe," she said, leaning back and letting her large leather chair swing, "Harlan never expected to make you an active partner in his politics. Twelve years in, you're still his lackey. Expected to throw great parties and enhance his social status, but shut out of making any significant policy contributions.

"Not that you aren't doing great things on your own—your painting exhibitions are phenomenal, you're becoming known. Hell, that Frenchman—who's supposed to be an international art specialist—Le Souche—who was in town last month even bought one. And working with abused women to restore the gardens at Oleander Creek is one heck of a worthy cause."

"But?"

"Elm, face it. Harlan's reneged on his part of the bargain. He's ignored your input. I mean, has he ever solicited your advice about any aspect of his platform? I didn't see him asking you about whether that massive waste-processing plant he green-lighted would have any impact on the environment. You'd think that since it's just up the creek from your plantation, he'd have sought your involvement on *that*, at least. He's just been using you—and you've let him."

"That may be partially true," Elm admitted grudgingly, regaining some of her poise. "Of course, perhaps if you'd seen fit to tell me all this sooner, I might have avoided some of it," she threw out reproachfully.

"Oh, for Christ's sake, Elm, who are you trying to fool? You know very well you wouldn't have listened to a word I had to say."

"I might have."

"Bull crap."

Elm swallowed, seriously shaken. All these years she'd carried the load of her inadequate, unsatisfying, empty marriage alone, convinced no one but she knew the truth. Now she felt cheated at her own game. "God, I just wish you'd told me how you really felt," she repeated, shaking her head, bewildered.

"Elm, honey, put yourself in my shoes." Meredith let out a gusty sigh. "How could I, in all fairness, turn around and tell you that Jennifer was bragging to anyone who'd listen that she's bagged Harlan MacBride, when it was obvious you didn't want to hear, or want to know, or want to see? Hell, we lunched last week and you were still singing Harlan's praises. The one and only time," she said through gritted teeth, "I ever came close to bursting your bubble was a few months ago, when you were recovering from that last IVF treatment and Jennifer was preening about Harlan taking her to the Cloisters for a romantic weekend."

"I can't believe he did that." Tears of rage and disappointment hurtled to the surface. "How could he?" she uttered suddenly, voice cracking. "How could he have been such a bastard?" She looked away, hiding her face with her hair, as the full implication of Harlan's deceit came rocketing home.

Meredith eyed Elm, wished she could console her but recognized she must make her friend face the whole truth. "He's damn fortunate your father didn't hear about it. Harlan seems to have a knack for getting lucky," she added dryly.

A nasty, creepy sensation stirred in the pit of Elm's stomach. "Go on. Tell me who was in line before Jennifer." She felt sick, yet she was determined to learn every last iniquitous detail.

"Well, she's the first who's really gone around flaunting it, but I understand there've been a few. Most of them were out-of-towners. He had a girl up in Charleston for a while, a secretary at a bank, I believe. He's been very careful. I think this is the first time he's done anything so public. I was pretty surprised. Heck, if something like this hit the tabloids, Harlan's chances of being reelected would be zilch." She held Elm's eyes for a full fifteen seconds, making sure Elm registered the full import of the words that had been in her craw for too damn long. Then she sat back and watched her friend carefully, feeling sad. Elm had been through a hell of a lot and didn't deserve this. She glanced anxiously across the desk.

"How did you find all this out?" Elm said, letting out a sigh.

"Tom told me."

"So, Tom knew. My God. I…Christ, this is all so crazy." Elm rose abruptly, dragged her fingers through her hair, her mind a mess of scrambled wires being gnawed at and shredded by persistent rodents. This couldn't be happening.

"What are you going to do?" Meredith asked slowly.

"Do?" Elm turned, glanced absently past her at the dull cream wallpaper plastered with Meredith's credentials—Old Miss, Harvard and Yale—and asked herself the same question. What was she going to do now that she knew, now that she was fully aware of the facts and couldn't hide behind blissful ignorance any longer? It had taken only seconds for the world as she knew it to fall apart. How long would it take for her to do what eventually would have to be done?

For a moment Elm's pulse raced, followed by a debilitating wave of dizziness. She'd had a few of these bouts lately. In fact, she'd been to see Doc Philips about them and he'd sent her tests to Dr. Ashby, a specialist in Atlanta. But this wasn't the same kind of dizziness, she reassured herself. This was different, caused by fear from the latest onslaught.

A new thought intruded in her already saturated mind. Surely her father, the redoubtable, venerated and oh-so-respected senator, couldn't have known any of this? Surely her father wouldn't have hidden the truth from her all these years? Surely Harlan's political future didn't mean more to him than his daughter's life? Her stomach lurched once more and she swallowed. That was impossible. She refused to believe that her own father could have been aware of Harlan's behavior. He would never have betrayed her, however dearly he hoped to put Harlan in the Oval Office. Or was she just trying to fool herself once again?

She collapsed rigid onto the chair, hands trembling.

"Elm, are you okay?" Meredith eyed her anxiously, wondering if she should get coffee, water or something stronger.

"I want to file for divorce." The words came tumbling out almost as an afterthought, as though someone else were speaking.

"Hey, wait a minute." Meredith sat up, startled. "That's a huge step, Elm. I'm not saying you're wrong, but you'd better think it over very carefully."

"My mind's made up." She sounded strangely firm and resolute.

"But, Elm, the election, the—"

"Fuck the election. I'm through. Get the papers together, Mer. And after I'm gone, you can tell him."

"Elm, I think you should consider the—"

"As of this moment, I'm hiring you as my attorney," Elm interrupted, pushing back the chair and rising.

"I can't. There's a conflict of interest, we're friends."

Elm shrugged. "You figure it out. I won't be here, anyway. I'm leaving."

"Where're you going?"

"To Gioconda in Switzerland. I'll stay with her at her chalet in Gstaad."

"But it's Christmas in two and a half weeks, Elm, you can't just walk out. Think of all your social commitments, the—"

"Frankly, I couldn't give a damn. Just don't let Daddy get a whiff of any of this yet."

"Elm, it's really not a good idea to make this kind of decision in the heat of the moment," Meredith insisted. "Are you absolutely sure this is what you want?" She came around the desk and laid an anxious hand on her friend's arm.

"I have to get out of here. It's the only way, Mer. Call me at Gio's when the papers are ready to sign. Please get it done fast. And thanks."

"For what, screwing up your life?" Meredith shook her head bitterly. "I shouldn't have come on so strong."

"Don't. We both know this had to happen one day. Everything you said was true. I just didn't want to recognize it. And now that I have, there's no way I can sit back and take it as I have all these years." She leaned over and gave her friend a quick hug.

Passing a worried hand through her pageboy haircut, Meredith sighed as she watched her friend leave. Elm was right. It would have come to this, anyway. Still, she was shocked and surprised at the rapidity of Elm's decision. She prayed she wouldn't regret it. She'd expected every sort of reaction—tears, anger, frustration—but not this. Not cold, rigid decision. My God, she realized, collapsing again in her chair, Elm had simply transformed into another being. For a moment she wondered if she should advise someone, even call Harlan or Senator Hathaway, the housekeeper—heck, anyone.

Then she realized she couldn't.

Technically, she was now Elm's legal representative and as such was bound to do what her client had requested: namely, prepare divorce papers and stay quiet about it.

She stared at the file she'd been working on, the legal challenge to the privatization of the Mogachee Municipal Waste Processing Plant, and sighed. Maybe Elm would calm down by tomorrow and realize she was being too precipitate. Not that Meredith blamed her for wanting rid of Harlan as fast as possible. Still, there were a number of things to be taken into consideration. Elm was a very wealthy woman, and the publicity…

Leaning back in her chair, she considered Harlan. He certainly deserved anything he got, even being dumped two weeks before Christmas. Still, she was herself a die-hard Democrat, and the party couldn't afford to lose Harlan's seat to the Republicans. On the other hand, Meredith had to admit, under all that boyish, suave, Kennedy-style charm, Elm's husband was a dirtbag who'd gotten lucky thanks to the old-boy network that functioned on past favors and future dues. She shrugged, wishing she hadn't been the one to confirm what Jennifer Ball, in her unsubtle, vindictive way, had let loose.

She could just imagine Jennifer, with those long, glossy legs she was so proud of, striding arrogantly over to Elm in full view of her less-well-endowed former classmates—now full-fledged veterans of the garden club, bravely fighting any incipient signs of middle age—and baring her capped white teeth at Elm. Jennifer had always loathed Elm, knowing she'd never have Elm's beauty, poise, wealth or privileged position in Savannah society, and she would have made darn sure her little entourage of doting admirers—including Hannah Ramsey, Tiffany Fern, and that two-faced bitch Elsa MacDonald—were present for Elm's humiliation. Jennifer had been divorced twice, and had had several affairs with notable local citizens. Luring Elm's husband to her side was a natural evolutionary step, and one that must have been especially satisfying. Not that Harlan needed much enticement, Meredith reflected grimly. The man apparently had a hard time keeping his pants on.

But divorce. Even she was shocked. After all, Harlan and Elm were an institution.

Did Elm have any idea of all that was on the line? Meredith wondered, concerned. With everything Harlan had to lose, there was no way he was going to take this lying down.

Tapping her pen rhythmically on her yellow legal pad, Meredith thought the matter over. Perhaps in a couple of days, when Elm had calmed down, she could talk to her reasonably, persuade her to wait at least until after the holidays, not make a rash decision in the heat of the moment. And then, if she was still determined to go ahead, then maybe Elm could have it out with Harlan and come to some kind of civilized arrangement. Not that he deserved it. Far from it. But in the long run, it would be better for all concerned.

When the phone rang, Meredith grabbed it as though her life depended upon the call. Anything right now, she figured, even old Mr. Tompson's estate case—which she loathed—would come as a welcome relief.

3

"**B**itch," Harlan MacBride muttered, then slammed down the phone so hard the antique mahogany desk shuddered. Had Elm gone fucking nuts?

Meredith Hunter's words echoed ominously.

Elm wanted a divorce.

It was unthinkable.

He'd never have guessed she had the guts to cross him this way, or that she'd take such a drastic step and then disappear. She'd been missing for days, making things damned uncomfortable for him—he'd only just now learned that she'd hightailed it to Switzerland, to that crazy Italian friend of hers whom he'd never liked, Gioconda Mancini.

Harlan flexed his fingers, eyes narrowed. Fuck Elm. She had no right to do this, no right at all. And fuck Jennifer for having opened her big sexy mouth. She was a great lay, and that tongue of hers could work wonders, but obviously he'd misjudged her ability to keep her goddamn trap shut.

He should have been more careful, he admitted, his lower lip twitching. But all those damn IVF treatments had been such a drag. Worse, he'd had to carry on the pretense of giving a shit—cosset Elm after the implantations, agree to the doctor's recommendation that he stay out of her bed—when he had far bigger matters on his plate. It wasn't surprising he'd let off steam with Jennifer. Any man would have. Elm should be grateful to him for being so understanding instead of flying off in a sulk.

And now she was threatening divorce, he reflected grimly. If he wasn't meticulous about defusing her snit, Elm could spoil his re-election chances. She of all people knew he'd won his House seat on a platform promoting strong, Christian family values. Hell, the goddamn campaign posters that were going out next week showed him holding her hand and surrounded by smiling kids. Not his kids, mind you, he reflected, annoyed.

He shook his head and muttered crossly. Elm was nothing but an unappreciative spoiled brat who should be thanking her lucky stars for having a husband like him, one who, despite the drawback of not having children, had been able to look past the negative and see the potential of the situation. That was something he'd learned early on: how to twist circumstances—however challenging—to his advantage.

Harlan leaned back in the deep office chair and a slow smile crept over his handsome features as he recalled the several newspaper and TV interviews where he'd tearfully confessed that God hadn't seen fit to bless them with kids, how maybe one day he and his wife would adopt. It had worked like a charm. Immediately the family-values freaks and the born-again Christians had come beating down his door, fists full of campaign dollars.

But they'd abandon him in a heartbeat if Elm's allegations ever got out, he reflected gloomily, the smile disappearing as fast as it had dawned. And so would Senator Hathaway's support, he realized, sitting up straighter. Much as he'd prefer to forget it, Harlan knew that, despite his charisma and eloquent Southern charm, it was Elm's father—the influential six-term senator from Georgia—who'd gotten him elected. Hathaway had made phone calls, calling in half-a-century's worth of favors, and the checks had followed. But even more critical was the family connection. Being viewed as the senator's political heir-apparent gave him instant clout. No way could that be jeopardized, he thought, sucking in his lean cheeks, bronzed from a weekend of sailing on his friend Tyler Brock's hundred-foot sloop. There had to be a way around this.

Harlan drummed the desk absently and pondered. At thirty-seven, he was everything old man Hathaway had once been: young, handsome, charismatic. But whereas Hathaway, for all his wealth and clout, had long ago had to content himself with the Senate floor, Harlan possessed that extra something that made him special, that rare and extraordinary political talent that made the White House a realistic goal. They both knew it, and that's why the senator had invested so heavily in him—because Harlan was his ticket to what he couldn't get on his own. No way was Hathaway going to let that dream die.

Of course, it helped that he had no clear idea of what state his daughter's marriage was in; the senator was very protective of Elm. Still, surely he could be made to understand, to see things Harlan's way? It might not be a bad idea to present himself as the injured party here, soliciting his father-in-law's sympathy, he reflected, fingering his Old Miss tie. It all depended on just how much Elm had blabbered.

Despite his nonchalance, he pulled the handkerchief out of his pocket and wiped a thin film of sweat from his brow. Old Man Hathaway was a rigid stickler for form, prided himself on being the goddamn Conscience of the Senate. Elm had to know she could wreak considerable damage with a tearful call to Dear Daddy.

Even as he considered that frightening possibility, he acknowledged that, for all her faults, broadcasting private matters wasn't Elm's style. Plus, Hathaway had been in the dark about his daughter's whereabouts, too. Maybe the better course here was just to come clean—well, not too clean, certainly, just enough to cover his ass in case someone saw fit to inform Hathaway of his son-in-law's little dalliances. He mentally sketched a speech—he'd act repentant, confide in him man-to-man, make the proper excuses. The senator was a player after all, a pragmatist. With any luck, he'd understand and let Harlan off with a scolding.

The idea grew on him. Not that its success was a given—

he'd have to tread carefully. Elm was the old man's only daughter, after all, and however much the senator might like and support his son-in-law, blood ran thicker than water. Particularly, Harlan mused, for someone like George Hathaway.

For a moment he surveyed his elegantly appointed office, the elaborate eighteenth-century frieze, the authentic antiques and Old Master paintings, the gracious bay windows reaching out onto the inner garden so carefully tended by Josiah, the Hathaway family gardener, all part of the image he'd so carefully compiled and cultivated. It was no less than he deserved, of course. Unfortunately, he reminded himself sourly, it all belonged to his beautiful, elusive wife. These offices, the house on Abercorn, were essential to asserting his status. Thank God very few of his constituents got to see that dumpy back office he'd been assigned at the Capitol, a sharp reminder that, in the bigger scheme of things, he still stood on the bottom rung of the political ladder.

But that was on the verge of changing.

If Elm didn't mess up.

He clenched his fingers and stared at the wall, plastered with endless photographs featuring flattering images of himself with everyone from Clinton and Bush to Magic Johnson and the king of Saudi Arabia. The sight soothed his sizzling temper and helped clear his head. He might still be only a junior congressman, but he'd already made many powerful friends and cultivated connections that he was certain would pay off in the future.

However, all that would be seriously at risk unless he fixed his little problem, he reminded himself. It was essential that Elm return. Harlan slumped in the chair and brooded. What did she want? he wondered. The divorce threat had to be a bluff. Still, never in a hundred years would he have imagined she'd go this route. Obviously he'd made a serious misstep in not acting suitably penitent the other morning. He should have realized when she disappeared to Oleander for those few days that something was up. But she was always buried over there, painting those weird canvases that the critics seemed to think were so hot and redoing the gardens with those freaks she'd recruited from the battered women's center.

With a shake of the head, Harlan rallied. He prided himself on crisis control, the power to compartmentalize and find effective solutions for any predicament. The present one required focus and action. He pulled himself up and began making notes on a legal pad, reviewing the circumstances.

Then a slow smile curved his lips, and he tapped his foot rhythmically, beginning to relax. Elm had recently complained of—what was it? Some sort of weird symptoms. Damn it, he couldn't quite remember. Never mind. She'd talked of visiting Doc Philips. *Bingo*. There was his excuse staring him right in the face: Elm was making all the wrong decisions because she wasn't feeling herself.

"Ha!" Harlan let out a harsh laugh and brought his fist down on the desk with a satisfied thud. If he played this right with Hathaway, he might just emerge smelling like a rose. *If* he played it right. It was essential to shoot dead on target.

Closing his eyes, Harlan conjured up the scene that would take place later in the senator's library, silently mouthing his words: Elm wasn't herself, needed help, had some sort of female problem that was affecting her decision-making. Maybe the last failed IVF treatment had hit her harder than they'd realized. He was sorry, so very sorry, he'd done anything to hurt her—his only excuse was that the stress of infertility had affected him, too. He regretted it bitterly, but surely she could forgive one little slip? And by the way, shouldn't they try to do something about this absurd divorce procedure that made no sense at all and that she would obviously regret the minute she regained her health?

He jumped up, excited.

It was perfect.

For a second he thought of the other measures he was implementing that one day, he hoped, would secure him his absolute freedom from the powerful Hathaway clan. But that was farther down the line. It was still too soon, he reminded himself. He shook his head. There was far too much at stake to take foolish risks. He owed it to the electorate to ensure his staying power, didn't he? After all, the future of the greatest nation in the world could not depend on the whims of a slighted woman.

Twiddling his gold fountain pen—the one with which he signed all official documents—Harlan glanced coldly at his wife's beautiful image smiling wistfully up at him from the silver-framed photograph. He would not tolerate her messing with him.

He felt better now that he'd decided on a definitive strategy. He stretched his arms and rotated his neck. Then he caught sight of himself in the gilt-framed eighteenth-century mirror above the marble mantel. Head tilted, Harlan surveyed himself critically. It wasn't just his boyish charm or rueful smile that captured voters, he acknowledged proudly. It was that blazing internal radiance that he'd learned to produce automatically, profoundly conscious of its effect. In simple terms, he had the power to seduce others! It gave him a rush to know he could subject them to his will. In fact, he was increasingly amazed at his own flawless charisma. Each time he spoke he absorbed the crowd's energy, its vibes, steeped himself in the atmosphere, then let the public set him on track, offer him their vision, so that he could pitch what they wanted back to them.

There was always a point—usually about five minutes into a speech—when he captured the audience's response, when he knew the bond had been forged. From then on, it was plain sailing and the gathered electorate was his. And that was his secret weapon—the magic touch that would lead him inevitably to his ultimate goal.

Straightening his shoulders, Harlan jutted his well-defined chin and remembered Jack Kennedy. A sudden vision of himself, ankles casually crossed on the desk of the Oval Office, sent a rush ripping through him. He rocked on his heels and basked in it. Then just as quickly, he stood still. He would get there, all right, but first he must get his ducks in a row.

He glanced at his watch, then at the battery of phones spread on the desk. Better get on with it and set up the appointment right away. There was no point in avoiding what had to be done.

4

Senator George Hathaway straightened the jacket of his immaculate dark suit and pulled from his waistcoat his grandfather's watch, the one that had kept perfect time since before the Civil War. He eyed it narrowly. Harlan was due here at six o'clock. If his son-in-law knew what was good for him, he wouldn't be late.

Crossing the somber library lined with several generations' worth of classics, he settled heavily into his favorite armchair, noting with surprise that his customary copy of the *Washington Post* was missing. Normally the morning edition was always set, freshly ironed, on the delicate side table. Then he recalled the servants had the day off for a Christmas event at the local Baptist church. George Hathaway encouraged churchgoing. He himself attended Christ Church, the oldest church in Savannah, as did Harlan and Elm.

But this past Sunday, Harlan had come to services alone.

At first he'd worried something was wrong with his daughter—Elm had been having strange spells of sickness in recent weeks, and he'd urged her to seek care. But when Harlan admitted that Elm had left Savannah, whereabouts unknown, it raised another disturbing possibility. There were troubling signs that things were deeply wrong in his beloved daughter's marriage.

The senator sighed deeply. In all the years Elm had been married to Harlan, he'd always believed her to be happy. Yet over the past few weeks something inexplicable had occurred and the marriage had clearly suffered. Elm had refused to explain. And now she'd gone away right before the holiday season, without an explanation, leaving no phone number, just a letter saying she needed some time and would call him.

It was irresponsible and selfish behavior, he concluded, shaking his gray head. Surely he'd brought her up to know better? His son-in-law was a fine young man with a promising future in which he himself had invested heavily. Harlan would go far—all the way to the White House, he hoped—but Elm's inexplicable actions could only serve as a hindrance.

Perhaps Harlan was right to think Elm's recent illness was the reason she was acting in a manner so unlike her usual dutiful self. Still, the senator suspected there was likely more to matters than Harlan was willing to admit. He'd heard a couple of rumors, things he'd have preferred not to have heard. Harlan was a handsome young fellow, he reflected, one who held a prominent position in society and a growing political power base, all elements that caused envy and inevitable gossip. They also attracted an inevitable bevy of women. But Harlan was a caring, loving husband. At least he appeared to be. Surely Elm was too bright to be put off by any silly nonsense?

Letting out a huff, he raised his tall frame from the deep maroon leather chair near the fire, too restless to read yesterday's copy of *Congressional Quarterly* and glanced into the hall at the Christmas tree standing forlorn in the corner. Ever since she was a wee thing, Elm had helped decorate it. The only other year the tree had remained bare until just before Christmas was the year Elm turned five and her mother had succumbed to cancer, he recalled with a sigh.

Checking his pocket watch once more, he noted with gathering impatience that it was one minute past six. At that very moment the doorbell clanged. With a small nod, the senator made his way across the marbled foyer floor and opened up the massive polished mahogany door.

"Ah. Harlan, m'boy, come on in."

"Hello, sir." Harlan gave him a tight smile.

Something about Harlan's attitude made the shrewd senator suddenly afraid that his suspicions were right and that he had somehow bungled things badly. He sent him a bland speculative glance before leading the way under the heavy crystal chandelier imported by the first Hathaway in 1820, and across the wide-planked pine floors of the library.

"Any news?" he asked, leaning over a silver tray decked with a splendid array of whiskey-filled Waterford decanters that sparkled invitingly. He poured two heavy cut-crystal tumblers of single malt and turned, handing one to Harlan, who stood, face drawn, next to the Adam mantelpiece.

"We've traced her, sir. She's staying with Gioconda Mancini in Switzerland."

"Thank God for that," the senator sighed, relieved, and sank back into the sagging leather. "I was getting concerned. So unlike her to disappear like this. Very odd." He sipped thoughtfully, never taking his eyes off his son-in-law.

"Well, at least now I know she's safe." Harlan threw back the whiskey in one shot, obviously deeply affected by his wife's sudden disappearance. He glanced at his father-in-law. "I just wish I knew why she felt this sudden need to disappear. I—" He looked down at the carpet, shook his head, then sighed. "I don't understand, sir. I've tried to be there for her, be a good husband. If I'd known she was feeling sick again I'd have gone with her to Doc Philips, but she never told me—"

"Hmm. I don't understand it myself."

"I guess we'll just have to be patient, give her the time and understanding she needs to get over this…this idea she's got in her head," he murmured, lips tight as he stared blindly through the window into the lush garden, past the camellias and the Roman fountain where two starlings perched, eyes fixed on the ivy-covered wall that for nearly two centuries had protected the Hathaways' privacy.

"Well. At least if she's with Gioconda we don't have to worry she'll be properly looked after. We should have thought of Gioconda immediately. It was the obvious place for Elm to go, now that I think about it." The senator eyed Harlan sharply. "You mentioned that she had some idea in her head. What was that, I wonder?"

"Oh, nothing serious. Just malicious gossip." Harlan shrugged dismissively. "They chatter too much over at the Tennis League. Unfortunately, sir, Elm appears to have been listening to some pretty outrageous lies."

"Hmm." Senator Hathaway sent his son-in-law another long, speculative glance. So something *was* up, after all.

"It was stupid of me not to have thought of Gioconda," Harlan said quickly. "I haven't called there, though. I thought—" he looked across at the senator and hesitated "—I thought it would be better to let her take the initiative."

"Perhaps." George Hathaway pondered the matter, not in the least bit fooled by Harlan's effort to shift the conversation. He didn't like it, not one little bit. It was so out of character for Elm to act like this. If Harlan had strayed— and it now seemed possible he had—why hadn't she just talked it over with him, had it out? Maybe sent Harlan to the doghouse for a few weeks, then patched it up, as all women did. And if she was sick, why didn't she stay close to her family? But as he watched Harlan, it was clear his son-in-law had more to say.

"There's another thing, sir." Harlan shifted, plainly uncomfortable.

"Go on," he said dryly.

"I got a call this morning from Meredith Hunter."

"Oh?" Something in the younger man's tone told him this was deeply serious.

"Elm's asked her to file for a divorce."

"Divorce?" The senator's glass came down on the small mahogany table next to him with a heavy thud, and he rose. "Why on earth would Elm want a divorce?"

"I don't know. It's utterly crazy. I could hardly believe it when Meredith spoke to me."

"What did she say?"

"That Elm had asked her to go ahead and prepare the papers," he said bleakly. "I just can't believe it, sir. After all these years. I thought we were happy."

"Are you sure? Something very serious must have occurred for her to take such radical action."

"Okay, we've had a couple of arguments now and then, and, well…I…well, I may not have always been a perfect spouse." Harlan shifted uneasily. "But nothing to merit this, sir, I assure you."

George Hathaway quelled a surge of anger at Harlan's oblique admission of adultery—Elm was his daughter, after all—but even more disturbing was the evidence that his son-in-law had been so foolish. There was too much at risk here to let one's libido rule one's actions, he reflected in disgust. His whole political future could be at stake. Smothering the pithy comments he would normally have delivered, he reminded himself that it was water under the bridge—what was needed now was crisis control. He paused thoughtfully. "Meredith Hunter, you say?"

"Yes. At least she's kept it close to home."

"Thank God for that."

"Elm doesn't seem to realize the implications of what she's done," Harlan ventured, "to all of us." There was a bitter edge to his voice that didn't escape the senator's sharp ears.

"Obviously not. Although it's rather clear you didn't take into account the consequences your, er…behavior might incur, either," he responded sarcastically, sending Harlan that piercing look that had been known to make the most stalwart opposition flinch. "But you and I will address that later. For the present, I think it's best that I have a word with Meredith."

"A word, sir?"

"Yes. This is a mess and we've got to contain it before it goes any further. I've known Meredith all her life. Her father, John Rowland, and I go back a long way, as you know. Perhaps she could be persuaded to delay filing, at least until the New Year. By then we must hope Elm will have had time to reflect on her rash decision and come to her senses.''

''You think she might?'' The hope in Harlan's eyes made the senator soften—very slightly. The boy had obviously been playing around. But, he admitted—honest enough to recall his own political past—it was almost inevitable in a position like his. What mattered was that he clearly regretted what he'd done.

''It certainly won't hurt to try. You leave Meredith to me, Harlan. I'll get in touch with her first thing tomorrow morning.''

''Thank you, sir,'' Harlan said gratefully. ''You'll keep me informed, won't you? I—I'm pretty anxious.'' He straightened his tie, looking uncomfortable and depressed.

''Of course.'' Elm shouldn't have put them in this position, the senator reflected, suddenly irritated. Whatever indiscretion Harlan had committed—and it couldn't have been that bad, or he would have learned of it from his own sources—she had no right to behave this way, no right at all. And just weeks before Christmas, when she knew very well Harlan would be expected to appear at every public function with her on his arm.

''Have there been questions?'' Hathaway lifted a steely brow.

''Well, yes. There have. I've taken it upon myself to say she's resting in a clinic in Switzerland. At least the last part's true, since that's where she is. I hope you think that's all right?''

''Good.'' He nodded, eyes narrowed, quickly setting up a strategy to contain the damage. ''Everybody knows she's been out of sorts lately. At least that should keep the gossips quiet. But not for long,'' he added with a significant look.

''I know. But Elm's health and well-being must come first.'' Harlan's brows drew together, forming an intense line over the bridge of his aquiline nose.

''Very right, m'boy, very right indeed. But she also needs to come back home where she belongs. We can't forget your career, Harlan. You can't afford to make the kind of mistakes that could cost you farther down the line, just remember that. We must take every precaution."

"I know, I—" Harlan rubbed a tired hand over his eyes. "Sorry, I'm kind of tired right now. I guess the last few days I haven't slept too well, that's all."

"I understand." The senator eyed him, bending just a little more. "But I'm sure that in a little while we'll bring Elm about. A few weeks in Switzerland with Gioconda may be just the right thing to cheer her up." He nodded sagely.

"You saying that makes me feel a heck of a lot better, sir. I've been—well, I guess I don't need to tell you how worried I've been the past few days." He gave a tentative boyish smile that expressed far more than words.

"So. What's on your agenda tonight?" the senator asked, feeling it was time to change the subject and lighten up. He'd made his point. Harlan would think twice before being careless again, and it wouldn't do to make the young man any more stressed than he already was. That would only serve to make matters worse.

"I have the Kaplan party, followed by a dinner at the Staceys'. I wish…well, I guess that's neither here nor there."

"Right. How's young Earl Stacey doing these days? Still thinking of joining the party? He could make a good running mate for you in the future, you know." The senator sent Harlan a thoughtful glance.

"You know, it's funny you should mention that, sir. I was thinking the same thing myself as I was driving over here. When I managed to think about anything other than Elm, that is," he added hastily.

"Have another?" The senator pointed to the empty tumbler in Harlan's hand.

"Thanks, but I'd better not." He glanced at his wrist. "I guess I'd better get moving. It's a black tie event so I've got to get home to change."

The senator heaved out of his chair, a tall, well-built man

with fine chiseled features and slate-gray eyes. "I'll walk you to the door. Patsy and Beau are off to church tonight."

They reached the massive door and he turned the heavy brass knob before throwing an arm casually over Harlan's shoulder. "You hang in there, Harlan. And learn from this episode," he said severely. "There's no leeway for mistakes in this business. Remember that."

"Yes, sir."

"What we need now is a lot of faith, a good strategy and patience. I'm sure that in a little while, Elm will see what nonsense this is, come home and all this will be behind us."

"I hope you're right, sir." Harlan answered fervently. "I'd do anything for that to happen."

"Well, just make sure this never happens again." He sent Harlan a brief nod, then watched his son-in-law walk dejectedly down the front steps, past the Roman columns and out into the street where his Cadillac Seville was parked. He seemed chastened, which wouldn't do the young man any harm. He just hoped his optimistic predictions about Elm were correct. He would definitely talk to Meredith about delaying filing in the morning then take it from there.

Harlan slammed the car door shut and sat for a moment in thought. All in all, it hadn't gone too badly. He'd gotten away with it, he reflected gleefully. The old man had given him nothing more than a slap on the wrist, and knowing the senator, he'd talk Meredith into delaying filing for the divorce. Which, in turn, would give him some time to sort matters out.

Harlan turned the key in the ignition and glanced at his mobile phone. He'd call Tyler Brock and tell him the good news. Elm wasn't going to be a problem after all. Still, a wave of unease wafted through him as he drove slowly down the street. There'd been an almost menacing tone in Brock's voice when he'd insisted Harlan get his wife back. He frowned. It was weird. Then he shrugged, and a few minutes later slowed before his home and swung into the courtyard. Pulling the keys out of the ignition, he ran lightly up the steps of the graceful white-columned mansion, a wedding present from the senator to his daughter, and walked through the high-domed hall to the study. There was no sign of anyone. Perhaps the servants were at the Baptist meeting, too, he realized, annoyed. The Southern Baptists seemed to do more churchgoing than anyone on earth.

Closing the door carefully, he moved across the room to the inlaid English cabinet, opened the mahogany door and quickly unlocked one of the thin brass-handled drawers inside. Then he picked up a small enamel box and tweaked open the lid. Tipping a thin trail of white powder onto the back of his hand, he closed his right nostril with the other. After a long, satisfying sniff, he switched to the other nostril before carefully closing the box and slipping it back into the drawer, which he closed and locked.

Harlan stood for a few moments, eyes closed, and rotated his head as was his habit, working the kinks out of his neck and shoulders. The cocaine began to take effect. He felt a sudden rush of clarity. Around him everything seemed starkly etched, the leaves greener in the garden, the tiniest details hitting him in the eye. He could think better, put things into perspective with the greatest of ease, and the slight wave of fatigue he'd experienced earlier disappeared completely. That felt a hell of a lot better, he reflected, throwing his blazer jauntily over the back of the chocolate leather chair and pouring himself a large whiskey, focusing with new intensity on the senator's words, recapping every detail, every nuance of the conversation. Earl Stacey, he reflected with a sneer. As pious as a fucking nun. When he chose a running mate, it would be someone of a different caliber. A player. Not that Earl wasn't a good guy. He was. Just not his style, he concluded, eyes falling on Elm's portrait above the mantelpiece.

He looked at it for a while, as he had earlier the photo in his congressional office, and sipped thoughtfully, feeling strangely detached. Up until now she'd been very useful and he'd never regretted the marriage. Still, if she went on acting up, she might become a liability. He thought of Tyler

Brock's strange words earlier today, then shrugged. He was probably just imagining things, but he could swear the man's tone had sounded almost like a threat. Well, fuck him. Brock needed him. He'd just have to see he remained essential.

Removing his gaze from his wife's picture, he turned his mind to Candice Mercier, that deliciously promiscuous little brunette who'd married old man Mercier not more than a year ago and was already setting her sights on ways of passing the time. Now that Jennifer and her big mouth were out of the scenario, he was only too delighted to oblige. Candice wouldn't cause any trouble—she didn't want to lose her meal ticket. For a moment the senator's words lingered. It was true that he couldn't afford any mistakes. But hell, a man had to live, didn't he? And Elm wasn't exactly a turn-on, what with her IVF treatments and the obsession about having a baby. Heck, he had a hard-enough time getting it up with her. Surely he must be allowed some pleasure?

Upstairs in the large marble bathroom he showered, then rubbed himself in one of the huge terry towels, sleeked his chestnut hair back and flexed his arm. He felt a new surge of energy induced by the cocaine and the shower and turned toward the mirror. He was in good shape, he noticed, pulling in his tummy, glancing sideways, then flashing a satisfied smile at himself. It was a killer smile that had never failed to rake in the votes. Lately, since Elm's disappearance, he'd added an underlying touch of melancholy that would make every woman in the room wish she could be the one to console him. It was sending Elm's ratings plummeting. Serve the bitch right for making a public fuss over something that should have been wrapped up between them.

His clothes had been carefully laid out on the bed. Reaching for his starched shirt, Harlan slipped it on, then did up his engraved cuff links in the lamplight of the huge master bedroom, with its stately mahogany bed and valuable antiques that had Elm and her heritage written all over them. His wife had excellent taste, he admitted grudgingly as he pulled on his pants, eyes narrowing as he approached the mirror to fix his bow tie. But Elm's irreproachable taste reminded him yet again that the house—and every damn thing in it—was in her name, just as were the accounts at the bank. Sure, he had access and was made to feel in charge. But he knew damn well that one false move and the bank manager would be on the phone to the senator so fast he wouldn't have time to breathe.

He adjusted the bow tie, gave it a final twist, then shrugged into the jacket of his tux and took another look at himself, pleased with the effect. Then he leaned forward, making sure his nostrils were free of any traces of white powder. You could never be too careful, he reflected, eyes narrowed. Then suddenly the day's troubles faded and he felt better. He looked good, felt good, was on a fast track to the top. Just as Jack Kennedy had looked good and been on a fast track to stardom. A pity he didn't have Elm to parade on his arm, he thought as he tripped lightly down the stairs, but that would all sort itself out. Elm, like Jackie, would be brought to heel and the waves of discontent would subside once more. Harlan smiled as he popped his cell phone into the pocket of his cashmere coat, threw a white silk scarf nonchalantly around his neck, and left the house.

As he descended the front steps his mouth took on a sardonic twist. Elm and her goody-goody ways. He didn't know what the hell she was up to in Gstaad, and cared even less, probably gossiping with that bitch Gioconda, whom he couldn't stand. But of the two of them, he gloated, he'd bet money he was in for a more satisfying night.

Part II

5

Sweat dripped from under the shock of Johnny's thick black hair, graying at the temples. It trickled past his bright blue eyes, down his lean brown cheeks and settled on his chin. Wiping it summarily with his wristband, John Mortimer Fitzgerald, the tenth Viscount Graney, shot a fleeting glance at the green neon numbers flashing on the digital panel of the state-of-the-art treadmill and jabbed the speed button. The pace upped a fraction and he fell into a faster trot. Another ten minutes or so of pitting himself against the machine might just do the trick, and finally allow him to let go of some of the tension.

Hell of a day, he reflected, feeling his muscles respond to the grueling exercise. Perhaps the correct term was *exorcise?* He smiled grimly at the pun and, breathing harder, stared out of the huge panoramic window of what had once been the chalet cellar, now expertly converted into a small yet well-equipped gym. He gazed down the white-blanketed slope, past neighboring chalet roofs partially hidden under a relentless flurry of chunky snowflakes that hadn't stopped all day. Skiing conditions tomorrow would be fabulous. About time he got the hell out of the chalet, away from his mother's hinting and nagging, his adolescent son Nicky's permanent sulking and his brother Liam's obsessive need to work at all times, despite the festive season.

Johnny regulated his breathing and continued to run. He loved Gstaad, the magic of the mountain that he'd known since childhood, but right now he longed for the freedom of Graney, for the peat bogs and the pungent smell of his Irish moors. He wished he could simply grab his old shooting jacket and stride out in the rain across the emerald fields, breathe in that bracing air that he only breathed back home in Ireland, instead of having to dress for dinner. Thank God his mother couldn't read his mind. He grinned suddenly. Okay, maybe he was a bit biased, as she kept reminding him, but Holy Mother of God, as his countrymen liked to say, he wouldn't exchange the limestone hills of Kildare for anywhere in the world.

The digital panel announced another three minutes, and Johnny ran on doggedly, determined to relieve the last shreds that the frustration of being cooped up indoors had provoked.

He was still brooding over the argument he'd had earlier with Nicky, he realized, eyes fixed on the lights beginning to twinkle through the twilight in the neighboring chalets. In the distance, he could just make out the MOB—the Montreux-Oberland train—winding its way faithfully up the mountain as it always had, day after day, year after year, with barely a change in the timetable for as long as he could remember.

Absently he pressed the button and the machine slowed its relentless pace while he followed the lights of the train plodding methodically on through the night. At last the mood that had stuck with him ever since he'd stepped on to the plane in Dublin had begun to ease. He smiled. There was something very solid and reassuring about the MOB. It transmitted stability and permanence, as though nothing, not even an earthquake, could change its routine. Its constancy and punctuality were entirely reassuring. He always felt better the minute he sat down in one of the pristine carriages, the gentle jog as the train pulled out of Montreux station. The signal to let go of the stress and let the mountain take over. He always, unfailingly, took the MOB instead of being driven by chauffeur to Gstaad.

The treadmill went into an automatic countdown, then slid to a reluctant halt. Johnny dismounted, wiped his face, then, tossing the towel over his shoulder, made his way to the steam room. Might as well pop in for five minutes before showering and getting changed for dinner. His mother, he recalled, grimacing, had guests coming over.

He stripped, threw his damp shorts and T-shirt on the slatted wooden bench and, wrapping a towel around his waist, opened the heavy glass door and penetrated the thick swirl of hot steam. Lowering himself onto the tiled bench, he sat down, his bronzed, lean, muscled frame supported by the upper bench and closed his eyes. Ah, that felt good. Already he could feel his muscles releasing, his whole body beginning to relax. His thoughts traveled home to Graney Castle, to Blue Lavender whinnying in his stall and all the plans he had in mind for him.

Sweat formed on his brow and limbs and he relaxed further, letting the image of Blue Lavender passing the winning post by several lengths take hold. At three years old, he was finally ready to realize Johnny's dreams. Already last year he'd picked up the Dewhurst Stakes, run over seven furlongs in England, meeting all his expectations and more. He'd bred a few Thoroughbred champions and had loved each one of them, but for some reason he couldn't explain, Blue Lavender meant more to him than all the others put together. Perhaps because he'd set such ambitious goals for him.

He leaned forward, flexed his arms and sank his elbows on his sweating thighs, holding the position for several seconds before the steam became suffocating and he knew it was time to get out. Closing the door behind him, he splashed straight into the small tiled pool of ice-cold water next to the steam room.

"Aargh!" He let out a groan of pain and pleasure while absorbing the shock, followed by the deliciously agonizing impact when he ducked. Thirty seconds later he stepped out refreshed. After a hot shower, he rubbed himself down with one of the huge white monogrammed terry towels that lay rolled in neat stacks on the pine shelves surrounding him. He glanced wryly at all the exquisitely packaged designer accessories, soaps and shower gels, creams and the rest that his American mother insisted on keeping available in what she liked to call the "fitness area." Rubbing his hair, he smiled benignly at her antics. There was even an in-house masseuse on twenty-four-hour call when she had houseguests.

Pulling on one of the heavy terry robes, lips still twitching fondly at his parent's whims, he regretted the sharp way he'd spoken to her earlier when she'd commented on his fight with Nicky. He knew she meant well, that it hurt her feelings when he snubbed her. For beneath that regally composed front lay a deep, sensitive and caring woman who had her family's best interests at heart. Particularly his son's.

He glanced at the clock on the wall. Almost seven. She'd be upstairs now in the living room, ensconced among the tapestry cushions of the deep velvet sofa that Juan Pablo, her Palm Beach decorator, had insisted on. She was probably wearing one of her endless collection of plush tracksuits and her habitual array of diamonds. Her feet would be tucked under the mink-and-cashmere throw before the flames of the blazing wood fire crackling in the grate, the latest copy of *W* magazine resting in her lap.

Well, that was "Mother," as she insisted on being called. She'd never been Mummy. All the years she'd been married to a peer—albeit, an Irish one—hadn't in any way diminished her all-American verve, Johnny reflected, tenderly amused, as he walked up the stairs. A ship in full sail was how he thought of her, with her gray hair perfectly coiffed, her manicured hands sporting jewelry consistent with her age and position. And one had to give it to her, he recognized. Widow of the ninth Viscount Graney, who had been the best Thoroughbred breeder in Ireland, and sole heir to the Pennsylvania Riley steel fortune, Grace was a legend in her own right. She had, he thought, peering at her now through the half-open double doors leading into the vast wood-paneled drawing room, the air of a woman entirely at ease with what and who she was. As though sensing his presence, she looked up and lowered her glasses.

"Hello, darling. Did you have a good workout?"

"Yes, thanks. And a steam." He moved across the room.

"Well, that's more than your brother has done," she remarked tartly. "I'd better warn you. He's having a fit."

"Oh?" Johnny flopped in the sofa opposite and hooked his ankles up on the ottoman. "Why?"

"The Brandt stock fell several points." She rolled her eyes and sighed. "Despite this tragedy, do you think he might be persuaded to remain here for the holidays as any normal civilized person would? You know, honey, I'm becoming increasingly concerned about Liam," she continued, brows creasing. "Instead of letting up, he seems to be more and more obsessed with work."

"I shouldn't worry," Johnny murmured mildly, avoiding being caught in a discussion concerning his sibling.

"That's all fine and dandy for you to say," Grace sniffed, "but I do. Of course I worry. It's a mother's duty to worry." She eyed him severely. "And what about Christmas, may I ask? Have you two lost every shred of family awareness? Liam with his stocks, you with those wretched horses you never want to be apart from, and Nicky sulking all day like a bad-tempered bear cub." She waved a disparaging hand. "There are times I wonder what I ever did to deserve such an ungrateful bunch of scallywags."

"Now, Mother," Johnny murmured soothingly, then leaned over and pecked her cheek. "We're all here, aren't we? Came at your beck and call as usual, dancing attendance as it were."

"Don't give me any of that blasé British lip of yours, John Graney." She reached for his hand and squeezed it affectionately. "But, yes, I'm glad you're all here. Christmas wouldn't be the same otherwise. After all, it's important to be together as a family. Particularly as you missed Thanksgiving," she added, sending him a meaningful look.

"Mother, first, I'm Irish and second, we've been over this

countless times for the past month," Johnny sighed patiently, drawing his hand away. "Blue Lavender had a swollen tendon. There was no way I could have left Graney right then."

"Of course not. Since you value horses above your family."

Johnny sent her a humorous glance, knowing how she loved to exercise emotional blackmail. Neither was he about to enter into another discussion about Graney, his horses— Blue Lavender in particular—their value and the fact that they constituted as important a business as any of the others in the Graney-Riley empire. Grace simply refused to understand. She hadn't even when his father was alive.

"Tell me about Liam's latest adventures with the stock market," he grinned, redirecting her thoughts and stretching his long legs closer to the fire. "By the way, have you seen Nicky anywhere?"

"He came in with a friend a couple of hours ago. I think they'd been snowboarding. Dear, far be it from me to interfere, but don't you think you should spend more quality time with him? He's your son, after all, and he doesn't see you that often since he's here at boarding school the better part of the year."

"Mother, he's sixteen years old, for Christ's sake. The last thing he wants is me hanging on to his apron strings," Johnny exclaimed, annoyed at being reminded of his paternal obligations.

"No, I guess not. Still…" she pondered, wishing as always that Nicky's mother, Marie Ange, hadn't died so young, or that Johnny could have found himself another wife as suitable as his first. Her grandson needed a mother, as well as his father, and the battles waging between the two of late concerned her. "By the way, what's her name—that woman—called." She waved a bejeweled hand disdainfully and sniffed.

"Mother, you know perfectly well what her name is." He clasped his hands behind his neck, teeth flashing.

"Yes, well, that may be so, but I don't choose to use it."

Grace exchanged *W* for the *Wall Street Journal* and, correcting the position of her designer reading glasses, pretended to read. She had little time for any of Johnny's girlfriends, particularly this Brazilian one, who in her opinion had lasted too long.

"Don't worry. She won't be around this year. Actually, I'm very surprised she called. Probably wanted her stuff shipped from the flat in Eaton Terrace," he remarked, swinging a leg over the arm of the chair and throwing an empty matchbox into the fire.

"What's that?" Liam walked into the room, clicking off his cell phone. "Did I hear you say Lucia wasn't coming to Gstaad? Why?"

"Nicky pissed her off."

"Kindly mind your language," Grace reproved automatically, then lowered her glasses, intrigued.

"Spill the beans." Liam sat next to his mother on the sofa and quirked a thick sandy brow. "Lucia never misses a chance to come to Gstaad. Must've been serious."

"It was. So you can breathe easy, Mother."

"Goodness, there must be good fairies after all," Grace murmured, lowering the paper.

"Come on," Liam urged, "shoot."

"Nicky went with me to St. Barthes during his school break. One of the horses took ill—it was just before the Arc de Triomphe—so I hopped on a plane to Paris early. Next thing I know I'm receiving hysterical phone calls and all hell has let loose back on the island." He glanced at his mother, saw a gleam in her eye and, knowing how she loathed his sophisticated Brazilian mistress, conceded, "You can relax, Mother, she's history."

"What made that happen?" Grace leaned forward, agog with curiosity.

"Nicky found a snake in the garden. He wrapped it in tissue paper, slipped it into a Cartier gift box and had it delivered by courier…with my business card attached," he added with a groan.

"No!" Grace let out a gleeful chortle.

Liam laughed. "Good old Nicky."

"You can laugh," Johnny said with feeling, "but I can assure you it was less amusing at the time."

"I'll bet. Cost you, huh?" Liam inquired, amused, peering through his glasses and switching the phone back on, unable to resist the temptation of glancing again at his messages.

"Put it this way, it turned into rather an expensive operation," Johnny muttered dryly.

"Well, if you're truly rid of her, all I can say is bravo, Nicky," Grace rejoined. "I'll have to give him extra allowance," she murmured, the thought of Lucia's perfectly manicured hands eagerly unpacking the snake too delicious to resist.

"Brandt stock's dropped another ten points," Liam muttered, frowning. "Still, I reckon it's hit an all-time low." He nodded decisively. "I'll call Rod and tell him to buy a chunk before the end of the day."

"Oh, Liam, leave that wretched telephone alone," Grace huffed, glancing disapprovingly at Liam's precious tri-band. "Now, Johnny, I hope you took Nicky to task about this snake business." Grace tried to sound disapproving but was obviously having a hard time. "It was very bad manners, after all."

"Mother, you're such a hypocrite," Johnny chided, eyes twinkling as he lowered his feet to the carpet.

"I certainly am not. I may not like the woman, but Nicky still had no business sending her a reptile." She winced at the thought.

"But it's so apt," Liam remarked, tongue in cheek. He winked at his brother and continued checking stock prices. "Ah, here's one that's lookin' good. Johnny, wanna buy some—"

"I don't want to buy a damn thing, Liam. You buy enough for all of us put together," Johnny interrupted, exasperated. "Believe it or not, this is meant to be a holiday—"

"Vacation, dear—"

"Whatever, Mother. Either way, it does not figure in Liam's vocabulary."

"Okay, okay, I was just asking." Liam raised both hands.

Grace let out a resigned sigh that expressed her feelings better than words. At thirty-eight and thirty-seven, her sons were able to take care of their own lives. Still, it was impossible not to wish and worry. Absently shifting the ornaments and ashtrays on the coffee table, she studied them, first Liam, then Johnny. Liam worked far too hard taking the many companies of the Graney-Riley group to further heights, while Anne Shellenberg, his girlfriend, seemed perfectly content to have reached thirty-five unmarried and COO of some company whose name Grace couldn't recall. After five years of hoping, both she and Avis Shellenberg—Anne's WASP mother—had long since given up dreaming of wedding bells chiming in the centuries-old chapel at Graney castle.

With an imperceptible turn of the head, she glanced at Johnny, the elder of the two, still lounging in the armchair and conversing with his brother, and her heart melted. He was her firstborn, the spitting image of his handsome father, those identical piercing Kerry blue eyes laughing as he spoke, and that glorious jet-black hair graying the same way at the temples. He was what, in her neck of the woods, was termed as Black Irish. So Celtic and handsome, charming and kind, just like his dad. Yet he lived like a semirecluse, spending the better half of his existence boxed up at Graney Castle raising those wretched horses, just like his father before him.

But of course, he'd never been truly happy since Marie Ange had died on that regrettable trip to Africa. That was still the crux of the problem. He could tell her he'd gotten over it until he was blue in the face, but she, his mother, would never believe him. She knew that he still blamed himself for the fatal tragedy after all these years. He did a good job of hiding behind a battery of shields erected over the years, mind you, but Grace knew better. And oh, how she wished he and Nicky could get over the barriers that all of a sudden seemed to have popped up between them. She groaned inwardly. Everything had seemed to be working out just fine until Nicky had hit his teens. Then suddenly it was one conflict after the other, leaving Grace dangling on emotional tenterhooks.

As she often did, she wished that Gerald, her late husband, was around to give her counsel. Raising two boys on her own hadn't always been easy. Not that she hadn't managed fine on her own; of course, she had. And was proud of the result, she reflected, smiling fondly at her boys. They were as different as oil from water. Liam was all Riley—he even looked just like her own plebeian Irish father, not too tall, sandy-haired and square-shouldered—and Johnny the opposite, tall, dark and aristocratic, a true blue-blooded Graney. But their differences had worked out fine, for she'd raised them well. She just wished Liam would let up a little and enjoy life, instead of being such an incurable workaholic.

"Speaking of girls, or women, rather," she said suddenly, glancing in the mirror and giving her hair a pat, "Jeanne and Louis de Melville's daughter will be here over the vacation. She's thirty-three, smart and independent." Grace infused enthusiasm into the statement.

"Who says we like smart and independent?" Johnny queried with a teasing gleam.

"Well!" Grace huffed. "Anything would be better than that creature you were parading at the Kentucky Derby last year."

"True, Mother, a mistake, I admit," Johnny conceded, remembering the model he'd invited at the last minute. "And as for trying to push suitable women in my direction, Mother dearest, please don't." He rose, shoved his hands in the wide pockets of the robe and sent her a laughing but firm smile.

"He's right, Mother, no canny little intros, okay?" Liam seconded.

"You're both impossible." Grace threw up her hands, sank among the cushions and shook her head. But she smiled all the same. "I suppose I just have to be thankful for small mercies," she sighed, referring, Johnny knew perfectly well, to Nicky's summary disposing of Lucia.

With a laugh he left the room and headed on upstairs, planning to get on with some work before the holiday really began.

6

Dusk hovered, enveloping the small old-fashioned mountain train as it began its gentle climb into the Swiss Alps, leaving Montreux and Lake Geneva below, shrouded in a veil of December evening mist.

Seated in the wide velvet seat of the carriage, tired after the exertions of the journey and the tension of the past few days, Elm leaned back, folded her hands and looked about her appreciatively, relaxed for the first time since boarding the plane in Atlanta. It was exactly as she remembered: the carved wooden bar serving hot chocolate and tea, the gleaming brass luggage rails and pristine starched white linen squares to lay your head against. She smiled, feeling her jet lag dissipate, strangely comforted by the discovery that time had preserved her memories.

Leaving Savannah and the plantation had proved much easier than she'd expected. In fact, as momentous as the step away from that world had seemed, actually taking it had been surprisingly simple, and she was almost dizzy with relief. Not even the lingering concern that her father would be disappointed and angry about what she'd done was enough to dim her newfound sense of conviction.

Harlan and the pain of his betrayal couldn't touch her here, she realized, her smile growing, illuminating her soft brown eyes and curving her full mouth. She savored the sense of freedom, suddenly grateful that she was seated by herself on the MOB and heading to Gstaad, a place where she'd gone to boarding school and spent so many happy moments of her adolescence. A month ago she wouldn't have believed it possible. But then, a month ago she'd still been drifting in a gray fog of denial. And now her vision had cleared.

Elm glanced around the carriage and wondered if all she'd lived through the past few days showed. Her lips twitched. She doubted that the plump gray-haired lady in the seat diagonally opposite, reading a newspaper through thick, purposeful lenses, was remotely interested in her carriage-mate's tribulations. The knowledge that no one here knew— that absolutely no one would send pitying glances, make catty or well-meaning remarks—was bliss. Not that those things should matter, she reminded herself. She'd followed society's rules and dictates for too long, and all they'd ever brought her was pain and anguish. From now on, she vowed, she'd make her own rules.

With a satisfied if still shaky sigh, she peered through the large train window, but the brightly lit carriage made it hard to see out. For a moment she stared at her own reflection with new awareness. She was filing for divorce, turning her well-ordered world upside down. But despite all the upheaval, the tension lines around her mouth had eased and her eyes held a glimmer of something—could it be hope?— that she hadn't seen for some time. Maybe it was just an illusion, but the mere fact she'd found the courage to come here filled her with a sense of optimistic expectation, as if she'd been given a new lease on life. She was thirty-four years old, yet inside she felt fifteen, suddenly young and ready to face her future all over again.

Pressing her forehead against the chilled windowpane, Elm bit her lip and gazed at the ice-covered stream hugging the railroad tracks. Above the stream, dark pine trees grew taller and taller as the train climbed, their thick branches sagging under the weight of sharp icicles and ten inches of fresh snow.

Elm swallowed and finally let out the long breath she'd been holding. She had every reason to agonize, but so many more to rejoice. After all, she'd faced the truth, confronted the fact that she'd been living in a sleepy world of illusion, and finally forced herself to wake up and take the upper hand. Her one regret was that it had taken her this long. Of course, the immediate future was easy—a long-awaited and much-needed vacation. Going back would be far more complicated. Aunt Frances—the one person other than Meredith whom she'd revealed her plans to—had said as much.

And Aunt Fran was right. There would surely be times ahead when she'd miss the stability, however stultifying, of her former life. Living on her own in her home city, where people would still think of her as Senator Hathaway's daughter and Harlan MacBride's wife, might prove very uncomfortable. There would be the inevitable snide comments and cold shoulders, perhaps even a tabloid assault full of distortions. But right now she didn't care about any of it. She'd face that hurdle when she came to it.

For frankly, she no longer cared what people thought. Savannah would just have to get with the new program or go get a life, she decided, breathing on the pane and drawing a smiley face on the glass with her fingertip. Then she remembered her father and her finger stilled, her ebullience fading. She loved him dearly, and the knowledge that he would never understand her reasons for divorcing Harlan, however valid, made her profoundly sad. She took a deep breath and sat back against the green velvet seat, acknowledging that this was the main reason, however cowardly, that she'd left Savannah without leaving word of where she was going. Aunt Frances had insisted, in her uniquely feisty fashion, that like it or not, Daddy was going to have to learn to put his daughter first for once. But Elm knew there was little use trying to explain. He would never listen. He'd merely offer irrefutable arguments about why her choices were all wrong.

The carriage door opened, cutting short her negative thoughts and the inevitable guilty feelings they aroused. Instead, Elm concentrated on the rotund, pink-cheeked ticket controller dressed in a neatly pressed navy blue uniform, a bright red leather satchel slung over his shoulder.

"Présentez les billets, s'il vous plaît."

Elm responded easily, happy to see her French wasn't too rusty, and produced her ticket. It felt good to hear that slow lilting Swiss accent once more, to know she was truly back. Then, as she returned the ticket to her large Hermès purse, another attendant appeared offering refreshments. She wasn't at all thirsty, but the idea of tasting steaming hot Swiss chocolate again was irresistible. So what if it was loaded with calories and cholesterol? Her personal trainer wasn't here to harp at her, was she? In fact, not one single person here would criticize or tell her how she should be leading her life.

Rebelliously tossing her hair back, Elm smiled at the woman and ordered a large hot chocolate with whipped cream. A minute later she was taking the piping-hot cup from the gracious attendant, breathing in the delicious, unforgettable aroma, eyes watering as she sipped cautiously. Savoring the familiar taste, she was able now to take a critical look back at her moves over the past few days. To her own amazement, she, who'd always been considered vague and fey, had proved immensely efficient. She'd found replacements for all her charity duties, handing over the garden project to Joan Murdoch, her competent assistant, who was more than happy to oblige. She had packed up her paints and canvases and left instructions for the staff at Oleander and the house in town, as though she hopped off to Europe at the blink of an eyelid every day of the year. She'd even managed to find someone to man her booth at the Daughters of the Confederacy bazaar—no mean feat, since the fund-raiser was notorious for being the most tedious event of Savannah's holiday season.

Incredible, she mused, relishing the rich, creamy drink and her own capabilities. Life had sent her an inside curve ball, and instead of despairing, she'd rallied and was experiencing an exhilarating rush of satisfaction. And it was incredibly uplifting to be free of Harlan's constant recriminations and barbs, and her father's subtle disapproval, she reflected ruefully. He always made her feel as though she could be doing better.

Placing her hand against the glass once more, Elm peered out again through the growing darkness to the twinkling lights of the distant chalets dotted on the snowy peaks. What must it be like to live up in a small wooden mountain dwelling, cozily ensconced behind red-and-white-checkered curtains, a blazing fire roaring in a rustic chimney? she wondered dreamily. She could easily imagine a family—little blond-pigtailed girls and boys in smocks—seated round a carved kitchen table, digging into large portions of *rösti*, the delicious Swiss equivalent of hash browns, and commenting on their day's work, their hopes and fears. The cows would be huddled in the barns for the winter now, each animal ensconced in a stall with its name carefully painted above, next to the huge bells that would be donned again in spring when they returned to pasture and joined the *poya*—the famous yearly trek up into the legendary Swiss Alps.

As she stared deep into the night, following a tiny beam of light flickering up on the mountain, Elm remembered that as a student here, she'd been drawn to the sense of timeless serenity the mountains exuded, to the quiet rhythms of alpine life, always envying its apparent simplicity. Of course, now she knew that life, no matter where it was lived, was never simple.

The train stopped at several stations. First Les Avants, where in May the slopes were covered in radiant white blankets of sweet-smelling narcissus. Then Château-d'Oex, where Aunt Frances and her mother, whom she could barely recall, had attended finishing school long ago. Then the train chuffed past Rougemont—wow, how the town had grown, there had never been that many lights before—with its ancient seventeenth-century chalets bordering the tracks, and on, down into the low-lying mists of the Saanenland toward her final destination.

It was snowing hard when the train finally pulled into

Gstaad station and Elm got up, excited, her tall, slim figure clad in elegant suede pants and a cashmere sweater, and hastened to the door of the compartment. She smiled and thanked a kind middle-aged man who stepped forward and helped her remove her luggage from the rack. Then, pulling on her long mink coat, she flung open the window and leaned perilously out before the train had come to a complete stop, watching eagerly as another slim, fur-clad figure hurried down the tiny platform, waving.

"Gio! Oh, my God!" She laughed, immediately recognizing Gioconda and waving back enthusiastically. As the train came to a halt she hauled her bags down to the platform and the two women tumbled into each other's arms.

"*Cara,* I can't believe it. You've finally made it! You should have let me send the car to the airport to meet you, darling, instead of using this uncivilized public transport," Gioconda exclaimed, enveloping her in a perfumed embrace before beckoning to the porter. "Take the bags to the car over there, please." She pointed and smiled, then turned once more, holding Elm at arm's length and looking her over critically. "*Bella.* How marvelous to see you. You look beautiful, as always. A little pale perhaps, but that will soon be taken care of. I'm so thrilled you came." She gave Elm another hug.

"So am I," Elm's eyes glistened as they linked arms and followed the porter under gently falling snowflakes to a gleaming four-wheel drive parked on the curb next to the yellow postal bus. Elm glanced at it nostalgically, welcoming yet another reminder of her school days.

While Gioconda chattered, Elm stared at her surroundings, allowing it all to sink in, still unable to believe she'd actually made it back to "her" mountain. She bit her lip and stood, hand on the car door, looking up through the snowflakes at the Palace Hotel, still rising like an enchanted castle, turrets brightly illuminated above the fairy-tale village, casting its magic spell over the wooden chalets lying peacefully below, their pointed eaves outlined by tiny trails of Christmas lights. Elm breathed deeply, filling her lungs with the chilly mountain air, and sighed. Already she felt like a different woman, as though she'd finally stepped out of a quagmire onto solid land.

"Stop painting pictures in your head and get into the car, *cara*," Gioconda urged, laughing, moving to the driver's seat while the porter placed the bags in the back.

Elm smiled absently and climbed into the vehicle. Barbra Streisand's "Memories" played on the CD deck. It was wonderfully appropriate. For a moment her eyes filled, and she leaned back against the soft leather seat, overwhelmed by emotion. Gioconda drove past the skating rink, where a group of young girls in bright, billowing ice-skating skirts twirled gracefully under the heavy flakes, like ballerinas in a music box. Elm swallowed hard, touched by how perfect it all was, how untainted and lovely and precious. Almost too good to be true.

Could seventeen years really have passed since she'd done figure eights on that same ice herself? And what had she achieved since then? she wondered. Then she pulled herself up with a jolt. It was pointless to get maudlin, as Aunt Frances would say. What mattered was that she was here now, almost as though she'd had to return to her beginnings to start all over again.

"I can't wait to introduce you to everyone," Gioconda was saying, bringing Elm back to the present. "There are several people already in town. A couple of old Roséens, Jim Talbot for one. Remember how fat he used to be?"

"No wonder. He lived at von Siebenthal's bakery eating doughnuts, if I remember correctly."

"Damn right. Anyway, he's quite slim now."

Elm shook her head. It all seemed part of another world and she felt suddenly ashamed that, barring Gio, she had not kept in touch with her old school pals.

"You'll never believe me when I tell you who I saw the other evening."

"Who?" Elm asked, grinning.

"Johnny Graney. Now, you remember *him*. You had a mega crush on him."

Elm frowned, then nodded, laughing. "Of course I remember. Is he still as devastatingly handsome? I used to lurk around the basketball court during practice, hoping for a glimpse of that killer smile. Gosh, how silly we were in those days."

"Deliciously, wonderfully silly," Gioconda agreed, driving through the tunnel, then out at the roundabout and past the *mölkerei*—the local dairy.

"Gee, it's still there," Elm exclaimed, delighted to see so little had changed. "Are the yoghurts still as scrumptious?"

"Absolutely. You'll have some for breakfast tomorrow morning."

They turned right and drove on, up past the Park Hotel. A few meters later the car veered right again into a small side road and Elm could see Gioconda's chalet twinkling through the layer of snow being swished rhythmically back and forth by the windshield wipers.

"I can't believe it," she exclaimed, a frisson coursing through her. "Everything looks exactly the same," she marveled as they turned into the driveway and she was able to distinguish the chalet properly. "Do you remember all those wonderful weekends and vacations we used to spend here, Gio? It seems like only yesterday."

"Don't remind me," Gio groaned dramatically, "I'll be thirty-four next month. Can you imagine? Me? Positively ancient."

"Rubbish," Elm laughed, "You're as gorgeous now, Contessa, as you've always been and you know it."

"Bah! *Non lo so.* The men seem to think so, but I have a mirror. I'm seriously contemplating some of those injections I hear so much about." Gioconda's eyes twinkled. Then she shrugged as only Italians can shrug and sent Elm a mischievous grin. "But, anyway, you'll be happy to know, *cara,* that the chalet only looks the same on the outside. I've redecorated the interior completely, thank God," she added. "Remember those dreadful brown velvet chairs of my grandmother's?"

"I do." Elm grinned back, recalling Gioconda's pithy

comments at the time. At fifteen, Gio had already possessed a tremendous sense of style, she realized, amused. "What color are they now?"

"Mercifully they don't exist anymore." Gioconda gave a dramatic shudder. "I donated them to the Salvation Army. And frankly, darling, I'm not even sure they wanted them." She pressed the automatic garage door, which opened immediately.

"Those doors always remind me of a spaceship," Elm remarked, tilting her head dreamily. "Like in those movies where a spacecraft opens and you get zapped inside and—"

"*Mamma mia.* You haven't changed in the slightest. Always that incredible imagination at work," Gioconda exclaimed, laughing. "Still painting a lot, *cara?* I loved your last exhibition. And by the way, Franco and Gianni are still dying to do that exhibit in Florence we talked about."

"That's not a bad idea," Elm mused. All at once, a project that a few months ago had seemed a logistically impossible project struck her as challenging and exciting.

"Well, that's a positive change," Gio remarked, surprised. "The last time I mentioned it, you spurned the idea outright."

"The last time you mentioned it, I was still living in La La Land," Elm answered ruefully as the vehicle crawled into the garage.

"Ah, *poverina,*" Gio exclaimed sympathetically. "I suppose escaping into your fantasy world was the only way to bear that self-absorbed husband of yours. I'll never understand why you married him," she added, shaking her head, her well-cut, silky, shoulder-length black hair swinging elegantly.

"I guess it seemed a good idea at the time," Elm replied with a noncommittal shrug. "But he won't be my husband for much longer."

"Thank God for that! When you told me you were leaving him and planning to get divorced, I made Umberto open a bottle of the vintage Crystal. We drank to your future and recalled all the good times."

"Umberto! It's amazing that he still works for you after all these years," Elm smiled, fondly remembering the Mancini family butler.

"You bet. He still bosses everyone around and makes a general nuisance of himself. *Nonno*—you remember my grandfather?"

"Of course."

"Well, *Nonno* offered to buy him a nice house in Umberto's village in Sicily, and take care of him and his family."

"And?"

"He was so insulted that the matter was never brought up again."

Elm laughed. "I can believe that."

"Frankly, I don't know what *Nonno* would do without him. They still spend hours going over the defeat at Monte Cassino. They're certain that if only they'd been the ones leading the Italian troops, history would have taken a different turn." Gioconda parked neatly next to a shiny red Ferrari.

"Yours?" Elm quirked an amused brow in the direction of the car.

"But of course, *bella*. I haven't changed. I'm still as extravagant as ever. Ah! There's Maria." Gio waved at the uniformed maid preparing to unload the car.

"Buona sera, signora."

"Good evening." Elm smiled back graciously, before following her friend up the carpeted steps.

At the top Gioconda pushed open the paneled wooden door and held it wide while Elm passed through.

"Benvenuto, cara. It's wonderful to have you back."

"It's wonderful to be back," Elm murmured, taking stock of the hall. "Wow, Gio, it's totally different, perfectly divine," she marveled, gazing appreciatively at the pine-paneled walls of the entrance, the regional antiques, the imaginative floral arrangements of wild flowers and berries. "That's fantastic," she exclaimed, enchanted, pointing to two heavy wax candles in wrought-iron stands flickering invitingly on an ancient wooden chest. "And that scent. I know that scent." She stopped, closed her eyes and sniffed, breathing in the subtle mélange of cloves, pine and something deliciously mysterious. "It's simply enchanting," she murmured, delighted, fingers trailing lovingly over the polished wood, "Just lovely. Trust you to do a perfect job, Gio."

"Glad you approve, *cara*," Gio pulled off her fur jacket and reached for Elm's coat. "Now, before we settle down to a well-deserved glass of champagne, I'll take you up to your room. Umberto, *siamo qui...*" she called, throwing the coats over the carved hall chair. "He can't hear a thing, poor old darling, deaf as a post."

"Signora Contessa?" Umberto, on the alert, appeared out of nowhere, the same picture of unaltered ancient dignity that Elm recalled so well.

"Look," Gioconda exclaimed, grabbing Elm's arm, "look who's finally returned to us!"

"Ah! *Signora, quanti anni.*" Umberto clasped Elm's hand, his creased face breaking into a delighted smile. Elm returned the pressure, eyes moist. It was like opening a picture book and finding herself back in her own personal fairy tale, a bittersweet reminder of just how much and how little had taken place since.

"It's marvelous to be back, Umberto," she murmured, deeply touched, smiling into his kind old face, remembering all the times he'd left the door unlatched for them, the midnight snacks and the scolds. It was like time travel, and again her eyes stung.

"Enough," Gioconda declared, grabbing Elm's hand. "Now we will make some fine new memories!" She winked, dark eyes flashing. "I have another surprise for you, *bella.* Come on." Like an excited child, she dragged Elm up the stairs, then down the tapestry-covered corridor to a door at the end.

Elm threw her head back and laughed, caught up in Gioconda's contagious enthusiasm. When she peeked inside as her friend opened the bedroom door, she caught her breath and clasped her hands. "Oh Gio, it's simply gorgeous," she exclaimed, stepping into the room.

"You like it? I had it completely redone as soon as you said you were coming. They finished yesterday," she giggled.

Enchanted, Elm moved about the room, touched more by the generosity of Gioconda's gesture than the actual, undeniable loveliness of the decor itself. A luxurious mink throw lay strewn over a long ottoman at the foot of the king-size canopied bed, draped with old rose Toile de Jouy curtains that matched the walls. Scattered lamps shed their gentle glow about the room, their reflections shimmering in the large pine-framed mirror above the antique dressing table. It was feminine and sophisticated, warm and welcoming, everything she'd dreamed of during the chilling loneliness of the past two weeks. Turning, she embraced her friend tight.

"Thank you, Gio. This means more to me than you can possibly know."

"Now, now, *cara*," Gio scolded gruffly, wiping a tear from her own eyes. "There's more."

"More?"

"Look." Gioconda moved and flung open another door. "Bathroom and walk-in closet, and over here," she continued, moving toward two heavy quilted curtains, "is your very own special little nook." She swept back the drapes with a flourish. *"Voilà!"*

Elm peered inside and let out a long sigh. "You've outdone yourself," she murmured, stepping into the cozy little sitting room lined with carved pine bookshelves. A plump love seat piled high with tasseled velvet and brocade cushions stood invitingly before a blazing open fire, while more fat wax candles guttered gently on the low coffee table next to an array of glossy magazines and a basket of scented potpourri. "What can I say?" she whispered, raising her manicured hands expressively. "It's perfect. I can't believe you did all this for me."

"If not for my dearest friend, then who would I do it for?" Gio laughed, thrilled at Elm's reaction.

"I guess all I can say is a huge thank you." The two women hugged again and Elm felt a warm glow of happiness.

"Now freshen up, *cara*. Umberto's probably already uncorking the champagne," Gio ordered. "And don't worry about unpacking, Maria will deal with it later."

Once she was alone in the room, Elm sank down, smiling, onto the well-sprung bed. She bounced on it twice, then sighed with pleasure. It was like waking up in a new world with no worries, no haunting shadows, and no doubts. It seemed that the mountain's peace was finally hers to share once more.

Jumping up, all her fatigue forgotten, Elm pulled a hairbrush out of her purse and dragged it through the long strands falling on the shoulders of her white cashmere sweater. She'd made up her mind to have a true break, hadn't she? To get her life in perspective before returning and facing the future. And that, she decided firmly, was exactly what she would do. She would live each precious moment of this blissful interlude to the hilt, savor each instant, engrave each sensation inside, then return to her own world a stronger and better person, able to face the decisions she would have to make.

And for the first time ever, she reminded herself proudly, those decisions would be hers alone to make.

7

Elm slid off the chairlift at the top of the Wassengrat run and straightened her ski poles. No more champagne anytime before Christmas, she swore, blinking and shaking her head, recalling the magnum her friends had insisted on opening last night to celebrate what her Old Rosey pals termed as her "return to the fold." There were several of them at the delightful brasserie and club, where she'd sat on the zebra bench, enchanted, as old stories were exchanged and fun times recalled, and also a little ashamed that she'd lost touch with so many wonderful people. But they'd scoffed at her embarrassment, and made her feel so welcome, so at home, as though she hadn't spent the past seventeen years away in a different world.

Now, after a long, delicious lunch accompanied by an excellent Bordeaux at the Eagle Club with Gioconda and several of her newfound friends—including Franco and Gianni, who were already excitedly planning the Florence exhibit of her paintings—Elm had spent what remained of the afternoon skiing with her pro, Rudy, whom she'd taken leave of at the bottom of the chairlift. Then, even though the hour was late, she'd decided to do one last run on her own.

It felt good to be by herself for a short while, skiing past the clusters of dark pines, taking her own lazy time to slide gracefully down the slope in the fresh virgin snow, feeling the cool wind whipping color into her cheeks and new life into her lungs. She'd often dreamed of these moments when things had been particularly dreary back home, when, lying languidly in the old canvas hammock, seeping in the damp summer heat under the protective shade of the live oaks, she'd picture herself shushing down the mountain, inhaling this crisp, invigorating air. Now that she was finally here, she felt revitalized.

It occurred to her that, since arriving in Gstaad, she'd had none of the symptoms that had so troubled her of late in Savannah. The dizzy spells had passed, the nausea subsided. Had it all been in her head? she wondered. Probably just a physical manifestation of the inner misery she'd been unwilling to acknowledge, she decided cynically.

She slowed, then stopped next to a knot of pines, watching the rays of soft winter sun indulge in a final flirt with the glistening white peaks before sinking gracefully into the valley. Although she'd left the States before learning the results of the extensive blood work ordered by Dr. Ashby, the Atlanta specialist Doc Philips had referred her to, she was certain now the tests would prove normal. Boy, was it good to feel like herself again. She smiled and gazed about her once more, capturing the beauty of the moment, the sun sinking behind the mountain, the range so clearly etched in the late afternoon light.

Elm prodded the snow with her pole and thought of Harlan. How strange that he already felt like part of her past. Indeed, everything that had formed her world back in Savannah, her daily activities and commitments, seemed distant and detached. Two weeks ago she'd been deeply involved in the garden project at Oleander that represented so much to her, listening to the heartbreaking stories of the women she'd recruited from the local women's shelter, admiring them for having the will to survive the abuse they'd suffered. She'd marveled then at the contrast to her own safe, sterilized world, where the worst thing she faced was the inevitable round of fund-raisers and photo-ops with Harlan.

And even though the veil of security had now been stripped away, she suddenly realized that she'd had more in common with those women than she'd have imagined possible. She hoped that, like them, she'd continue to stand firm and tap into some well of inner strength to carve herself a new life. Of course, her life was made much easier than theirs. She had financial security to lean on. But that didn't make it easy, all the same. The main thing was she'd made a start, she admitted proudly. Since the moment she'd told Meredith to file the divorce papers, she hadn't had one doubt that she had made the right move.

Elm wiped her glasses and gazed about her. Perhaps she should just stop questioning herself and enjoy the time away.

Although her toes were slowly going numb, Elm adjusted her woollen cap and glasses and gazed about her once more, nose tingling. Her painting had made her an acute observer of her surroundings, but she'd never dared to focus that intense vision on herself. Now was as good a time as any to change that. After all, you could live a whole lifetime in a second, she reflected, drinking in the beauty; it was all up to what you saw, what you made of it, how you let it touch you. And now she was determined to see it all, feel it all, absorb each detail from the trees to the snow and the flickering lights already shining in the village below, which reminded her how late it must be.

The run was empty, she noticed, reflecting that the other skiers were probably sipping *glühwein* and hot chocolate at Charlie's Tea Room, or listening to strains of the piano before the vast open fireplace at the Palace Hotel.

Moving her right ski tentatively on the snow, Elm realized uneasily that conditions were fast turning icy. Better get going, she decided, setting off down the hill, anxious now to reach the bottom and make her way back to Gioconda's chalet.

She was about two-thirds down the slope when she felt her left ski slide out of control. Desperately she tried to recover her balance but without success. Then, to her horror, Elm watched another skier appear out of the trees and glide straight into her path.

Oh, my God! She tried to shout a warning but no sound came.

Next thing Elm knew, she lay tumbled in the snow entangled with a complete stranger, wincing at the string of oaths she heard. Her victim was male and expressed himself in British English. There was no doubt he was seriously upset. Dragging her arm free, Elm mumbled an embarrassed apology and managed to get up.

"I'm so sorry," she said, mortified, reaching for a fallen ski pole. The man rose, too. He stood several inches above her, likely a good six foot two. Elm cringed, watching as he shook off the excess snow like a goggled St. Bernard, and wished the earth would swallow her up.

"I really am so sorry," she repeated, not knowing what else to say.

"Don't you look where you're going?" he muttered, flexing his right arm before removing the pair of shiny goggles and a black woolen hat.

"I'm afraid my ski got caught on the ice and I went out of control. You're not hurt, are you?" she enquired anxiously.

Their eyes met and all at once he grinned. "Nothing a hot bath and a drink won't cure," he replied, scrutinizing her.

"Thank goodness," Elm murmured, relieved, struck by his dark good looks, bright blue eyes, chiseled features and thick dark hair graying at the temples. He seemed strangely familiar, she realized, frowning. Then, removing her woolen cap, she shook out the snow, tousled her hair and took off her glasses, which had misted up after the fall.

"You sure you're okay?" he asked, eyeing her carefully.

"Fine," she answered, tucking her hat into her pocket. "Look, again, I'm dreadfully sorry. It was all my fault. I lost control of my skis on an icy patch up there."

"That's okay." He glanced at the darkening sky around

them. ''Better get to the bottom before we end up skating down this thing, though. I'll lead the way.''

Elm was about to protest at his arbitrary attitude of command when a quick look at the ominous shadows cast by pine trees changed her mind. Perhaps it was no bad thing the stranger wanted to lead the way. With a shrug she followed him. He was obviously an ace skier, though she had no difficulty following him to the bottom of the slope, despite the increasingly icy conditions. She just wasn't going to break her neck trying to prove herself, she decided, shushing down the run after him.

Leaning on his ski poles at the bottom of the slope, Johnny Graney watched appreciatively as the slim, white-clad figure crossed the last few hundred yards, then made a neat sharp stop next to him.

''Okay?'' he inquired solicitously.

''Fine.'' Elm pressed the tip of her pole into the back of her binding. Johnny followed suit, wishing she'd remove her glasses once more so that he could catch another glimpse of those incredible brown eyes, such an unusual contrast to the blond mass falling about her shoulders. At least if he was going to be rammed into by a strange woman, he reflected philosophically, then by all means let it be by a beautiful one.

As though guessing his silent wish, Elm stood in the snow, shook her skis, then removed her glasses. For a moment he frowned. He knew that face, was certain he'd seen it before. Was she an actress? Someone he'd met in London or New York? He flexed his memory while removing his own equipment, determined to find out who she was.

''How about a *glühwein* or a hot chocolate in the village?'' he threw casually, surprising himself.

''Oh, I really don't think—''

''You said you were sorry for running into me.'' He grinned, eyes flashing in his bronzed face. ''Make up for it by joining me.''

Elm was about to refuse when she suddenly realized that,

actually, she wouldn't mind having a drink with this handsome stranger. It was Gstaad, after all, not Chicago. Everybody knew one another.

"Okay, why not?" She smiled.

"Great. Maybe we should introduce ourselves. In a formal manner," he added, lips twitching as he removed his right glove.

Elm grinned ruefully and did the same.

"You first," he urged in a smooth British accent.

"Elm Hathaway from Savannah, Georgia."

"Pleased to meet you, Elm Hathaway from Savannah, Georgia. I'm Johnny Graney from Ireland slash Pittsburgh, U.S.A." A warm tingle coursed through Elm's fingers. Then all at once, memory jogged, realization dawned and she drew them back quickly.

"Johnny Graney?"

"Guilty." He sent her a curious glance. "This sounds like a line, but haven't we met before?"

"Uh, as a matter of fact, we have," Elm responded, feeling as if she'd been thrown into a time warp. Johnny Graney had been her first serious crush, the boy she'd mooned over some twenty years earlier. It came as something of a shock to realize just how much time had elapsed—and, apparently, how much she must have changed, she reflected with a touch of humor. Johnny was clearly having a hell of a time trying to place her.

"I'm dreadfully sorry, but I—" He raised his hands in a gesture of defeat. "I'm afraid I just don't remember."

"How flattering," Elm replied dryly. "But it makes sense. At the time, you were only peripherally aware of my existence."

"I was?" His face took on a look of comical horror. "You must be joking," he added, throwing up his hands. "If I'd ever met you, even for a split second, I'm certain I'd remember."

Elm burst out laughing and watched his face color with polite embarrassment. He'd been a dangerous flirt back then, and every girl's hero. She couldn't resist teasing him a little longer. "I can see I made a lasting impression on you," she said, glancing down. "It's kind of cold. Shall we move?" Picking up her skis, she acquiesced when he immediately insisted on carrying them with his own.

"Look, I feel awful. At least give me a hint," he begged.

"Should I?" she taunted, eyeing him playfully, deliciously aware that she was flirting, something she hadn't done in years.

"Come on, be a sport. Heck, you almost massacred me back there. Are you planning torture, too? What kind of a woman are you?" He raised an amused brow, and Elm smiled sweetly.

"It's too cold for conversation."

"Okay. The Palace Hotel—I promise a table next to the fireplace if you tell me who you are and where we met."

"That's blackmail."

"Elm Hathaway from Savannah, Georgia," he said thoughtfully, placing their skis on the back of a new silver Range Rover. "I know that rings a bell somewhere."

"This is really quite demoralizing," she pouted, sighing heavily as he held the door of the vehicle for her. "To think I've changed to the point of being unrecognizable—"

"I never said that, I merely—"

"I know," she continued, enjoying the game. "You meet so many women it's hard to keep track. Don't worry, I understand." She sent him a sympathetic, pitying look.

"Hey! Hold it," he exclaimed, coming around and getting in the driver's seat, rallying as he turned the key in the ignition. "If it was a long time ago as you're implying, maybe you were a skinny, gawky little thing. A sort of ugly duckling who's since turned into a swan."

"A skinny ugly duckling—" Elm spluttered, laughing, "I was never an ugly duckling."

"In that case, you'll just have to help me out," he insisted, driving out of the parking lot.

"I don't know." She eyed him thoughtfully. "Seeing you strain your memory is rather satisfying," she remarked, leaning against the cream-colored leather, remembering the numerous times she'd haunted the basketball court and the soccer field, just waiting to catch a glimpse of him.

"I give up," Johnny declared dramatically as the four-wheel-drive vehicle wound down the mountain and back toward the village.

"What, so easily?" She raised a brow and looked him over with a sly grin. "I seem to recall a certain basketball team captain rallying his players with a speech about never giving up and fighting until the death, et cetera, et cetera…quite dramatic stuff, really," she added with a sigh, "and so disappointing to know it no longer holds true."

The car braked abruptly. "My God." He turned and stared at her. "Now I remember. Little Elm Hathaway, the Southern belle from Savannah. You had a picture of me under your pillow—" a slow wicked grin dawned "—and that bitch Janine whatever-her-name-was stole it and showed it to the whole school at dinner."

"Yes, well, we don't need to dwell on that," Elm muttered hastily, blushing despite herself. It had proved the most lowering experience. "Uh, I think there's a car behind you," she added, trying to divert his attention.

Johnny took his eyes off her and drove once more. "Well, well. It's a small world indeed." He flashed her another sidelong grin. "My only excuse for not recognizing you at once are the developments since then."

"Developments?" Elm eyed him suspiciously.

"Put it this way, you were, uh…proportionally different."

"Proportionally?"

"Mmm-hmm."

As he watched her expectantly, clearly daring her to take the bait, it occurred to Elm that she was way out of her depth. This man was obviously a practiced playboy and entirely too aware of his own appeal. But boy, this was fun. Curiosity won and she raised a questioning brow. "Okay, I'll bite. So tell me, was I a freak?"

"No," he said, turning into the parking lot of the Palace, then drawing up under the porch where the valet hastened down the steps. "But even you must admit that you were a bit of a gangly girl—lovely, of course, but gangly all the same. Whereas now," he drawled, "you look every inch a woman—with certain inches being especially impressive."

She blushed. Well, she'd asked for that, she realized, feeling his gaze intent upon her and grateful that the valet had opened her door, providing her with a quick escape.

Elm alighted from the vehicle and strode up the steps toward the hotel entrance, ruefully aware that the passage of twenty years had done nothing to strengthen her defenses against Johnny's charm. Thankfully, he didn't mean anything by his nonsense; he'd probably used that line a thousand times. Johnny Graney, she reflected with a grin, was obviously a serial flirt.

And luckily, she assured herself, she was smart enough to realize it.

8

Two hours, and two *glühweins* later, Johnny returned to the family chalet, satisfied that he'd extracted from his old schoolmate a promise to meet for dinner. He was intrigued by the unexpected encounter and smiled to himself as he walked upstairs. Elm Hathaway was charming and intelligent and genuinely fun. A pleasant change from the majority of women he came across.

He knew he had a reputation as a playboy—his mother had asked him point blank if he was auditioning ladies for a harem—but the truth was he just plain lost interest in most of them after the first date. Beneath their flirtatious smiles and eager questions was an obvious fascination with his title and the size of his bank account; sometimes he'd barely get the woman out the restaurant door before she was bluntly offering to share his bed. No wonder he was happiest at Graney Castle—at least there he didn't feel like a piece of prime horseflesh on the auction block.

He grinned, suspecting his teenage son Nicky would tell him to "get over it." And, admittedly, being the object of enthusiastic female pursuit had its pluses. Still, he found himself hoping for something more. Not that he was looking for a serious relationship—his heart always had and always would belong to Marie Ange—but in certain dark moments he recognized in himself a deep loneliness, a yearning for quiet companionship.

And whose fault is that? he reminded himself sharply, feeling the inevitable pull of the past, the memory of what he'd lost. He drew himself up, determined not to let the contentment of his afternoon with Elm fade. He'd ring up the Chesery and make a reservation for tomorrow night. At least they could talk there without being constantly interrupted, and the food was delicious. He frowned. Usually he avoided being too chummy with his old Rosey friends because they reminded him of Marie Ange, of the past. But somehow Elm was different.

He shrugged and proceeded down the corridor, wondering if Nicky was home. He must make a call to Graney, too, and talk to O'Connor before he left for the evening, to get the latest report on Blue Lavender. He'd ponder the unexpected appeal of Elm Hathaway later.

She most definitely would not "go for it," Elm reflected, amused, recalling Gioconda's excited outburst when she'd told her of the encounter. But now, as she sat across from Johnny in the intimate yet elegant ambience of the Chesery, she was glad she'd accepted his invitation to dinner. The Chesery was one of Gstaad's best traditional restaurants and it was almost impossible to get a table.

Pretending to study the menu, Elm eyed the man sitting across the table. It was easy to see why she'd fallen for him all those years ago. It wasn't just his patent good looks or seductive charm or lethally athletic figure that attracted, but the warmth and intelligence that lay behind his smile. Although he came across as somewhat guarded in his manner—not distant, exactly, for he was quite playful, as she'd learned yesterday afternoon—she sensed that he was simply a man who didn't reveal himself easily to others. And this atmosphere—superb quality and efficiency enveloped in an intimate yet highly sophisticated setting—suited him perfectly. Her mouth curved and she surveyed him and the appetizer, *oeuf surprise,* a delightful concoction of scrambled egg placed in an eggshell and topped with caviar. Johnny looked deliciously elegant in a blazer and tie, and utterly at home in this charming restaurant where waiters addressed him by name and he called the shots.

Harlan would hate him, she thought wryly, for Johnny was the type of man Harlan could only pretend to be—effortlessly confident and in control, someone whom others instinctively looked to as a leader. Harlan had his own brand of power, to be sure, but the truth was, his backers—including her father, she reminded herself with a twinge of unease, remembering this morning's stilted phone conversation with him—could take that away as quickly as they'd given it to him.

She had sensed the concern in her father's voice, but already he seemed, albeit reluctantly, to have accepted the fact that she'd had to get away, even if he didn't agree with it. But then, he still didn't know the real reason for her departure. Her divorce from Harlan was going to be a bitter pill for the senator to swallow, and she wanted to tell him herself when the time was right.

But enough of that, she decided, determined not to spoil the evening, and bit back a smile at a sudden vision of Gioconda, wagging her finger and admonishing her not to waste her thoughts on a failed marriage, or on a faithless, feckless man like Harlan, when she had such a magnificent specimen within arm's reach.

And she was right. For Johnny was proving to be an amusing dinner companion, regaling her with hilarious stories of his son Nicky's escapades. She felt young and carefree as she laughed at Johnny's hilarious description of Nicky's unfortunate decision to host a sidewalk sale of Grace Graney's prized collection of Ming porcelain—at decidedly bargain prices—realizing that she'd laughed more since being here in Gstaad than she had in the past twelve years. And that laughter was something she'd missed.

The meal was delicious, but by the time they'd reached dessert, even Elm, with her lack of experience, could sense that Johnny hadn't invited her out just to talk about their old school days. Most definitely not. The realization that he was obviously attracted to her was remarkably enticing, she admitted, savoring a shudder of excitement and a tiny spoonful of delectable chocolate mousse. More surprising was the recognition that she, too, was drawn to him.

Not that she could act upon that attraction, of course. She hadn't come to Gstaad for romance. She was still a married woman, after all, one who'd never thought of betraying her vows even at the worst of times. Yet Johnny was making it plain that he found her company very pleasant—and he struck her as the type of man who didn't hesitate to go after what he wanted.

The thought was so shockingly alluring that Elm nearly choked on the mousse. Before, whenever she'd sensed that a man was interested in her, she'd distanced herself automatically. But then, she'd been married—really married, not filing for divorce—and living behind a wall of Southern protocol, the subtle protection offered by her husband and her father's position and the strict rules of the society she lived in. She'd let those walls imprison her, separate her from the hopes and dreams she'd once aspired to.

And suddenly she longed to break free.

This, even more than her own growing fascination with the man across the table, made her realize she must be very, very cautious. She didn't want to be one of those women who left their husbands, only to enter into a series of scorching relationships that ended with them burned and bewildered several months later. Better to just enjoy this pleasurable evening and allow herself to bask in the feeling of being admired, not criticized, and then give Johnny a firm handshake of thanks and farewell.

As he entertained her with stories and listened to her laugh, Johnny couldn't remember the last time he'd enjoyed a woman's company more. Elm Hathaway was certainly a welcome surprise, especially during what had been shaping up to be a tedious Christmas, thanks to Nicky's sulks.

As a discreet waiter topped up their champagne glasses,

he studied this beautiful, understated and elegant woman, simply yet chicly dressed in black velvet pants and a high-necked cashmere sweater that defined her excellent figure. Her jewelry was exquisite and unobtrusive. Apart from her obvious beauty there was something very enticing about her, he decided, something in that sexy, soft Southern drawl that charmed.

"Tell me about your home," he said, interested in learning more about who she was, what she thought, how she felt. There was a rare unspoiled quality about her that struck a chord.

"Home? That'd be Oleander Creek, my family's plantation." She tilted her head thoughtfully. "It's a wonderful old place that belonged to my great-great-grandmother. It used to be in the country but now it's practically on the outskirts of Savannah. Although I also have a town house in the city, Oleander Creek is my real home and I love it dearly," she sighed, and twirled her glass, eyes soft. "It's one of those rare places where it's possible to find real peace." She glanced at him and he nodded.

"I know exactly what you mean. It's the same way I feel about Graney."

"Graney." She pronounced the word carefully. "That sounds dreadfully grand," she countered, a smile hovering about her lips.

"Not really." He shrugged. "It *was* originally a medieval Irish castle, so I suppose that makes it fairly impressive. But behind those thick stone walls lie a plethora of problems, believe me. Trivial things," he grinned, "such as outdated plumbing and unreliable electricity. Helps scare off unwanted guests." He took a sip of champagne and smiled when she let out a gurgle of laughter.

"Sounds just like Oleander. Believe me, I've scared off my share of unwanted guests, too."

"Do you have many of them?" he queried, interested to learn more.

"In politics, they swarm like bees to honey." She let out a little sigh. "Harlan, my hus—soon to be ex-husband—"

she corrected hastily "—hates that the place is so old," she added, blushing. "*Decrepit* is the exact term he uses."

Johnny laid his glass down and pricked up his ears. She'd mentioned earlier that she was getting a divorce, and from her description of her husband, it was no wonder. "Likes things in good order, huh?"

"Oh, yes, only the best," she said dryly, folding her hands on the table and staring absently at the cloth. "He considers Oleander rather shabby, despite all the restoration work I've put into it. He wanted to bring in a New York decorator to smarten the place up and make it presentable for his Washington cronies, but I refused." She shrugged and their eyes met. "Maybe it was wrong of me—it really is an ideal spot to entertain—but I couldn't bear the thought of it being picture-perfect and used only for fund-raisers, or as some kind of *Gone with the Wind* prop for PR purposes. It's my sanctuary and I love it just the way it is, with the stairs that creak, the layers of old dust up in the attic, the shutters that bang relentlessly in the storms during the rainy season. To me it's just home."

"Sounds like the old place has a lot of stories to tell."

Elm laughed. "Many more than you can imagine. I had some pretty outrageous ancestors. My great-great-grandmother Elma is practically a legend in Savannah—the original Steel Magnolia."

"Steel magnolia?" Johnny repeated blankly.

"It's an expression that means a certain combination of Southern grace and inner grit. In Elma's case, she had both in spades." He watched her take a quick sip of champagne and settle back in her chair. "As Sherman's forces were advancing on Savannah, a forward scouting party of maybe a half-dozen soldiers made their way to Oleander Creek and were preparing to force their way into the house when one of them slammed his rifle butt into the front step and cracked the stone. Well, Elma thought this was unpardonably rude and confronted them at the door, saying there was no way they were getting inside unless they cleaned themselves up and remembered their manners. Apparently she gave those

Yankees such a tongue-lashing that they left without even looking for the gold Elma and her slaves had hidden in the bottom of the well.'' She smiled and took another sip. ''The crack in the step is still there.''

''Sounds like Miss Elma was an enterprising woman. Do you take after her?''

''Me? Oh, no, although I'm named after her. But she was far more courageous than I've ever been or had to be.''

''Did she survive the war?''

''Oh, yes.'' She smiled, her eyes soft in the candlelight. ''The tale goes that the Brigadier General commanding the Yankee scouts was none too pleased when his men came back empty-handed. He arrived at Oleander later the same day, ready to do battle with the terrible harridan his men had described, and torch the place if necessary.'' She leaned her elbows lightly on the pristine white cloth and continued the story. ''Instead, he found Elma in the hall, decked out in a beautiful evening gown and welcoming him and his officers to dinner in the most ladylike fashion.''

He grinned at the image. ''What did the general do?''

''What could he do?'' She spread her hands and laughed. ''He was just a Yankee—not up to all Elma's Southern charm. According to local historians, he sat down to dinner, enjoyed a few glasses of excellent vintage brandy, then left, loudly proclaiming the graciousness of Southern hospitality. Of course, the uncensored story passed down by one of Elma's slaves is that he spent the night with Elma after she'd extracted his promise to furnish her with supplies and protection when Sherman reached Savannah.''

''Ah, not just an enterprising woman, but a practical one, too. And did the general keep his promise?''

''Well, Oleander's still standing, so I guess he did. My estate manager, Ely, who's a direct descendent of Elma's favorite slave, still insists you can't trust a Yankee as far you can throw him, but even he admits that the general must have been a gentleman.'' She smiled at him, then lowered her gaze to her empty dessert plate.

"Do you all have a thing against Yankees?" he asked casually. "That could pose a problem."

"Why?" she asked, frowning.

"My mother's a Yankee. Good Irish stock from Pittsburgh. I believe her family, the Rileys, didn't arrive until after the Civil War, but still, I wouldn't want you to think I was hiding my origins from you," he teased.

"It's certainly a thought," she responded, eyes filled with laughter as she leaned back. "But I guess the general paved the way for you by holding his promises. Also, if I remember rightly, you're an aristocrat. As far as Southerners are concerned, that's definitely a plus."

"You relieve my mind, madam," he said, taking her hand and raising it gallantly to his lips. "For a moment there I thought I'd cooked my goose."

Her laugh sparkled as their eyes met for a fleeting moment before Elm withdrew her hand. "Okay, your turn," she said quickly. "What makes you spend the better part of your time at your castle, I wonder?"

"Same thing that sends you scuttling off to your plantation, I should think," he murmured with a challenging grin, eyes seeking hers. "The desire to flee the madding crowd. Plus, I love the place. It's home, just like Oleander is for you."

"You never thought of moving to Pittsburgh?" she countered.

"Uh, actually, no. I love the States but I'm an Irishman through and through. Give me Dublin any day. Anyway, I have a business to run in Ireland."

"Really?"

"Graney is a stud farm. I breed Thoroughbreds."

"A stud farm. That must require a lot of patience."

"It does. And I must warn you not to get me going on the subject of horseflesh. My mother claims that I can become a dead bore."

Elm laughed and as she did so, Johnny leaned back, sipped his brandy and relaxed. All in all, it was turning out to be a very agreeable dinner.

* * *

Elm grinned, enjoying the easy intimacy between them, so deliciously alien yet somehow also familiar. She was deeply intrigued by the reserve she sensed behind his relaxed manner. Gioconda had said something about having a long story to tell her when they had a moment. And she supposed he must have been married at some point, since he had a sixteen-year-old son.

"What about your ex-wife?" she asked suddenly. "Didn't she like it at Graney?" The words were out before she could stop herself. Deeply embarrassed by her rude question, she cringed as his eyes shuttered and he carefully chose a cigar from the waiter, who happened to stop by the table at just that moment with a humidor.

"Do you mind?"

"Of course not, go ahead." Elm wished the floor would open up and swallow her as the end of the cigar was carefully clipped off and lit. Perhaps she should just change the subject. How could she have been so gauche? It was none of her business what his ex-wife liked or didn't like.

"I've never been to a place like your castle. I've visited quite a few English country houses, but that's not the same, is it?" she remarked hastily.

"Very different," he agreed blandly, fully concentrating on pulling on the cigar. "Actually, when Marie Ange was alive, we didn't live there. We split our time between London and Paris."

A rush of horrified realization made Elm look straight at him. "I'm so sorry. I had no idea. I—it was extremely bad manners of me, I—"

"Don't. He reached across and laid a hand over hers. "How could you possibly have known? It was a natural conclusion to think I was divorced. You may remember Marie Ange. We met at Rosey. Anyway, it all happened a long time ago, so don't feel bad." He squeezed her hand.

Elm mustered a smile, still chiding herself. Then she glanced uneasily at the snifter the waiter had placed before her. It was foolish to accept an after-dinner drink, but she could use it after her faux pas.

"Now, tell me some more about your life in Savannah," Johnny said, deftly redirecting the conversation. "I imagine a politician's wife has an inordinate amount of duties to perform?" He quirked a brow and raised his glass.

She shrugged, thankful for the change of subject. "There are lots of political and social functions, but I try to limit my involvement where I can. I far prefer to work on my own projects. At present, I'm restoring the gardens at Oleander with the help of some residents from the local shelter for abused women."

"That sounds very laudable."

"Not at all. I hope I can help restore some harmony in their lives, that's all."

"I didn't mean to sound condescending. I'm sure it's a very worthwhile thing you're doing for these women. And the gardens," he added with a smile.

"Well, I discovered the original garden plans purely by accident while cleaning out the attic one day and that's how the idea was born, thanks to a good friend of mine who runs the shelter. We both agreed it might be a wonderfully therapeutic experience for these women to be involved in the restoration project."

"And what do you do with the rest of your time?"

"Oh, the rest of the time I paint."

"What medium do you paint in?"

"Oils. I do some abstract, but mostly landscapes. The occasional portrait."

"Do you exhibit?"

"Now and then. But organizing an exhibit is time-consuming. Somehow, other things always end up taking precedence." She paused a moment, staring into the distance. Then she shrugged and gave him a rueful grin. "I'm not going to let that happen again. Let things get in the way, I mean. Indeed, Gioconda won't let me. She's been trying to persuade me to commit to an exhibit in Italy—I'm half afraid she's going to lock me in a room with only my paintbrushes until I cry uncle and allow her to organize the opening party for me in Florence.''

Johnny watched as she eyed the cognac, biting her lip as though deciding whether or not she should drink it. The gesture was so unintentionally erotic that he almost lost his focus.

"This meal was perfectly delicious," she said, laying her napkin on the table. "You'll have to roll me out of here if I'm not careful. I haven't stopped eating since I arrived." She glanced about the restaurant, seemingly enchanted by the atmosphere, the open fireplace, the low-beamed ceiling and the intimacy.

"That's what Gstaad's all about—relaxing, eating and having fun."

"I guess you're right," she agreed. "I'd forgotten how people here in Europe know how to enjoy life." Her huge chestnut eyes had taken on a wistful expression that gave her an air of vulnerability. She was a compelling and complex woman, he decided, with an intriguing layer of uncertainty beneath that well-bred confident exterior. She was also perceptive, he mused; she'd sensed his discomfort at discussing Marie Ange and had immediately tried to redirect the conversation. Usually he deeply resented personal questions, and yet he hadn't minded Elm's. For some reason he didn't feel threatened—although part of him knew he should, for she was entirely capable of upsetting his well-ordered world.

He hadn't come to Gstaad for a fling, but he felt a surprisingly strong sexual attraction to her, and he hoped that the subtle undercurrents he'd sensed signaled an equal interest on her part. The question was whether either of them was in a position to do anything about it. The prospect was both alluring and dangerous. He'd be willing to bet that if they acted on their impulses, they'd both be getting far more than they bargained for.

He watched as she took a fleeting look at her wrist. "Oh,

dear. It's almost eleven-thirty. Time's flown. Maybe I'd better be getting back to Gioconda's.''

"Already?" he asked, surprised at the regret he felt that the evening was coming to an end.

"It's getting late."

"Really? Gosh! I'm dreadfully sorry. I didn't realize Gioconda had turned into such a stickler—an eleven o'clock curfew's pretty strict."

Elm laughed. "I'm sorry. I'm afraid I'm not good at this," she admitted, pressing her long, smooth hands together again in an elegant yet nervous gesture. "It's been a long time since I went out to dinner with anyone except my hus—ex—oh, God, when will I get this right? Soon-to-be ex-husband."

"How long?" he asked softly.

"Well, let's see." She twiddled the snifter. "I married Harlan right out of college, so a long time. Twelve years, still more if you count the engagement." She gave a nervous laugh and glanced quickly up as the waiter hovered solicitously, seeing if they needed anything.

Smiling, Johnny reached across the table and took her hand in his, casually turning her fingers. "I was thinking that perhaps we could either go to the Bellevue—probably meet up with some of our old pals." He grimaced comically. "Or preferably we could go somewhere else on our own for a nightcap. That is, if Gioconda won't get too worried about the lateness of the hour."

"Oh, shut up," she giggled, allowing his bronzed hand to stay put over hers,

"Well?" he prodded, "any thoughts on the matter?"

"Perhaps," she murmured cautiously, and he wondered if she was conscious of his fingers lightly clasping hers.

"I've got a perfect compromise," he said temptingly. "How about going to the Green Go at the Palace Hotel for old times' sake?"

"You mean dance as if we're teenagers again?"

"Hell, why not? Let's go relive our youth."

"Your youth, perhaps, not mine," she chuckled. "I can

assure you that we never danced together as teenagers—I expect I would have expired from the thrill.'' She drew her hand away, pausing for a moment. He could read her hesitation, her doubt that this was all happening too fast, then sensed the moment when she was ready to take the plunge.

"Shall we?" he asked.

"Yes. Why not?"

Late that night, Elm curled under the duvet, her feet aching deliciously from hours of dancing, unable to wipe the silly grin from her face. Johnny was handsome, gallant and wonderful and not at all daunting. Still, all evening she'd been conscious of his strong masculine aura, the magnetic pull of his personality; all the things she'd imagined he would be when she'd scribbled her longings and dreams in her tattered high-school diary. It seemed so ridiculous, like a soppy novel, that he was turning out to be exactly the kind of man she'd imagined in her fevered schoolgirl dreams. She thought of the chaste kiss he'd dropped on her cheek as he brought her to Gioconda's door, and realized wistfully that had she not married Harlan so young and for all the wrong reasons, she might have instead built a life with someone like Johnny.

She tucked her arms under the pillow, propped up her neck and stared at the silver moon piercing the crack in the curtains, picturing what people back in Savannah would say if they knew she'd danced the night away in the arms of an Irish viscount. She burst out laughing, imagining the shocked murmurs, the conjecturing gleam in the eyes of her peers, the rabid curiosity. It was liberating to realize she didn't give a damn. In the past weeks her priorities had suddenly changed, and kowtowing to Savannah society, with its petty, restrictive rules, wasn't even on the list.

Thinking of Savannah brought Harlan to mind, and she sighed heavily. Of course, the divorce wasn't de facto yet. There would probably be some bitter battles up ahead, she acknowledged. Harlan wouldn't easily relinquish all their marriage had brought him. For him, it had meant an entrée into a world that would otherwise have been far harder to broach. It wasn't her that he'd wanted, she thought angrily, but rather everything that she represented. And if she hadn't been so blind, so determined to maintain the fiction that her marriage was fine, she might have recognized sooner that, emotionally, it had been over for a while.

Had she ever really been in love with Harlan, or had she just fallen for his good looks and suave manner? Surely she'd felt true affection for him at the beginning? He'd been so charming and ambitious, had seemed so much like her father. Indeed, the two men had taken an instant liking to each other; they supported the same causes, and Harlan had flattered George Hathaway with assurances that he was the younger man's role model. She'd known that by marrying Harlan, she'd be able to give her father the son he'd always wanted, one who could fulfill the ambitions he hadn't believed his daughter could meet.

Of course, it hadn't taken her long after the wedding to find out just how selfish Harlan could be, and to realize that his boyish good looks and suave manners were all part of the same facade he used with his electorate. And if you looked carefully enough you'd realize that his smile never reached his eyes.

Still, she'd spent a good part of her life at his side, and there had been some great times together. Moments of affection and intimacy that she still believed were real, especially before his political career took off and he'd begun to spend so much time in D.C. She sighed again. It was sobering to realize there just hadn't been enough of those moments to make the marriage worth fighting for.

In fact, all that was left of her relationship with Harlan was the print on their marriage license, and soon that, too, would be gone; even now, Meredith was working on finalizing the details and paperwork for the divorce.

As for Harlan, it was undoubtedly the political ramifications of the divorce that would bother him most. Probably her father as well, she noted sadly. He didn't know yet, and she would have to tell him soon, perhaps after Christmas.

He had such high hopes for Harlan, she knew, feeling guilty for being the cause of such disruption and wondering if it was fair to do this to them when an election was around the corner. Harlan, for all his faults, was truly a brilliant politician, and had done a lot of good for the people of Georgia. Daddy was right. He had what it took.

Elm sighed and turned on her side, recognizing that there was never a right time and that she must go ahead, whatever the consequences. She'd spent a lifetime trying to please them all, trying to be the perfect daughter, wife and hostess—she would have tried mother, too, had life offered her the chance.

In a strange way, her evening out with Johnny tonight had helped clarify the issues for her. Her marriage was truly over, and she now had the freedom to make her own choices. It would be hypocritical to deny the riveting attraction she'd experienced tonight as Johnny had twirled her about the floor to the infectious beat of salsa, false to pretend she didn't want to enjoy something more than Harlan's selfish bursts of sex. The temptation of discovering what it felt like to be properly held in a man's arms—a man who might actually think of her pleasure and happiness before his own—was devastatingly alluring. She swallowed, throbbing with anticipation, shocked to find her mind running ahead of itself when all they'd done was dine and dance together.

A smile touched her lips as she recalled the walk home afterward in the bitingly cold, starry night, arm in arm, sliding down the hill, catching each other on icy patches and laughing like kids. What if Johnny was right and, as he'd whispered when they'd parted, their paths had crossed again for a reason?

Elm sat straight up and tucked her knees under her chin, pulled the duvet closer and wondered what sort of a lover he would be. Generous? Giving? Tender? God, she was thirty-four years old and the only man she'd ever slept with was Harlan, her first real boyfriend. Still, she mustn't let her naiveté run away with her. It was all very suave and sophisticated to have a passing fling with someone—if you were like Gio, that is, and that was the kind of world you moved in. But it wasn't hers and somehow Elm wasn't quite sure if she was ready for this yet.

With a yawn, she snuggled under the goose-down cover, half ashamed of her silly recurring schoolgirl fantasies as she recalled the feel of his arms about her as they'd swayed on the dance floor, the scent of his aftershave and the strange comfort it had afforded her. Maybe that was it. Maybe she was just seeking a comfort zone.

But Johnny was a gentleman and would never make a move without her consent, she realized. If she wanted something more than casual friendship, she'd have to signal that. What would he do, she wondered suddenly, if she let down her guard and was frank about her interest?

Realizing she would never get to sleep, Elm switched on the bedside lamp and popped a pill, still toying with the idea of crossed paths and destiny. Just before her eyes closed, she wondered about the consequences of flouting destiny.

Then she let out another sleepy yawn. There was no end to the justifications you could come up with if you really put your mind to it, she reasoned drowsily. The real truth, she acknowledged, eyes closing, was that even if she were bent on seducing Johnny, she wouldn't have the first clue how to go about it.

9

She had a sensational body, Harlan reflected, letting his hand slide over Teresa's voluptuous naked butt. And boy, could she move it. What a great piece of ass, he sighed happily. Now he understood why Tyler Brock had moved her into his Skidaway mansion so fast. She was as hot as chili pepper, even if she couldn't speak a damn word of English. Anyway, who needed language to have good sex?

She stretched on the large bed like a cat, her dark hair brushing against his skin, and moaned in satisfaction. Turning her around, he lay back against the pillows and let her come down on him, her tongue playing havoc with his balls. Then she straddled him, and he let her guide him inside her, delighting in her damp heat, the way she rode him and the sensuous roll of her hips that caused all sorts of indescribable sensations. Closing his eyes, Harlan indulged himself. Then two delectable realizations hit simultaneously; that he was fucking a hot little whore in Elm's very own bed, which was no more than she deserved for all the trouble she was causing, and that there was something wonderfully empowering about screwing a woman while Brock unknowingly picked up the tab. The combination made him come in a quick, hot spurt that left him incredibly satisfied.

Boy, Teresa was a good fuck. Best one he'd had in a while. And Brock couldn't be taking care of business for her to be fucking like this off the record, he reflected smugly as he lay in the aftermath, the girl's head on his shoulder. Brock might go on believing he was at the helm, that his donations to the campaign made Harlan subservient, willing to answer his beck and call. But he was wrong, Harlan concluded, a grin covering his face, damned wrong. Still, it served its purpose to have the man stay on his ego trip for now, at any rate. Once he was reelected and the funds were in, things might be different. Or they might not, he recognized ruefully. There would always have to be men like Brock around, until he was absolutely sure of his own power base. They were, after all, a necessary part of an up-and-coming politician's entourage.

He sighed, then yawned and, giving Teresa's butt a friendly slap, sat on the edge of the bed.

"Time to leave, baby."

"Leave?" She frowned.

"Yeah, you know, bye-bye, adios. But not for long. I'll call you on your mobile." He pointed to her cell phone lying by the bed next to her handbag. *"Sexo, muy bueno,"* he added in his minimal Spanish, wiggling his eyebrows suggestively at her.

Teresa laughed, threw back her long black hair and flashed a row of perfect white teeth. *"Muy bueno,"* she agreed, arching her tits toward him provocatively.

"Oh no, hon, no more today," he said, shaking his head sadly, then grinning. *"Mañana."*

Teresa pouted and nodded and let her hand play with her breast, eyes holding his. For a moment he was tempted to fuck her again, but then thought better of it. It would mean he'd be late for the Historic Savannah Preservation Society dinner. Leaning over, he gave her nipples a quick pinch and a taunting lick. Then, straightening, he motioned to her to get dressed before moving toward the bathroom.

Hmm, he pondered, if it weren't so damned inconvenient for other reasons, Elm's absence was something he could definitely get used to.

* * *

The next morning Elm woke to a bright day peeking through the drapes, and the delicious smell of freshly baked croissants and strong Italian coffee floating up from the dining room. She stretched, realizing something was vaguely different this morning. Then she recalled the night before and smiled sleepily before jumping out of bed and pulling back the drapes. Sunlight burst into the room, settling in a puddle on the duvet. A knock on the door made her look up.

"Come in." She turned, rubbed her tousled hair and smiled at Gioconda, who had popped her head around the door.

"Good morning, *bella*. Have a nice evening?" Gioconda glided into the room, already dressed in her sleek black-and-white Prada ski suit and a crimson sweater. "I'm joining a group on the glacier today. We're going up in the chopper. I'll be gone all day. So, tell me—" she sat down on the edge of the bed and studied an errant nail as Elm slipped on her dressing gown and slippers "—how was your dinner last night?"

"Great."

Gioconda stretched out on the bed, long, lush and feline, and propped her chin thoughtfully in her hands, her mischievous eyes black as two ripe olives. She let out a husky low laugh. "Is that all, just great? From what I heard, you came in late enough." She quirked a well-groomed brow.

"Umberto," Elm said darkly. "Back to his old tricks, I see."

"He's worried about you being out late with a strange man. I told him Johnny wasn't strange, that you've known him for twenty years. He felt happier about it."

"Gee, thanks! Anything else you'd like to share with the class?"

"No, but before I leave I want to know what happened." Gioconda sat up straight, glanced at her Chopard diamond watch and moved her hands impatiently.

"Nothing happened."

"Nothing? Not one itsy-bitsy teeny-weeny kiss?" Her

hands dropped in patent disappointment. "*Madonna mia*, I had a better opinion of Graney than that."

"Gio, don't be ridiculous. We had a nice, pleasant, civilized evening, that's all. Stop trying to make this into something it's not." Elm tried to sound convincing. It was true, of course. It had been a delightful evening. But to deny the undercurrents would be to fool herself.

"Are you going to see him today?"

"He said he'd call." Elm glanced at her friend doubtfully. "But perhaps it would be better if I didn't see him, Gio. I don't need problems right now. I've got enough to cope with already, and I didn't intend to—"

"Ah!" Gioconda rose from the bed, triumphant. "So nothing happened, but you know very well that it could happen if you let it, right, *cara?*"

"Lordy, I don't know." Elm threw up her hands in despair. "It's too early in the morning to be talking about all this. Can't I at least have a cup of coffee?" she countered. But as they made their way down the wide staircase and approached the dining room, Elm came to a sudden halt on the last step. "You know what Aunt Frances would say about all this, don't you?" she asked.

"No, tell me."

"That Johnny Graney has trouble written all over him and that one should always avoid what's bound to end up in tears."

"*Va bene*, I'll say no more." Gio shrugged, cast her eyes heavenward and mumbled in Italian as she led Elm into the dining room and poured her a large caffè latte.

"It's not that I don't like him," Elm continued, "I do. In fact he's—well—terrific. I just think I should back off a bit," she murmured after the first long sip, "before he gets any ideas, you know…" She threw her friend a pregnant look.

"I know exactly what you mean." Gio wiggled her black brows expressively and laughed. "Loosen up, Elm, you're on vacation. You came here for a break, to get away from that idiot paranoid husband of yours and have fun. Let this be a fresh start. A little flirtation can't do you any harm. Quite the opposite, I should think. Now, instead of blushing like a Victorian virgin, you should be thinking when and where you're going to get him into bed.''

"Gio! It's not like that," Elm exclaimed, setting the large blue-and-yellow china cup down in the saucer with a bang. "We're just old schoolmates. I mean, he hasn't even kissed me."

"Who are you trying to fool, *bella?*"

"I…" Their eyes met, Gioconda's filled with wicked understanding and laughter.

"Go for it, Elm. You're young, beautiful, single—nearly—and it seems to me it's about time you caught up with all you've missed while you catered to Harlan Machiavelli MacBride. Why, you've about as much idea of men as you had when you left school. And *Dio,* that wasn't saying much," she added with feeling. "Besides, I'd be willing to bet Harlan was selfish as hell in bed."

"Really, Gio," Elm sputtered. "I don't think it's appropriate to be discussing this over breakfast." Somehow discussing her husband didn't seem right, even if he was out of the picture.

"Really, *cara?* And when, exactly, do you consider it an appropriate time?" Gioconda asked, spreading her tapered, scarlet-nailed fingers on the table, eyes brimming with affection.

"Oh, I don't know! Why don't you go skiing and leave me be," Elm complained. "If Harlan was, well, not the world's most exciting lover—though as you've pointed out, I don't have much room for comparison—I always thought it was well…okay." She shrugged. "It could have been my fault, too, you know," she ventured. "After all, it takes two to tango."

"Oh no, you don't!" Gioconda jumped up, hair flying. "You're not going to take the blame again. No way, *bella.*" She wagged a finger firmly. "All these years I've heard you convince yourself that everything wrong in that marriage was your fault. I didn't say anything at the time because it wasn't my place. But now, *basta*. No more. You've got more guts than that. Elm, recognize the truth,'' she implored. ''Harlan used you, just as he uses everybody, for your money, your father's position and anything else he thought he could suck out of you.''

''You're right. Though I like to think that, at least at the beginning, we were…well, I guess 'in love' seems like a big statement after all that's happened since, but—'' She looked away, the years of criticism and self-doubt rolling before her. ''Anyway, Johnny's probably just out for a good time,'' she remarked, fiddling with the edge of the tablecloth.

''Isn't that what you're out for, too? You're both adults. Where's the glitch?''

Elm smiled briefly. ''I guess there isn't one. I'm just not as worldly as you, Gio. I need to adjust. It seems kind of… I dunno.'' She shrugged once more and downed some more coffee.

''Whatever.'' Gioconda shook her head. ''I have to go.'' She blew Elm a kiss from the door. ''Just don't take forever making up your mind about Viscount Graney. It's—'' she glanced at her watch ''—my God, already the twenty-second of December today, and the vacation will be over in a couple of weeks. If I was you, I'd make my mind up fast.'' She winked. ''And remember, men are only good to have fun with. Enjoy it while it lasts. No commitments, no until-death-do-us-parts, just plain old fun.''

''You make it sound like I just want a handsome lover.''

''Frankly, *cara,* I think a handsome lover—and from the reports I've heard, Johnny's pretty remarkable in that department—is exactly what you need.''

''Reports?'' Elm squeaked, suddenly uncomfortable. It made her feel cheap, another notch in a well-used belt.

''Oh, stop getting uptight.''

''But you said—''

''*Niente,* nothing to worry about—'' Gioconda waved dismissively ''—just things one hears along the grapevine.''

A car horn hooted outside and Gioconda grabbed her anorak from the chair. ''I have to get this show on the road if I want to catch the chopper. Bye, *bella,* have another coffee and relax. And remember, you're not in Savannah anymore, there's no need to be looking over your shoulder wondering what people are thinking. It's your life. Live it. *Ciao.*'' She waved goodbye.

The phone rang just as Gioconda closed the door, and Elm could hear Umberto's deep voice answering the call. Her heart beat faster as she wondered if it was Johnny.

Confirmation came thirty seconds later. ''*Buon giorno, signora,* the telephone is for you.'' Umberto handed her the portable phone with a little bow then disappeared into the kitchen. Elm managed to quiet her pulse, but couldn't suppress the grin covering her face from ear to ear.

It was at lunch on the sunny terrace of the Sonnenhof—a gorgeous chalet atop a mountain above the village of Saanen with a cozy wood interior, low pine beams, a killer view and food to die for—that Elm realized just what a hypocrite she'd been that morning. For sitting across from him, slowly sipping her Kir Royal, she couldn't stop her vivid imagination from picturing them together, preferably somewhere quiet and undressed. The thought was deliciously shocking.

Johnny had picked her up at ten sharp and they'd driven up to Shönried, then done several runs down the Horneggli before ending up, well exercised, at the Sonnenhof. They'd laughed a lot, she reflected with a satisfied little sigh. Perhaps their conversation wasn't terribly profound—they certainly hadn't dug into world politics, which, after Harlan, was just fine by her—but he was amusing, charming and easygoing. Being with him wasn't a strain. She didn't have to think of what to say or wonder if he thought she was stupid, as she so often did with Harlan's supercilious Washington cronies and the pseudo-intellectual group he liked to have hanging around him, parroting his opinions. This was simple, and reminded her of who she really was. Gio and Meredith were right, she concluded, she'd become so focused on catering to Harlan's every whim that she'd lost touch with herself.

They had just ordered when she saw two men approach the table. One was of medium height, sandy-haired, in his mid-thirties, and obviously American, the other a boy who could only, she decided, be Johnny's son. They were like peas in a pod, she reflected, realizing with a stab of nostalgia that it was like seeing a replica of Johnny all those years ago.

"Elm, this is my brother Liam, and my son, Nicky."

"Hi." They shook hands.

"Mind if they join us?" Johnny asked.

"Of course not." She moved over on the corner bench and smiled invitingly at Nicky, who eyed her warily then sat down. Liam and Johnny sat opposite.

"So, you're from Georgia?" Liam inquired.

"Savannah."

"Beautiful city."

"Dad, can I order a Coke?"

"Of course." Johnny hailed the waitress. "I guess you'll be having your usual, guys?"

"Yep." Liam leaned back and smiled. "Only decent steak you can get in this town. He brings the meat in from Argentina. That's the trouble in Europe, you can't get—"

"Did you ski with my dad?" Nicky asked her suddenly.

"Yes, we skied the Horneggli."

"You must be good," he conceded reluctantly. "Dad's a pretty advanced skier."

"And you?"

"I snowboard mostly. I'm on the Rosey team."

"So was your father, if I remember rightly. The ski team, I mean."

"You went to Rosey?" Nicky eyed her with new respect. "Bet that was a while ago, huh?"

Johnny met Elm's eyes and they laughed. "It certainly doesn't seem nearly twenty years, does it?"

"No, it doesn't," Elm agreed, determined to include Nicky in the conversation.

"My mother was at Rosey, too," he said. Elm caught the edge of defiance in his tone.

"I know. I remember her. She was very beautiful and had great grades. She won the prize for drama, I recall." She noticed the quick look exchanged between Liam and Johnny. Something wasn't right. There was an uneasy undercurrent when Marie Ange was mentioned. She could almost feel the tension coursing between Johnny and his son.

Liam was studying his cell phone. He sent her an apologetic glance. "Just need to check some stock prices. Haven't had time this morning. This vacation has put everything on hold."

"Uncle Liam, get a life," Nicky exclaimed.

"Nicky's right," Johnny said. "Leave that damn phone at home, Liam, and enjoy yourself. Elm, we have this major family problem here." Johnny leaned toward her, laughing. "Liam never has time for anything except work. We're trying to convert him—unsuccessfully, I might add—to pleasure."

The lunch proved to be deliciously entertaining. Elm enjoyed the interaction between the brothers, amused at how different they were, the one so dark, Irish and aristocratic, the other a strong-willed workaholic American businessman. And Nicky. He was sweet and bright and sulky and all the things she imagined an adolescent would be.

They left the restaurant ready to hit the slopes, although after a huge *steak à l'ardoisek,* a couple of Kir Royals and two bottles of delectable local Swiss wine, Elm was amazed any of them could even move. Nicky challenged her to a run and by the end of the afternoon they'd become fast friends. She made him promise to show her some of his snowboarding moves before she left for the States. By the time Johnny dropped her off at Gioconda's chalet, she was wonderfully tired and ready for a hot bath.

"It was a delightful day, thank you. Your brother and son are great."

"How about tonight?" He leaned back against the car door and eyed her thoughtfully.

"I think I'll take a rain check. I'm pretty beat and I have some calls to make to the States." It was ridiculous, of course, to refuse his invitation when she'd like nothing more than to accept, but she needed to catch her breath, to assess just where she intended to go with all this. A quiet evening seemed like just the thing.

"You're sure I can't persuade you? We could go to the movies, if you don't want to be late. I could see what's on and call you," he said, his smile deliciously persuasive.

"Well, I…look, why don't we have a rest and then see in a little while," she countered, dying to accept, but not wanting to give in too fast. Oh God, this was all so difficult. She could feel him drawing her like a magnet. She had never felt anything quite so strong, so intense or alluring. If she'd read about it in a book she would have thought it was nonsense.

But it wasn't.

She reached for the car door. "Thanks for a wonderful day. It's been truly great. And I'm still reeling from lunch."

Johnny jumped out of the Range Rover and, removing her skis from the back, came round and helped her out. Then he walked her slowly to the chalet.

"Well, perhaps dinner tomorrow, then," he said regretfully. "I'll give you a call."

No use insisting, he realized, although he was surprised how urgently he'd wanted her to say yes. Elm was proving addictive. What was it about her that was so intoxicating? But perhaps she was right and they should take it one step at a time. The more he saw of her, the more he knew he wanted her. And not just in the usual way of conquer, enjoy, discard—or allow himself to be discarded. This was different. There was an underlying intensity, a sweetness and depth to Elm that attracted him far more strongly than he'd reckoned for.

He wasn't sure he was ready for that kind of relationship. No, he corrected, he knew he wasn't. Perhaps an evening at home might remind him of that.

* * *

Johnny looked up from the papers he'd been pretending to review at his desk. In fact, he was thinking about Elm, still trying to fathom why her simple refusal of his invitation to dinner bothered him so. Perhaps it was just the novel experience of being turned down, he admitted—although, actually, it was rather pleasant to know there were still women out there who didn't jump when he snapped his fingers. But then, the kind of women he usually met knew the name of the game and had no illusions about his intentions. They understood it was a passing interlude and nothing more. Elm, he suspected, didn't play such games.

A knock on the door made him raise his head.

Liam peeked his sandy head around the door. "Mind if I come in?"

"Go right ahead."

"Thanks for lunch," Liam remarked, glancing at his brother. "Nicky loosened up a bit. Seems like a nice gal, that Elm Hathaway."

"She does, doesn't she?" Johnny replied with a noncommittal smile.

"But I have to say," Liam remarked, his tone suddenly serious, "I wouldn't fool around with her if I were you."

"Excuse me?" Johnny sat up straighter. His brother never, ever interfered in his private life. "Why on earth not?"

"For one, because she's married."

"Getting divorced," he countered.

"And—" Liam leaned against the doorjamb as though he hadn't been interrupted "—I'll tell you something else."

"Yes?" He eyed Liam coldly. Elm was his affair.

"Her father is Senator Hathaway of Georgia. Surely you must have figured that out."

"Actually, I hadn't thought about it."

"He's an old acquaintance of Dad's from way back when."

"I know that."

"So you should realize that he's a very conservative man—the conscience of the Senate, so to speak. I doubt he'd take kindly to the discovery that his yet-to-be-divorced daughter is shacking up with you.''

''Look, don't you think you're jumping the gun?'' Johnny bit back icily. He wasn't going to ''shack up'' with Elm…was he? It sounded so insulting. ''My friendship with Elm is purely platonic and—''

''Sure. But for how long? I ain't stupid, bro. I know the way you operate. She's far too gorgeous to just let slip away. And I happen to think she likes you. Anyway, it's just a friendly brotherly warning, that's all. I don't want Mom having a fit.''

''Great. Any other good news?''

''No.'' Liam sighed and turned. ''I'll see you later.''

Trust Liam to be the bearer of bad tidings. Damn Senator Hathaway—and Elm's husband, too, for that matter.

He passed a hand absently over his chin. Not that there was much point in shaving again if he wasn't going out. It was ridiculous that going out should be contingent on Elm's plans, though, he reasoned, getting up and walking into the bathroom, where he pulled a razor out of the cupboard.

At the sound of another knock on the door, Johnny stopped the blade halfway down his foam-covered cheek. He looked up to see his son in the mirror.

''Do another run?'' he asked casually. Nicky had been aloof the past few days. He just wished the boy would open up, and wondered suddenly if perhaps Nicky was in trouble. But as Elm had pointed out when he'd touched on the subject after lunch, it wouldn't do to ask. He'd just be rebuffed once more. What was it she'd said? That his son would come around in his own good time.

''So. How've you been?'' He glanced at Nicky in the mirror again, the razor gliding smoothly on down. As he rinsed the blade, he noticed Nicky's foot nervously drumming the side of the tub where he'd perched.

''Something troubling you, son?''

''Sort of.'' He glanced up briefly, his expression full of worry and doubt. ''I need to tell you something, Dad. Something that happened the night before school vacation.''

"Shoot."

"You're not going to like it."

Johnny threw some water on his face before grabbing a towel and turning. "Why don't you come in the bedroom and tell me about it."

"Okay." Nicky followed his father reluctantly into the bedroom and flopped into one of the oversize armchairs while Johnny dashed on some aftershave. *Let him take his time, don't press him. Give the kid a chance.*

"I—you're going to be really pissed off, Dad."

"More pissed off than when you sent Lucia the snake?"

A mischievous grin lit up Nicky's face and their eyes met. "Boy, was she angry. I wish you could have seen her."

"Thanks, but no thanks. I was very glad I was several thousand miles away. Anyway, what's troubling you? Whatever it is, I'll try to help you solve it," he said quietly, seating himself opposite the boy.

"The trouble is, you can't help, nobody can," Nicky burst out, his eyes—so like Johnny's own—flashing wildly.

"Hey, calm down. There's nothing that can't be dealt with in life. Now, come on," Johnny urged, leaning forward. "Why don't you just get it off your chest."

"I guess I might as well. They're going to call you, anyway," Nicky mumbled, falling back against the cushions and scowling. "We had this party, you see. Jim Padrone, Hal, Peter and I."

"Go on."

"Yeah. Well, we got all this booze. Whiskey, beer, Hal even brought a huge bottle of sangria."

"Jesus," Johnny murmured sympathetically, "I hope you didn't drink any of that. Bottled sangria is bloody awful."

"No, I—hey, you're not angry?" He looked up, surprised.

"I presume you're going to tell me you got busted?"

"How'd you know?" Nicky looked at him in awe.

"Been there, done that."

"You're kidding?" Nicky looked at him wide-eyed. "Did Grandma find out?"

"Actually, no," Johnny replied, recalling the incident.

"How come?"

"I got Liam to cover for me."

"How did he do that?"

"I shouldn't be telling you this," Johnny murmured uneasily, but the sudden look of complicity, absent for so long in his son's eyes, was too much to resist.

"Come on, Dad, tell."

"Okay." Johnny sighed and conceded reluctantly, "When they called from school, Liam pretended Mom was out and that he was my uncle. He tutted in that way he knows how, and sounded dreadfully serious and adult. And they believed him. I guess I still owe him one."

"Wow! That's cool. But the thing is, there's more to this, Dad." He looked away again. "There were girls."

"Ah." Johnny tried to keep the grin off his face and failed.

"Trish, she's a really fine chick. Texan. Well, we were playing strip poker and she lost. She was doing this dance thing and…well, to make it short, Dad, she was in boots, a bikini and a Stetson and not much else, dancing on the stage, when Mr. Roach walked in."

"You mean you were doing this on school property?"

"Uh-huh."

"Great. What next?" He needed to laugh but stored it for later, the thought of sharing this with Elm somehow appealing. After her kindness toward Nicky at lunch, he was sure she'd appreciate it.

"Roach had a fit. We were in the gym. Well, you know how they have that stage thing there?"

"Yeah."

"We were hidden so he couldn't see who was there. I threw Trish a sweatshirt and since the other girls were all crying and acting up, we split. Bottom line is, Trish was the one who got caught."

"I see." The smile disappeared from Johnny's face.

"They called her dad. He's very strict and she was scared as hell. She's an only daughter and he thinks the world of her."

"Not after this, I imagine," Johnny murmured dryly, glad he didn't have a sixteen-year-old daughter. "What happened after that? And why haven't I been called yet?"

"Because you weren't reachable and they've all left on vacation." Nicky lifted his chin belligerently. "Jim, Hal, Pete and I went to the headmaster and told him we were the ones with her, and that if he was kicking her out, he'd better kick us out, too."

"I see." Johnny eyed his son with new respect.

"And I don't care if you punish me, I'd do it over again. Trish's a great kid. It wasn't fair she should take the fall on her own. I'm sorry if I've disappointed you, Dad. I didn't mean for this to happen, but I couldn't let her take the blame alone."

Seeing the boy was getting worked up, Johnny leaned over and squeezed his knee. "I'm not cross. I'm proud of the way you behaved. You stood up like a man. I might be furious with you for other things, but never for doing what's right."

"But what about school? They still haven't decided if we're to be suspended or kicked out."

Johnny rose and switched on the lamp while Nicky watched him anxiously. Johnny took his time. The next few words could be vital to help breach the distance that had been steadily growing between them of late.

"Nicky," he said carefully, facing his son and looking him straight in the eye, "you've made rather a hash of things. But you also faced up to what you did and stood by your friend when she needed it. That says a hell of a lot about who you are. I'm damned glad to see you're turning into a man who knows his values. You've done what we all did at some point. But you were stupid enough to do it on school property and get caught. That carries a price. Now, I'm not encouraging you to start fooling around again. Far from it. But I'd be willing to bet your headmaster is relieved to know he's making decent men out of you guys."

"You mean you think he'll take us back?"

"I have no idea. That's his call."

"Dad, do you think you could try to talk to him?" Nicky leaned forward, biting his finger. "Maybe try to get him to take Trish back, too. Maybe that way her dad would give her a break."

"I'll call up and see what I can do. It's weird I haven't any messages on my phone. Or didn't you give them my cell?" he asked perceptively, not waiting for an answer. "I hope she keeps her clothes on, if and when she gets back," he added severely.

"Wow! Thanks, Dad. I thought you'd be real mad at me."

"What? For doing what I did?" Johnny leaned over and ruffled Nicky's hair as he used to when he was small. "We all make mistakes. The trick is to learn from them."

"I guess." Nicky got up and gave him a thoughtful look. His eyes were glistening.

Johnny rose and, unable to resist, flung an arm around the boy's shoulder and gave him a tight hug. "I love you, Nick, don't ever forget it."

"I love you too, Dad," he muttered, returning the hug.

Even though she was thirty-four, had attended Yale law school, was married with two children and had a thriving law practice, Meredith Hunter always felt about ten years old when she had to speak to George Hathaway. When he'd called her to request a meeting about Elm, she'd instinctively known she'd be at a disadvantage and had tried to tip the balance in her favor by having the meeting on her terrain.

But some good that had done.

Now, sitting on the opposite side of her desk from Uncle George, she wondered what it was that made him so intimidating. He was kind and urbane, one of her father's oldest friends, and she loved him dearly. Just as she did Elm. And, she reminded herself, it was Elm's interests she represented here, not his.

"Uncle George, I feel as badly as you do about Elm and Harlan," she lied, knowing that Elm was breathing for the first time in years. "But I've been hired as her attorney, and as such I have to comply with her wishes.'' She tried to sound professional, hoped she looked it with her glasses perched on the end of her nose and her chestnut hair pulled back in a strict French twist. She'd even donned a sleek gray suit that spelled business.

"Well, I know you're right, Merry Bell," the senator responded, using her childhood nickname, "but sometimes we can't follow the rules to the letter, can we? Believe me, I know. Sometimes it can be hard. Sometimes we feel guilty. But in the end, we understand that what we did was for the good of God and country. This is one of those cases."

"God and country? I fail to see—"

"Now, Merry. Remember when you and Elm were small and that poor handicapped little Joe Farrell entered the egg-and-spoon race even though, because of his disability, it would have been physically impossible for him to win?"

"Uh, I remember." She tried to guess what he was getting at and wondered if Harlan was behind this sudden visit. She sighed inwardly. This wasn't going to be easy.

"Joe couldn't have won that race in a thousand years. Yet it meant so much to him. And what'd y'all do?" A smile lit up his gray eyes at the memory. "Y'all dropped your eggs. One of you fell, the other stumbled and Hal Raeburn developed a mysterious limp. Joe hung in there and won the race. And do you know how much that meant to poor little Joe? To his parents?" His eyes went misty. "More than you'll ever know. Probably helped the boy's self-esteem for the rest of his life."

"I remember. But I really don't see what it has to do with Elm's divorce." She shifted, caught his eye and looked away. *Be professional, Meredith.*

"Well, just that sometimes what appears to be inevitable doesn't have to be. If we can just slow things down a bit, the people who deserve to win will find a way. And Harlan and Elm deserve that chance, Merry Bell. All I'm asking is for you to hold off filing until after the holidays. Elm's not well," he continued, lowering his voice. "We still don't know what's wrong. It's probably nothing serious—a nervous complaint, the doctor says—but she needs time, time to see that running away and shirking her duty isn't right."

"But I promised, Uncle George. I have the papers ready. I can't lie to her."

"I'm not asking you to lie, I'm asking you to postpone," he continued patiently, making her feel like a small child again. "Let's be reasonable about this, Merry, and give her time to come around, give Harlan the time to woo her back." He reached across the desk and gave her hand a fatherly pat. "Elm's upset. Harlan may have made a small mistake and she took it badly because of the way she's been feeling. Nothing really serious. I'm sure you and Tom have had misunderstandings. Most couples do. The thing is," he said, frowning, "if you file the divorce papers, then things'll take on a different twist and become far more difficult to undo."

That, at least, was true, she had to admit. And, like Uncle George, she wasn't altogether certain Elm had fully thought through her actions. The decision to file for divorce had been so hasty. Still… "I really don't know," she murmured, caught between the devil and the deep blue sea.

"Once those papers are filed," the senator insisted, "there'll be no going back. It'll get out. People will begin to talk. Pride and opinions will get in the way. Let's you and I at least give 'em a chance at solving this little hitch on their own."

"But how can that happen if she's in Switzerland?"

"I've been thinking about that. I'm going to recommend Harlan takes a trip there in the early New Year." He winked across the desk at her. "I'd be willing to bet big money those two lovebirds will be on that plane home together, none the worse for wear."

Meredith let out the breath she'd been holding and cautiously felt her way. "Uncle George, it would be unethical of me to hide this from Elm. She was adamant about wanting to file. As for Harlan wooing her back, as you put it, well, I don't know if that's possible." She shook her head doubtfully, not liking to break the news that Elm and Harlan were history ten years ago. Here was a man who, as far as she knew, had been faithful to his dead wife for more than thirty years. He probably wouldn't understand, anyway.

"You're absolutely right, Merry Bell, and I respect you for it."

Ah, shit. Now Meredith knew she was truly screwed. When Uncle George started down that track there was no escape.

"But still, dear, what would a few days' difference make in the course of the divorce?"

"Not much," she conceded grudgingly. The holiday was upon them, and the court would be closing until after the New Year, anyway.

"And yet, those few days might make a lifetime's difference for them, mightn't it? Which is why, young lady, I'm asking you, not just as Elm's attorney—and a fine choice she made—but as her old and beloved friend, to overcome your natural and rightful inclination to follow the rules by the book, and to consider the hearts and lives of those concerned."

"Yes, Senator."

"Don't you 'yes Senator' me, young Merry." He smiled and patted her hand once more. "You're a good girl, Merry Bell, and I know we understand each other. Now, I won't be taking up any more of your time," he said, making to rise. "I appreciate you meeting with me like this on such short notice." He stood up.

She rose as well. "But Uncle George…"

"Yes?" He looked down at her from his great height, his bow tie perfectly knotted, his white hair immaculately combed, his smile gracious, the epitome of a Southern gentleman. She'd never stood a chance, she realized with a sigh. But perhaps he was right and a few weeks wouldn't make a difference. And what if Elm and Harlan did suddenly get back together? You never knew what could happen in a marriage. Then she'd feel like shit.

"Okay." She let out another deep breath. "I'll wait till court reopens. But I can't drag it on any longer than that."

"Of course not. I wouldn't dream of asking such a thing," the senator exclaimed, smiling down at her benignly and took her hand in his. "It's a good deed you've done today, Meredith Hunter. I'm proud of you." He squeezed the hand he was still holding as she led him to the door. "And how are those two fine young rascals of yours?" he asked.

"Great. Keeping me on my toes as usual." She reached up and kissed his cheek, her memory suddenly stabbed by the smell of his cologne, the same one she remembered from her youth. There was something solid and permanent about Uncle George that she couldn't resist. He really was a gentleman of the old school, the type on which the myth of the South had been built. And he infallibly reached his goals with that subtle steely charm, she thought, waving goodbye as he turned to have a word with Ross Rollins. She faced Ally at her desk, mentioned that she planned to leave early today so she could finish her Christmas shopping, and then closed the door behind her.

Settling back down at her teak desk, Meredith wondered if she should phone Elm and tell her about the delay, or just leave it as it was. Harlan would apparently be there in Gstaad soon enough, anyway.

For a moment she wondered if Elm was right to have left so abruptly. Then she slammed her palm down on the desk and swore. It was her damn life, wasn't it? And she'd had precious little of it between Uncle George and Harlan maneuvering her from pillar to post. Let Elm live a little. Hopefully she'd find a man and have some fun. Serve Harlan right for fucking around with Jennifer and God knows how many others.

Still, Uncle George might be right. Maybe Elm did just need some time to come around. Who knew? Maybe this would actually shock Harlan into behaving. Boy, was she glad her Tom wasn't in politics and a womanizer.

Then, pressing the button, Meredith sighed and buzzed her secretary. It was time to get on with some work.

10

"I love you, too." Elm laid down the receiver and sighed. Daddy was having a hard time understanding her actions. She could feel the disapproval reaching her through the phone line.

Thank God she'd decided to come to Gstaad. Had she been at home, all her well-founded resolve would have evaporated in the face of her father's displeasure. He had a way of making her feel so small, so guilty and worthless, as though what she'd done was nothing but a selfish act perpetrated by a spoiled child to cause discomfort to others. He hadn't actually voiced the words, but she could hear them in the long silences.

"Aargh!" Elm let out the frustrated exclamation as she rose, annoyed with herself. What was the use of being here if she allowed herself to wallow in the same self-doubt she was determined to leave behind?

It had turned dark since she'd begun her calls, first to Meredith and then her father. She rose from the deep love seat of her gorgeous sitting room, switched on the lamps and glanced at the clock. It was nearly six. Johnny had said he'd phone, but he hadn't. She shrugged, swallowed the little pang of disappointment and headed into the bedroom. He had other commitments as well, of course, and she was the one who'd refused him when he'd asked her out, she reminded herself.

Two hours later, with Gioconda off to dinner, Elm had convinced herself that spending an evening in a comfy tracksuit, bare feet curled under her in front of the fire in the lovely upstairs living room was exactly what she needed. She poured a glass of white wine, grabbed the book she'd been reading and then sank down among the fur-and-velvet cushions of the deep sofa, trying not to wonder what Johnny was up to.

Gioconda had mink-trimmed curtains, she noted. If anyone had told her that before seeing them, she would have squirmed and considered it the height of bad taste. Yet, looking at the dark green velvet bordered with honey-coloured fur, she had to admit they were gorgeous. Regal. Like a king's robes, yet more low-key and terribly Gioconda. She smiled, gazed past the flames at the crackling logs and shook out her hair, which she'd just washed. It was almost dry when she passed her fingers through it.

The phone rang and she waited for Umberto to pick up, then remembered that it was his night off and that Maria's boyfriend had come to pick her up half an hour ago. Hastily she rose and grabbed the receiver.

"Mancini residence."

"Elm?"

"Oh, hi." The sound of Johnny's voice left her slightly breathless.

"I'm sorry to call so late."

"That's fine."

"It's a bit late to go out, I suppose, unless you'd still like to." So he hadn't made alternative arrangements, or maybe his plans had fallen through. For a moment she hesitated. Then she had an idea and blurted it out before she could stop herself.

"You're right, it's kind of late. Plus, I just washed my hair. But why don't you pop over here?" she offered. "I could whip us up an omelette or something."

She caught the moment's hesitation and wondered if she'd

been right to issue the invitation. But surely there couldn't
be any harm in having him over for a bite to eat, could there?

"That'd be great. I'll be there in about half an hour."

"Fine. See you then."

Elm laid down the receiver, grinning. She'd never invited
a male friend to dinner, she realized, except Brad Havisham,
but the date had been innocent enough. Brad was gay.
Switching on the CD player to smooth jazz, she hurried upstairs to change. What should she wear? Nothing too formal.
She looked feverishly through the closet, grabbed a pair of
plush blue velvet pants and a matching sweater, and held it
against herself, staring in the mirror. No, too…maybe the
green ones, maybe they'd look better. After several tries and
a pile of rejected garments strewn around the closet, Elm
decided on her first choice and slipped them on. Then she
ran to the bathroom and dabbed on a little lipstick and
makeup before grabbing the hair dryer. God, why wouldn't
her hair do what it was supposed to? She twisted the round
brush again, determined to get it right this time.

What would she give him to eat? She'd never really been
in Gioconda's kitchen, which was very much Umberto and
Maria's territory. Still, there must be eggs, she assured herself, and bread and wine and cheese and enough things to
get a simple meal together. Elm held the hair dryer in midair
and wondered if she'd made a tremendous gaffe. Should she
have asked Gio's permission? she wondered. What rubbish,
she realized, smiling. Gio would be the first to encourage
her to invite Johnny to dinner. In fact, she'd probably think
dining at home represented a stroke of genius. So much easier to find a bed afterward.

Elm caught a glimpse of her beet-red face in the mirror.
Good Lord, surely Johnny wouldn't interpret this as an invitation to sleep with her, would he? She slowly switched
the dryer off and gave herself a mental shake. Nothing
would happen unless she wanted it to. But, of course, that
was just the problem—she didn't know what she wanted.

Enough. She glanced at her watch. My God, he'd be here
in five minutes.

Skipping downstairs, Elm rushed into the dining room. Then she had an idea. Why not eat in the library, as she and Gio did sometimes, on the round table with the long paisley cloth? It would be so much cosier. She slipped through the living room and into the adjacent library. Good, the fire was even lit, as though awaiting them. She was arranging the table—flowers grabbed from the sitting room, a candle as the centerpiece—when she heard the doorbell ringing. With a quick glance at her handiwork, Elm headed toward the foyer, denying that this was anything more than a casual evening spent with a friend. After all, she reasoned, as she crossed the hall, the man hadn't even kissed her.

Johnny stood in the open doorway, looking incredibly handsome. He wore the same sheepskin coat he'd worn the day before. His dark hair was covered in snowflakes and he held a bottle of champagne.

"Hello."

"Come in. I didn't realize it was snowing again." She held the door wide and he moved inside, leaning over to peck her cheek in a friendly manner as he looked down at her.

"Sure I'm not invading your privacy?"

"Of course not. It'll be fun to have a quiet evening. There're a bunch of DVDs in the den."

"Great." He handed her the bottle and shook off his coat. "It's chilled. If you tell me where Gio's champagne flutes are, I'll pop it open."

"This isn't going to be a very grand dinner, I'm afraid. In fact, I don't really know what's in the refrigerator at all. And I'm not even sure I can find the flutes." Elm sent him a somewhat embarrassed smile, blushing.

"That's fine. We can order from Wally's. That's the latest Rosey takeout—great burgers, I have to say. How about it?"

"Not a bad idea," she agreed, the thought of a juicy burger suddenly striking her as rather appetizing.

They moved into the sitting room. Elm located two champagne flutes while Johnny deftly popped the cork. God, he looked great in those black jeans and a black cashmere sweater she could swear was Armani. Almost devilish. She held up the glasses and he poured expertly.

Then Elm sat on the couch and Johnny in the wide armchair opposite. A comfortable silence reigned, broken only by the soft jazz and crackling logs.

"You never finished telling me about Graney Castle and Ireland," she said, suddenly embarrassed at the lack of conversation.

"Best land on the planet," he said staunchly, adopting a brogue, "and I wouldn't change it for the world."

"Hmm." Elm grinned, relaxing as she let the champagne linger on her tongue.

"Joking aside, Ireland really is a great place. It can be wild and passionate, or soft and giving, like its women. Its people are proud, with a long memory that yields grudgingly and bears many scars. The Irish are both rebels and poets."

"And horse traders," she said, tongue in cheek.

"And horse traders," he agreed. "We're like Joseph's coat of many colors."

"Well, you're poetic tonight, aren't you?" she teased. "But actually, I can imagine it. It must be truly wonderful. Soulful, and special," she murmured now, her eyes turning soft.

"You're painting it in your mind," he exclaimed.

"How could I not, with that brogue? I have to say, Johnny Graney, you sure have a touch of the blarney in you." She sent him a mischievous grin, the initial tension of his presence alone with her in the house dissipating.

"Now, pray, what self-respecting Irishman doesn't have a touch of the blarney?" he protested, eyes twinkling.

"Well, blarney or no blarney," she said, raising her glass, "Graney Castle sounds perfectly divine."

"Perhaps you'd find it less divine the day the plumbing gives out," he muttered wryly, remembering their conversation at the Chesery.

Elm shrugged and laughed and he watched her lean back, fixing his gaze on her. Did she have any idea how seductive she looked sitting there, feet curled under, the soft blue of her velvet pantsuit setting off her light tan and hair to perfection, those huge brown eyes that one moment sparkled with amusement, the next with tentative doubt?

"Graney and Ireland are obviously to you what Oleander and Georgia are to me," she said, suddenly serious. "You can't replace that special place in your life," she continued rapidly, "the place you've laughed and cried in, that holds all the scents, the joys and pains, the images you carry inside. They're all yours and yours alone. That's why one finds it hard to share."

"You're right, he murmured, touched by her perception and deep sensitivity. Graney was exactly that.

She smiled tentatively. "I guess we all have memories we cherish. I can still just remember my mother—I must have been about three—in the garden. Sometimes when I'm working I think I feel her there, near me. Probably just my imagination. But I don't want that precious memory overrun by strangers. Each time the camellias blossom in the spring and I smell that pungent scent of damp earth at dawn, the magnolias and the freshly cut grass on a hot sultry summer's day, I just know I'm home. Like you said," she added, looking at him from under thick lashes, "I wouldn't change that for the world." Then abruptly she blushed. "Sorry, I'm getting carried away."

Johnny sipped champagne and studied the plethora of emotions flitting across her face, surprised at how her sensitivity had provoked an unprecedented rush of emotion he hadn't felt in years. He cleared his throat. "I know exactly what you're saying." Then, sitting up straighter, he set his glass down on the big leather ottoman before the fire. "So, what about ordering those burgers?"

"Sounds like a good idea," Elm responded. For a moment, the mood had changed—there'd been something intangible in the air, a closeness coursing between them, as though much more of themselves was being shared than just a conversation. She felt deeply relieved now that they were back on neutral territory.

Johnny watched her as she picked up the phone and

placed the order, the mass of wild gold hair cascading about her face. He sensed that underneath that easygoing demeanour, she was not altogether happy. A divorce was never easy, he reminded himself. He should leave her to her thoughts. Yet he couldn't, trapped by the need to step further into all he sensed lay hidden behind those long dark lashes. She put up a good front, he realized, but he could read beyond the well-bred smiles and natural grace to the hopes and fears and uncharted territory he was certain lay beyond.

And he wanted to dive right in.

Elm turned and Johnny, shocked by the sudden intensity of his thoughts, tried to pull himself together. Whoa! This was ridiculous. He needed to get a grip. Now. What was wrong with him? He hadn't even kissed this woman, yet tonight he felt something he'd not known since... Marie Ange's image sprang before him, and he caught his breath.

Shaken, he poured some more champagne. "I should have brought milkshakes, not champagne," he remarked, watching her grin.

"That's a tempting thought."

"Is everybody out?" he asked, eyes narrowing.

"You're not thinking of raiding Gioconda's kitchen, are you?"

"The thought had crossed my mind. Do you think she has any ice cream and milk?"

"I know she does."

"Then what are we waiting for?" He grabbed her hand and pulled her up, laughing and hooking his arm around the champagne bottle. "Hamburgers always give me a craving for milkshakes. I hope it's vanilla ice cream," he added as she followed him downstairs. "I make a mean vanilla shake."

They reached the kitchen and Elm switched on the lights. Two small shaded lamps glowed low, sending shadows dancing over the painted cupboards and the gnarled beams. The cozy eating nook with red-and-white-check cushions welcomed. The sound system was installed here, too, and the strains of smooth Latin jazz swirled around them as

Johnny deposited the champagne on the kitchen table and reached for her, pulling her close and twirling her into a light rhythm that eased into a slow sway. Her body tensed and he rubbed a hand up and down her spine, soothing until her head lay on his shoulder and they were barely moving.

This was precisely what she'd told Gioconda shouldn't be happening. And precisely what she most wanted, Elm thought, allowing him to hold her close, delighting in the feel of his body, the firmness of his grip, his hand slowly massaging her lower back. She felt alive, tingling with unexpected emotions.

"This feels good," he murmured, nuzzling her hair in a way that left her feeling vulnerable.

"Yes," she answered into the crook of his shoulder. She gripped him more tightly, feeling almost dizzy with delight at being held so firmly, yet so gently. For a second she panicked. She couldn't be having one of her spells again? Surely not. She hardly remembered what they were like. *Not now, please.* She grabbed his shoulders, afraid she might fall, then slowly relaxed. This wasn't the dizzy, nauseous state she'd learned to dread over the past few months, but rather a heady, light feeling, like nothing she'd ever experienced. The sensation grew as his hand snaked to the back of her neck, fisted in her hair and gently tilted her head back, making her gasp with a sharp longing.

"I want to make love with you," he murmured, voice husky, searching her face, stark desire flashing in his eyes.

And so did she.

It was wondrous, frightening and exhilarating. When his lips touched hers, her mind blanked and her body gave way. This wasn't a tender, yearning kiss like yesterday's, or the polite pecks Harlan had delivered over the years, but a rough, ragged demand for satisfaction.

He ravaged her mouth, fired her senses, left her breathless, wanting and in tatters, all fear forgotten as they came together, bodies demanding each other with an urgent intensity. She filled her hands with his thick dark hair, felt her breasts taut and aching against his hard muscled chest and craved the touch of his skin. She let out a quick gasp when his hand slipped down her back and pressed her close, and she felt him hard against her. God, he wanted her.

And she him.

He kissed her eyelids, her nose, her mouth, his hands slipping under her sweatshirt, causing another sharp intake of breath when they glided upward. She heard a low growl of satisfaction as he realized she wore no bra. Then he touched her nipple, and any attempt at sanity disappeared. Elm dropped her head back, arched and gave way to the rush of heat that left her limp and wanting.

"The kitchen's not the best idea," he whispered, drawing her toward the door, but she stalled him, dragged him back. With something between a laugh and a groan, he slammed her against the refrigerator door, moved against her.

Elm clung, intoxicated, afraid that if he let up it might all go away, not caring if he took her then and there.

Raising her arms, he lifted her sweater. She tugged at his sweater and he helped her pull it off, slipped his hands under the waist of her pants, slid his hands over her buttocks, then reached between her thighs.

Elm moaned, stopped tugging his shirt and gave way to the delight, the sheer unadulterated glory of his fingers expertly seeking her core, searching, discovering, sending her soaring on a wave of pleasure. Then, just as she thought the ecstatic agony would never end, she shattered, crashed, let out a cry and collapsed against him, breathless.

Johnny soothed her, held her, whispered as she leaned against him, his lips kissing her tenderly now, fingers stroking her hair.

"Let's go upstairs," he said in a hoarse whisper, straightening her clothes gently.

Then the light went on in the porch and they froze, eyes locked.

"My God, it must be the burgers," she whispered, half giggling, half horrified.

"Don't panic."

"But what about the food? The guy's waiting."

"Forget them. He'll leave them on the porch."

"But—"

"Shush."

"Oh, my God, this is totally crazy," she hissed as the doorbell rang once more. Then, before she could protest, Johnny grabbed the discarded garments, slipped his arms under her and hoisted her into his arms just as she heard the key turning noisily in the lock. "Oh, Christ, it must be Umberto. Hurry, please," she urged, looping her arms around his neck, heart racing. Never, in her whole sedate life, had she lived such an adventure, she realized as he raced up the stairs.

"Where's your room?" he whispered breathlessly when they reached the landing. "God, I'll kill my trainer. He assured me I was in top shape."

Despite her fear of being caught in this embarrassing state, Elm stifled a giggle and pointed. "Second on the right," she whispered, grinning up at him. He looked down at her, grinned back and dropped a kiss on her mouth before marching to the bedroom. She'd left the door ajar and he pushed it easily with his shoulder, then kicked it shut before carrying her to the bed. Their eyes locked, then he dropped her down among the pillows.

"Hey," she protested, seeing the look in his gleaming blue eyes.

A warm glow radiated from the shaded bed lamps, a scented candle on the dresser burned low, its reflection flickering in the mirror as he joined her on the bed.

"Close call," he murmured, the grin replaced by something hungry and intense as he lowered his mouth once more to hers. She felt his warmth, the taut, knotted muscles rippling under her fingers as they glided over the breadth of his shoulders, traveling down his back until they met the waistband of his jeans.

"No," he whispered, prying her fingers away gently. "This isn't how I want our first time to be, rushed and secretive." He dropped a kiss on her forehead and caressed her face. "This isn't right. You'd feel terrible tomorrow morning. And I don't want you to regret anything we do together.''

He was going to have to find somewhere for them to meet, he realized, watching her, playing absently with a strand of long, silky hair that glistened in a shaft of moonlight.

God, she was lovely, beautiful, wild in a way he would not have expected. Yet there remained an innocence in her naked passion that told him all too well she'd probably not experienced anything quite like this before. She wore her emotions in her eyes, in her body, in each fluid movement of her limbs, and that, more than anything, made him hesitate. It was important to remember that this was, at best, a passing affair. And the unschooled heat of her response was all the confirmation he needed to know she had never had an affair before.

He smiled down at her, reining in his own raging desires and forcing himself to stand up. From the little he'd seen of her, he realized she was used to leading a tailored life, bolstered by rules and sobriety. He didn't want her to be embarrassed by anything they did.

And he didn't want to hurt her.

If and when they spent a whole night together, he knew it must be right. Whatever the reason—and right now he wasn't about to start a psychological inventory—it was important.

''I don't think we should do anything either of us might regret in the morning, do you?'' he asked, adjusting his sweater. He touched her cheek lightly then dropped another kiss on her lips.

''I guess not,'' she said with a smile and a sigh.

''Good night, beautiful, sleep tight. Sorry about dinner.''

''That's fine. And you're right. I don't want to make mistakes. I've made enough already,'' she said, causing him to frown as he wrapped the duvet around her. But watching her snuggle obediently as he tucked her in and kissing her gently alleviated any fears that her words might have sparked.

* * *

Elm watched as he slipped silently from the room, torn between longing and the deep-rooted knowledge that he was right, of course. This was not the proper time or place. She was touched that he'd been so thoughtful, realizing that she would have quite happily given way to her baser instincts. And that, she reflected, might have ended badly. She sighed and closed her eyes, although sleep would be impossible for a while. Johnny, she realized ruefully, was turning out to be quite a surprise.

Johnny departed discreetly from the chalet, then headed home on foot. An owl hooted somewhere in the distance and snow lay fresh on the ground. The soles of his fur-lined boots crunched the unsullied white blanket as he trod down the hill toward the silent village. As he passed the parking lot, the church clock chimed the half hour. Crisp, heady air scorched his eyes and cheeks as he began the climb back up the hill.

When he reached home he moved quietly, fiddled in his pocket for the key and inserted it in the lock, grimacing when it squeaked. The last thing he needed was his mother asking questions he was in no mood to answer.

Grabbing an apple from the kitchen table, he went upstairs, munching, and wandered thoughtfully to the window, assimilating the unexpected events of the evening. He'd never imagined Elm could be capable of such raw, unfettered passion. There was something unspoiled and almost innocent about her, which surprised him in a woman in her mid-thirties.

That husband of hers must really be a selfish bastard.

Several hours later, sleep still eluded him. With an irritated yawn Johnny put his book aside, got up and moved toward the window. A smile flitted over his face as he pictured Elm, curled under the duvet as he'd left her, fast asleep like the village below. Leaning on the windowsill, he watched the glistening falling flakes, magnified in the circle of light cast by the street lamp, and tried to piece together the unexpected rush of emotion for a woman he barely knew, and this strange instinct to protect rather than take. He shifted, uncomfortable at his own reaction.

Hell, weren't they both playing the same game? Both seeking to escape for a little while? Elm's life obviously held some challenges that would need ironing out. It would be natural for her to want to enjoy the time away, not get involved talking about her life back in Savannah. What annoyed him was his own curiosity, when the last thing he needed was to become entangled.

He stifled a yawn and gazed out into the calm, peaceful night, a Christmas card in the making. Their little interlude seemed a bit unreal, he reflected pensively. It would definitely be up to him to keep his feet well grounded and not let things get out of hand.

He stretched, glanced at the clock and thought of breakfast only a few hours away. Soon the slumbering village would wake. The baker would pile fresh croissants and rolls into the oven, the milkman would begin his rounds, and Gstaad would blink open its sleepy eyes to a new day. He rubbed his eyes, yawned again and realized all at once that Christmas Eve was upon them. What, he wondered, did Elm and Gioconda have planned for Christmas?

More to the point, where was he going to take her to continue what had begun so intensely last evening? Even though the safest thing would be to run like hell in the opposite direction, he knew he wouldn't…couldn't. He needed to see her again. Then, as he climbed back into bed, he had an idea. It was a crazy idea, he reflected, but nevertheless he would think about it. She was, after all, someone who appreciated the out of the ordinary, and, he decided with a sleepy grin, he aimed to please.

11

"What's the big deal?" Gioconda asked, surprised, carefully observing Elm's reactions across the breakfast table. "Where's the glitch, *cara?*"

"There isn't one, I guess, except the obvious ones, like I'm still married and perhaps I should wait before throwing myself into bed with the first man who opens his arms. I mean, think about it, Gio. A month ago, this would have been inconceivable. Plus, I don't think two people should do it without some sort of—"

"Commitment?"

"Yes. No. I don't know." Elm shrugged, irritated by her own lack of decision, and trying to come to terms with the events of the previous night. One moment she felt happiness at the sheer physical intensity of the orgasm she'd so unexpectedly experienced, next she was coping with guilt. She'd woken at dawn, vestiges of her old self surfacing to whisper quite loudly that she had no business getting involved in a casual affair when her life was tottering in a precarious no-man's land.

"I think what bothers you is not being able to justify your emotions," Gioconda summed up.

"No, that's not what I meant," Elm protested, knowing deep down that Gio was exactly right.

"Of course it is. You want grounds for a good old guilt

trip, and you're having a hard time coming up with them,"
Gioconda continued relentlessly. "*Madonna mia,* when will
you realize that Harlan and your marriage are history?" Gioconda cast her eyes to heaven, shook her head and poured
herself another cup of strong coffee. "And the last thing you
need right now is a commitment, Elm. Get real. You're just
getting out of a twelve-year marriage—"

"You see? You said it," Elm pounced. "I'm still getting
out, the divorce isn't filed yet—Meredith said something
about the court and the holidays. I should at least wait for
that to happen before contemplating a relationship, don't you
think?"

"Why? This is a simple holiday fling we're talking about,
not a life sentence. In fact, it's a necessary step in helping
you get free of Harlan," Gio explained patiently. "Look,
Santa's being good to you this year, and he's brought Johnny
as a divine little gift."

"A little gift?" Elm murmured unhappily. Last night he
hadn't felt remotely little. She'd been so swept away, she
hadn't had time to think at all. Now, in the morning light,
doubt loomed.

"Exactly what I'm saying. A perfect, guilt-free gift. And
the sooner you understand that, the better. You're not com-
mitting a major sin, or lowering your standard of behaviour.
This is about finding out a little more about yourself. What
kind of woman you truly are, what you really want. How
will you know unless you try? You'll never discover your
likes and dislikes—in bed or out—unless you experiment."

"Gio, I don't know. Maybe it's different for you. You're
sophisticated, worldly. I just don't think it's that way for
me."

"Rubbish, *cara.* It's that way for everybody," Gioconda
dismissed, reaching for some wafer-thin toast.

"Well, I hope I'm not so lost to propriety that I don't
know who I am anymore," Elm muttered tartly, spreading
some strawberry jam on her croissant. "I hope I have some
idea of what my principles are—though I guess after my
behavior last night, I should question that, too."

"Oh, please, don't let's get into values and principles," Gio responded, exasperated. "I'm referring to your feelings. Didn't you say it felt marvellous to be in Johnny's arms?"

"Yes...no...I don't know." She let out a huff. For some reason she didn't want to share last night's intimacy over coffee.

"I'll bet my bottom euro you didn't know what hit you." Gioconda grinned smugly, before sinking her teeth into her toast. "Say, *cara,* do you think I should wear the red Gianfranco Ferré outfit tonight, or the black Armani?"

"Gio, you'll look fabulous whatever you wear," Elm answered vaguely. "What do you think will happen now that we've...well, you know, that things have gone further, so to speak. Do you think he'll just naturally assume I'll go to bed with him? I could hardly blame him if he did. God, that would too embarrassing for words, I—"

"Elm, will you stop blowing this thing out of proportion? *Dio,* we're in the twenty-first century. A woman can decide the time and place, what she wants, how far she's willing to go. Forget all those old-fashioned Southern notions and get with the program, girl. You're the one in control."

"I'm well aware of all that," Elm replied stiffly. "Still. It all happened rather quickly. Unexpectedly."

"Because it was meant to. Because you both wanted it to. Anyway, didn't you just say he was a perfect gentleman and tucked you nicely up in bed without taking advantage of the situation?"

"Yes, he did." Elm said, a little smile spreading as she remembered how nice it had been.

"Well then, *cara?* What are you worried about? Just accept last night for what it was, a great evening." She glanced at Elm's troubled face and decided it was time to lighten up the conversation. "By the way, perhaps you can explain a large package containing hamburgers sitting on the doorstep when I got home last night?" She sent Elm a questioning grin, determined to make her see that the spontaneous events of the previous night were not a drama, but rather an amusing interlude.

"Oh, Lord, the burgers. I forgot." A reluctant grin spread over Elm's face as she recalled the doorbell, her own horror and Johnny's quick reaction. "Umberto almost caught us red-handed in the kitchen, you know."

"You're kidding!"

"He came home at what can only be termed as a critical moment. Thank God he rang before he unlocked the door."

"Wise old bird. He always rings. If it's before eleven, that is. *Mamma mia,* I wish I'd been a fly on the wall of that kitchen." Gio's black eyes sparkled with laughter.

"Gio, do we have to get into this again?" Elm squirmed, embarrassed.

"Of course not, *cara.* And frankly, I'm truly happy for you. Johnny's a very nice man. I'm happy for him, too," she added, rising and straightening her ski suit. "I have the feeling he leads a rather lonely life. I know he keeps a British stiff upper lip, but he's never been the same since his wife died. And that was a long while ago." She sent Elm a speculative glance. "Sure you don't want to come skiing with us? We're going to the Wassengrat, then lunching at the club." Gioconda pushed her chair carefully in toward the table and picked up her mail expectantly.

"No, thanks. I'll take a rain check. The weather's not great today."

"Okay. And *bella?* Enjoy it while it lasts." Gioconda winked and blew her a kiss. "And whatever you do, for goodness' sake, don't think! It's always fatal."

"It's all right for you," Elm retorted darkly, "you've been playing this game for as long as I can remember."

"Well, it's about time you learned, too, isn't it? Ciao, have a great day."

Elm watched her departing figure, reached for the coffee-pot and tried to put her life in perspective. It was barely three weeks since the Jennifer Ball incident, barely two since she'd made the life-changing decision to get divorced and come away to Gstaad. And here she was getting intimately involved with a man.

She poured more coffee, then sank her forearms onto the

table and sighed. Was she just making a damn fool of herself? Was this "fling," as Gio kept calling it, a terrible mistake that she would sorely regret? Or, as her friend seemed determined to describe it, a part of the process? What if someone back home found out, told Harlan and spread it about that she was sleeping around? Not that she had or necessarily intended to sleep with Johnny, she reminded herself hastily. But if they did find out, what would her father say? Could Harlan's chances of re-election suffer if there was a scandal?

These thoughts and many more hammered relentlessly until the phone rang. She reached across the table to where Gio had left the receiver, lying next to her half-drunk cup of coffee, and picked up.

"Good morning, Mancini residence."

"Hi. How are you today?" Johnny's deep voice, firm and unwavering, scattered all her looming questions. Her pulse beat dangerously faster. "Any plans for today?" he asked.

"Well, not really. I need to do some Christmas shopping."

"Me, too, actually. I forgot that it's almost Christmas. Still, would you have time to take a drive? There's a place I'd like to show you."

"Oh. Uh, where?"

"It's a surprise."

She experienced a moment's doubt then glanced out the window. Was she just inviting more problems? Silence reigned while she hesitated.

"The weather doesn't look too promising," he continued persuasively. "I thought we could have a bite somewhere, then I'd show you the surprise."

It was tempting. Terribly tempting. And she couldn't help wondering what his surprise was.

"Elm? Are you still there?"

"Of course."

"Well?"

"Okay. I'll go."

"Good. Then that's settled. If you like, I can pick you up

in the village at around twelve, give you a chance to do your shopping. I'll bring us some lunch. Would that suit you?''

"Perfectly. Thanks.''

"And Elm?'' She caught the moment's hesitation, the way his voice lowered, and her heart gave a sudden lurch. "I hope you don't regret last night?''

"No. No, of course I don't,'' she replied, taken aback.

"Good. Because I certainly don't.'' A long silence followed in which she flushed and tried desperately to think of an intelligent answer.

"Right.'' He sounded brisk now. "I'll see you at twelve in front of Hermès. Bye.''

Before she could reply the phone went dead.

Fingers trembling, she laid it down on the table. What was she letting herself in for? Perhaps it wasn't a good idea at all. Yet it was also so exciting and wonderful and deliciously illicit, and for the first time in years she was truly enjoying herself.

With a smile she got up. Harlan, her father and Savannah's precepts were fading mysteriously as she hurried upstairs and, scooping her hair up with a pen, entered the shower. All at once she decided to shake off any lingering misgivings and take Gio's sensible advice. She would stop worrying and let things take their natural course. She could always say no, after all. The main thing was to enjoy every minute of the interlude—for who knew when there'd be another?

After a fifteen-minute drive heading southwest through the Alps, past the tiny hamlet of Gsteig, the Range Rover headed up the Pillon pass, into the mountains. Just as she was about to ask where they were going, the car stopped opposite the first cable-car station that traveled up the glacier.

"You want to go up the glacier?'' she asked doubtfully, wondering if her anorak would be warm enough. "It must be twenty degrees below up there.''

"No.'' He slewed sideways and grinned at her.

"Then where?" Elm glanced at a small wooden edifice above a double garage and raised a questioning brow.

"This is the surprise," he smiled smugly, and removed some keys from the pocket of his sheepskin jacket. "Come on."

They exited the car, and after pulling a picnic hamper from the back, Johnny walked her up the steps at the side of the garage and unlocked the door of the hangar. He hadn't been back here for ages and the lock was stiff. How long had it been? Two or three years? Certainly he'd never dreamed of bringing anyone here. But Elm was one of the few people who would probably appreciate the Chalet Wildhorn, his father's mountain retreat hidden in the middle of nowhere. Now, as he pressed the button of the little old-fashioned cable car that served the chalet, he hoped he was right. This was, after all, a place he'd kept very private, a vestige of his past, a past that didn't even really belong to him, he reminded himself, but rather to the man he'd loved so dearly and had lost too soon.

"Climb in," he said when the ancient gondola finally stopped. Once they were seated opposite each other, he pressed a button and the lift took off lugubriously, swaying gently between the pine trees. A cold blast made her raise her face and breathe in the pure, unpolluted mountain air, relishing the feeling of it entering her lungs. Then she gazed down at a half-frozen stream trickling below. As the lift ascended, the trees grew sparser and the thick blanket of virgin snow increased, marked only by tiny paw marks that disappeared among the trees.

"Those belong to the resident foxes and badgers," Johnny remarked, following her gaze. "There are quite a number of animals up here. Now, look."

Elm watched in wonder as a lovely old chalet came into view, nestled in the middle of the mountain.

"Wow! That is incredible," she exclaimed, taken aback by the uniqueness of the spot. "Who owns it?"

"It used to belong to my father," Johnny said, relieved that her reaction was all he'd hoped for. "I haven't been here for quite a while, although there's a wonderful old care-taker who looks in on the place for us.''

''It's lovely.'' ˘

''I think so. Mother wanted to sell it after Dad died. She never uses it. But I begged her to keep it, so she did. It's quite old and needs work done to it, but my Dad used to love coming up here to ski and write. It was here he finished his last book on Thoroughbreds.''

As soon as the lift ground to a halt, Johnny alighted and gave her a hand down. Elm looked about her, enchanted. The walls were painted with amusing cartoonlike figures representing tourists of different nationalities.

''This is quite amazing,'' she laughed, amused by the car-toon painting of Jeeves the butler, standing next to the front door. Above it read ''Was your journey really necessary?''

Johnny unlocked the wooden door and held it open for her to enter. And as she did her earlier qualms dissipated completely. The hominess—old ski boots and walking sticks, faded anoraks and gloves lying in the entrance—re-assured her to no end. This was not a fancy bachelor pad, or an impersonal hotel, but exactly the kind of spot she loved. Her fears about how he might have interpreted the previous night vanished, replaced by a warm wave of sur-prise that he'd understood her so well so fast, that their long conversations about Graney Castle and Oleander Creek had meant more to him than mere small talk. She was touched, too, that he was willing to share what was evidently a very special part of his past with her.

As she moved inside the hall and followed him over to the panoramic window of the bright, airy living room, she understood something else that boosted her confidence: this was not a place he'd brought other women, but somewhere he believed she would somehow understand and appreciate.

As she watched him set the hamper on the floor and pull back the drapes, Elm's eyes softened and she swallowed. Never, in all the years of their marriage, had Harlan shown any signs of even trying to understand who she really was deep inside. He hadn't cared enough, she supposed. Yet in the space of a few days, Johnny seemed to have captured an important facet of her being and acted upon it.

"Come over here and take a look."

She joined him, stared out over the majestic glacier, amazed at the vista. It was a unique and magnificent spectacle. Not a cute, charming or typically Swiss view like the ones lower down in the valley, but a whole other face of the mountain, with all its perils and challenges, a rugged and fierce yet glorious face that rose, proud and imposing, its jagged peaks reaching determinedly toward the fast-moving cluster of cloud swirling overhead.

"It's…awe-inspiring," she murmured. She placed her hand on the back of a well-worn velvet chair that looked as though it had been here forever and smiled, filled with the uniqueness of the spot.

"It's a bit chilly in here," he remarked, moving toward the large whitewashed fireplace that dominated the room and placing logs expertly on the wrought-iron holders. "The place hasn't been lived in for more than twenty years. Thank goodness Hans comes in to clean the place and make sure the pipes are okay. Still, it could do with some work, couldn't it?" He glanced up at the ceiling where a fault line rippled and grinned at her.

"I think it's just perfect as it is, but a fire would be lovely," she exclaimed, rubbing her hands and crouching next to him as the small branches of light wood snapped and crackled and the flames took hold.

"That should do it." He leaned back on his heels, then held out his hand and pulled her up. Slipping an arm loosely about her shoulders, he drew her toward him.

"It's delightful," Elm murmured, leaning into the crook of his arm. "It's so different from any other chalet I've known," she added, "not fancy or sophisticated but simple and cosy."

He squeezed her a tad harder and dropped a kiss on the crown of her head. "I'm glad you think so."

"I do, I really do," Elm reassured him, drinking in the ancient pine paneling, old sofas and worn needle-work cushions, the huge crackling fireplace and an endless array of bookshelves stacked tight with paperbacks, hardbacks, magazines and photographs, some framed, others lying loosely against the books, of children at different stages of growth, and statuettes of racehorses and silver trophies. Looking about her, Elm felt it told her a lot about Johnny's father. And a lot about Johnny, too, for having preserved this place just as it was for all these years. He obviously held his past close to his heart.

But it was also, she supposed, a kind of shrine. Did he do the same thing with his wife's things? she wondered suddenly. That was really none of her business, she reminded herself, enjoying the strength of his arm around her and glancing once more at the fireplace, experiencing that same warm, tingling glow that had lurked since last night when he'd tucked her into bed, relieved that he'd made no attempt at any physical intimacy.

"Let's take a look at the kitchen and see if there are any plates for this feast Gretchen put together. I told her to stop by Pernet, the delicatessen, and pick up some smoked salmon. I'm afraid it's a cold lunch as the appliances need updating."

"It's fun like this, just as it is. Did your dad spend a lot of time here?"

"When he wanted to get way from Gstaad and the social buzz. In those days, when I was at Le Rosey, my parents spent the whole winter here. He said he needed a refuge."

"He must have been a very special person," she remarked thoughtfully.

"He was. I still miss him." Johnny smiled at her over his shoulder as he placed the hamper on a counter. Elm smiled back, understanding. She knew exactly what he meant, for she missed her mother, too, even though she'd barely known her.

He started to unpack the picnic basket, then paused.

"This can wait a minute. I forgot to show you the view from upstairs." He led her quickly out of the kitchen and mounted the threadbare carpeted stairs that tilted crookedly.

''You may have noticed that the chalet tilts slightly. It's because of the glacier. Lots of landslides and avalanches in these parts. One day it'll end up down by the road, I should think.'' He laughed, that rich, low, warm laugh that awakened a rush of simple pleasure mixed with a pinch of trepidation as they reached the landing and Johnny opened the door of a large bedroom. He walked over to the windows and drew back the drooping blue curtains. Elm noticed a large bed made up with plain, serviceable white linen and surrounded by more stacked bookshelves and photographs.

Just as an image of her hair spread out on the white pillows flashed, Johnny turned, saw her glancing about, and caught the fleeting uncertainty in her eyes. He pulled himself up short, quickly banishing the vision of them both cuddled under the enormous duvet that sank down on each side of the bed, and looked away, afraid he'd betray himself.

He mustn't rush things. For both their sakes. Bringing her here had been the right thing to do, he thought, pleased, but he mustn't forget that this was, after all, only an interlude, nothing more.

''I'm glad you like the chalet. Not very grand, I'm afraid, but—''

Elm touched his hand and smiled as his arm came so naturally back around her shoulders again.

''I think it's perfect. Thank you for sharing it with me.''

He glanced at her and experienced a jolt. She had understood. It left him elated, yet uneasy.

Elm turned silently toward the window and they gazed once more at the glacier, at the square blue cable car, dangling like a toy box as it climbed to three thousand meters up the steep, treacherous face of the mountain, over the gorge, dangling above furrowed, icy grooves that in spring gushed forth, transformed into turbulent waterfalls. Overhead the impressive whorl of clouds still loomed, laden with oncoming snow.

''Better open up and air the place out before it begins snowing again,'' Johnny remarked, unfastening the window and letting in the cold air. Elm leaned on the windowsill, breathed in the rarefied atmosphere, the raw scent of impending snow, the still peace of nature. A robin and two bullfinches perched on the sill of the crooked little birdhouse on the terrace below, pecking carefully at the seeds, while others sought shelter in the naked branches of the shrubs. Was it Johnny who saw to it that the birds were fed? she wondered. Each revelation told her a little more about this man with whom she'd shared such an intimate moment the night before, but whom, in truth, she hardly knew.

"You know, even though I've been coming here ever since I was a kid," he remarked after several minutes spent in companionable silence, "I don't think I'll ever tire of it."

"I know exactly what you mean. I spent those great years at Le Rosey, then never returned until now, yet all the while I've been away I've never forgotten. Some of my happiest memories are here on the mountain," she replied simply.

He nodded, glad that he'd brought her. He didn't want the Palace Hotel, room service, champagne and caviar. Rather a simple lunch of baguettes and pâté, or perhaps pasta whipped up in one of those ancient copper pots and a bottle of good Bordeaux from his father's cellar, providing the cooker worked. This was the first time, he reflected, somewhat taken aback by the realization, that he'd ever contemplated sharing anything so intimate with anyone except back in the days of Marie Ange. Yet it didn't seem like a violation of his past, or his wife, or anything they had shared together. Now, as he stood with Elm by the window, it seemed right.

Then it occurred to him that not even Marie Ange had visited this spot. It was, in fact, the one place that had remained totally intact, unexplored, a place he could begin again and start afresh.

"I'd better close the window or you'll catch your death," he said, drawing her quickly away, appalled by his rambling thoughts. His life was a well-organized, well-orchestrated affair and he planned for it to remain that way.

"It is quite chilly," she agreed, smiling brightly, eyeing the bed from the corner of her eye with a mixture of trepidation and longing. Was this why he'd brought her here?

Elm moved quickly back across the room, leaving him to close the window. But to her relief he made no attempt to restrain her, and they made their way back down the stairs and into the living room where the fire was blazing away nicely.

"Drink?" Johnny offered.

"I'd love one."

"How about a glass of red wine? My father used to keep some excellent claret here. You sit by the fire and I'll get it, then I'll see what's in that basket."

"Great." Elm descended the few steps into the nook before the fireplace. It was deliciously cosy and she curled up into the cushions, imagining what Johnny's father must have been like. Perhaps his son was very like him. Already their conversations in the past days had touched on many varied subjects, and she liked it that he held intelligent, strong views, and backed up what he believed. They'd even enjoyed a heated debate about American and British politics over lunch the other day up at the club.

She sank back and enjoyed the warmth. Several minutes later Johnny returned with an open bottle of Château Latour and two large wineglasses, which he set on the ottoman before the fire. "Fairly drinkable, I should think," he said, showing her the bottle.

"I should say so," Elm exclaimed, reading the date. "What a treat." She felt increasingly at ease now that they were downstairs again, the inevitable tension produced by the unspoken knowledge of what they'd shared the night before disappearing as she sipped the delicious wine and they sat close, gazing into the flames. That was another thing she appreciated about him: how gentlemanly he was. Harlan had always acted gentlemanly in public, but unfortunately, his manners in private lacked finesse—anywhere and anytime was always the right time for sex, as far as he was concerned.

Johnny, on the other hand, seemed perfectly happy to sit near her, not even trying to take her hand, just calmly absorbing the moment. And she felt certain, peeking at him, that he was truly enjoying himself, just as she was. The knowledge allowed her to relax and take real pleasure in her charming surroundings.

"When did you last come here?" she asked, curious as to why he hadn't adopted the place as a haunt of his own.

"I was just trying to figure that out. It must be almost three years. And even then, I've only come up to check on things. But last night I had the sudden urge to see the old place again." He glanced at her suddenly, smiled ruefully, then leaned over and took her hand. "It seemed appropriate to come here with you. I haven't the faintest clue why, but for some reason it just did." He lifted her fingers to his lips and dropped a light kiss there.

Elm nodded and let out a sigh. She felt strangely honoured, touched that he'd wanted to share this with her. She left her hand lying in his, enjoying the warmth of his fingers. When he drew her close she didn't shy away, merely allowed her head to rest on his shoulder and let him stroke her hair tenderly, secure in the knowledge that this was one of the most tender moments of her life.

12

As a full-fledged member of the yacht club, Harlan entered the exclusive Skidaway Island community with a wave in the direction of the guardhouse, then headed directly for Tyler Brock's mansion. You couldn't miss it—Greek revival, ten bedrooms, painted candy pink with white trimmings. How the hell Brock'd gotten approval to build the thing from the usually conservative design review board, he'd never know.

Still, the man gave great parties, no one could dispute that, he reflected as he got out of the Cadillac and made his way to the front door. Elm usually refused to frequent Tyler's shindigs, but that was okay by him. The less Elm knew about Tyler, the better. Particularly the company he kept. Even he'd been surprised when the night before, during a lavish dinner at the mansion, Brock had introduced him to a couple of questionable Latin Americans who reminded him only too well of the pictures he'd seen in the papers around the time of Noriega's arrest.

The encounter left him ill at ease. But Tyler had brushed the men off and the dinner had ended up being a good one, with plenty of booze and other preferred items available, and Harlan had conveniently forgotten about the more questionable guests. Especially when he and that saucy little tramp, Teresa, managed to find time for a quick slap and tickle in the guests' cloakroom. He supposed that had been unwise—they could so easily have been caught—but that had only added to the sexual thrill. The memory made him go hard, and he forced himself to draw a long breath. *Forget that for now and remember the purpose of this visit.*

A uniformed maid answered the door and led him through to the vast marble-floored living room filled with overlarge sofas and lots of gold leaf. French eighteenth-century mirrors and ornate decorative furniture lay strewn about, glaring harshly in the morning light, with no guests to disguise the scene. Harlan winced at the sight. Elm had a point. Tyler's taste was decidedly bad, what she would term as nouveau riche. And, he recognized sourly as Tyler, dressed in plaid Bermuda shorts and a silk polo shirt, waved to him to sit while he talked loudly into the portable phone, she'd be right.

Harlan slid onto the sofa and accepted the offer of coffee from the maid. He glanced at his watch. It was almost eleven and he had a lot to do this morning. It bothered him that Tyler wanted to see him today at such short notice—it had sounded more like an order than an invitation. Then he shrugged mentally and watched the real estate tycoon in action. The guy was brash and uneducated but he also had an unlimited flow of funds behind this distasteful front. It was unfortunate, Harlan knew, that he'd found himself obliged to introduce Tyler into certain circles, when he'd rather not have. But hey! It was a small price to pay for the man's support, the flowing cash, the ever-growing vision of freedom at the end of the tunnel. All he seemed to have to do was hint to Tyler that such and such a project needed funding, and next thing he knew a check was on his desk.

It was a novel experience for Harlan. Up until now, he'd depended exclusively on the senator's goodwill to pull in favors and produce funds. And he found it very agreeable to dispose of large sums of money without having to render accounts to anyone. Not that he hadn't kept strict accounting; of course he had. You never knew when a guy like Tyler might suddenly turn around and demand an audit, and he wasn't about to come out not smelling like a rose. Still, it gave him a true sense of his increasing power and clout to be able to commandeer this kind of cash flow.

"So…" Tyler laid the phone down next to him on the white and gold couch and folded some papers. "How's it going, Harlan? Everything running okay with our plans for the election? Any news of when your wife's getting back?" He raised a bushy blond brow inquiringly. His eyes were small and gray, almost like a pig's, Harlan thought, and his mottled red complexion was definitely unprepossessing. Of course, his belly flopping from beneath the polo shirt didn't improve matters any.

"Election's on track and Elm is doing fine," Harlan answered with one of his winning smiles, "enjoying Christmas shopping with her girlfriend over in Europe. Women! They never get enough of it, do they?" He smiled at the maid as she refreshed his coffee.

"Would seem so," Tyler said slowly, sucking in his fat cheeks, a peculiar glint in his piggish eyes. "How long's she planning to be away, do you reckon?"

"Oh, I don't know. She'll be back soon enough." Harlan took a sip, then laid the cup carefully back in the saucer, anxious not to appear unnerved or annoyed by Tyler's unexpected question. How did he happen to know Elm was away, anyhow? He hadn't mentioned it in any conversation that he could recall.

"She'll be coming home for Christmas, I guess?" Tyler eyed him closely. Too closely.

"Well, maybe, maybe not. She hasn't been doing too great health-wise," he said, measuring his words. "The senator and I both feel it might do her good to have a rest. The Christmas season's pretty exhausting. Of course, if she doesn't return I'll be joining her as soon as I can," he added, remembering the senator's recommendation, which at the time he hadn't taken seriously but now seemed very apt. "It'd be nice to spend a few days away together. Kind of like a second honeymoon." He smiled nostalgically. "We rarely get a chance to be on our own with all my commitments," he added, a shadow flitting across his face, as though he were seriously sorry to be deprived of his wife's company.

"Doesn't spend much time with you when she *is* around, though, does she?"

"What do you mean?" Harlan looked up, taken aback.

"Spends most all of her time up there at that old Hathaway plantation, as far as I can make out."

"She's very fond of the place. It's been in the family for centuries."

"Uh-huh. Pity you don't use it more often for fundraisers. I guess it's kind of run-down, huh? Place like that could be made into a fucking palace with a couple of million to smarten it up."

"It sure could," Harlan agreed fervently, wishing that by some mysterious act of God Oleander Creek could suddenly become his. He could just envisage pouring some of Tyler's money into it. It was exactly what he needed to top off his image as a man who hailed from the old South, but had a unique understanding for the new.

Tyler, who apparently didn't own a handkerchief, sniffed loudly and threw his arm over the back of the couch and yawned. "I was talking to our manager over there at the waste-processing plant the other day, and he was telling me we need a certificate, a clean bill of health, so to speak. It's for the fucking Environmental Protection Agency. Apparently that initial waiver you arranged for is about to expire. We need to get them off our back. You can get that rolling along, right, Harlan?"

"Sure thing. If you can get me the required documentation, I'll see what can be done."

Tyler eyed him then, taking his time, speaking slowly. "Sure, we'll get you the documentation. Might have to be a little flexible in some areas, though. Nothing to worry about, of course, nothing significant. Just these motherfuckers over at the EPA are so tight-assed—if they had their way, everyone in this goddamn country would be living in sterile respirator rooms, like that bubble boy." He laughed and got up. "How about a drink, Harlan? That coffee won't get you far."

"Sure, why not?" Harlan followed him out onto the terrace, happy that Tyler would once more be in his debt. He listened as Brock shouted to the maid to bring them two strawberry daiquiris. Harlan winced. He didn't drink strawberry daiquiris, preferring straight Scotch, but he stayed quiet. Sitting down opposite Tyler with a broad smile, he stretched his legs, then broached a subject he knew would appeal to his audience.

"Say, how's the sailing going, Tyler?"

13

"**G**io," Elm popped her head around the door of Gioconda's lavishly decorated bedroom and smiled at her friend, stretched out on the Toile de Jouy daybed. She looked deceptively languid, but actually her attention was fully riveted on the *Economist*. Gio pretended to be an airhead, superficial and worldly, when in truth she was very well read and smart as a tack.

"Come in," she waved. "Back from another day's frolicking and lovemaking in the Alps, *cara?*" she teased, lowering the magazine.

"Oh, shut up." Elm laughed and sat down on the edge of the vast bed. "You know very well I've been skiing."

"No little stopovers on the return journey?" Gioconda persisted remorselessly. She had been thrilled to hear about Johnny taking Elm to his father's retreat on the mountaintop. She hadn't thought of him as a romantic man, and she wondered now if she'd underestimated him.

"Only a hot chocolate stop at the bottom of the run, I'm afraid. Sorry to disappoint you. Now listen, Gio, I need to know what we're planning for Christmas."

"*Mamma mia, cara,* thank goodness you mentioned it. As for doing something, well, to be frank I hadn't thought too much about it. *Nonno* won't be here, so we're just the two of us. I'll give Umberto the day off, of course. He likes to spend Christmas with his niece, who works in another chalet. I suppose we can do something for dinner on the twenty-fourth, though,'' she continued vaguely. ''Why?''

''Because,'' Elm said, leaning forward and pulling at her ski gloves, ''Lady Graney—Johnny's mother—has invited us both over for Christmas lunch on the twenty-fifth.''

''You're kidding?'' Gio sat up straighter.

''I kid you not.''

''Why both of us? Why not just you?''

''Because the woman knows perfectly well that I'm staying with you. We'd hardly split up on Christmas, would we?'' she replied witheringly.

''No, I suppose not.'' Gio gave one of her Italian shrugs and made a moue. ''*Va bene.* Let's go.''

''You sure you think that's a good idea?'' Elm hesitated.

''Of course it is. Well, what are you waiting for? Call the woman up and tell her 'thank you very much we'd love to.'''

''But that's just it. I'm not certain we should,'' she said carefully.

''Elm! Why on earth not?'' Gioconda bounced up, silky black hair flying. ''Of course we have to go. Don't you want to know what the rest of his family is like? Particularly his mother? One should always inspect the mother.''

''I thought we'd agreed this was just a simple holiday fling,'' Elm said. ''If that's the case, why would I want to get involved with his family?'' she countered.

Gio shrugged once more. ''Oh, I don't know, *bella.* Curiosity, I guess. Well, don't you want to know?'' Her piercing eyes bored into Elm's. ''Come on, tell the truth, you're dying to go.''

''Of course I'd like to meet them. I mean, apart from anything else, Lady Graney knows my father—or did, many years ago—so if for that reason only…'' Her voice trailed off.

''Elm, cut the BS. You know you want to go because you want to spend Christmas with Johnny and his family. Forget the rest.''

"Well, I guess that's true," she conceded ruefully, a slight flush tingeing her cheeks as she smiled. "It just seems, well…kind of personal. I mean, Christmas is an intimate family occasion, I don't know if—"

"Elm, stop second-guessing yourself. Did Johnny sound as if he wanted you to go?"

"Yes. Very much."

"Well? What's stopping you? Apart from all these righteous motives you've come up with." Her eyes narrowed shrewdly.

Elm let out a deep sigh. "I guess I feel bad about Harlan and my dad and Aunt Frances. It seems wrong to be having fun, celebrating Christmas away from home, when I know they'll be unhappy back there without me. I didn't even trim the tree before I left," she murmured guiltily.

"In that case, you should have stayed in Savannah," Gioconda said firmly. "What earthly use was it coming here, if you're going to keep on worrying about what's going on over there?" Taking a practical approach seemed best, Gio decided, watching Elm's troubled eyes.

"You're right. I'm being stupid."

"Not stupid, sensitive." Gio smiled, her eyes softening. "All your life you've worried about others. The thing is, *cara,* now it's time to worry about you. Believe me," she added dryly, "if Harlan thought that leaving you alone for Christmas would help his damn re-election, he'd do it without blinking twice."

This last was true, Elm recognized. "Okay, you've convinced me." She got up, laughed and stretched. "I'll go make the call right away, before I change my mind."

"Good." Gio picked up her magazine once more.

"Of course, there's still the problem of what we're going to give the Graney family for Christmas. I mean, what does one buy a sixteen-year-old? I have no idea."

"*Santa Madonna,*" Gioconda wailed, wringing her hands dramatically, "is there anything else she can find to complicate matters?"

* * *

As it turned out, the presents proved less of a problem than Elm had feared. A gift certificate from the CD and video store seemed a suitable present for Nicky. A quick drop in at Hermès revealed a lovely collection of cashmere shawls, designed only for the Gstaad store, portraying the celebrated decoupages of Madame Rosat, a local artist whose beautiful cut-paper pictures depicted local scenes that were famous in the region. Having never met Johnny's mother, Elm had no idea what colors she wore. In the end, she chose a shawl with a russet border she considered suitable for a sophisticated older lady, confirming with the saleswoman that Lady Graney could change it if she didn't like the color.

Then there was Johnny. What did one buy for a man one, well, had feelings for, that one wanted to make love with but who wasn't one's husband? Her face flushed at the awkwardness of her task. Nothing too personal, she decided resolutely, but nothing too casual, either. Hermès again proved helpful and she selected a pale blue cashmere sweater that she thought would match his eyes. For Liam, whom she barely knew but who seemed to spend a large amount of time glued to his cell phone and Blackberry pager, she acquired a pen with all sorts of gadgets on it at Cartier. Gioconda's gift was the only one she felt certain about, for she'd brought it with her from home—a canvas painted especially for her friend, tucked in the bottom of her largest case. She'd even managed to keep it hidden at the back of her cupboard where it lay wrapped, awaiting the big day.

In the haste of departure, she'd forgotten to get gifts for any of her friends and family back home. How could she have been so thoughtless? Elm wondered. And was there anything she could do to remedy the situation? After a long debate, she decided the best thing would be to have flowers delivered with special messages. Not to Harlan, of course. Certainly not. Still, it was hard to recognize that all the small habits one had taken for granted were no more. Here she was driving back up the hill, the back of the Range Rover piled high with gifts for people she barely knew, while her own family—

"Stop it," she exclaimed out loud, as she veered the car into the small, snow-packed road leading to Gioconda's chalet. She'd bet good money that the last thing on Harlan's mind was her Christmas gift. Unless, she winced, it was part of his new strategy to bring her back home. He seemed determined to try to resume their life together. She'd stopped taking his calls, leaving instructions with the staff to say she was out and didn't know what time she'd be back. What a nuisance Meredith hadn't been able to file the divorce before the holidays. But so it was with court procedure, Meredith had explained; inevitably there were delays.

Cruising into the garage, Elm parked next to the bright red Ferrari, determined to shake off the blues that were overshadowing her day. With a toss of her head she grabbed the collection of shopping bags from the trunk and climbed the stairs. As Gio had rightly pointed out, there was little use being here if she was going to sit around moping.

The Christmas lunch was, as Gioconda said afterward, *perfetto.*

The Dowager Viscountess Graney had welcomed them warmly. "Please, call me Grace," she said as they shook hands, "it makes me feel like one of those stiff old English women in corsets when I'm called by my title. You can take the girl out of Pittsburgh," she added with a wink, "but you can't take Pittsburgh out of the girl." She laughed, showing them into the lovely pine-paneled drawing room, where Christmas decorations abounded.

"It's exquisite," Elm exclaimed, tempering a moment's nostalgia at the sight of all the holly and candles.

"Oh, that's my butler Roberto's doing. He just loves all this. He's Spanish," Grace added, as though that explained Roberto's decorating skills. "Now, where are the boys?" She frowned. *"Roberto-o-o,"* she called in the direction of what Elm presumed must be the kitchen, "where are Johnny and Nicky and Liam? I tell you," she said, turning back to

Elm and Gioconda with a shake of her wonderfully coiffed silver hair, "those boys are just impossible. I told them to be on time. But will you believe it? I had to stop them from going up the mountain this morning. No sense whatsoever of what's due for Christmas and the family. But what can I do?"

She was interrupted by the sound of male voices on the stairs.

"Ah, finally. John Fitzgerald, the least you could do is to be here to receive your guests," she reproved.

"Yes, Mother." Johnny winked broadly at Elm and Gioconda and gave them each a kiss. Nicky followed suit and Liam shook hands.

"This is my friend, Gioconda Mancini," Elm introduced, watching as they sized one another up, Liam polite, Gioconda producing what Elm thought of as her social smile.

"Well. Where's the champagne, Mother?" Johnny asked as they moved by the fireplace and sat down on the large couches. The tree had been strategically placed in the far corner next to the window that overlooked the snow-covered village and was surrounded by gifts.

"I've brought a few gifts. May I place them by the tree?" Elm inquired of her hostess before she sat down.

"Why, you shouldn't have," Grace exclaimed, smiling.

"I'll fetch them," Johnny said.

"Thanks." Their eyes met, lingered a few seconds before he went to the hall, retrieved several packages and together placed them under the tree.

"You didn't need to get us all presents," Johnny remarked, glancing at a tag with Nicky's name written on it. "It was very thoughtful of you."

"It's the very least I could do, when your family has so graciously invited us to join you at Christmas. After all, it's a family affair."

"It is, isn't it?" he said, glancing over at the group by the fire. Oddly, Elm and Gioconda's presence didn't seem out of place. Quite the contrary. He'd had several moments of misgivings over the past forty-eight hours, wondering if this wasn't moving things too fast, but he was glad now, hearing Gioconda's musical laughter trill as she talked to Liam, who was asking whether she was part of the Mancini olive oil family business, that they had joined them. Did she know any of the details regarding the merger they'd just finalized?

"Now, Liam, leave the poor girl alone," Grace exclaimed. "This is Christmas, after all. Surely we don't have to talk business. Leave all that for when you get back home to the U.S."

"I was just asking," Liam said with an injured look.

"Actually, I know all the details of the merger that took place earlier this fall," Gioconda responded. "I'm on the board."

"You are?" Johnny watched as Liam, surprised, took a closer look at Gioconda. He grinned inwardly. She didn't seem like the kind of woman who would be on any board of directors, unless it was for some glamorous charity. But he knew Gioconda well, knew there was a quick brain behind all that languid Italian sophistication.

Then Nicky came and sat on the arm of the sofa, chatting comfortably with Elm. It was amazing how at ease she seemed with his son, despite having no kids of her own. He wondered all at once if not having children bothered her, and what the reason was. Choice? Or an inability to conceive?

Very soon Roberto emerged from the kitchen. Lunch was announced and they trooped, chatting, into the low-beamed dining room. There were three van Goghs on the wall, Elm noticed, their frames topped with holly. She was charmed to see such illustrious art mingling freely with Christmas decorations. The Graneys struck her as an amusing family, each totally different: Grace very much the matriarch in her pearl gray velour pantsuit and diamonds, Liam the serious American businessman and Nicky the hyper kid. And Johnny, she asked herself, what about Johnny? she wondered, taking a peek at him as they settled at the table.

"Now, who's going to say the blessing?" Grace inquired of the table at large.

"How about Elm?" Nicky said helpfully. "When my mom was alive she used to say it. Isn't that right, Dad? That's what you told me."

Elm noticed Johnny's abrupt change in demeanor, the stiffening. Flushing, she turned hurriedly to Grace. "I'm sure one of you would do a much better job."

"Oh, well, how about you, Liam," Grace said quickly, then bent her head, as did the rest of the table. Elm swallowed her embarrassment as Liam said grace and lunch began.

"Ah, here's Roberto with the turkey." Grace smiled brightly as the butler offered Elm the platter and conversation returned to normal. Was Johnny still so very affected by his wife's death? Certainly the incident moments earlier would suggest that he was. She felt a stab of pity, remembering Marie Ange had died fourteen years earlier. Johnny was always charming, thoughtful, sensitive to her wishes and amusing. But she got the impression that part of him remained shielded, perhaps even from those who knew and loved him best.

Gioconda was entertaining Nicky with some of her more daring Rosey adventures when Johnny interrupted Elm's thoughts.

"How is everything? Okay?"

"Wonderful," she replied, her bright smile belying the sudden stab of regret she was experiencing as she remembered the Christmas lunch that would take place several hours from now in Savannah. Her father had told her, somewhat reproachfully, that Harlan would be joining him and Aunt Frances. The intimation had been that he was a better Hathaway than Elm.

Oh well, she'd made her choices. There was little use regretting her decision and spoiling her day. Later she would phone them and say Merry Christmas—even to Harlan. But right now, she was determined to enjoy the time with the Graneys.

It was after coffee, after they'd unwrapped the gifts, exchanged thanks and exclamations of laughter and appreciation, that Grace moved over to the couch next to her.

"Well, that's all gone quite well, I think. You really shouldn't have bothered getting me such a lovely gift," she added, gesturing to the Hermès shawl draped around her shoulders.

"Yours was gorgeous, too." Elm lifted the box containing a variety of soaps from Rancé, the famous perfumers established in 1795. "I love these. And thank you again for having us."

Grace patted her arm and lowered her voice. "I'm sorry Nicky made the remark about the blessing. Children can be thoughtless. Of course, he's unaware of just how badly Marie Ange's death—that was Johnny's wife—affected his father."

"I understand."

"Yes, well, it was a sad story." She sighed, pleated the shawl. "Johnny's always felt it was his fault that she was killed. He seems to forget that he was the one who warned her to stay put. But she was very stubborn and insisted. You know what the French can be like. Very sweet girl, of course, and we all loved her dearly, but imagine wandering off in the desert to sightsee without a proper guide? And just look at how it all ended up. The thought of that poor child's death still leaves me shuddering." She let out a long breath. "Oh well, no use harping on about the past, is there? Now, how about charades, Nicky?" She waved at her grandson across the room. "Why don't we organize some games?"

"I tell you, Liam, he has feelings for that woman," Grace exclaimed after seeing Elm and Gioconda out and returning to the drawing room.

It had turned into a happy, hearty Christmas lunch, she reflected. Roberto had surpassed himself and the food was splendid. And once Nicky had finally loosened up, he'd entertained them with charades and absurd imitations. Altogether, it had proved a delightful day. Even Elm's Italian friend, whose grandparents Grace knew vaguely, was charming. Now Johnny had disappeared to play a video game with Nicky, much to her delight, and she and Liam were relaxing in the aftermath of the pleasant afternoon.

Grace sighed and repeated her fear.

"Nah, Mother. He's just having a good time. Elm's a nice gal, don't you think?"

"Perfectly lovely," she said, dolefully. "Do give me another glass of champagne, darling. At this rate, I'm going to need it." She shook her head and dropped onto the sofa with a sigh. "It's not Elm but the circumstances I'm worried about. I hate to think what George Hathaway, who's always been a stickler for convention, would say if he thought Elm and Johnny were—" She looked up at Liam as he poured, her hand stopping in midair as a thought occurred to her. "Darling, you don't suppose they're sleeping together, do you?" She sent him a horrified look.

Liam merely continued to pour. He looked at her cynically over the rim of his glasses as if to say "dumb questions don't merit answers." Grace closed her eyes and lifted a hand.

"Okay. Don't tell me. If they haven't yet, they will. You just have to see the way they pretend not to look at each other. Oh, my goodness gracious, what a pickle. To think that all these years I've been hoping, praying to St. Anthony, the patron saint of marriage, that one day Johnny'd find someone suitable to replace Marie Ange. And now look what's happened."

"Mother, slow down. They're just dating." Liam handed her the champagne flute.

"Really, Liam, sometimes you make me want to—don't you understand?"

"That they're two grown adults having a good time? Of course I do. For Christ's sakes, Mother, give Johnny a break. I really don't see what there is to get uptight about," he added, flopping into the armchair and rolling his eyes.

"But don't you see? She's still married," Grace explained

in a plaintive wail. "As Roberto was flambéing the plum pudding, I suddenly remembered who her husband is. I almost choked, I might add."

"I know exactly who her husband is."

"Then why didn't you say so?" Grace exclaimed indignantly. "He's that handsome young congressman from Georgia, Harlan MacBride, isn't he? I remember seeing pictures of him in *W*."

"I didn't think it was important."

"Not important—" Grace broke off, casting her eyes heavenward. "You're hiding something. Have you met the man?"

"He came to my office not that long ago with our local congressman, Bernie Mankowicz, in search of funding for some ecological project in Georgia. I believe we gave him a check."

"Oh, Lord. Imagine that. Married to a congressman we support!"

"From what I gather, she's getting divorced from the man. She calls herself Hathaway," Liam reminded her. "That should tell you something."

"Maybe. But I haven't heard of any divorce and I'm sure if anything as important as that were going on in Savannah, my friend Mary Ramsey would have mentioned it over the phone."

"Well, maybe she's not getting divorced," Liam countered patiently. "Maybe she's just taking a marital break."

"Liam, for Pete's sake. Congressmans' wives don't take 'marital breaks' and well you know it. Particularly someone with her political background. Mark my words," she said darkly, "Elm is clearly a woman groomed her whole life to fill a certain role. For her to abandon that role, to even contemplate divorce, means there's something very wrong going on." Her brows furrowed. "I think Elm's delightful, but I'm not sure I want Johnny to get involved with her. A lot of people are going to get burned."

"Lord, Mother, stop getting uptight. It's just a holiday fling, after all. In the New Year they'll each go back to their lives, with no one the worse for wear.'' He let out a long-suffering huff. He was getting bored with the subject of Elm and his brother. He wished it were a working day, that he could check the markets instead of having to mooch around making small talk. At least Gioconda Mancini had given him some interesting details regarding the merger.

"You know, I sometimes wonder," Grace commented in a conversational aside, "how someone as sharp as you can be so incredibly stupid when it comes to the obvious.'' The withering look accompanying her words spoke volumes. "It would be plain to a blind bat that Elm means more to Johnny than just a *fling*, as you put it. My God, Liam,'' she murmured, her eyes softening and her voice more gentle, "I haven't seen that look in his eyes since before Marie Ange died.'' She took a sip of champagne, deflated, the thought leaving her suddenly sad and tired. "It does seem unfair that when he finally meets a potentially suitable companion—for she certainly strikes me as that—it has to be a woman who can only bring more heartbreak into his life.''

"Mother, this is ridiculous. You've met her for…what? Four hours? You know nothing about her, whether she'd be perfect for Johnny or not. And here you are ranting and raving as if they'd announced a wedding date. Don't you think you're jumping the gun?''

"Maybe. Possibly. It's just a feeling I have.''

"Anyway, why are you so worried that she'll bring him heartache? She's getting a divorce. She'll be a free woman. Johnny's a free man. Not that he's looking to get hitched, mind you, but he's certainly available for a little fun. What's the harm?''

"Oh, I don't know," Grace interrupted. "It's just a hunch.'' She shook her head and sighed. "I must be getting old, but I just don't believe things will be as simple as you suggest.''

"Well, I like Elm," Liam said staunchly.

"So do I,'' Grace sighed woefully. "I couldn't think of a more charming woman for Johnny if I searched the entire planet. But not under these circumstances, Liam. Mark my words, honey, there'll be trouble before this vacation's over. I can feel it in my bones."

"That sounds so Irish."

"Well, I am originally Irish and I respect my gut feelings, so don't you give me any of your lip, Liam Graney." Grace wagged her bejeweled finger. "I know what I'm talking about."

"Right. Well, we'll just have to wait and see, won't we?" He heaved himself out of the chair. "I think I'll go play a video game with the others."

"Liam, really, when have you ever played a video game?" Grace exclaimed, exasperated.

"Uh, never. It's time I broadened my horizons." He grinned sheepishly. "That's what Nicky keeps telling me."

Grace smiled affectionately, knowing perfectly well he was escaping. Oh well. It was one of the trials of being a parent.

"Off you go then, darling. And please don't let Johnny give Nicky any more champagne. It's not good for him."

"We're in Europe, Mother. Kids here are breast-fed on the stuff. Be thankful it's not Guinness."

"Oh, just go," she said with a wave before sipping the last of the champagne. All she could do was hope the romance was, as Liam had put it, a holiday fling with no consequences. But she was genuinely concerned. Elm was not the type of woman to spend Christmas away from home—despite her smooth explanation—or to be running from her marriage without a good reason, and the last thing she wanted was her son entangled in the middle of a messy political divorce.

Setting her glass on a copy of *Country Life,* she flipped mentally through her address book. Who did she know in Savannah, apart from Mary Ramsey, who was well informed and discreet enough to give her the scoop?

Why, Louise Murphy, of course. And what better time than today to wish her old friend a Merry Christmas?

14

Frances Hathaway Irvington Bell, the senator's twice-widowed elder sister, sat opposite her brother across the long Georgian dining table. Harlan sat between them. The table was decked as befitted the occasion, with the family sterling and crystal, and Beau stood in attendance in his white jacket and bow tie, passing the array of warm dishes gracing the sideboard.

Between dainty bites of turkey, Frances took a look at the two men seated with her at the table. She'd never much liked Harlan MacBride and had even told her brother so, discreetly—of course, she never imposed her views, rather let them be subtly absorbed—but, as usual, he hadn't listened. He didn't want to listen now when she'd remarked, more sternly than usual, that she wasn't surprised matters between Harlan and Elm had come to a head. She'd heard a different version of Harlan's tale from her sources and it tallied very little with the one her brother was inclined—for all the wrong reasons—to believe. How George could be so blinded by political ambition for the creature was beyond her. He would have done a lot better to worry about his daughter's happiness.

Unfortunately, he seemed to believe these were one and the same thing.

She placed a delicate forkful of sweet potato into her

mouth, wishing that she could swipe that smarmy sad little
smile from Harlan's irritatingly handsome countenance. Jennifer Ball, indeed. She itched to stick his face in the gravy
for humiliating her lovely niece. It had made her stark raving
mad to hear Elm, blind as a bat to Harlan's flaws, defending
him after all these years, when Frances knew for a fact that
the poor child was miserable. Oh, she'd made a life for herself, of course, that was Elm's way, and she was proud of
the courageous way she'd dealt with a potentially horren-
dous marriage. And she had her painting and her garden
project, of course. But that, as Frances well knew, wasn't
enough. As a Southern belle herself, one who'd been briefly
but happily married twice and then elected to stay single
despite a number of very flattering offers of marriage, she
knew a woman needed something more sustaining in her life
than just a sense of duty. Elm, she concluded, barely listening to her brother's comments on the upcoming election,
needed to discover true love.

God, he wished he were somewhere else, Harlan reflected,
stifling a yawn as the interminable Christmas lunch lingered
on. He could feel the eyes of that old bitch Frances boring
into him from behind that smooth smile, that perfect, soft-
skinned, fine-featured face framed by its styled gray hair.
She looked like a charming, elegant, harmless old lady, but
that, Harlan knew, was far from the truth. The woman was
a venomous viper and he blamed her for many of Elm's
defects. He was certain it was she who'd encouraged Elm
to take the trip to Switzerland. Why, he wouldn't be surprised if the old cow hadn't come up with the idea herself.
Elm was too much of a wimp—or had been, up until now—
to take such a radical course on her own. And what about
the divorce? he wondered, ploughing through the turkey. For
all he knew, the old witch was behind that, too. She'd always
hated him, and had let it be known in that overly polite,
measured, indirect manner of hers that made him feel
strangely inferior and left him seething inside.

Forcing himself to remain in control, Harlan smothered

his anger, careful to listen attentively to his father-in-law and occasionally disagree with him—just enough to capture his interest—then appeared to let himself be won over by the senator's compelling arguments, giving the old man the satisfaction of thinking he was still in control. But not for long, he vowed.

He'd see to it the waste plant got a clean bill of health, proving to Tyler he was worthy of his confidence, and more dollars would flow. Of that he was certain. He glanced around the ample, high-ceilinged dining room and smothered a smile. It gave him a rush of satisfaction to think that, if he was lucky, this might be the last Christmas he'd have to spend stuck between these two, playing the same game he'd been playing for so long, a game he'd outgrown and that no longer held its original appeal. Then he reluctantly remembered that he wanted—needed—Elm back, at least temporarily, and grimaced inwardly. He would probably have to face a few more Christmases.

But the end result would be well worth it, he assured himself, hiding his inner glee, well worth every fucking bite of turkey, every charming smile in Aunt Frances's direction and all the kowtowing he'd had to do to over the years. Not long to go now, he vowed, exclaiming as Beau and Mae triumphantly carried out the tray with the flaming plum pudding. Here were two votes he knew were secure, and the First Baptist Church could pretty well be counted on with Beau in his pocket. He'd better make sure his nephew, the local postman, got a raise.

He watched the senator swallow a sigh. The table must seem terribly empty without his little girl, the seating order altered for the occasion. It was usually Frances who sat to his right and Elm who graced the head of the table. But not today. Apparently she'd phoned earlier in the day, sounding cheerful, and said she'd spent Christmas with Dowager Viscountess Graney, whom the senator remembered from the old days. George had remarked to Harlan that at least she was with fellow Americans on Christmas Day and maybe the time away would end up doing her good. He'd mentioned that he'd been careful not to criticize or spoil the day for her, encouraging her instead to enjoy herself, then sent her his love and wished her a happy Christmas. A hint, Harlan supposed, directed at how he should talk to Elm himself. Well, the senator needn't concern himself. He had no wish to alienate her further right now.

When he'd arrived, he'd seen Aunt Frances on the phone, and the quick glance she gave in his direction. She'd spent quite a long time chatting with Elm in a low voice out in the hall, while Harlan had eyed her impatiently from the armchair in the den. He'd made sure the senator noticed his discomfort, and he jumped up eagerly to pick up the phone when Aunt Frances finally called him, let the glimmer of hope in his eyes show.

"More pudding, sir?" Beau leaned over with the dish and the senator scooped up another spoonful.

"This is a terrific Christmas lunch, Beau. You tell Mae I said so. Everything was simply perfect."

"Delicious," Frances agreed, delicately dabbing her pink lipstick with the white linen napkin. "Tell me, Harlan, what are your plans for the New Year, now that Elm's away?" she asked in that well-bred innocent tone that didn't deceive him one little bit.

"Oh, just the usual rounds," he answered vaguely. "I'm not too keen on going out at all, but I guess I'll have to show up. It's expected of me."

"Why, of course you have to go to all the usual events, Harlan. It would make a mighty odd appearance if you didn't," the senator cautioned.

"I know. It's just…well, it seems so strange to be there by myself."

"I'm sure you could find someone to take along," Frances murmured, her soft gray eyes resting on him for a moment. "What about your cousin Loretta, isn't she back for the vacation and on her own? I'm sure she'd be grateful for the company. Is this her third or fourth divorce? I've lost track."

"I don't know," Harlan answered shortly. "Anyway, I'm

going to Switzerland to spend a few days with Elm after the first of the year.''

''Really?'' The senator looked up, pleased. ''That's a good idea, boy, very good idea indeed.'' He indicated to Beau to serve more wine and smiled.

''Well, that should be an interesting trip,'' Frances commented mildly, lifting her glass, her eyes meeting Harlan's over the rim. ''Are you planning to stay at Gioconda's chalet?''

''Actually, I thought of staying at the hotel.''

''Oh. Well, I hope you find room at the Palace. It's usually packed at this time of year.''

''I'm sure my congressional office can do something about that,'' Harlan responded, trying not to sound withering.

''Hmm. I hope so.'' She sounded doubtful, leaving him doubly annoyed and determined to get the best fucking suite the damn hotel could offer.

''Elm sounded in excellent form,'' Frances continued, pricking the plum pudding—a family tradition—with her fork, ''better than I've heard her in a long while. Incredible what a break away will do for one. I have always been a great believer in foreign travel. It expands the mind so wonderfully. I'm sure Elm must be enjoying getting together with all her old Rosey friends, don't you think, George? Did she tell you she met her old pal Geoffrey? Such a nice young man,'' she continued dreamily. ''I can remember his father way back when. Always so distinguished, well-mannered and polite, and of course quite devastatingly handsome. So nice when a man is that good-looking but with no artifice. A rare quality, don't you agree?'' she addressed Harlan, forcing him to acknowledge her words. ''And then, of course, Gioconda is such a social butterfly and will want to introduce her to *all* her friends. She moves in a very *haut monde* circle, which is just the kind of company Elm needs right now. A nice change from here,'' she added. ''I'm sure she must be out every night at all those wonderful dinner parties. And Europeans entertain so superbly, I always find. Did you say she was lunching with Lady Graney today?''

''That's right. She's the heiress to Riley Steel, you know, up in Pittsburgh. Why, Harlan, you were up there visiting not that long ago, isn't that right?''

''Yes, in fact, I think Liam Graney's office gave us a check to help with our cleanup of the Kemira Acid Spill Superfund site. We've linked it to a sister project up in his area and he's very sensitive to environmental causes.''

''Good, excellent. I'm sure Elm will be able to chat to him about it. Did you mention it to her?''

''Uh, actually, no. But I will,'' Harlan said quickly.

Frances eyed him and smiled. ''Having a wife as smart and lovely as Elm is certainly an asset, isn't it, Harlan?''

''Of course. I'm very aware of all her qualities.''

''Are you?'' She raised a brow so slightly he might have imagined it, ''Well, that's nice, isn't it? Now, shall we have coffee in the living room, George? I think that would be lovely.''

The next few days flew by as though Elm were in a magical dream. Skiing with Johnny, dining with Johnny, laughing and having the best time of her life with Johnny and their friends. It *was* a dream, of course, an interlude, but oh, what a special one. The time had cast a glow over her stagnant existence, bringing new life, a fresh energy and strength to go forward.

On New Year's Eve they joined a group of friends at the Palace Hotel. The party was superb, the buffet incredible, champagne and caviar flowed and the guests were in a suitably festive mood. At midnight, competing firework displays filled the Gstaad sky, and as the last colored spray died, Elm let out a sigh as friends kissed and hugged, wished one another Happy New Year. It was, she realized, not simply a new year, but a whole new beginning, the first year on the fresh path she'd so abruptly and unexpectedly chosen.

She thought over the past months, the rude awakening of her senses—in more ways than one—and the unknown future lying ahead. There was still much to be faced, she reflected, watching the exquisite crowd, elegant and bejeweled, couples kissing, flashes going off, friends and strangers greeting one another, embracing, wishing one another much luck and happiness for the year to come. It seemed astonishing that for the first time she wasn't experiencing that daunting sense of awe that before had overwhelmed her when she thought of what lay ahead. Instead, she welcomed the new chance to start over. The planning of her exhibition in Florence next autumn was a landmark she looked forward to. It would be the consolidation of many years of the work that she'd always had to relegate to second place, but that would now take on a primary position in her life.

She glanced at Johnny, standing next to her, so handsome and debonair tonight in his tux, hair slicked back. Yet underneath she sensed a withdrawal, as though he, too, were evaluating, weighing, contending with his own inner thoughts. They'd talked little of their personal lives, she realized, giving way rather to the trifling amusements afforded by the time of year. The company and the leisure-seeking was what they'd all come here for: to forget reality, she realized suddenly. That was what this was all about, to be able to relax for a few short weeks, let go of the everyday burdens and responsibilities and pretend, if only for a while, that life was a never-ending fairy tale of fun, parties and joyous laughter in horse-drawn sleighs and glistening ski slopes.

And she didn't regret it.

Again Elm recalled that evening at Gioconda's and, for the hundredth time, wondered what might have happened if Umberto hadn't rung the bell. Would she have given in to those insistent urges Johnny had sparked within her? Well, thankfully she hadn't and could look herself straight in the mirror without dying of embarrassment. And fortunately Johnny had made no other attempt to push things any further. Even that magical afternoon spent up at the chalet had been nothing but a delightful interlude.

Her thoughts were interrupted by an elegant couple wishing her a Happy New Year. She smiled and laughed, but realized that she wished they could leave now. She needed some peace, some tranquillity. It had all been so delightful and carefree, but, she realized, too much of this could begin to pall, too.

She thought again of her itching desire to get back to her work. Johnny had been so admiring of the painting she'd offered Gioconda for Christmas, which now hung above the fireplace in Gio's living room and had not seemed at all taken aback when she'd told him she planned to make a career out of it.

"Shall we leave?" he asked quietly, slipping an arm about her and leading her back to the dance floor where the orchestra was playing "Fly Me to the Moon."

"Leave?" Moments earlier she'd wanted just that, but she felt a stab of disappointment that he wanted to end the evening.

"Did you think I was about to drop you off at home?" he asked, eyes softly amused as he glided with her around the floor, then lightly touched her cheek, leaving her breathless by the gesture's sheer intimate tenderness.

God, Elm looked lovely tonight, Johnny reflected, ethereal in that white sheath with the delicate silver trim. And her skin, that glorious skin he so wanted to touch and to discover, but which he'd held himself back from, suspecting that, once he'd touched it, he might never be able to stop. And those incredible brown eyes, wide, beautiful, tender eyes that contrasted with her sleek, naturally blond hair.

Elm looked up and he tightened his arms about her waist. "I have an idea," he said, banishing his doubts.

"Oh?"

He stared deeply into her eyes. "Would you consider spending the night with me at the Chalet Wildhorn?"

Elm swallowed. "I…?"

He held her gaze, leaving her no doubt as to what lay ahead if she accepted.

"It's entirely up to you," he added, twirling her once more, then slowing the pace, eyes still riveted to hers. "If you prefer, we can simply stay here until the party ends and then I'll drop you off at Gio's.'' He smiled gently, slipped his fingers casually through the strand of hair that had fallen on her shoulder and waited.

Oh, God.

Elm hesitated, her feelings so utterly conflicted she could barely breathe. Should she give in to her desires and go with him? Or should she do the sensible thing and go home without allowing herself a taste of temptation?

For a while she let him rock her gently around the dance floor, eyes glued to the satin lapel of his tux.

Then slowly she raised her eyes and made a snap decision. Wise or not, she was going to do it. She would spend the first night of this year in his arms, hidden away in that magical spot. It would provide a fitting baptism for her new self, her new life. And even if this was all she ever had of him, it would be enough.

''Okay,'' she murmured, ''let's go. I'd better tell Gio.''

''Forget Gio, she's down in the Green Go, dancing the night away. Believe it or not, she even got Liam onto the floor.'' He smiled down at her and drew her closer. For a while they danced, cleaved together, welcoming each other's warmth, wanting to prolong the pleasure, make the dream last as long as possible.

When the music stopped he touched her lips gently with his. ''Ready?''

''Yes.'' She nodded, happy now that she'd made up her mind. She followed him out into the lobby, the trepidation replaced by a feeling of inner peace and satisfaction. Johnny collected their coats, wrapped Elm's mink about her, and they waited on the steps for the valet to bring the Range Rover.

Then they were driving through the night, snow pelting into the lights and the windshield as they left the village and headed toward the glacier. The flakes grew heavier as they climbed slowly round the hairpin mountain bends, tires crunching.

But at last the car stopped in front of the garage. Silence

reigned. There was not a soul within range, just the snow and the night and the glow from the lamp illuminating the small wooden stairway leading to the private cable car.

"Careful," he warned, seeing her flimsy evening shoes. "Wait there a moment." He alighted from the car, and before she could stop him, opened her door and lifted her in his arms.

"Johnny, I can walk."

"You'll get your feet frozen," he said, climbing the stairs, then opening the door to the car and depositing her on the rug-covered seat. "Now, hang on while I lock up."

In a moment he was sitting opposite her and the little cable car took off into the mountain. They leaned forward and huddled together, watching the ever-thickening snow-flakes fall so peacefully, so gently, piling higher and higher on the ground below.

"I may have to dig us out of here tomorrow morning," Johnny remarked, eyeing the birdhouses, their tiny roofs weighed down with a good thirty centimeters of new snow.

"It's magical, so utterly peaceful and undisturbed," Elm murmured as they entered the chalet. She watched Johnny turn on the lights and light the fire in the sitting room as she removed her coat. Dropping the mink on a chair, she slid beside him onto the sofa.

"Another drink, darling?"

"Oh no, thanks. I've had enough champagne to last me the rest of the year. I wouldn't mind a cup of tea, though." He'd never called her darling before and the endearment sent a tingle up her spine. She gazed into the flames, smiling, listening to the domestic sounds of the kettle hissing in the kitchen. She looked up as he handed her the mug of tea, which she cupped in her palms before taking a long sip, savoring the warmth and the moment, capturing the tender buildup of expectation. She would never forget this as long as she lived, she decided, letting her head rest on his shoulder, determined to relish each instant.

"What a perfect way to begin the year," she murmured.

"Yes, it is," he replied. "Any big plans for this one, Elm?" he asked softly.

She shrugged. "I guess. It'll be a decisive year for me, that's for sure."

"You mean your divorce?"

"Uh-huh. And my exhibition in Florence." She didn't want to say any more, simply smiled into the fire. "And what about you?" She turned her face up.

Johnny gazed down at her and dropped a light kiss on the tip of Elm's nose.

"Cold nose," he remarked, rubbing it, "healthy puppy."

"Come on, tell me what your big project for the year is. Actually, I think I know," she murmured archly.

"Really?" He quirked a brow.

"Yes. Having Blue Lavender win all the races you enter him in."

"Ha! Right on target. I have great hopes for that horse, though winning *every* race might be expecting a little too much of him. Still, I really believe this year is going to be a good one. That horse is ready. I just know it."

"Spoken like a true Irishman." She let out a low laugh. He'd talked a lot about his horses, and she felt as if she knew them. She could picture Graney Castle, the well-tended stables, bracing Irish mornings with Johnny riding through the swirling mist, putting the horse through its paces, then pausing by a white-picket fence, the horse edging against it, exchanging long conversations with men in tweed caps and green Barbour jackets, weighing their options, their hopes for the champion.

She laughed tenderly when he passed his tongue over her upper lip. "What were you thinking about, my lovely?"

"You, and Ireland and Blue Lavender. I'm sure he'll win."

"How do you know? Have you cast a spell on him? Got the fairies and leprechauns afoot, have you? Been up to some of that Southern witchcraft Savannah's famous for?"

"You don't need any of that," she murmured softly, delighting in the trail of soft kisses down the side of her temple.

"Well, it won't be for lack of training or trying," he murmured, his hand slipping to her low-cut neckline, "but of course, you never know. A win depends on so many factors," he muttered, fingers playing havoc with her sanity. He caressed her breast and she gave way to delicious sensations, to mindless delight as he roamed, seemed to know exactly when and how to follow the rising spiral of desire that grew within her.

A shudder ripped through her as his lips came down on hers. Then, as though by common instinct, they reached for one another and she was wrapped in his arms, his hands coursing up and down her body, holding her close, murmuring tenderly. Her fingers dragged through his hair. She breathed in the musky scent of cologne, his scent, basked in the strength of his sinewy taut muscles. Then gently he laid her back on the couch, set her head against a cushion and Elm knew she couldn't make him stop even had she wanted to.

His fingers traveled under the thin gauze of her evening gown, outlining the curve of her breasts, grazing her aching nipples that longed for his touch. She let out a ragged moan, felt herself go liquid inside, experienced an increasing longing, rising as he caressed her. She closed her eyes, unable to do more than float on this ecstatic wave of newfound pleasure that she could hardly bear, it was so sweet. Then expertly he slipped her gown aside and lowered his lips to her breasts, suckling where before he'd touched, taunting playfully, drawing her nipples gently between his teeth until she cried out with unabashed desire, each delicious, tumbling sensation stronger than the previous, until she could endure it no more.

Oh, God. It was wonderful. So wonderful. Too wonderful. Somewhere in the recesses of her mind Elm wished this could go on forever, that his lips would never stop, that the fire would go on crackling, that the wondrous joy of discovering her body and being so utterly indulged would never ever end.

She wanted him to go on and on kissing her, to block out everything but the soft soothing sanctuary of his arms, reach out once more and touch that part of her being she'd never before known existed. Her breath caught, as magical thrills traveled her being, leaving her weak and wanting. Then she leaned toward him, fisted the front of his shirt and, tilting her head back, let out a cry of delight.

But now she wanted more, wanted to feel him deep inside her, to be his, only his, to give him all she had inside, fulfil all he'd awakened within her. She wanted to experience all that unrestrained energy, that underlying wildness she sensed so close beneath the surface that he held back, perhaps afraid of frightening or hurting her. Tonight, she vowed, she would have every ounce of him, body and soul.

As soon as he recognized the feral light in her eyes, Johnny knew it was time. She'd passed a benchmark, wanted what he wanted.

In one swift movement, he lifted her off the couch and marched up the crooked stairs and into the bedroom, confident that tonight he would make her his, if only for a while.

He laid her silently down on the bed, eyes locked when she pulled him down with her, tearing off his bow tie, unbuttoning his shirt, her lips trailing down his chest. Pulling off the half-divested evening gown, he threw it to the floor, reveling in the touch of her body, taut and wanting, groaning as she kissed each part of him until he lay weak with pleasure.

Elm savored, laved, filled herself with the taste of him, wanting to know every inch of his body inside out, feel the ripple of each muscle quiver under her curious tongue and fingers.

Then in one fast movement he found her, cupped her, caressed her. When she all but climaxed, he brought her down on top of him, entered her hard and fast, thrusting so deep she thought he'd touched her soul. There were no tender words, no soft caresses, just a frenzied, furious converging of desires as he grabbed her hips and she rode him, head thrown back, hair wild, and together they ravaged, demolished every last barrier of restraint as they fell, crying out, into an endless ravine of never-ending pleasure.

Afterward Elm rested her head on Johnny's damp chest, and sighed. She couldn't move, couldn't speak, couldn't do anything but lie basking in the aftermath. It had been so incredibly physical, so intense and primal, even deliciously savage at times.

And wonderful.

Simply, gloriously wonderful.

As she lay sheltered in the crook of his arm, she suddenly recalled her wedding night with Harlan and shuddered at all she'd missed all these years.

"Are you cold, darling?" Johnny shifted and moved the duvet over them, then reached for his cell phone on the bedside table and switched it off before holding her close again, lips tracing her brow.

"Mmm-hmm." She snuggled closer and laid an arm lazily across his chest, knowing she'd just attained the unattainable. She was tired, deliciously, delectably tired, and so exquisitely sleepy. Then her cheek sank into his chest once more, and her eyes closed. Her last thought as sleep took over was that this was a truly perfect way to begin the new year.

Johnny leaned back against the plumped goose-down pillows and stroked her hair gently, absorbing the intensity of what had just occurred.

He'd never dreamt it could ever be this way again, that he could feel with that same unique force of years earlier. Yet tonight the impossible had occurred: for the first time in fifteen years, he'd felt something, a fierce tenderness that stirred a part of his being he'd believed dead with Marie Ange in the Sahara Desert.

Elm, he marveled, had helped him remember what it was like to feel whole again.

* * *

She awoke wondering where she was. Then, feeling an arm thrown over her, she quickly remembered and a slow smile dawned. This was perhaps just a pleasant interlude, a fling, as Gioconda had so rightly termed it, but it had marked her. She sighed and looked down at Johnny's sleeping face and tousled dark hair. She must not, she reflected, fall into the deadly trap of believing it was anything else. But, by God, was she glad to have lived it, to finally know what it felt like to be made love to by a man who gave as much as he took.

Gio was right. She definitely needed to gain more experience. She had no real knowledge of men, nothing really beyond the realm of the life she'd led within the protected ambit of her own little world. Pulling the duvet carefully, so as not to wake Johnny, she turned. Whatever the future, she would always remember this precious moment they'd shared and be grateful to him for having made it so perfect, so sweet and so intense, for having chosen to share the silent peace of "his" mountain with her.

Johnny woke, bleary-eyed, and blinked. He switched on his cell phone and read the time. Two o'clock in the afternoon. Jesus, how had he slept this long?

Then slowly the events of the previous evening tumbled into place. Not surprising that he'd overslept, he realized ruefully. He turned swiftly, saw the empty bed beside him and wondered where Elm was. Then the aroma of fresh coffee reached his nostrils and he smiled and passed his palm absently over his chin, noting that he could do with a shave.

With a yawn he got up, pulled on an old cashmere robe of his dad's still hanging on the back of the bedroom door and made his way quietly down to the kitchen.

For a moment he stood silently in the kitchen doorway, watching her standing with her back turned, wearing her evening gown and an ancient cardigan he remembered from the old days. How lovely she was, all woman, unfettered, and how much he enjoyed her company and her being. His thoughts were followed by a sharp twinge of regret, that the interlude must inevitably come to an end.

He cleared his throat. Elm turned and smiled at him. She looked deliciously tousled yet domestic, holding the kettle in one hand, the coffeepot in the other.

"Good morning. Happy New Year." He came over, dropped a kiss on her brow and sniffed. "That smells delicious. Where did you find it? I can't believe that coffee can still be good."

"Well, as it's all there is, we'll just have to try it and see," she reasoned, tilting her face up and smiling mischievously.

"Okay, okay, I bow to your better judgment." He laughed, getting out two mugs. "Let's make a fire and have it in the living room, it's bloody freezing in here. Aren't you cold?" He reached for her, rubbed her back and together they went into the living room, carrying the coffee and the mugs. It felt, Elm reflected, as though they'd been doing this forever.

She pulled herself up quickly. Those were the kind of thoughts that could only lead to trouble.

"How," she asked, watching him rekindle the fire, "are we going to go back home dressed like this?"

He looked up and eyed her, amused. "That's a small detail I didn't take into account last night."

"Well, I'm going to look mighty intelligent when I ring the front door bell and Umberto opens up. I can just imagine the man's face." Elm shuddered. "This is going to be so embarrassing."

"Don't worry about it," he responded blithely, finally getting the fire going, "we'll find an answer."

Just then, the cell phone he'd tucked in his pocket gave a loud ring. "Oh, boy," he muttered with a wry smile, sitting down on the tiny old Welsh milking chair by the fire. "Here goes our peace and quiet. Hello?"

The immediate change in his body language told her something was wrong. She stiffened as she saw him clench his fist, heard him murmur assents into the phone. Her pulse beat faster as he signed off and turned, white-faced, toward her.

"That was Liam," he said, voice harsh. "Nicky's on the way to the hospital."

"The hospital!" She blanched. "What happened?" she exclaimed, jumping up, horrified.

"Appendicitis is their best guess. We'll know once they get there. I'm afraid we'll have to leave right away."

"Of course. We must go at once," Elm agreed, all other concerns forgotten as they hurried upstairs and pulled on their shoes and coats in silent haste.

Never had Johnny felt so worried and impatient. And nothing cooperated with him. First the key got stuck in the lock, then the cable car jammed twice. Once it finally worked, it seemed to take ages to get back down the mountain. All he could do was try not to panic, accept the offer of Elm's soothing hand as they rushed to the car, then race down the icy mountain, through empty villages to the Saanen hospital, where Nicky was about to enter surgery.

Elm's pulse raced as they drew up in front of the hospital. She barely considered what they must look like, still dressed in their evening attire. All that mattered was Nicky.

Then Johnny grabbed her hand and together they hurried toward the emergency entrance, their only thought to reach Nicky's bedside.

15

"At last." Grace exclaimed, astounded, despite her worry, to see Elm and Johnny hurrying down the corridor still dressed in their evening clothes. "Where on earth have you two been?"

"How is he?" Johnny asked hoarsely, ignoring her question.

"Dr. Kunz is about to operate. I've been trying to reach you since nine o'clock this morning when the pains started, but you were nowhere to be found. I tried everywhere, on your cell phone, the car phone, but there was no answer. Oh, darling, I've been so worried." Grace suddenly collapsed, face crumpling, onto one of the plastic chairs.

"Where is he?" Johnny asked, patting his mother's shoulder, but thinking only of his sick child and trying to master the overwhelming sense of guilt. He'd been making love, thinking only of himself, when Nicky could have died.

Liam pointed to the door of a room. "They asked us to leave while they prepare him for the OR. He's fine, bro, stop worrying. It'll all be all right." He smiled reassuringly.

Johnny turned and flung open the room's door.

"Nicky." He rushed across the room and grabbed his son's hand. "Are you all right? Oh, God, I'm so sorry I wasn't there." He leaned over and hugged his son, hands shaking, feeling that same terrible fear he'd experienced only once in his life and never wanted to go through again.

"I'm fine, Dad." Nicky looked pale but he smiled bravely. The tranquil faces of the hospital staff clustered around the bed filled Johnny with relief. "It'll be okay. And they say I get to eat ice cream and stuff afterward." He gave his father another valiant little smile.

"Of course you will," he murmured, caressing his son's brow, containing his own agitation.

"At least I won't really miss any school," Nicky added, as the nurses rolled his bed out of the room and down the corridor. Johnny glanced anxiously at the wide doors of the operating theater.

"Why's that?" he murmured absently, still gripping the boy's hand.

"Well, it fits in with the suspension," he whispered confidingly.

"The what? Oh, yes, the suspension." All at once he remembered, rubbed his son's dark hair, so very like his own, and gave a hoarse laugh. "I wouldn't worry about that right now," he whispered. "Will you forgive me for not being there when this all happened?"

"Excuse me, Lord Graney, but Dr. Kunz is waiting."

"Of course, sorry." He hadn't realized they'd stopped pushing the bed, and continued walking beside it.

Then Nicky tugged at his hand. "Stop worrying, Dad, you're worse than Grandma. You couldn't have guessed I'd have appendicitis. No one could. By the way," he asked in a voice so low that Johnny had to bend over to hear him, "how's it going? You and Elm, I mean?"

Johnny swallowed and masked his surprise. "Great," he replied, trying to regain control of his frayed nerves as they reached the operating theater and Grace and Elm appeared on the other side of the bed. Grace bent over and kissed Nicky's brow.

"I'll be here, darling," Grace murmured. Elm waved and winked and Liam squeezed his hand.

"You hang in there, son," Liam said bracingly as the

wide doors opened and the bed with the small figure was swallowed up inside.

Johnny stared at them a moment, then leaned against the wall and let his head drop.

"He'll be fine," Liam said, gripping his brother's shoulder.

"Of course he will." Grace adjusted her fur-trimmed cloak and took a deep breath. "Now, let's go find some coffee. Though how you two can go anywhere dressed like that," she said, eyeing Elm and Johnny disapprovingly, "I really don't know. You'll catch your death in that dress, dear."

Elm blushed to the roots of her hair.

Grace was now back at the helm and without further ado she marched them to the elevator and down to the coffee shop. Elm trailed behind, wallowing in embarrassment. Her evening clothes made it painfully obvious that they'd spent the night together, she reflected dejectedly. When Liam's hand touched her arm, she smiled gratefully.

"I feel terrible," she whispered. "This is so uncomfortable and inappropriate. I should have taken a cab home or something and changed before coming over. It's just that we were so worried and there was no time and—"

"Don't mind her," he said, "she's just overwrought about Nicky. If you need a ride I'll drive you home in a little."

"Thanks," she smiled gratefully, "I'd hate to have to drag Johnny away." Liam returned her smile and they directed their attention back to Grace and Johnny.

"And, anyway," Grace said, speaking in a calmer tone now, "there's no point in being negative. I heard somewhere that positive thinking helps the outcome of an operation."

"Mmm-hmm."

"And of course, I called Father O'Connor back home, as soon as I knew this was happening."

"That's ridiculous," Johnny replied, letting loose his anxiety. "This isn't a damn funeral, Mother. You must have woken him in the middle of the night."

"Well, that's just too bad. I've donated more than a million dollars to that church. He can perfectly well lose a few hours' sleep on behalf of my grandson."

"God, I don't believe it." Johnny cast his eyes heavenwards and flopped into a chair opposite Elm and Liam.

"A few extra prayers won't do any harm," Grace sniffed, undaunted. "Nicky will be fine. The doctor comes highly recommended."

Two hours later they were still waiting. Elm, seeing how worried Johnny was, had refused to leave. Now they sat, a forlorn, oddly clad little group, anxiously awaiting the pending outcome of the operation.

"Something's wrong," Johnny said, pacing the corridor, agitated. "An appendectomy can't possibly take this long. Why doesn't anyone give us a briefing?"

"Look, the doors are opening." Liam pointed to the operating theater and they converged upon the emerging doctor, who was just removing his surgical mask and gloves. He was closely followed by the bed, rolled out by two nurses, where Nicky lay still and sedated.

"Your son is fine," Dr. Kunz said, addressing Johnny. "A good thing we caught it in time, though, it was blowing up. We'll keep him for a few of days, but he'll be all right. You can all go home now." He smiled briefly at the assembled group.

"Thank you, Doctor, but I'm staying," Johnny said firmly.

"I'll get the nurse to provide a cot in the room, then."

"The sofa will do fine."

"As you wish." Dr. Kunz smiled, accustomed to anxious parents.

"Thank you for coming out on New Year's Day and taking care of my boy."

"It's a pleasure. And don't worry about Nicky, he's strong as a horse and doing great. This will keep him out of mischief for a few weeks."

Johnny smiled, and shook the other man's hand gratefully. Then, dragging his fingers through his hair, he turned to Elm.

"You must be exhausted. You'd better let Liam take you home. And what about you, Mother?"

"I can stay."

"No, please, I think you should both go home. I'll stay with Nicky."

"Are you sure?" Elm asked anxiously. She hated the idea of leaving Johnny and Nicky here on their own; on the other hand she didn't want to seem like she was imposing her presence when perhaps they wanted to be by themselves. Perhaps it would be better to go and let Gioconda know what was happening and return later. The realization that she still had to make her New Year's calls home hit as she kissed Johnny goodbye. She glanced at Liam, who nodded.

"Come. Let's get going, Mother," he urged.

Grace was still looking affectionately down at Nicky, eyes glistening. "He looks awfully pale," she said.

"He's fine, Mother. Now, come along with Elm and let him rest. Johnny will stay and I'll be back in a little."

"Don't worry, Mother, I'm not going anywhere."

"So I should hope." Grace's tone left no doubt as to her opinion of his previous absence. Liam stood behind her, raising his brows conspiratorially at his brother before shepherding Grace out the door, while Johnny dropped a kiss on Elm's brow then turned her toward the exit.

"I'll call you later. Thanks for staying." He smiled deep into her eyes and a knot formed in her throat as she followed close on Liam and Grace's heels.

After a refreshing bath, Elm knew it was time to forget her present worries and call home to wish the family happy New Year. Her first call was to Aunt Frances, who after the first greetings proceeded to inform her of a piece of news she hoped was very wrong.

"What do you mean, Harlan's coming here tomorrow night?" Elm squeaked into the phone as she sat, swathed in her terry robe, hair wrapped in a towel, on the sofa of her sitting room before the crackling fire.

"Just that, honey. There was no stopping him. I know he wanted it to be a surprise," Frances said dryly, "but under the circumstances, I thought it better to advise you."

"Oh, thank God you did, Aunt Frances. I can't think why he's coming, unless…"

"Well, dear, I don't know what he thinks he's going to achieve. But you know how tenacious he can be. That, and he has a very high opinion of his own person. According to your father, he has some notion that you'll be coming back home with him and all this business will just blow over, and the two of you will get back together, snug as two bugs in a rug. Sometimes men can be so inordinately stupid," she added with a sigh. "I just hope your mind is made up, Elm dear, whatever it is you've decided to do."

"Don't worry, Aunt Frances, it is. I've realized in these past few weeks just how empty and purposeless my life was. And I plan to change that. Radically."

"Good. That's the best New Year's news you could have given me and I'm very pleased to hear it. Now, don't you let Harlan wangle you into thinking you're the guilty party here. Men—and Harlan in particular, with all that smart political talk—are all too good at that."

"I won't, I promise." She smiled into the phone.

"If he even tries, just you remember Jennifer's odious face. I saw her at the Chatham Club the other day. Not looking quite so confident anymore."

"Oh, well, that's good, I guess." Not that she cared anymore. "I still can't believe Harlan's making the trip over, though. He hates traveling to Europe."

"I know. I was very surprised, too. My advice is to have a meeting with him in some discreet but public place and make your position perfectly plain right from the start. If you give him any leeway at all, he'll slip into the cracks like a woodworm."

Elm chuckled. "You really don't like him, do you, Aunt

Frances," she said, her curiosity whetted. "How come you never said anything all these years?"

"It's really not my affair, darling, and after all, he was—is still—your husband. I didn't want to interfere or prejudice you in any way."

"No, I suppose not," she conceded. "But don't worry about that anymore. I assure you, my eyes are wide open."

"And long may they remain so. You know, it may actually be a good thing to get this whole thing straightened out away from home, honey, on neutral territory, so to speak, come up with some sort of civilized arrangement you can both live with until this damned election your father goes on and on about is over with."

"God, don't remind me of the election. Always the election. Does Daddy ever think of anything except Harlan's political future?" she asked bitterly.

"I wonder that myself at times," Frances replied grimly, "but I'm sure your happiness comes first."

"Are you? I wonder." Elm paused, stared into the flames. "You know, sometimes I think Daddy's main concern in life is getting Harlan to where he never managed to get himself."

"I won't say I think you're entirely wrong about that," Frances answered carefully, "but right now you need to concentrate on yourself. You've spent far too long worrying about George and Harlan and putting your own life on hold. And," she added mischievously, "I'll look forward to hearing the details of this trip of yours once you get home."

Elm didn't even pretend not to understand.

"Oh, Aunt Frances," she said, biting her lip, "I really don't know if you'll approve. I don't quite know if I do myself."

"That's beside the point. It's about time you let your hair down and had a little fun in life. Is he gorgeous?" she added in an undertone.

"Very gorgeous. Irish. But it's not serious. Just a fling, so don't worry."

"We'll see," Frances replied cryptically. "Well, good-bye, dear, and take care, won't you?"

"I will. Bye-bye, Aunt Frances, and thanks for the warning."

She hung up and straightened the towel on her head. However disagreeable the prospect, perhaps her aunt was right and it would be better to sit down face-to-face with Harlan and get this situation straightened out. After all, they were adults. Surely they could talk without things deteriorating into a quarrel?

Elm sighed, determined to face whatever she must.

Then her thoughts turned back to Johnny and Nicky and her heart sank. The last thing she needed right now was Harlan here. But it looked like she didn't have a choice. There was nothing for it except to get it over with, as soon as possible.

Afternoon turned into evening and Johnny still stood next to the bed, gazing down at Nicky. He'd woken briefly, complained that his tummy hurt, then gone back to sleep. As he gazed at his son, Johnny remembered the day Nicky was born, the delight on Marie Ange's lovely face when she'd shown him the baby, that wondrous, unique sensation of holding his child in his arms for the first time.

He recalled other times, too, the bad times, the awful day when he'd come home to the flat in Paris and looked at his motherless child for the first time. It was only then that he'd taken full consciousness of Marie Ange's death, truly realizing that she was never coming back. Shortly afterward, to the disapproval of his mother and brother, who'd said he was isolating himself, he'd moved to Graney Castle for good. He'd buried himself there, thrown all his energies into improving the stud farm, making it one of the most respected in the country.

When Nicky had been ready to go to school, he'd considered leaving, moving to either Dublin or London, though not New York as his mother wanted. But he'd thought better of it and Nicky had ended up attending the village school.

That had turned out well, for now Nicky wasn't isolated when he returned for vacations but rather had a number of friends in the vicinity. Nicky's presence had also helped dispel the invisible yet inevitable class barrier separating the castle from the village, for Nicky was a popular, hospitable child and had filled the centuries-old fortress with life. Children's voices had echoed through the great hall as they played at medieval warfare, careened up and down the stairs and onto the ramparts. All in all, it had been a good decision.

But when Nicky turned twelve, Grace had insisted that he get what she called "a decent education." Johnny had protested, assured her that Ireland had one of the best educational systems in the world and that he didn't see why he should send his son away. But in the end Grace had won, and Nicky was sent to Le Rosey, for it was true, Johnny conceded, that he needed some friends and a social life among his own class as well as in the village.

The first months had been lonely. Knowing the strong bond between them was going to change had not been easy, and the first couple of years of adolescence had proved particularly difficult. But since the episode before Christmas, he and Nicky had rediscovered some of the closeness they'd once shared, and the feeling that they were establishing a new phase of their relationship was heartwarming.

Now, staring down at the pale face on the pillow, he knew he could never, ever have forgiven himself if something had happened to Nicky.

"So I'll go straight back and join them," Elm told Gioconda as they enjoyed a quick, light snack of cheese tart and a glass of wine that Gio had insisted on.

"I'll come with you to the hospital," she offered.

"Thanks. Johnny's very upset he wasn't with Nicky when it happened. He should have been at home, not spending the night with me," she said guiltily.

"Don't be ridiculous. It's not as if anyone could've guessed Nicky would have appendicitis," Gio dismissed.

"I guess not. Still, Johnny wasn't there when his son

needed him. I'd feel guilty as sin, too, if it were my child. Especially as he hasn't got a mother.''

"No, but his uncle and grandmother were there, so don't let's make this into a soap opera, *cara*. The kid's sixteen, not six.''

"You're right, I guess... By the way, Gio, I forgot to tell you—Harlan's arriving here in Gstaad tomorrow. I couldn't believe it when Aunt Frances called me.''

"You're kidding.''

"Oh, God, I wish I were.'' Elm let out a sigh. "I'll just have to get it over with.''

"I suppose he wanted to surprise you. Thank God he didn't try to call here. I loathe that smarmy tone of his....'' She grimaced.

Elm's fork clattered to her plate as a thought occured. "Please don't invite him here, will you?''

"You have to be joking? Harlan, here? In my home? No way, *bella*,'' Gio responded with a scathing sniff. "And if he calls here asking for a hotel recommendation, I'll send him to the Bernerhof, the station hotel, which will do perfectly for the likes of him. Plus, it's very cozy and nice,'' she added smugly, sinking her teeth into some brie.

"Cozy and nice?'' Elm grinned, despite her annoyance. "I just imagine his face. Though I'll bet you anything that by the time he gets here he'll have pulled every string in D.C. to find him a room at the Palace, even if it's in the attic. Lord, but it really is a pain in the butt, him coming,'' she added, surprised that the only real sentiment his arrival caused was irritation, not guilt or self-recrimination. In fact, the realization that she'd moved on so far in such a short period of time left her upbeat.

Then she thought of Johnny, alone at the hospital. "Oh, God. What'll I tell Johnny? Gio, we finally, well...made love last night. This doesn't seem like the best moment to tell him my husband's popping in for a visit and—''

"Was it wonderful?'' Gio interrupted, eyes glinting.

"Yes. But shut up and please listen. What am I going to say to him about Harlan? He's got enough to cope with right now. Not that this is terribly important, is it? After all, he knows I'm getting divorced.''

''Frankly, I don't see that it's any of Johnny's business what you do, *cara*. I shouldn't think Harlan will be here long, do you?''

''Oh, no. As soon as he realizes that I'm not getting on the plane back home—and believe me, I plan to make that abundantly clear—he'll be off again in a sulk... I hope,'' she added with a grimace.

''Then I'd not bother mentioning it to Johnny at all. As you just pointed out, he'll have enough to deal with in the next couple of days without having to worry about you and your ex.''

Elm took a sip of wine and nodded. ''You're right. Unless an appropriate moment comes up, I'll deal with this alone and get it behind me. I don't want anything interfering with the wonderful time Johnny and I are having together.''

''That's the spirit,'' Gio encouraged. ''Maybe you should go back to the hospital by yourself and I'll go over there later on,'' she added. ''I have a couple of things I need to do in the village before the stores close.''

''Sure. That's fine.''

They finished their snack, hugged, and after calling home and leaving a message for her father on the answering machine, Elm drove the Jeep over to the hospital.

It was dark by the time she arrived and stepped into the reception area. The nurse, familiar with Elm by now, sent her straight on up to the room, where she knocked softly.

The door opened. Elm looked over at Johnny. He was still in his tux, a five o'clock shadow covering his chin, and she was shocked to see how strained his eyes looked. ''Oh, darling,'' she whispered, moving quickly to his side and instinctively pulling his head down to her shoulder, where he let it rest. ''Are you okay?''

''The truth is, I should've been home with him, Elm.''

''I know. I feel just as guilty as you do. But there's no use dwelling on it. You're here with him now, and that's all that matters.''

"Not that I didn't want to be there with you," he added quickly, raising his face and flashing her a quick, intimate smile.

"I know, I know, I understand," Elm laughed, determined to lighten the atmosphere.

He grinned for the first time all day, then dropped a kiss on her lips and drew her farther into the room. "I think Nicky's forgiven us already. He's acting very mature about the whole thing."

"Poor baby." Elm went to the bed as Johnny turned on the farthest lamp. Elm gazed at Nicky through the shadows. Her eyes misted with an unexpected rush of tears and her heart ached with an emotion she'd never before experienced. This must be akin to what it felt like to have a sick child of your own, she reflected, shocked at the ferocity of her emotions. She felt a sudden longing to hug Nicky, to straighten his sheets, protect him, make sure he was okay—that they were both okay, she realized, raising her eyes and meeting Johnny's across the bed. Then, with a deep breath she banished the thought, determined not to be silly and sentimental.

"The doctor says he'll be fine in a few days."

"Of course he will." She smoothed the sheet, touched Nicky's forehead gently. "He looks a perfect angel lying there so quiet, so young, so innocent."

"Not all that innocent. Don't forget Trisha and the suspension," Johnny said with a touch of humor.

She laughed softly, thought all at once of Harlan's imminent arrival and for a moment was tempted to tell him about it. Then the door opened and the nurse entered with a small metal tray, and the moment passed.

"*Guten Abend,*" she smiled. "Your son will be fine, but don't expect him to wake until the morning. He'll probably be a little grouchy. Will you and your wife be spending the night here?" she asked, turning to Johnny and Elm.

"We will," he said, taking Elm's hand in his and squeezing it before she could protest that she wasn't Nicky's mother.

"I understand." The older woman smiled back at Elm

sympathetically. "It's always such a worry when they go through these childhood ups and downs. But better now than later, *ja?*" She bid them good night and closed the door, and Elm let out an embarrassed laugh.

"Are you upset she thought you were his mother?" Johnny turned her toward him, slipped a finger under her chin and looked at her with a curious smile.

"Of course not," she dismissed. "I just didn't want there to be a misunderstanding."

"It doesn't matter. Too much trouble to begin explaining. Do you mind not having children, Elm?" he asked suddenly.

"I did. For a while, I fought the truth with every fiber of my being. Now it really doesn't matter anymore." She hated herself for the betraying tremor in her voice, but she couldn't help it.

"You could have adopted, I suppose."

"Harlan didn't like the idea."

"Why couldn't you have children?"

"Look," she said curtly, "they don't really know, okay? We tried all sorts of methods that were extremely disagreeable and difficult but they didn't work. I really don't see why it's important." She knew she sounded irritated, but this was a subject she didn't want to discuss.

"I'm sorry," he said, with a contrite shake of his head. "I don't know why I asked. None of my business and damned insensitive of me. I didn't mean to upset you." He touched her cheek fleetingly, then dropped a kiss on her brow.

"It's okay," she mumbled.

"You've been such a good sport about all this," he continued. "I'm sorry my mother was so rude this morning."

"She was just upset about Nicky."

"You're right—" he cupped her face and gazed into her eyes "—but thanks for being so supportive, anyway. I appreciate everything you've done."

"It's nothing. I'd do it for anyone."

"Would you?"

She flushed, moved away from him, back toward the sterile hospital bed, and made a big deal about adjusting Nicky's pillows as he moved fretfully in his sleep. She didn't want to think, to care, to have feelings of any kind. After all, she might never see these people again. And she had enough on her on plate to deal with, what with Harlan appearing on the scene out of the blue, reminding her only too pointedly of all the responsibilities she'd left behind in Savannah, the many things that soon—very soon—she would have to face.

He had no desire to go to Switzerland, Harlan realized crossly. But the talk with Tyler had left him uneasy. Brock seemed so intent on Elm returning to Savannah, as though all their projects depended on it. It made no sense, but then, the man was weird in more ways than one. Now it seemed somehow essential to get Elm back home. It was a damn nuisance but had to be done. So here he was, on the first of January, flying to a destination he had no desire to visit, to persuade his errant wife to return to him. Thank God his old friend Butch Smith had gotten him an upgrade to first class or he couldn't have borne it.

After a long session of string-pulling, he'd finally arranged a room at the Palace Hotel in Gstaad. He realized, annoyed, that he had probably been shoved into the worst accommodation in the hotel, but still. Also, it might not do any harm to have some pictures taken of him and Elm, the glamorous young couple on a lovey-dovey vacation in the snow. The thought pleased him and he stared into the clouds sipping Scotch and water, and jotted a note for Marcy, his secretary, whom he'd phone on arrival to make sure all the right papers and magazines knew exactly where to find him. Elm's disappearance, which he'd viewed as a liability, could still be put to good use.

There might even be a few celebrities he knew hanging around Gstaad, he reflected, perking up. Yet another detail for Marcy to ferret out tomorrow. You never knew who might be where, at just the right moment. The thought cheered him considerably.

He tilted his seat back, confident things would work out

exactly as he'd planned. His mind drifted to the PR stunt Charles Ensor, his campaign manager, had helped him arrange last week. Usually he and Elm were a fixture at the various New Year's parties around town, but her irritating absence had put a wrench in that plan. So instead, he'd refused all invitations, explaining that he'd be spending New Year's Eve in a midnight vigil at Christ Church praying for world peace. The crowd at the church hadn't been particularly large—that had been a disappointment—but by remaining on his knees long after the service was over, he'd made sure everyone there noticed him. He'd heard the approving whispers, the murmurs about how the congressman was such a good Christian, such a serious and sober young man.

Of course, the only way he'd gotten through the damn ordeal was by imagining feisty little Teresa on her knees before him, but then they'd never know that. He'd phoned a source at the paper this morning who'd told him they'd be running a piece in tomorrow's paper in praise of politicians who weren't afraid to wear their faith on their sleeves; the church's rector had provided several flattering quotes about the good example Harlan had set.

Even as he congratulated himself on another superb performance, Harlan realized it wouldn't be enough. Elm's support was still a key part of his re-election strategy—and that meant getting her home.

"Damn her," he whispered, his well-tended fingers longing to reach out and twist that long, swanlike neck of hers, wishing he could just order her on a plane and be done with it. Instead, he contented himself with imagining the day, not too far distant, he hoped, when she'd be expendable.

But not before the election, he remembered, taking another long sip and signaling the flight attendant for another drink. Certainly not before the election.

16

"Harlan, please try to understand," Elm said beseechingly, unfolding her hands and reaching for the glass of champagne he'd insisted they enjoy in the vast lounge of the Palace Hotel, seated at the far end by the window overlooking the Alps.

"I just don't understand why you can't forgive me. Heck, Elm, we've been married for twelve years, that's a lifetime. Surely you owe it to us to try again?" He reached over, touched her arm, smiled in that persuasive manner she knew only too well.

"Harlan, it's no use," she said, pulling away, the feel of his fingers on her arm leaving her strangely uneasy. "I'm not going back to Savannah right now and I'm still determined to go ahead with the divorce. This isn't about one affair you've had, it's about what our marriage really was: a sham. We've grown apart, we have virtually nothing to say to each other, and frankly nothing to share."

"I don't see it like that," he argued belligerently. "What about all the plans we used to dream about in the early days? Have they just flown out the window?" He sounded suddenly bitter as he snapped his fingers. "I don't suppose you've given a moment's thought to how this might affect my chances in the election?"

"Of course I have," she said in a softer tone, feeling

suddenly selfish. "Which is why we must proceed carefully. I realize we have to do this divorce in a civilized manner. I don't want to damage your career."

"Then at least come back and live with me until the election's over. God, Elm, you know how conservative most of my constituents are. One sniff of scandal and I can kiss my career goodbye."

She hesitated, then shook her head sadly. "I'm sorry, Harlan, but I can't come back and live with you just to save face."

"But why, Emmy?" Harlan leaned forward, dropped his hand on her knee, and his voice grew softer. "I'm sorry I messed up, sweetie, but all that IVF stuff was hard for me, too. I couldn't come near you, and when I did, you shied away." He smiled at her helplessly, beguilingly, with that boyish frankness that had worked so well in the past.

"I just can't. It's impossible." Elm shook her head, determined not to be drawn into his web, reminding herself that he was playing a game.

"There must be a reason," he insisted.

"No specific reason. But I want other things out of life now than just being your wife. In fact, I'm holding an exhibition in Florence in the autumn."

"Well, what's to prevent you going ahead with that?" he said reasonably.

"Harlan, stop it," she snapped defensively, "You know it's not like that. You hate my painting. It's time to move on now. I'll help you all I can with the election, but I won't come home."

"Is that a definitive answer?" He drew back, face and body language suddenly changed.

"Yes, it is."

"I see. Well, in that case, I guess there's really no point in my sticking around here trying to persuade you." He raised his hands in a gesture of defeat.

"I can assure you I won't change my mind."

"Okay!" He shrugged. "If that's the way you're determined to play it, then so be it. I just hope you don't regret this, Elm, and that you're not letting third parties who have no real notion of what our life is all about influence you,'' he said darkly, referring, she was sure, to Gioconda and Aunt Frances.

"This decision has been entirely my own," she said deliberately, "and I'm not likely to change my mind any time soon."

He looked at her for a long moment. "Then so be it." He signaled the waiter to pour them more champagne and smiled as though nothing had taken place.

Elm sighed, relieved, and accepted the champagne. She was grateful he'd conceded gracefully; he was taking it all much better than she'd expected. The least she could do now was try to end their meeting as agreeably as possible. For all she knew, she thought, swallowing, the next time she saw him might be in court.

"Jesus, that was a long night," Johnny exclaimed to Liam, stifling a yawn as they walked into the bar of the Palace Hotel for a quick bite to eat. Grace had taken over dealing with a fretful Nicky while Johnny went home to shower and change.

The two men sat down at the bar.

"Scotch?" Liam suggested. "You look as if you could use one."

"Good idea." Johnny swiveled the bar stool and looked around the room. Then he stiffened. Surely that couldn't be Elm over there by the window?

His eyes narrowed, and he fought the urge to rub them. She was sitting sideways on one of the leather sofas. A man was leaning over, talking to her, laying his hand on her knee in an intimate manner. Then he watched as the man lifted her fingers and raised them to his lips.

A rush of unprecedented anger gripped him. What the hell was she doing here chatting with this man, whoever he was?

His fingers tightened around the tumbler and he took a long sip of whiskey, eyes hard and narrow.

"Something wrong?" Liam asked, noting the change in his brother.

"Take a look. Over there." He jerked his head in the direction of the window.

Liam followed his brother's gaze and saw Elm. She was talking intensely to a youngish, handsome man.

"I'm leaving," Johnny exclaimed, pulling out his money clip and slamming a hundred franc bill on the bar.

"Hey, hold it," Liam exclaimed. "Why are you so upset?"

"I should have thought it was pretty obvious," he retorted witheringly.

"What? You're upset because Elm's talking to a man? That's ridiculous," Liam laughed. "Why don't you go over there and say hi?"

"Why don't you? I'm too damn tired. Besides, she doesn't look as though she needs company."

"Now, cool it," Liam said, gripping Johnny's arm. "You're tired, you're wound up and you've been worried as hell about Nicky. But that doesn't mean you can start reacting like a temperamental teenager."

"I'm not."

"Yes, you are. Don't you think you owe Elm the benefit of the doubt? Think of all Elm's done for you. Hell, she even went over to the hospital in her evening dress and took shit from Mother. How do you think she felt, parading in front of all of us, when it was obvious you guys had spent the night together?"

"Apparently not embarrassed enough to prevent her from seeing someone else the minute my back's turned. I'm going home for an hour's sleep, then I'm going back to the hospital," he replied stiffly.

"Oh, bro, you've got it bad." Liam shook his head. "Just remember that the days of branding a woman as your personal property are over." He reached for another sip, only to stop the glass in midair. "Hey, you know what?" he said, slipping on his glasses, "that guy she's with seems familiar."

"Great," Johnny threw sarcastically, wanting to deny Liam's words, scared that he could feel so possessive of another human being.

Liam's eyes narrowed behind the lenses. "Wait. I know who he is. It's her husband. He was in my office a while back," he exclaimed.

"Well, maybe you'd better go over there and reintroduce yourself. As far as I was aware, she was getting divorced from her husband. But from where I'm standing, they look as if they're getting on like a house on fire!" Johnny snapped. With that, he turned on his heel and marched out of the hotel before Liam could stop him.

When he got home, the message light was blinking. Elm's voice came onto the answering machine asking about Nicky, asking if she could return later to the hospital. He eyed the machine skeptically, but the message helped to quell some of the irrational anger he'd experienced. He was probably being ridiculous. Anyway, what did he care how many men Elm lunched with or talked to? It was none of his damn business, now that he came to think of it.

Still, if Elm thought she could fool with him, she was mistaken, and the sooner he told her so, the better. After prowling the room for several minutes, unable to rest, he grabbed his jacket and decided to make his way back to the hospital. She could ring him there on his mobile if she really wanted to get in touch. And if she wanted to come over, well, she knew the way.

He got in the Range Rover, dialed the hospital and got the latest news from his mother. Nicky was taking a nap and doing fine.

After driving aimlessly for several minutes, Johnny wondered if it might not be better to talk to Elm as soon as possible. He dialed Gio's number, asked Umberto when she was expected back and was told that she'd phoned five minutes ago and should be returning in a half hour. *Fine.* He would see her at Gio's instead of in public.

Again the irrational anger flared. If this was the way she

planned to behave behind his back, it was probably better
to pack the whole thing in and call it a day before he got in
any deeper. There was no room in his life for this kind of
shit. He should be grateful that he'd observed her little ren-
dezvous at the Palace Hotel. It was a much-needed wake-up
call, reinforcing all the reasons he hadn't wanted to get involved with her in the first place. Their lives were eons apart,
she was still married and—if today's exploits were anything
to judge by—the decision to divorce was a sham.

He drove around aimlessly, giving her time to make it
back home, then headed slowly up Gioconda's street while
he mentally worked out exactly what he planned to say. By
the time he came to a halt in front of the gracious chalet, he
felt more in control. This was the sensible thing to do, he
reflected, sitting a moment longer in the Range Rover. Some
small part of him still wondered if this was really a good
idea—words said in anger were always regretted. But inside
he knew he wouldn't rest until he'd spoken his mind.

If this was the kind of game she wanted to play, then she
was well matched, for he knew the rules better than anyone.
Smothering a sigh, he acknowledged that he'd been nurtur-
ing the secret hope that with Elm it would be different,
which proved how foolish it was to dream.

His right to dream had died long ago.

For an instant, he faltered. Then, determinedly refuting
any lingering doubts, Johnny got out, walked up the stone
steps and rang the doorbell.

When she got in, Elm decided to take a few minutes
curled on the sofa before returning to the hospital. Umberto
had said that Johnny had phoned a few minutes earlier. She
smiled, relieved and feeling lighter, glad the meeting with
Harlan had gone relatively smoothly. She only wished now
that she'd told Johnny about the visit, so that she could share
her relief and rid herself of any last doubts. But that
wouldn't be fair, she reflected, not with all he had to deal
with. And Harlan was leaving this evening, having apparently realized there was little sense in staying. Gioconda was

right. It was silly to make an enemy out of an ex-husband unnecessarily. Much better to find a civilized solution.

She heard the doorbell and looked up, overjoyed when seconds later Umberto showed Johnny in.

"Why, Johnny." She unfurled her legs from under her, laid down her book and rose to kiss him. When he stood rigid, she backed away, frowning. "Is something wrong? Nicky?" She held her breath.

"He's fine." Turning away, he took off his jacket and flung it on the chair. "How's your husband?"

Elm froze. *So that was it.* "He's fine," she replied cautiously. "He's leaving tonight."

"Thanks for telling me that he was in town," he remarked tartly, walking over to the window and staring out over the snow-covered landscape.

"Johnny, I didn't tell you because there hasn't been an opportunity, and you have enough to contend with right now without having my problems to worry about, too."

"Oh, sure. Naturally, he arrived unannounced."

"Don't be sarcastic." She came up behind his stiff back, stopped and swallowed. "I didn't know that he was coming until yesterday."

"Of course not."

"How could I tell you when we were so worried about Nicky? I didn't think it was appropriate, or even a priority, for that matter."

"Really?" He whirled round and faced her, eyes smoldering. "You spend the night in my arms, then walk out as cool as you please to a date with your ex? Oops, I forgot, you're still married to the man. Perhaps you never intended to leave him? I can assure you that from where I was standing, the two of you looked awfully cozy."

"What on earth are you talking about?"

"I happened to walk into the Palace with Liam at lunchtime today. Unless I'm much mistaken, you were on a sofa by the window of the lounge, smiling at someone who was kissing your hand. You didn't seem too upset about it."

She drew back, shocked at just how angry he was. "Har-

Ian came here to try to persuade me to return to Savannah—he's worried that my absence makes him look bad. I told him that wasn't an option. We had lunch and now he's leaving again.''

"Just like that?" he sneered.

"What exactly are you saying?"

"That what I saw was very different from what you're describing."

"Look, I'm sorry I didn't warn you. Maybe I should've said something, but we were so worried about Nicky I didn't think about it, and then when I did, it didn't seem like the right time."

"So you were just going to forget about it and not say anything?"

"I intended to tell you when you arrived now. In fact, I wanted to share it with you."

"Gosh, thanks a lot!"

"I wish you'd stop acting in this ridiculous manner," Elm exclaimed, flushed. "You'd think I'd committed some major crime. All I did was have lunch with my soon-to-be-ex-husband, iron out a few details that needed to be ironed out, and send him on his way."

"Do I look stupid?" Johnny asked conversationally, hands stuffed in the pockets of his corduroys.

"No, you look jealous," she retorted, matching his tone. "And with no reason to be."

"Jealous? Ha! Why on earth would I be jealous? After all, we're just having a holiday fling, aren't we?"

"Yes. I suppose we are," she replied quietly, looking him straight in the eyes.

He shrugged. "We both had quite a lot to drink the other night. I probably said a number of things I didn't mean."

Elm held his eyes for a second longer, then looked down, anger and pain battling the knowledge that he was truly upset. But she wasn't about to be treated as though she'd sinned. She knew all about being made to feel guilty and was not disposed to begin all over again.

"I'm sorry if I hurt you, Johnny. I was wrong and should

have told you this morning that I had to meet with Harlan. But I'm not your chattel and I don't owe you any explanations. I'm choosing to give them, which is totally different. If you can't handle that, then perhaps we shouldn't see one another.''

She looked out the window, biting her lip. Maybe it was for the best; maybe it was time to get back to reality.

''If that's what you really feel, then I agree wholeheartedly,'' he responded stiffly.

Eyes swimming, Elm turned away. ''Fine. I'm sorry it's ended like this.''

''So am I.''

''Thanks for all the—the lovely times we spent together.''

''Nothing to thank me for,'' he replied gruffly.

Her back was turned and forbidding as she stared out the window. For a moment he experienced a sudden urge to go over to her and simply soothe away the pain. Then he realized it just wasn't worth it. There was no future for them. And he was damned if he was going to let her get close enough to break his heart. Better to end it now, before things got too serious. ''Well, I'd better be going,'' he muttered. ''I'm due back at the hospital.''

''Of course.'' She turned slowly, arms crossed protectively across her chest. ''Give Nicky my love.''

''I will. Perhaps you could see him sometime.''

''I'll be leaving as soon as I can arrange it.''

''Won't you go by the hospital before you leave? He'd be awfully disappointed if you didn't.'' He fought the impulse to tell her she was wrong to leave, to please change her mind, determined to ignore how empty he suddenly felt.

''Of course I'll go to the hospital and say goodbye.'' She summoned up a polite social smile that didn't reach her eyes. ''I'll give you a ring beforehand to make sure it's convenient.''

''Right.'' He nodded, shifted from one foot to the other, part of him wanting to leave, the other compelled to stay. ''Well, I suppose I'd better be off.''

''Good luck with Blue Lavender,'' she murmured as they

stood across from each other, separated by the length of the room, so irretrievably distant when only hours earlier they had been so close.

"Thanks. Good luck with the painting." He gestured toward the canvas on the wall above the fireplace. "I'm sure the exhibition will be a great success." He cleared his throat, and wondered where all his righteous anger had disappeared to. For a last second he contemplated crossing the room and kissing her one last time, but common sense and her manner forbade it.

"Goodbye, Elm," he said at last.

"Goodbye, Johnny."

With a quick nod, he turned brusquely and stepped into the hall, closing the door carefully behind him, not seeing how close she was to bursting into tears.

Elm stood, drained and forlorn, staring at the closed door, dashing the tears angrily from her face. There was no point in crying, she chided herself. She'd be a lot better off making her plane reservation and getting the hell on home before she got herself into any more messes. Not that this was a mess, of course, it was just a passing flirtation and she'd been a silly sentimental idiot who was overtired and—

Leaving her book open on the table, Elm fled the room, rushed upstairs to her bedroom and, throwing herself on the bed, indulged in an uncharacteristic bout of tears.

She'd go home—not to Savannah—but home to the plantation, the one place she really belonged, the place from which she could begin again, start the new life that now stretched out so lonely before her.

Fifteen minutes later she rose, dried her tears with her old lace handkerchief and after a long sniff, called the airlines and booked her flight home.

Part III

17

The end of March and beginning of April was always a busy time at Graney, and Johnny found himself spending the better part of his time either out on the moors exercising his horses, or in his office in the east tower of the castle, dealing with paperwork.

For the past three months, since returning from Gstaad, he'd plunged into the usual barrage of activities, grateful for the familiar bustle. The Graney stud, which had been founded in 1860 by his great-grandfather, had for many years now been associated with some of Ireland's greatest Thoroughbreds, producing a long sequence of top-class stallions whose lineage could be traced back to Hyperion. The burden of maintaining Graney's legacy of excellence now fell on his shoulders, and it was a task he welcomed. Especially now, because the work kept his mind occupied, allowing him a measure of distance from the holiday interlude he refused to think about.

He kept an orderly existence, getting up early, throwing himself into the day's rhythm, stopping briefly for lunch. But today he had other plans.

Johnny looked at his watch. Nine o'clock. If he left now, he would be at Kevin O'Connor's stables by ten, just when the second group of horses was due to go to the training gallops. He hadn't been able to go to England to see Blue

Lavender win his first race as a three year old, but the horse
had come back to the stables two days ago and O'Connor
had assured him he'd taken the race well. Today Johnny was
keen to see his first proper workout.

Reaching the stables, he parked the Bentley in the usual
spot by the hedge and walked down the front row of stalls
on the way to the office, surprised to see Blue being rubbed
down in his box.

O'Connor came out, dressed as always in his ancient
tweeds, a well-worn cap covering his grizzled hair, his side-
burns needing a trim, and greeted him cheerfully.

"Good morning, my lord," he touched his cap. "As you
can see, he's in fine fettle."

"Good morning. I thought he would be going out with
the second lot at ten," Johnny remarked as the two men
shook hands.

"No, sir, I had him out first lot at eight-thirty, and he
worked very well, very well indeed. Yesterday he only had
a light canter, but today he worked well at three-quarter
speed and pleased me greatly," O'Connor remarked in his
rich Irish brogue.

"Good." Johnny eyed the horse thoughtfully, then turned
back to the trainer. "I suppose we must now think seriously
about the 2000 Guineas," he remarked, watching carefully
as O'Connor hesitated, shoving his hands in the capacious
pockets of his sagging tweed jacket, then clearing his throat.

"I've been thinking, sir. Blue won his last race by only
one length, but he was going very strongly at the end."

"Yes?"

"Well, I felt certain that after another hundred yards he
would have drawn clear from the field."

"I see." Johnny eyed Blue meditatively for a moment.

"He's a fine horse, sir—a real credit to the Graney stud.
His running and his breeding tell me that his best distance
would not be one mile, but at least a mile and a quarter."

"I see," Johnny noted, masking his excitement. "And
what conclusion do you draw from that?" he ventured.

"Well, sir, the 2000 Guineas is one mile and the opposition at this distance will be strong,'' O'Connor continued in his ponderous manner.

"I suppose the Maktoums will run Kabul."

"Exactly, sir, that's what I heard. And what I'm hearing here is that young Aidan O'Brien could run two good 'uns from his powerful stable."

"I see. So what do you propose?"

O'Connor took his pipe out of his pocket and tapped it thoughtfully on the gate. "Well, we have the option of running next in the Kentucky Derby over a mile and a quarter, and although the American-trained three-year-olds appear to be a good lot this year, frankly, I'd rather take our chances over the longer distance. Plus, of course, there's the potential prestige and greater stallion value in the future,'' he murmured.

"Hmm. Still, it's a much greater risk to take on the best American horses,'' Johnny pointed out, anxious not to appear too eager.

"Well, sir, you've taken risks before and, I must say, things haven't worked out too badly,'' O'Connor replied with a grin.

Johnny nodded. "You're right. Let me think this over."

"Of course. Coffee, sir?"

"Yes, please."

As the two men made their way into the office, Johnny's pulse beat a tad faster. The Kentucky Derby. This was what he'd worked for, what his father and grandfather and great-grandfather before him had strived to achieve. Now O'Connor was telling him it might be just within his grasp.

Sitting down in the old armchair to which the trainer directed him, Johnny thought hard. He trusted O'Connor's judgment implicitly. And anyone could see that Blue was a special horse. But the Derby. That was something of a plunge into the unknown, as far as he was concerned. Still, he realized, mind racing, this would be the chance to put everything they'd worked toward to the test. Blue had, in a very real sense, been bred for this challenge.

The horse was the end result of almost a century and a

half of selective breeding in a favorable environment, the splendid consequence of sticking to predetermined goals without faltering, of not allowing doubts or fears to sway him from the vision on which his great-grandfather had built the Graney stud. Maybe O'Connor was right and this would be Blue's season of triumph, he reflected, imagining Jim Hurley, his jockey, dressed in the pink-and-blue Graney colors and riding the horse to a triumphant finish. Then, with a half smile, Johnny tried to visualize himself in the winner's circle, accepting the congratulations of the roaring crowd.

He was shocked, and a little irritated, to realize the picture he'd painted in his mind included Elm by his side.

As he drove home, he acknowledged that he hadn't been entirely successful at eradicating all thoughts of Elm. In fact, he admitted it was impossible not to think of her—she kept popping into his head, the sun prompting a sudden memory of her smile, the wind somehow carrying an echo of her laugh. Often he managed quite well at pushing her to the back of his mind—it was, after all, a skill he'd perfected in the years following Marie Ange's death—but then something would waken the dormant memories he so carefully avoided, and she'd linger in his vision as if she were just inches away.

Today's lapse should be credited to his mother, he decided, annoyed. She'd phoned him last night and mentioned, oh so casually, that she'd seen a picture of Elm and her husband in *Town & Country.* Why on earth had she thought he'd care? He was far too busy to be thinking of Elm at all, what with Blue and now this news of the Kentucky Derby.

Would she be there? he wondered. It was, after all, one of the most important sporting events on the American social calendar, and she'd talked of her father's keen interest in horse racing. Then he reminded himself sternly that Elm's presence didn't matter to him one way or another.

After parking his car at the converted carriage house, he felt too restless to tackle the paperwork waiting for him in the east turret and decided to check in at the stables for a look at the foal birthed last week. A brisk breeze filled the late morning air was brisk as he walked down the gravel path where crocuses and daffodils bloomed and on toward the paddocks. He felt strangely distracted, and it took more effort than it should have to focus his thoughts as, eyes narrowed under his tweed cap, he peered through the drizzle at the young stock grazing in the limestone-enriched pastures that spread out like green velvet around the ancient keep. New York and London might be where the action was, he reflected with a half smile, but as far as he was concerned, Graney was the center of the universe, the place where the landscape, the people, the air and the horses spelled home.

Pulling the collar of his Barbour jacket higher about his neck to avoid the increasing rain, he trudged on down the path. Two of the stable hands on horseback trotted by, tipped their caps, then broke into a canter.

Johnny watched them disappear across the moor, two mystical figures shrouded by the fabled Irish mist that made it so easy to recall the legends of the land, the lore that anywhere else would seem ridiculous, but that here still remained interwoven with the reality of everyday life.

For a moment Johnny stopped, propped his shooting boot on the lower rung of the fence and leaned against it, pensive. This was his destiny, and instead of brooding after what he couldn't have—didn't really know if he wanted, anyway—he should be satisfied with the hard-won peace he'd found here. He couldn't afford to be distracted.

Removing his foot, he straightened and continued on his way, reminding himself that there was still a lot to do today. He glanced at his watch. He had three meetings to attend.

After checking in at the stables—the foal was doing wonderfully—he wandered back up the path toward the castle. But as he walked in the shadow of the ramparts, he came to a sudden stop, glancing toward the tiny cemetery by the chapel, which for centuries had constituted the final resting place for the Graney family members. He rarely visited, except to make sure the place was properly tended, that flowers were placed on the graves.

Slowly, as though compelled, he made his way there, opened the creaking iron gate and stepped into the graveyard, glancing at the grave stones, some of them so ancient they tipped crookedly. Walking automatically to the far end, where his father and Marie Ange were buried next to each other, Johnny stopped and stared down, remembering.

It had been a battle to have her buried here, he recalled, crossing himself before the simple marble slab that carried her name, but he'd insisted, despite her family's desire to take her back to their château in Sologne for burial. Now he wondered if he'd been right to deny them the comfort of their daughter's presence. He'd been so desperate to have her here on Graney soil that he'd been blind to the realization that they mourned her, too.

He crouched before the grave, straightened two drooping daffodils, and thought about the woman he'd loved so dearly and who'd died fourteen years ago. They'd had so little married time together. Only three and a half years. How, he wondered, would their relationship have grown had she not fallen victim to a horrible, sudden death at the hands of rebels in the Sahara? Would their marriage have continued being the fairy tale he had projected all these years—as though imagining anything else would be to blaspheme Marie Ange—or would her stubborn nature have worn the relationship thin in the end? His own question surprised him, and he realized it was the first time since her death that he was able to think of her in perspective.

He stood up abruptly and stared at the plot, and for the thousandth time relived the circumstances of her death, her stubborn determination to wander off with her camera to take pictures of the natives, how angry he'd been when he'd returned to the tent to find her gone. Then the Bedouin rushing into the camp several hours later, saying she'd wandered into the camp of a rebel group and had been taken hostage.

Johnny passed a hand over his eyes and hunched his shoulders as the rain came down harder. For as long as he lived, he would never forget those three terrible days: the negotiations, the certainty that she would be returned to him, and the utter horror when her body was discovered riddled with bullets not far from their camp.

But there was nothing he could do to change that now. She was gone and he would have to live with it, just as he had all these years. He was able now to recognize the mistakes that had been made—her brother's determination to dictate the terms, the French family's certainty that because of their experience in Africa they knew better how to deal with rebels than he did. Had he been right to concede? All these years, he'd chastised himself for allowing them to take charge, had lived in the decision's lingering shadow. But now—and for the first time it didn't seem like a sacrilege— he stood before Marie Ange's grave wondering if the outcome would have been any different had he intervened personally.

With a last look, he turned and moved back across the grass. He glanced at his father's stone and smiled sadly. He still missed him, always would. But as he walked back through the iron gate he felt lighter, as though a weight had been lifted.

On reaching the castle he shoved open the small green side door that led to the gun room and the pantry. Once inside, he hung up his coat with the other macs and shooting jackets hanging haphazardly on pegs, pulled off his comfy, worn boots, and set them among the eclectic assortment of wellies, shooting boots and brogues filling the old cloakroom. Then, slipping on a pair of well-worn loafers, he made his way up the back stairs and into the great hall where Maeve, the housekeeper, was vigorously polishing the intricately carved oak banisters of the grand staircase with two girls from the village.

"Hello Maeve, hard at it, huh?" He smiled and nodded to the girls before disappearing into the library where breakfast was laid at the small round table near the window.

He sat down, spread the large white napkin, then, removing the silver cover off the generously laden plate of bacon, eggs and sausage, enjoyed the smell of a true Irish breakfast. As he spread a thick slice of soda bread with rich, creamy butter brought up from the home farm and poured himself a cup of strong tea, he wondered again why the thought of the Kentucky Derby and his mother's coincidental mention of Elm had so disturbed him. Because she was back with her husband—so what? he decided irritably, tucking into the eggs, determined to obliterate her image. He was damned if he was going to let her intrude or diminish his appetite.

Elm was a thing of the past, a pleasant enough interlude while it lasted, but which was over and done with. There was no room for regret. Jesus, Mary and Joseph, as his countrymen were prone to saying, he should be thanking his luck and the good faeries. His son was well and thriving, his horses were in fine fettle and life was going along very nicely, thank you very much. He should be happy, instead of hankering—well, not hankering exactly, he never hankered after anything except a win on the race track—instead of *permitting* juvenile thoughts to tamper with his well-being. Elm, thank goodness, was safely back in Savannah, which she probably never should have left.

What really grated on his nerves, he realized, reaching for the marmalade, was the fact that she'd used him. He could see that quite clearly now. He'd been nothing more to her than an experiment, a chance to see what it would be like to be with another man. Well, he reflected, mouth curving into an ironical smile, she'd discovered just how good it could be, that was for sure. He knew when a woman was satisfied, when he'd taken her places she'd never been before.

He took a long sip of tea, the thought affording him some small satisfaction, then ploughed through the rest of the eggs and sausage. Serves her right if she found it hard to stay with her handsome congressman hubby. Maybe she'd learned a thing or two on those few occasions they'd become more intimate.

Of course, if he were inclined to be honest with himself, he'd admit he had, too.

Johnny stirred his tea thoughtfully, stared out the window and wished that today he could banish her image as efficiently as he seemed to have done for the last couple of months. But something in the way his mother had spoken of her had conjured up such vivid images, that, before he could prevent it, all those singular feelings he'd experienced with Elm were tumbling through his mind, jostling for priority. The same feelings, he admitted savagely, that he'd believed safely dead and buried more than a decade ago.

He scraped his chair back abruptly and rose. Enough daydreaming. He had work to do, horses to breed, meetings to organize, any number of important issues that needed dealing with.

On that unsatisfactory note Johnny left the library and made his way past the diligently polishing girls in their jeans and T-shirts and on up the narrow spiral stairway that led to his office in the turret. He was determined to get through the mountain of paperwork sitting on his desk. And nothing—least of all his mother's unwelcome phone call—would stop him.

Elm steadied herself, balancing on her heels, then rose from the flower bed, trowel in hand and leaned against the live oak. She blinked as, head spinning, the familiar nausea rose inside. It couldn't be happening again, she argued, surely not. Yet for several days she'd found it hard to work in the garden, almost impossible to paint, and at times felt as if she was living in a fog. And then this morning as she got up and looked out of her window toward the Little Ogeechee River, she remembered that she'd never received those test results from Dr. Ashby, the specialist in Atlanta.

Perhaps, she reasoned, drawing herself up, determined not to give way to weakness, it was time she found out what the tests had revealed. Surely by now they'd been delivered by post to the house in Savannah, as she'd requested when she left for Gstaad. But she'd picked up all her mail and there had been nothing. Most likely that meant there wasn't anything special to report. Still, maybe she should give the doctor a call and check in, anyway.

"I'm going inside for a while," she called to Julie, one

of her favorite women on the gardening project, who was happily planting bulbs a few paces away.

"Fine. I'll stay here—I'm determined to finish this bed," Julie answered, looking up and wiping the sweat from her forehead.

As she carefully made her way up the stone steps, Elm experienced a moment's satisfaction. Julie was one of the people who had most benefited from the project. When she'd first arrived at Oleander, she'd been frightened, battered and bedraggled, an abused waif with little hope. Now, several weeks later, she was clearly thriving; her skin shone, toned and brown from being outdoors, and a new glimmer lit her eyes, as though she'd rediscovered the will to live. And Elm liked to think the garden had helped her find her way.

She pushed the screen door open and stepped inside the porch, short of breath. What on earth was wrong with her? She hadn't felt a thing all the time she was away in Gstaad, or in those first difficult days after her return to the plantation, when, despite her delight at being back in the home she loved so dearly, she'd felt bereft and alone, struggling to understand Johnny's abrupt rejection. Then, just when she'd found her feet again and put the events of Gstaad behind her, she'd begun to experience the same symptoms she'd had in the fall, leaving her languid, weak and exhausted.

She collapsed into the rocker with a sigh of relief, longing for a large glass of iced tea to assuage her thirst. "Isah," she called, hoping the maid could hear her from this distance.

"Yes, Miz Elm." The small, gray-haired black woman came smartly onto the porch, arms akimbo, and studied Elm with a frown. "What are you doin', sittin' like that in those ol' clothes in your grandma's rocker? If she was alive today she wouldn' approve, no, ma'am," she muttered reprovingly. "Somethin' ain't right with you, Miz Elm. You ain't been doin' good ever since you started diggin' up that there garden with those women," she added with a sniff.

Isah had no sympathy or understanding for the project

Elm had so fiercely undertaken. She could not understand why the women had to be housed and fed here on the plantation when, in her view, they could quite easily take care of themselves. But it was typical of her girl to act this way, always helping others, always ready to take on some new task. "What you need," she recommended sagely, "is a good rest. This is what all that runnin' around in foreign parts—which you ain't got no business doin'—'ll do for you. I know you've got a lot on your plate right now, Miz Elm, what with Mr. Harlan playin' his games and so on and so forth, but that don't mean you can't mind your health."

"Isah, could I just have a glass of iced tea, please? I'm so very thirsty," Elm pleaded, eyes shut, knowing the scolding would continue for a good twenty minutes if she didn't bring it to a close. Isah had helped out in the nursery when Elm was born, and tended to forget her charge wasn't a child anymore.

"Of course, I'll get some tea, honey, right away. Now, you stay sittin' right there. Don't you move, y'understand?" She wagged a withered finger and Elm smiled weakly, reaching for the phone book in the hopes that she'd had the sense to jot down Dr. Ashby's number. But of course it wasn't there. With a sigh she rang 411.

Several minutes later, she dialed the doctor's number and glanced around the enclosed porch, at the array of half-finished canvases lining the walls, at her easel and paints that she'd abandoned for the past few days. There was so much to do to prepare for the exhibition in Florence, but right now the mere thought of picking up her paintbrush was overwhelming.

Finally she got through. "Doctor Ashby? Hi, this is Elm Hathaway. I'm sorry to bother you, but I never received the results of my tests."

There was a pause on the other end of the line, and Elm wondered for a moment if she'd lost the connection.

"Well," Ashby said finally, "actually there's a reason for that."

"Oh?"

"Yes. I had some results that didn't make much sense. I'm really sorry, but frankly, I need to make sure there wasn't a lab error. I'd like you to come to my clinic here in Atlanta so that we can make sure these tests are done right."

Elm smothered her annoyance. "Okay. But couldn't we get Doc Philips to take some more samples and simply ship them to you? It's kind of hard to fit a trip into my schedule right now."

"I understand. Unfortunately, I'd really prefer to have my own laboratory process the results. The samples taken by your Dr. Philips were sent to an outside lab and may have been corrupted. I don't want to take that risk again."

"I see."

"How are you feeling, by the way?"

"Well, I was perfectly fine up until a couple of days ago. Then I started experiencing the same symptoms again."

"I see. In that case, I think I should definitely see you sometime soon." The doctor sounded grave and she frowned.

"Is anything wrong, Doctor?"

"No, no. But I'd prefer to see you in person, not talk over the telephone. Could you come in, say, sometime next week?"

"Well, I guess."

"Actually, Mrs. MacBride, it is important. I need to check your new results, compare them with the first lot, and make sure we get this right."

"But is there anything serious?" A shudder ran down her spine and she swallowed. Was there something the man didn't want to tell her?

"I just don't have enough information to make that determination at this point, so we'll consider this visit a routine checkup. But since you're feeling unwell, it certainly would make sense to have you come in as soon as possible, don't you agree?"

"Of course," she said, smiling her thanks as Isah laid the glass of chilled iced tea next to her on the little wicker table.

The doctor put her on hold a minute, then came back on

the line. "My scheduler informs me we've got an opening at three o'clock next Thursday. Will that work for you?"

"That would be fine," she answered, jotting down the date. "Thank you, Doctor. I'll see you then."

Elm hung up and took a long draft of tea. "Ah! That tastes so good."

"What doctor you callin'?" Isah stood firmly next to the chair, rubbing her hands on the white apron of her uniform. "If you're sick, why don't you visit Doc Philips?"

"I already did," Elm responded. She didn't feel up to arguing with Isah right now. "That was the specialist in Atlanta that Doc referred me to. Remember when I wasn't feeling well, just before I left for Switzerland?"

"I sure do." Isah frowned, looking at her with narrowed eyes. "You better go get yourself some rest, Miz Elm. You go lie over there on the couch."

"I think I will. Just for a little. Did Meredith call?"

"Not today, no, ma'am."

"God, I just wish this whole divorce and the election was over and done with, Isah. I get a stomachache just thinking about it all. I'm sure what I'm feeling is caused purely by nerves. I hate having to play these games, pretending to the electorate that everything's all right, appearing at events like the garden fete the other day with Harlan. It's so hypocritical. And it beats me why I ever said I'd accompany him to the Derby. I must have been drinking that day!"

"That may be so, but if the bossman thinks it's the right thing to do, then it's the right thing to do, Miz Elm, and no mistake about it. He ain't been a senator all this time for nothin'. Now, you go lie down and rest on the couch an' I'll bring you some more tea in a little."

Elm gave in and moved over to the couch, where she stretched her legs gratefully. She still felt dizzy and weak. Perhaps she'd leave the garden alone for a while and try to get some of her paintings finished before she went to Kentucky. She grimaced. If she was feeling anything like this, she wouldn't get to the end of the street, let alone Louisville. Which might not be a bad thing.

The race reminded her of Johnny—not that, of late, it took much to remind her. She wondered if Blue Lavender would be running. He hadn't mentioned the American races. She sipped and pondered. Perhaps he only did the European circuit. Then a sudden longing gripped her and she closed her eyes, and tried unsuccessfully to shut out the vision of him, the feel of him, the strong, gentle way in which he'd…

Leaning her head back on the old, flowered cotton cushions, she let out a sigh. She must forget those moments, that incredible night, for whenever she recalled the time spent in his arms up in the wilderness, a stab of such utter loneliness gripped her that she was left dizzier and sicker than she already was.

Elm huffed. Since returning from Gstaad she'd tried desperately not to think of him, not to wonder what he was up to at precisely that moment, not to check her watch and calculate what time it was in County Kildare. Still… She glanced surreptitiously at her wrist. It must be, what, 4:00 p.m. in Ireland? Maybe he was with his horses or having tea in the castle, or maybe he had a girlfriend and was flirting with her, or perhaps—

"Aargh!" She groaned in frustration and, turning impatiently on the cushions, indulged in one last vision of him seated before a huge open fire, legs resting on a well-worn ottoman, a couple of snoozing dogs at his feet as he sipped a whiskey and read the *Irish Times*. It was silly to think of him, but there were times when she just couldn't help herself. Their departure had been so abrupt, so horribly unexpected, so terribly cold and impersonal as they'd stood at opposite ends of the room, oceans apart, when only hours earlier they'd been locked in each other's arms.

She let her arm drop to the floor and sighed once more. Perhaps she was just too worn down by Harlan's constant wheedling that she return to the house in Savannah and her father's insistence that she accompany him to public events until the election was safely past. Thank God Meredith had filed the divorce papers, despite Harlan's protests, and of course Aunt Frances had backed her up. Oh, she knew people looked at her strangely, criticizing her, and that the whole city was conjecturing. But she didn't care. Nothing would compel her to return to the town house to live under the same roof as Harlan. She would, she'd agreed, appear with him in public when necessary, but that was all, and once the election was over the divorce would be finalized.

Needless to say, Harlan wouldn't accept the situation. He had argued with her till he was blue in the face. He'd whined, threatened and blustered. But it was to no avail. Having made the decision, she was determined to stick by it.

Elm drank the rest of the tea and gazed toward the river. She could hear the birds twittering in the live oak by the door; wreathed with Spanish moss, it was the same tree the Yankee soldiers had camped under. The moss needed trimming or it would soon be too close to the house, she reflected vaguely, her thoughts returning to Johnny. How could she simply banish him from her mind as though nothing had taken place between them? Or forget those moments spent in his arms? Of course it had been only an interlude, she knew that. This was ground she'd covered over and over. Still, not one phone call, not a postcard to say hi, not even an e-mail.

Had he banished her so categorically from his mind that he didn't remember who she was?

Despite her resolve, Elm couldn't smother the intense stab of pain caused by his complete silence. Perhaps, she concluded bitterly, this was the manner in which he conducted all his affairs. And it served her right for getting involved with him in the first place.

Taking a last long sip, Elm finished the tea. Then, climbing to her feet with effort, she decided that if she was going to travel to Atlanta next week she needed to get organized. For a moment she wondered if she should tell Aunt Frances or Meredith about the visit to Dr. Ashby, then decided against it. There was little use worrying either of them when probably the doctor would give her a tonic and she'd be feeling much better in a few days time.

* * *

God, the bitch was driving him nuts.

At first, when Elm had followed him back from Gstaad so quickly, Harlan had been sure, absolutely certain for forty-eight glorious hours, that he'd won, that she was coming home properly chastened, and that now all would fall back into place.

What a mistake that had been.

Not only had she not returned to the house, but she'd set herself up at the plantation, making it clear that she had no intention of returning to him now or ever, and putting him in a fucking impossible situation.

People in the know were starting to talk. Harlan swiveled in the large leather chair, remembering the call from Tyler Brock. Brock had seemed mighty upset that Elm wasn't living under the same roof as her husband. What he couldn't figure out was why Brock even cared. Of course it was important to project a family image, and Elm was critical on that front, but he still had the senator's unwavering support and his own growing popularity, didn't he? None of Brock's little ventures would be imperiled if Elm was out of the picture.

Maybe Brock had the hots for Elm. He didn't quite like the notion, Harlan realized—he might not want her anymore, but that didn't mean anyone else could have her. In any event, he'd made a hundred excuses and explained that this was how they lived. Still, he couldn't keep fielding questions. He had so much to do and couldn't waste precious time worrying about Elm's whereabouts and activities.

At least Brock was lending him his Gulfstream V for the campaign, which would make his and Ensor's life a hell of a lot easier. Still, the last time he'd asked—well, not asked, exactly, but hinted—that he needed more funds, they hadn't been forthcoming. Obviously, Brock had been signaling his displeasure. But it wasn't as if things weren't getting done, he reflected indignantly. He'd even arranged a wetlands waiver for one of Brock's real estate subsidiaries so that it could use landfill to develop some marshland property—and that wasn't exactly easy these days, what with all the regulatory interference from the Army Corps of Engineers. He shook his head, reminding himself that at least there'd be another cut for him in that deal.

Harlan smiled, despite his preoccupations, and dreamed for a few minutes of the dollars being deposited in the Cayman account Tyler Brock had opened for him via his Miami lawyers. It all seemed so simple. He wondered why more folks didn't do it. And this was his money—not George Hathaway's, not Elm's. It signaled freedom and a bright future—as long as he could keep his silent partner happy enough to keep the money flowing. Which meant, he realized, circling back to the source of his present problem, that he had to get Elm under control.

But how?

The telephone rang—not the blue one but the chrome one; his private line. Very few people were in possession of that number and he picked up quickly.

"MacBride speaking."

"Harlan, hi, this is Abe Ashby."

"Why, hello." Harlan sat up straighter and paid attention. He and Ashby had worked out a plan for Elm's upcoming visit to Atlanta. Ashby would insist that Elm admit herself to the clinic for a few days, which would give Harlan a chance not only to keep her controlled and in one place, but also might help goose his approval ratings. He was rather looking forward to playing the distressed husband, worried sick about his wife, knowing the press would eat it up.

"Yes, well, I'm calling because I had your wife on the line earlier today."

"So everything's settled? She's coming this week?"

"Well, no. I'm afraid she phoned to tell me she's not coming in for the testing. Says she feels much better and plans to leave it until after she returns from Kentucky."

"Shit." Harlan paused a moment, regrouped, realized her presence at the Derby could only help him. "Well, I'll be with her in Louisville. I'll simply insist she stop in Atlanta on the flight back. What excuse did you give her about the tests?"

"That the lab had messed up," the voice down the line responded dryly. "But I'm sure any new tests will just show the same thing. By the way, did you ever have those soil tests run?"

"Of course," Harlan snapped. "The place is clean."

"Oh. All right. I'd been hazarding a guess that she's been reexposed to the same triggers as before."

"Look, Ashby—" Harlan was thinking fast "—I already told you there's no fucking connection, okay? Can we get that clear?"

"Crystal."

"Good. Then let's keep it that way, shall we?"

"Sure. There may have been an error. Perhaps it wasn't what I thought it was. I'd like to verify, in any case."

"Yeah, well, you tell her that and let me know. No results to her before I see them, understood?"

"Harlan, I don't like this. This is all highly unethical—"

"Yeah, well so is snorting coke in between cases, Doctor. If you want to hold on to your license, you'll do as I say, got it?"

A silence followed. "All right." The reluctance could be felt on the line, but he really didn't care, Harlan reflected as he hung up. An opportunity had come his way. How he would use it, he wasn't sure yet, but use it he would and to his extreme advantage.

He rose, rotated his neck, then moved over to the door, which he locked silently. Then swiftly he took the tiny key that he always carried in his pants pocket and slipped it into the lock of the inlaid cabinet. He would need every ounce of focus, he realized, and coke helped him focus like nothing else could. Lately he'd been sniffing two or three times a day, just to make sure he didn't lose his edge. As he opened the drawer he was filled with that sense of relief that came each time he got close to it. He sighed as he reached for the tiny white package.

A few minutes later, the door unlocked once more, he called Marcy and went to work with a vengeance. He had to be in D.C. for the budget vote. He'd also been invited to speak at the National Press Club. That, he reflected proudly, would raise his political profile to an entirely new level. The prestigious luncheons were always well attended by national and international journalists, and the fact that he'd be standing at the same podium from which both Carter and Reagan had announced their candidacies was a gratifying indication of his own destiny. He'd have to make sure Ensor wrote a kick-ass speech.

After running through a dozen phone messages and signing off on a mountain of correspondence, Harlan headed for a lunch date at the Chatham Club, feeling he'd had a wonderfully productive morning. Unfortunately, his chipper mood was dampened when he walked into the club to see Elm, lunching with that old bitch Frances Hathaway. It took all his sangfroid to stay calm and greet them. He dropped a kiss on Elm's cheek, which she could hardly refuse, even sat down for a couple of minutes, laying his hand on hers briefly and asking how she was feeling, before he moved to the table the bell captain always saved for him.

As he greeted Judge Wetherspoon and Remer Gibson, two of the city's most respected citizens, he was glad he'd made the effort to show folks things with Elm were just fine. Now the word would go out to their notoriously gossipy wives that any rumors of marital problems in the MacBride household were completely false.

Thank God the Derby was just around the corner. He always made a point of going to the famous May race in Kentucky—there were always deep pockets there to be charmed—and Elm had promised to go with him this year. He had to say this for her, she never welshed on her word. Maybe in Kentucky, Elm would discover just what she'd been missing, he thought with a grin.

By the time he dug into his usual lunch of fried shrimp and grits, Harlan's mood had cheered considerably. He moaned with pleasure as he bit through the crispy, well-seasoned crust to the tender shrimp inside.

Those idiots in the kitchen at least knew how to cook, he reflected, passing his praise on to the maître d'. And vote.

18

At the center of Kentucky's bourbon and whiskey country, the Seelbach Hilton stood as a landmark to a golden era. The grand old structure had been Louisville's premier luxury hotel since its opening in 1905, inspiring F. Scott Fitzgerald and, in the days of Prohibition, attracting notorious figures like Lucky Luciano and Dutch Schultz. The king of bootleggers, George Remus, became Fitzgerald's model for the character of Jay Gatsby.

Over the years, its refined Southern hospitality had attracted many famous faces, including eight U.S presidents and, in his heyday, Al Capone. Now, as it did every year, the hotel buzzed with the contemporary rich and famous, rubbing shoulders amid turn-of-the-century artwork and antiques, come to witness the most legendary race of the year, the Kentucky Derby.

But as she walked through the lobby next to Harlan, Elm had no eyes for the past glories of the hotel as she smothered her increasing irritation. How hadn't she noticed before that Harlan never missed a chance to engage complete strangers in conversation, so long as he thought they might prove useful to him? Leaving him talking earnestly in the middle of the marble-floored lobby, she made her way to the reception desk and smiled at the attractive black receptionist. "We have a reservation under MacBride. A two-bedroom suite?"

"Just a moment, Mrs. MacBride, I'll pull that right up for you." The young woman glanced at the computer screen, then frowned. "I show a one-bedroom suite, Mrs. MacBride, with a request for a king-size bed and—"

"Excuse me?" Elm laid her handbag and white gabardine jacket on the desk and turned to Harlan, now approaching, still in deep conversation with two younger men. Incensed, she turned back to the receptionist. "There must be a mistake. Perhaps you could move us to a two-bedroom suite?"

"I'm sorry, ma'am. I'm afraid there aren't any other suites available. We're sold out for the Derby, ma'am." The woman smiled apologetically.

Elm flexed her fingers, finding it increasingly difficult to mask her anger. She should have been on her guard and checked the damn reservations herself. But the past few days, once she'd begun feeling better, had been solely dedicated to catching up on her paintings for the upcoming exhibition.

Harlan reached the desk. "Everything okay, honey?"

"Actually, no, it's not okay. There seems to be a mistake with the reservation."

"Oh?" He raised a brow and turned to the woman behind the desk. "What's wrong, Betsy?" he asked, glimpsing her name badge and giving her his best grin.

"Well, it seems Mrs. MacBride wanted a two-bedroom suite, but I'm afraid—" She looked at them, embarrassed. "I'm afraid there's no more availability."

"Oh. That's too bad. I'm sure that we reserved a two-bedroom." Harlan frowned, turning to Elm with a dismayed, apologetic look that made her want to slap him. "I'm so sorry, honey. What'll we do?"

"Right now we'd better go up," she said between gritted teeth. "I don't think you want to hear what I have to say here in the lobby."

Harlan smiled easily at Betsy as Elm stalked toward the elevators, barely containing her fury. She would leave immediately, find a motel or whatever, but she would not, she vowed, spend a night in a king-size bed with Harlan. He'd had it all figured out, she reflected, jabbing the elevator button, feeling like a fool.

"Honey—"

"Do me a favor and don't call me that. And by the way, don't bother having my bags delivered, since I'll be leaving."

"Now, Elm, calm down, please," he pleaded, glancing quickly about, hand on her arm. "Let's be reasonable about this."

"I see nothing to be reasonable about. We cut a deal. I kept my side of the bargain. You didn't. Now I'm through."

The elevator opened before he could answer and they stepped inside. "Elm, this is ridiculous," Harlan exclaimed, brushing off her protests with a laugh. "It's only two nights, for Christ's sake. Surely you could at least do that for me?"

"Actually, I can't. I think you planned this whole thing. There was never a two-room suite reserved, was there?" she queried, eyes bright.

"You really hate me, don't you?" he countered sadly.

"No, Harlan, I despise you."

He flushed and his lip twitched. "I don't see why the hell you need to be so darned aggressive about something so trivial. I'll sleep on the couch if it makes you happy."

"If you thought for one moment I would agree to this underhanded arrangement, you were dreaming," she continued.

"I don't know what you mean," he blustered as the elevator reached their floor and Elm marched out.

"Harlan, do me a favor and cut the crap," she exploded, stopping in the middle of the wide, empty, ornate corridor.

Harlan threw her a venomous glance. Bitch, he thought inwardly, fucking bitch. When the hell had she turned into such a shrew? And why couldn't she just do as she was told? With a supreme effort, he dominated the desire to slap her face hard, get her inside the suite and throw her on the bed for a little lesson on who was boss here. He smiled briefly at the bellboy, who'd come up in the adjoining elevator with their bags and slipped him a tip as they entered the living room of the well-appointed suite.

"Would you like me to show you how to use the—"

"No, thanks," they answered in unison.

The door shut and Elm threw her jacket down on the sofa. "Harlan, why did you bother to do this? You know very well I have no intention of sleeping with you ever again. Why can't you just accept that and the divorce and let us get on with our lives?"

"Look, Elm, there's been an error, okay? Believe it or not, I'm not to blame. So why don't we try and make the best of it?" he smiled, a conciliatory, sheepish smile. "Come on, Emmy, it's only two nights, for Pete's sakes. Surely you can manage?" He raised a brow, lips curved. "I swear I'll sleep on the couch and not bother you."

Elm turned and stared out the window. Was she making too big a deal out of it? If he slept on the sofa and she locked the door of the bedroom, what was there to fear?

"I'll sleep here," he insisted, dropping onto the wide couch and testing the cushions. "Seems comfortable enough to me."

"I haven't made up my mind yet," she answered grudgingly, feeling slightly foolish. "What time is the Barnstable Brown party tonight, anyway?"

"About 8:00 p.m. Look, I'll give you all the space you need to get ready. I promise I won't bother you one little bit. But please, Elm, this is important," he said, leaning forward, hands clasped on the knees of his light gray suit, his tone cajoling. "A lot of my supporters are here. So are a number of people whose endorsement would make all the difference in my re-election campaign. I need you to help me look good. You do want me to win, don't you?"

"Yes, of course," she conceded, turning back into the room and rummaging in her handbag for her cell phone. "I said I'd appear with you in public at certain events and I'll keep my word," she added reluctantly. "But you cross the threshold of that room tonight and this is the last time I help you out, Harlan MacBride. Is that clear?"

"Crystal, honey. Now, shall I call up for some champagne?"

* * *

Johnny moved about the beautifully decorated room, cocktail in hand, exchanging greetings, colliding with movie stars, socialites, sports celebrities and hangers-on, and watched amused as a dignified, portly black waiter served mint juleps from a silver samovar. Then he spied a majestic figure clad in crimson silk and diamonds at the far end of the room and, realizing it was his mother, made his way toward her.

"Hello, Mother, you look magnificent tonight." He dropped a kiss on her powdered cheek.

"Well, thank you, darling, you don't look too bad yourself, handsome." Grace smiled affectionately and patted his arm. "You won't believe who I just saw, Tom Crui—oh, my God, is that who I think it is?" She peered across the room and tapped his arm. "Look."

Johnny followed his mother's gaze across the shimmering crowd and suddenly his pulse raced. Could it really be Elm? Of course it was. And on second glance, he recognized the attractive fellow with her, the same one she'd been sitting next to on the sofa in Gstaad. He stiffened. It was unlikely he'd forget that smarmy grin any time soon.

"Darling, did you see? Surely that's Elm over there."

"Yes, Mother, it is. Now, can we step into the other room, please?"

"But, darling, it would be very rude not to say hello. Oh, and look, that's Senator Hathaway. I simply must say hi."

"Mother, please—"

But she was already gliding across the room in full sail. "Senator!"

Oh, God, he didn't need this. What should he do? Talk to her? Avoid her? He watched his mother exchange greetings with a tall, elegant, white-haired gentleman, then saw Elm approach them, saw her smile and greet his mother. Ignoring his racing pulse, he studied her, registering how perfectly lovely she looked in pale blue silk cut low, a delicate diamond choker round her neck and diamond studs in her ears. As beautiful and elegant and understated as he re-membered. He swallowed, still unsure how to act. The hus-band seemed to have disappeared. Should he say a casual good evening to her, or nip outside and spare them both embarrassment?

He was just deciding on the latter option when Elm looked up. Their eyes met, locked, and time stood still. Even if he'd wanted to, he couldn't have moved away as memories swamped him. Everything came hurtling back: the taste of her, her scent, the way she'd writhed, wild and unfettered, in his arms, her joyous cry when at last he'd released her.

Then all at once the space between them narrowed as he moved toward her through the crowd, until at last they stood face-to-face, only inches apart, and Johnny experienced an indescribable longing to take her in his arms, to crush his mouth on hers and feel her heart beating close to his.

Instead he heard himself saying, quite naturally, "Good evening."

"Hi. I didn't realize you'd be here." Elm smiled, embar-rassed, wondering if he could hear her heart thumping in her chest so hard it hurt.

"It is one of the season's most important races," he mur-mured, smiling.

"Yes, of course, so stupid of me. Is…is Blue Lavender running tomorrow?" She gripped her bejeweled evening bag tightly.

"Yes. His first real test this season. I have great hopes for him."

"Really? That's wonderful. I hope he does well." She flushed and looked away, biting her lip, tried to breathe and not let him see how much his presence had affected her.

"How long are you stay—"

"Elm, honey, sorry to interrupt, but there are some people I'd really like you to meet." Harlan sidled up on her left and slipped a possessive arm around her waist. "Hi, I'm Harlan MacBride, Elm's husband." He reached a hand to-ward Johnny.

"How do you do." Johnny grudgingly shook the other man's hand. Then he caught sight of Elm's discomfort—actually, she looked rather angry—and with a nod turned on his heel and walked away.

Elm pulled herself away from Harlan's grip. "How dare you interrupt my conversation?" she hissed. "Where are these people, anyway?"

"Oh, right over here. Who was he? I don't like you talking intimately to other men when you're with me," he added, slipping his arm around her waist again in proprietary fashion.

"Look, I'm here, aren't I? Isn't that enough? Surely I'm allowed to talk to whomever I want."

"As long as you keep up the show, baby." There was something strangely unnerving in the manner in which he spoke. It sent a shudder through her. Maybe she was imagining things, but that look of his just now... She turned away, needing some air, only to catch a glimpse of Johnny's back disappearing into the next room. Her fury resurfaced, driving away the fear. "Let go of me," she muttered as Harlan paraded her among the glittering bejeweled guests, "or I'll walk out on you right here."

Harlan glanced at her. He didn't think he'd ever seen Elm look quite so livid. It afforded him a rush of satisfaction and slowly he dropped his arm. Smiling brightly at her, he dropped a kiss on her cheek before she could stop him. "I'll see you in a little, hon," he said, loud enough for anyone close by to hear, "and we mustn't be too late, darling, I don't want you getting too tired."

Seething, Elm turned and headed for the garden. If she stayed inside one moment longer, she'd suffocate. Making her way toward the open French doors, she stepped thankfully onto the terrace.

Where was Johnny, and what must he have thought? That she was back with Harlan, of course. She could have screamed with frustration. Why had Harlan appeared just then? She wished she could explain things to Johnny, tell him that this pose of being happily married was nothing but a farce. Suddenly, explaining this to him seemed desperately important, even though, of course, it wouldn't change anything between them. Still, if he believed she'd never had any intention of divorcing her husband, then he must utterly despise her for having made love with him under what he would consider false pretenses. It made her look cheap, tacky, and she didn't want him to hold such a low opinion of her.

Sinking onto the balustrade, Elm blinked back the tears stinging her eyes and let out a shuddering sigh, remembering the shattering look they'd shared. It was the same look his eyes had held when they'd made love. She'd sensed a world of emotion coursing between them, and she could have sworn that he cared, that like her, he was unable to forget. But that, she realized sadly, had been short-lived, any remote chance at reconciliation nipped in the bud by Harlan's unwelcome intrusion.

If only she'd had a chance to explain, Elm lamented, wishing suddenly that she could smash something, throw a stack of plates or a tray full of champagne glasses onto the lawn, anything to assuage the terrible frustration burning within.

They reached the hotel shortly after one and silently rode the elevator to their floor. Elm had her feelings under control now and was not about to give Harlan the pleasure of seeing her upset.

"Good night," she said with a polite smile that disguised her inner turmoil. "Need an extra pillow? Oh, and here's a blanket." She handed the items to him quite pleasantly, wishing she could hurl them at his head.

"Elm, are you sure you don't want some company? I—"

"Don't even think about it," she said, closing the door neatly in his face and locking it firmly on the inside. She could hear him muttering sullenly as she prepared for bed but paid no attention. All she could think of as she climbed under the freshly ironed coverlet was Johnny, that

intense look in his bright blue eyes, that sudden flash of—
was it hope? Oh, God, she wished it was so.

Sleep was impossible.

Where was he staying? she wondered. Here at the Seelbach? No, probably with friends of Grace's, or at one of the
stud farms. That would make sense, for he'd want to be near
Blue Lavender the night before the race. She propped her
head on her elbow and wondered briefly if her Blue really
had a chance to win the race tomorrow. But mostly she
asked herself, over and over, what might have happened
tonight if Harlan had stayed away.

After several more hours of tossing and turning, Elm finally fell asleep. But her dreams were troubled, haunted by
strange images, a handsome, dark-haired medieval knight
with bright blue eyes snatching her from the ground and
carrying her away on a chestnut stallion that flew like the
wind. She didn't know if it was passion or anger that drove
the knight, whether he carried her to heaven or to heartache,
but in his arms she felt utterly secure.

If only dreams could come true.

Two floors up, Johnny looked in the bathroom mirror,
thoroughly annoyed with himself. "Fool," he said out loud,
"you bloody fool. Surely you don't want to go back for
more, Graney?"

But his head and his heart didn't seem to see eye to eye.
His mind was filled with a vision of Elm, of her tremulous
smile and her shy eyes meeting his from across the room.
Despite his efforts to banish her from his brain, she kept
intruding, like a sweet-voiced Circe calling him to destruc-
tion. And fool that he was, he wanted to follow her, even
welcomed the chance to fall back under her spell.

With a snort of disgust, he clicked off the bathroom light,
walked across the room and settled into his turned-down
bed. Tossing one pillow to the floor, he scrunched the other
behind his head and vowed to stop thinking of her. He
needed to concentrate on tomorrow's race, on Blue's

chances of running his last furlong fast enough to win. That, he reminded himself over and over, was all he really cared about.

But his vividly erotic dreams suggested otherwise.

19

"Darling, that must be room service," Grace murmured, gliding across the large living room of the three-bedroom suite, her beige silk robe flowing in her wake.

"I'll get it, Mother." Johnny, still in his dressing gown and pajamas, opened the door and let the waiter pushing the breakfast table in. He hovered impatiently while the young man set it up, then tipped him.

Grace smothered an elegant yawn. "I'm getting too old for these late-night affairs," she remarked, sitting opposite Johnny at the table. "Liam is still fast asleep. Did you have a good night, dear?" He looked a bit weary, she thought, as though he hadn't slept well. Probably worrying about Blue. She lifted the cover from the plate and sighed. "A real Southern breakfast." She smiled nostalgically. "I can't look at a plate of grits without remembering your father and how much he loved them. Each time we came to the Derby we'd stay right here at the Seelbach and enjoy a long breakfast on the day of the race. Do you remember that?" She sighed, trying not to recall the awful day her husband had died.

"I remember, Mother," Johnny said shortly.

"Well, there's no need to be so bad-tempered," she responded sharply. "I have a right to my memories," she added with a sniff.

"I'm sorry, Mother, I know you do," Johnny smiled.

"And you're right, those were very good times. Remember the year Seattle Slew won the Triple Crown?"

"Of course I do. Your father was furious because he lost, but then, so were all the other owners. Still, it was a great win. What a horse. Takes me back a while."

"He's still one of the best breeding stallions about," Johnny remarked, reaching for a Danish.

"Seeing Senator Hathaway brought back old times, too. The last time we met was here, shortly before your father died."

"Hmm." Johnny made a noncommittal sound and bit into the pastry.

"By the way, did you ever get the chance to speak with Elm last night? I thought she looked lovely," she added casually, peeking out of the corner of her eye as she spread a sparse layer of butter on her toast.

"Yes, very briefly," he answered shortly, pouring a large cup of black coffee.

"I was surprised to see her and her husband here," she continued. "I mean, if they really are getting divorced, it seems strange that they would be here together, don't you think?" She did not add that Louise, her friend in Savannah, had informed her that general gossip had Elm spending the better part of her time at the Hathaway family plantation.

She let out another little sigh. Breakfast here was always tinged with memories. Still, she couldn't help but be curious about her son's reaction. "Did you get a chance to catch up with each other?"

"Not really. Her husband turned up pretty quickly," he remarked dryly.

"Ah! I see. Well, you never can tell with these political marriages, can you? So much is done for appearances' sake."

"Mother, Elm is back in Savannah living with her husband," he said deliberately, "so please don't play match-maker. We're through."

"Oh, I see. Well, I'm so sorry. I just happened to hear something different, that's all."

"What do you mean?" He looked up and frowned.

"Nothing at all." She rolled her eyes heavenward. "Are you going to see Blue this morning?"

"Of course I'm going to see Blue this morning, Mother. In fact I should already be over there."

"My, my, you got out of bed on the wrong foot this morning, didn't you?"

"Mother, surprising though this may seem, I'm worried about the race. It's only natural, don't you think?" He downed some more coffee.

"Why, of course, darling. Just don't get all British and cynical on me, I can't stand it." But something else was bothering him, for she knew her son. He was usually disconcertingly calm before a race.

The door of the third bedroom opened and Liam appeared, knotting the cord of his cashmere dressing gown.

"Morning. Newspapers arrived yet?"

"They're over there." Grace waved to a pile of papers lying on the coffee table before the fireplace. "But please, darling, not at breakfast. Remember, your father always used to say that breakfast together was sacred. And he was right."

With a regretful glance at the papers, Liam joined Johnny and their mother at the table. "Guess who I ran into last night?" he said, lifting his cup for Grace to pour him coffee.

"Don't tell me," Johnny said witheringly, "Elm Hathaway."

"Yes. How did you know? Did you tell him, Mother?" He reached for the jam.

"Is Elm the only person you guys saw last night?" Johnny asked irritably. "There must have been hundreds of people you knew at that party, so how come we keep talking about her?"

"*Sorry*," Liam cast his mother a quick glance and she drew her brows together.

"I'm getting dressed and going over to Churchill Downs." Johnny finished his coffee, folded his napkin and got up. "You coming along?" he asked his brother.

"Sure, I'll come with you."

"Okay." He glanced at his watch. "See you in twenty minutes, then. Time now to shower and shave."

"What bug bit him?" Liam asked once the door had closed on his brother.

"I don't know, darling. I guess he's still sweet on Elm but won't admit it," she sighed. "I wish I knew what was going on. It's a funny thing, you know, her being here with her husband. A friend in Savannah told me they're not living together anymore."

"Oh. Did you tell Johnny that?"

"Not really."

"Why not?" Liam looked at her over the breadbasket, surprised.

"Well, I figure it's a complicated situation and best left alone." She sighed again. "A pity, of course, such a charming young woman and so very suitable. But when things aren't meant to be, as your father used to say, it's better to let sleeping dogs lie."

"I guess you may be right," he answered doubtfully.

"What's meant to be will be. You know, *que sera sera*, it's all up to fate and destiny."

"Here we go again," Liam muttered, reaching for the coffee.

"It's the memories, darling. This place is full of them. I half expect your father to come walking straight out of that door."

"Now, now, Mother, don't get maudlin."

"I'm not," she said briskly, seeing the wistful look in her son's eyes that he was trying to hide. "Now, you go get ready and accompany your brother, while I go to my hair appointment. I'll meet you both later on at the track."

The odds against Blue Lavender were five to one when Elm had cast her bet. Harlan, as was to be expected, bet on the coincidentally named Harlan's Holiday, and the senator, who had no horses racing this year but enjoyed the sport, had hedged his bets.

"Where's Harlan?" the senator asked Elm as she joined

him in the box, which belonged to Walker Terence, one of George Hathaway's oldest friends and a legendary horse breeder in Kentucky.

"Oh, out and about, talking to people. As usual."

"Well, Emmy, that's what he's supposed to do." He frowned, concerned that Elm showed no sign of reconciliation. He sincerely hoped she and Harlan would get over this little speed bump soon. The whole mess was becoming increasingly risky, but nothing he'd said up until now seemed to have any effect on her. That was unusual—she'd always been such a dutiful daughter. He really must have a serious talk with her about her responsibilities once they got home.

He shook hands with friends and Elm smiled and chit-chatted, her eyes never leaving the track. Johnny must be in the barns with Blue, she figured. It felt so odd, strange, knowing this might be one of the most important days of his life and not being with him, she reflected sadly. But any chance of that had been killed by Harlan's untimely intrusion. She and Johnny were through, and despite that moment of emotional connection last night, his terse departure had been a clear demonstration of his feelings.

"Well, what a pleasant surprise." Elm turned to see Grace Graney entering the box, dressed in pearl silk and flaunting an extravagant hat decked with ostrich feathers. Liam followed behind. "Hello, Grace. I'm so excited for Johnny. This must be a momentous day for you all."

Grace took full stock of Elm, admiring the diaphanous, wide-brimmed hat and matching see-through beige coat that covered her elegant cream dress. She wore a pearl choker, matching earrings and discreet designer shades. Perfectly appropriate, she thought admiringly. "Now, tell me, dear, does your father have a horse running this year?"

"No." Elm shook her head and kissed Liam, who squeezed her hand in a firm, friendly manner. There was something very nice and steady about Liam Graney, she realized, something constant and comforting, despite Gioconda's disparaging remarks. Maybe he did talk a lot about business, but he was also as solid as they came.

"There's a raging disagreement going on about the star quality of this crop of three-year-olds," Liam remarked. "Let's hope Blue Lavender runs a great race. Johnny's been working him hard. That horse is in phenomenal shape. O'Connor's a seasoned trainer and his jockey's got terrific hands."

"I hope so, too," Elm agreed fervently. Somehow Blue's success had become paramount. She felt as tense and excited as if the horse were hers. Despite longing to know the answer, she stopped herself from asking him where Johnny was and whether he planned to join them in the box. Instead, she trained her binoculars on the horses that were beginning to trot onto the course.

"There goes Blue," Liam exclaimed. "He looks good. There's still about ten minutes to go," he added, glancing at his watch. "Here, take a look through my binoculars."

Elm raised the glasses and watched Johnny's horse. She didn't know much about horseflesh but could tell, just by looking at the glossy coat and perfect proportions, that he was a beautiful specimen. Next to him trotted Harlan's Holiday.

As the horses slowly lined up at the gates, the crowd paused in expectation. Elm, standing at the front of the box next to Liam, didn't notice when Johnny slipped into the back. He edged his way to the front of the box, never taking his eyes off Blue. The horse had drawn the seventeenth post position, which meant he'd have the luxury of a hard, fast track, but would also have to contend with a lot of traffic. Johnny grimaced. Jim Hurley, his jockey, was going to have to pick his way through a cluttered field. Now that the moment he'd invested so much in was finally here, he was desperately worried something would go wrong.

At that very moment the gun went off. The crowd sent up a roar, and the most exciting two minutes in sports began. Johnny gripped the balustrade and watched anxiously as Blue bounded forward and a crowd of horses rushed inward to gain position. Blue was pinched back into ninth as Harlan's Holiday edged ahead, leading the field at record speed into the first turn.

"Come on," he whispered, fists clenched and his excitement

pounding as Blue began picking off one horse, then another. When Ryan Kennedy edged up on Pick of the Month close on Harlan's Holiday's heels, Hurley banked Blue and pushed him through an opening five feet off the rail. The crowd exclaimed as suddenly Blue Lavender surged ahead, gaining on Harlan's Holiday as the horses came roaring around the clubhouse, then turned onto the front stretch.

Nails dug in his palms, Johnny watched anxiously, worried that Harlan's Holiday was setting a suicidal pace, and that Hurley would be lured into matching it. It was a general rule of racing that no horse could sustain its maximum speed for more than three eighths of a mile, and Blue, with more than half a mile still to go, already appeared to be running full out—he looked impossibly fast. Luckily, Hurley sensed the possible trap and held his position. He stared at the leader's churning hindquarters, waiting for him to fold. Sure enough, at the top of the stretch, Harlan's Holiday faltered. Blue was now level and pulling ahead, but was joined by two other horses that had started their final effort. Within a second, there were just two front runners, Blue and Pick of the Month, neck on neck.

"My God, I think he just might do it," Liam muttered, binoculars trained on Blue Lavender as he edged ahead of Pick of the Month's blistering pace.

"Oh, I hope so, he must," Elm exclaimed excitedly, causing Johnny to take his eyes off Blue for one precious second. So she was here. But there was no time for conjecture as the crowd let off another shout of amazement and Blue Lavender, having already run at an astonishing speed for most of the race, accelerated into the final stretch, almost as if he were just now breaking out of the gate. Johnny smothered a shout and held his breath, suddenly wishing his father could be here to witness this magnificent horse, the outcome of all they'd invested so much time and love in, pulling at such a stunning pace. He gripped the railing, pulse pounding, as Blue Lavender pulled ahead by two lengths from Pick of the Month.

When Blue Lavender flew past the winning post by three

lengths in what would become a legendary victory, Johnny let out a shriek.

"You've done it," Liam shouted, clapping his brother's shoulder. "You've done it, bro."

Johnny stood stunned, gazing at Blue, barely able to believe that this horse, his creation, had actually won the Derby—and set a new course record in the process. Blue's wonderful blend of stamina, ability and heart had worked a miracle.

"Oh, Johnny, that's fantastic, congratulations." Elm turned to him, eyes glistening.

"Thanks." In what felt like a supremely natural gesture, Johnny reached over and hugged her.

"What a race!" the senator exclaimed. "That'll end any debate about this year's three-year-olds." He clapped a hand on Johnny's shoulder and congratulated him as others swarmed round, all wanting to express their admiration.

"Go get your trophy, Graney," Walker Terence shouted with a loud guffaw. "Great show—what an incredible display of raw speed. Just terrific. Haven't seen a Derby like this in years." The pink-cheeked, white-haired veteran pumped Johnny's hand enthusiastically. "Now, off you go to the winner's circle, young man, and make sure that magnificent horse gets his roses."

Johnny grinned, gratefully accepting compliments and accolades as he edged his way, slightly dazed, toward the entrance of the box. Then suddenly, he turned and faced Elm.

In a spontaneous gesture, he grabbed her hand.

"Come on."

Elm's face broke into a radiant smile. "I'd love to."

"Then let's go. Meet you there, Liam," Johnny called over his shoulder, and, tugging Elm's hand, made a beeline out of the box.

There was no sign of Harlan. Elm knew he really didn't care for the race, just sought the opportunity to see and be seen. But right now she didn't care what he would think when he saw her with Johnny; she was engulfed by the excitement and thrill of the moment, the happiness of knowing that Johnny had achieved his goal, so spectacularly.

Soon they were being guided into the winner's circle. O'Connor and Hurley stood proudly next to Blue, patting him as they dressed the winning horse with the famous blanket of roses. There were more congratulations, more handshaking and exclamations.

Then it was time for the trophies. Elm stood proudly next to Johnny as the speeches were delivered and O'Connor raised the large silver trophy triumphantly for the crowd to see. Then he handed it to Johnny, who, holding it reverently, walked over to Blue and lifted it before the horse's bright eyes, wanting him to share their triumph. After an emotional pause, he turned and hoisted the trophy toward the sky, basking in the wild cheers of the crowd.

Elm felt a knot in her throat, knowing how much it all meant to him. And this, she realized excitedly, was just the beginning of the season. There was still Belmont and Ascot to be run. Blue could well become the season's champion.

It was another half hour before Johnny managed to escape from the admiring crowd and take her aside.

"Look, Elm," he said quickly. "I know we may not have much of a chance to talk tonight, but I…well, I need to speak to you."

Their eyes met and held once more, and Elm made no pretense of not understanding what he meant.

"You're right. We need to talk," she murmured.

"Then how about lunch tomorrow? Are you free? Could you manage that?" His eyes pierced hers with new intensity.

"Yes, that would be wonderful."

"How about the Oak Room at one o clock?"

"I'll be there."

"Good girl." He squeezed both her hands and his face broke into a smile. Then he raised her fingers to his lips and dropped the lightest of kisses on them. "I have to go now. I'll see you later. Will you get back to the box on your own all right?"

"I'll be fine. Now, go," she said, sending him on his way as the horse was led toward the barns, and Johnny joined

O'Connor, Kennedy and the others in the triumphant march across the turf and back to the stables.

She let out a long sigh and closed her eyes behind her sunglasses for just a moment. Suddenly the crowd faded and she was back on their mountaintop, feeling the joy of Johnny's arms about her. He cared. Despite all the months spent agonizing, trying so desperately to pretend to herself that he was nothing more than a passing fancy, fate had brought them back together. Despite their bitter parting in Gstaad, the pull had been stronger than either of them could resist.

She opened her eyes again and realized she must get back to the box, that Harlan would be looking for her. But even that couldn't dampen her excitement. There was something so utterly perfect about the day. She thought longingly of lunch tomorrow. Harlan was flying to D.C. in the morning, so there was no fear of him interfering with their meeting.

"Shall we go back and see if we can find the others?"

At the sound of Liam's voice, Elm jumped and turned.

"Oh! I didn't realize you were still here," she exclaimed, seeing him standing next to her, shading his eyes from the sun with his racing card.

"Blue made a pretty packet this afternoon," he remarked. "Did you bet on him?"

"Of course." Elm laughed, feeling more lighthearted and happier than she had in months. "Did you?"

"Yep. Let's go cash in our winnings."

"Good idea."

Elm glanced wistfully in the direction of the stables, wishing she could have shared Blue's triumph to the end. Then, with a contented sigh, she linked her arm with Liam's and together they made their way to the bookie stands.

The race was over by the time Harlan hurried into the box. Not that he cared. Horse racing didn't interest him in the least, and his time was far better spent chatting up potential donors on Millionaires' Row. Besides, he'd run into Bo Derek—wow, what a rack that woman had. Even in her late forties, she was incredible-looking. With any luck, she'd call the number he'd slipped her.

Sighing, he remembered that he wanted some photos taken with Elm for the papers back home. Stepping into the box, he heard the excited chatter and learned that Blue Lavender had won. Where was Elm? he wondered, looking around the box. Then he edged his way to the front, peering over to the winner's circle. And scowled. What the hell was she doing there?

"How come Elm's down there in the winner's circle?" he asked the senator.

"Oh, she went down there with Johnny Graney, the horse's owner."

"I see." Harlan's eyes narrowed. "May I borrow your binoculars?"

"Sure." The senator pulled the binoculars from around his neck and handed them to Harlan. "You'll still get a good glimpse of Blue Lavender. Absolutely incredible race. One of the best Derbies I've ever attended," he added.

"Thanks." Harlan donned the binoculars and focused them on Elm. *Damn.* He should be down there, too. That would have made a perfect picture for the magazines. Now she'd probably be featured with Graney. He adjusted the lens for a better view. Wasn't that the same guy she'd been speaking with last night? His eyes narrowed. Christmas. Hadn't she spent it with them, too? What the hell was going on? It had never crossed his mind that Elm might be having an affair of her own. Now suddenly he wondered.

Lowering the binoculars, Harlan stared at the turf thoughtfully. Maybe that was why she was so averse to sleeping with him. She'd been too busy banging other guys. Which meant it was entirely likely she really did plan to go through with the divorce after all. An icy shudder was instantly followed by a hot rush of anger. Double-crossing bitch with her sanctimonious attitudes, making him beg her forgiveness for his affair when all the while she was probably fucking around. He quickly raised the binoculars again and trained them on the Irishman. Handsome fellow. And wasn't that

Liam Graney next to him, the industrialist he'd visited in Pittsburgh, the one who'd promised to think about contributing to his campaign?

He shrugged, determined to brush off the unease all this caused. Maybe he was reading too much into it. The fact she was standing next to the guy didn't mean anything. Besides, he could swing things, couldn't he? And if Elm really wanted out of the marriage, then why not? All he needed was for her to toe the line until this election was won, make sure the senator was still on his side, and then she could go her merry fucking way. The sooner the better, actually.

Then he hesitated, reluctantly acknowledging the truth to himself. Things were more complicated than that. It certainly wouldn't do his image any good to have her scampering off straight after the election with some fancy aristocrat. That, he realized, was something he hadn't counted on. People might even think he'd been jilted. He'd have to seriously think about whether he could allow that.

He watched as she disappeared from view. Shit, he'd better go try and find her if he hoped to catch some pictures. There were always photographers grateful for shots. He handed back the binoculars to his father-in-law, and smiling graciously to the other guests, slipped from the box in search of his errant wife, annoyed that he was being put to the trouble.

Then he came to a cold stop in the corridor, assailed by another disagreeable thought. Hopefully Tyler Brock hadn't been watching the race and seen Elm standing in the winner's circle with another man. Brock was so damn uptight about making sure Harlan flaunted the Hathaway connection. It was none of Brock's damn business, of course. But still, the thought of his displeasure left Harlan uneasy. Quietly divorcing Elm after the election might not be a viable long-term solution after all.

He definitely needed to give the matter some serious thought, Harlan decided. There was simply too much at stake to leave anything to chance. Problem was, what was the solution?

20

Johnny stepped into the Oak Room, its fine, hand-carved lion's head columns, ornate wood accents and brass chandeliers reminiscent of the gentlemen's billiards hall it once used to be. He had little notion of exactly what he planned to say to Elm. But as the head waiter led him to one of the alcoves—a suitably private venue for what he hoped would prove an important conversation—he knew he would have to tell her the truth: that he was finding it bloody hard to get through life without her.

He sat down facing the dining room and waited for her, his mind wandering back to the night of the party. When he'd seen her eyes across the room, he could have sworn they'd been filled with as much longing as his own. But looks could deceive. Daylight often brought a change of heart, he considered uneasily. But then again, hadn't she joined him in the winner's circle with such delightful spontaneity, clapping so fervently, eyes glistening as though Blue Lavender were as important to her as she was to him?

Johnny flipped absently through the menu. He would just have to risk it, he realized reluctantly. He didn't relish the possibility that he might get hurt—especially since he'd spent most of the last fourteen years erecting barriers to prevent that very thing—but he also realized what he stood to lose. He glanced at his watch. It was one minute to one.

He did not have to wait long.

At precisely three minutes past, Elm arrived, dressed in a pretty, pale-pink suit and silk top that even he recognized as Chanel. He rose automatically as she moved toward him, her long, lithe body gliding with the same infinite grace he always associated with her. When she stood next to the table, he raised her hand to his lips and tried not to imagine her soft, silky skin under his.

He cleared his throat, struck anew by how very beautiful she was. "Thank you for joining me," he said as the head waiter deferentially pulled back her chair.

A bottle of chilled champagne stood in an ornate ice bucket next to the table. The waiter popped the cork and poured. Elm smiled softly. She'd been so nervous, so anxious after the excitement of yesterday and an evening spent on tenterhooks, knowing that she wanted to see him today more than anything she could remember. The restless anticipation had barely allowed for sleep.

Now that she was finally here, she found it incredible that it should feel so natural, so entirely right, to be seated opposite him once more, a glass of champagne in her hand, drinking to Blue's health, as if they hadn't spent the past months without exchanging so much as a telephone call. It was almost as if they were a couple, she recognized, suddenly a bit nervous of the implications, separated by circumstance but now back together, picking up their usual routine.

Johnny sat across the table silently watching her, enjoying each familiar gesture: the way she touched her hair, her smile, the wide dark eyes, flecked with gold, that shone so bright and were so revealing. There was no need for words, no need to tell her how much he was enjoying just being with her, for he knew simply by looking at her that she, too, was absorbing this closeness, filling in the lonely months spent apart. It was as if a calm recognition of what they meant to each other hovered over them, requiring no excuses, no regrets.

And no pretense.

When he reached his hand across the table, Elm slipped

her fingers into his and a little sigh escaped her. And for a short while they remained thus, hands linked across the well-laid table, savoring their reunion.

"I know I was a bloody fool that day we parted," he murmured at last. "Can you forgive me, Elm?"

"We were both stupid," she responded softly, delighting in the feel of his fingers stroking hers. "I should have explained about Harlan arriving."

"Can you fault me for feeling just a tiny bit jealous?" he asked with a sheepish grin.

"Just a little?" she queried, a gentle smile breaking over her face.

"I hate to admit it, but I still am jealous," he admitted, gripping her fingers just a little tighter. "It's hard to think of you with another man, Elm."

"Why are you so sure there's another man?"

"Well, what else could I conclude?" He drew back, but she held on to his hand, eyes pinning his.

"Looks can be deceiving, you know."

"What do you mean?" His brows came together in a thick dark line over the bridge of his nose.

"Well, not everything is always exactly as it appears. Sometimes you can jump to wrong conclusions."

"Let me get this straight." He leaned forward. "Are you telling me that you and your husband aren't together any longer? That just doesn't make any sense. I mean, you're even staying in the same suite, for Christ's sake." He felt a tug of annoyance. Surely she wasn't trying to take him for a fool, was she?

"That," she replied, her voice hardening, "was not of my choosing. But, anyway, it's beside the point. What I'm saying, if you'd let me finish," she remarked, looking him straight in the eye, "is that I'm still divorcing Harlan. Nothing has changed."

"But you're allowing people to believe you're happily married? Sorry, but I'm finding this slightly hard to follow."

"It's politics as usual," she sighed. "My father begged me to appear at certain public events with Harlan. A divorce right now might cost him the election, and frankly, although I don't want to stay married to him, I don't wish him any harm, either.''

"So you're not living together?" Johnny squeezed her fingers tighter, as though needing to hear the right answer, then he loosened his grip just as suddenly, lest he betray too much.

"I'm living by myself at Oleander Creek," Elm replied. "You can't have much of an opinion of me," she added, "if you imagined I went from your arms straight back to my husband's."

"Look, I'm sorry." He disengaged his fingers and dragged them through his hair before draining his champagne glass. "I hate to admit it, Elm, but that's exactly what I thought."

"I realize that. For a while it upset me a lot. I believed—well, hoped—that even though we'd spent very little time together, you knew me better than that."

"Touché." He signaled the waiter, who filled their glasses promptly. He raised his with an apologetic grin. "To you, my dear. You must pardon my stupidity, my boorish behavior. I suppose it comes from living alone too long, and having turned into a bit of a misanthrope."

"You're not boorish or a misanthrope, Johnny, you just find it hard to trust people."

"Hmm." He nodded briefly. "You may very well be right," he admitted, surprised at the realization. "Elm, I know that this is all my bloody fault, but—and stop me if I'm wrong—I think, despite the fact that we both have a lot to contend with in our past, we feel the same way about each other." He paused, closed his eyes a second, then continued. "God, when I saw you the other night at the Barnstable Brown party, I—well, it's hard to put into words exactly, but I just knew that I need you with me, need to get to know you properly, with no barriers between us. I want you with me when I wake up in the morning, to see that light in your eyes, not have to imagine it. God knows I've tried to forget you—"

"Gee, thanks," she murmured, lips curving.

Johnny laughed, half amused, half exasperated. Part of him wanted to beg her to come away with him and continue what they'd left off in the mountain. But common sense told him they were past that. He hesitated. Did he really want this…emotional entanglement? To have his head ruled by his heart? But the realization that he might rise from the table without some sort of commitment—a promise that he would soon see her again—made the risks pale.

"I need to ask you something. I know it may not be easy and I don't expect an answer right away—" he paused, wondering if he sounded crazy "—but I would like you to think about it."

"Okay," she said, wanting him to continue, afraid that he wouldn't, afraid of what he might ask. The moment was far too important to keep up pretenses, or deny the intense, palpable desire hovering between them. Their need for each other, irrespective of all the difficulties that any kind of relationship between them entailed, filled the atmosphere like a heavy, musky, unavoidable scent neither wished to escape.

"I realize this is perhaps premature," he said slowly, eyes fixed on her face, "but would you consider spending some time with me at Graney?" He leaned back as she removed her fingers from his grasp and sat straighter.

"You mean go to Ireland and stay with you at the castle?" she asked, surprised.

"That's right." He nodded, his eyes intense. "I want you to come to Graney, to see where I live, to understand what my life's all about."

"I—I'll have to think about it. Right now there's so much to do. I have the exhibition to prepare, I don't have nearly enough canvases ready. Then there's the shipping to consider, the hanging of the paintings—"

"But that's in the autumn, isn't it?"

"Yes."

"Then why are you so worried? There's enough time."

"I know, but there's my garden project, too, I don't know if—" She knew she was blabbering nonsense. What scared her was the sudden twist that whatever lay between them was taking. He was asking her to come and share time in his home, in the place he held sacred.

Instinctively she knew he had never asked this of any other woman. She was certain that, except for his wife, he had never offered another woman anything that smacked of commitment or permanence. Her heart jolted. Part of her longed to say yes, here and now. But how could she?

After all, she wasn't even divorced yet. Did she really want to enter into a relationship when she was only just beginning to find her own feet? When she was just learning to trust the woman she'd become? Most important, could she stand the hurt and pain if things fell apart again? She swallowed, her mouth suddenly dry, knowing she must think this over. It was absurd to get so involved but, God, she was tempted. "I'll really have to think about it," she finished lamely.

"I'm aware of that. I'm not in a hurry. Though if you take too long to make up your mind, I may just show up one morning on your front steps at Oleander Creek," he said, with a spark of the old mischief she remembered.

She let out a low, shy laugh and shook her head. "I'd love for you to come to Oleander, but not right now. My life is pretty complicated at the moment, what with the election, then the divorce."

"I was just joking. Perhaps I shouldn't have suggested Ireland at all," he said stiffly.

"No," she answered quickly, seeing him retreat behind that icy, impenetrable barrier of doubt. "I promise I'll think about it. I—I love the idea, it's just…it's just…" She glanced at him, begging him to understand without a hundred explanations.

"Of course." He smiled, reached again for her fingers and caressed them lightly. "No pressure, Elm. I get the feeling you've had enough of that to last you a lifetime, that it scares you more than anything. I want you to be happy and at ease, not burdened. Now," he murmured, picking up the menu with a smile that eased the tension, "shall we order some of the bluegrass chicken stuffed with Colonel New-some's country ham? I've heard it's delicious. They say that if you can only have one meal in Louisville, then the Oak Room is the place to have it. Let's see if the critics are right,'' he said lightly.

She smiled back, grateful that he understood, and was giving her the time and space to come to her own decision.

It was the first time in her life, she recognized ruefully, that a man hadn't tried to make up her mind for her.

In the hours and days that followed, Elm thought a lot about the luncheon. As the flight taxied into Savannah's air-port in the pouring rain and she picked up her car and headed out to Oleander Creek, her brain was full of everything they'd discussed.

Ireland. From the moment he'd spoken the words, her heart and mind had been spellbound, as though he'd turned on a bright new light that revealed to her just how much she'd secretly longed to enter his world. She wanted to see his home, to see him at Graney, to see whether she fit there, too. She'd done little else but relive each moment of the meal, savoring the memory of each tiny gesture, and the way he'd pressed her close when they'd finally parted in the lobby, not passionately or insinuatingly, but close in a way that told her more than anything how deeply he wanted her—not just her body but her companionship.

He'd neatly tossed the ball into her court, she realized. The choice was hers. It was all she could do to remind her-self that she must not act on impulse. After all, it wasn't easy to simply up and leave again. She had commitments, didn't she? Her work in Savannah, the divorce and the damned election. And that trip to Ashby's clinic for the tests that she kept putting off. Not to mention the exhibition, looming ever closer. How would she have enough canvases ready by the autumn if she kept disappearing? Though the thought of painting in Ireland was tempting.

Then there was her father and Harlan. What excuse would she give them for yet another visit to Europe? She supposed she could always invoke the exhibition as justification. But as she veered off the two-lane highway and onto the dirt road, through the arc of ancient oak trees draped with dripping Spanish moss and on past the old fields that spread wide and far on either side of the road, she knew she was not prepared to make excuses anymore. The days of deceit were over. As she drove past the old railroad track where trains still hauled their consignments of raw and manufactured goods to and from Savannah's port, she knew the answer. She wouldn't worry about what anyone thought—she'd simply make the decision for herself, in her own time, based on her own needs and concerns.

As she approached the white clapboard plantation house, sunlight finally pierced the clouds, its rays flirting gently with the brick foundation that held the old house high above the crescent of outbuildings. Elm slowed the Jeep and let out a sigh. She was home. Yet for the first time she sensed that Oleander was no longer enough for her. Somewhere along the way, a void had developed that couldn't be filled merely by a home, however lovely, however dear.

Isah stood at the top of the steps and waved.

She waved back. This was her life, she reminded herself, the place she'd been born and bred. But did that mean there couldn't also be room for growth, for her life to branch out in new directions?

After exchanging a few words of greeting with Isah, Elm strolled around the house and faced the river. Then she turned and glanced back at the house, at the grander riverside facade with its wraparound porch and double galleries designed to enchant visitors who in olden days had sailed up the river from Savannah. They'd have reached Oleander via a path that led from the dock through a small forest, to the grassy clearing that provided a dramatic setting for the house.

Elm dragged her fingers through her hair, then shoved her hands into her pant pockets. Tapping her foot on the paving stone, she glanced wistfully toward the half-finished garden project and remembered her time with Johnny, recognizing that yes, she wanted more. She enjoyed everything about him, his smile, his voice, his presence, his company, every-thing from his sudden frowns to their endless conversations on so many subjects.

So what was she so worried about? she wondered. What was to stop her from going to Ireland? Meredith had the divorce under control, didn't she? Nothing was going to be finalized till after the election, anyway. Harlan would be spending the next couple of weeks on the road campaigning like mad, and she had made it abundantly clear that she was not joining him on the campaign trail, despite Ensor's rec-ommendations.

But to travel to Ireland, to stay at Graney...

She suddenly imagined Grace and her father's reaction if they should find out, and despite her inherent embarrass-ment, a slow smile lit up her face. She really must stop thinking like a fifteen-year-old and grow up. She and Johnny were adults with every right to decide with whom and how they wanted to spend their time.

She entered the house and passed through the dining room into the hall. She must phone Aunt Frances; her aunt hadn't joined them at the Derby because she hadn't been altogether well the past few weeks, which was a worry. And Gio. She owed her a call, too. And like it or not, there was that ap-pointment that she'd cancelled and needed to set up again with Ashby's office. Not to mention the guys over in Flor-ence organizing the exhibit, too. Gosh, what a lot to do. And of course, there was the garden project to deal with. She was needed there, too, she reminded herself as she climbed the stairs and headed for her bedroom, wondering how Johnny was managing his qualms, if he wasn't regretting the invi-tation.

For she was under no illusions that this step had been easy for him. Inviting her into his home had to have been as significant for him as it was for her. Graney was his refuge, the place where he hid from the world, that insulated him from the memories of a very painful past. It couldn't be simple, she recognized, to open a door he'd closed so firmly.

And yet he'd somehow worked up the courage to let her in, hoping that she wouldn't hurt him, believing that the risk was worth taking. Even more amazing, by leaving the ball in her court, he was trusting her to make the right decision for both of them.

It was a weighty responsibility, she acknowledged, taking a seat at her bedroom window and staring at the small gray-ish pink brick walls, remnants from the original garden that were being worked into the project. After all, if she did go to Ireland, she'd be taking a huge leap into the unknown. And although she was longing to ignore convention, pack her bags and leave, something still held her back.

"Are you serious, Mel? How many cases are we talking about?" Meredith leaned back and twiddled her pen, her eyes on the young journalist from the *Savannah Morning News,* who sat on the opposite side of her desk. Vaguely, she wondered who her next client was and hoped it wasn't the Jennings case, since she'd barely had time to review the file.

"I dunno, exactly. That's why I want to investigate. But there's definitely some sort of trend. Several people in the Ogeechee area have been showing up at local emergency rooms, reporting nausea and fatigue. They're being told there's a nasty flu bug going around."

"Well, maybe there is," Meredith shrugged. Mel Bamberger was inclined to go out on a limb about anything that he thought might be in any way suspicious. "Yes? Come in."

Ally peeked around the door. "Your next client's in five, Meredith."

"Thanks, Ally."

"I'll just slip the file on your desk."

"I'll take it." Meredith reached out her hand and glanced at it. "Oh God, I knew it. The Jennings case. Mel, I'm sorry, but I'll have to shove you out of here," she remarked as Ally closed the door.

"Fine, but just listen one minute, okay?"

"Okay, but be quick." She began taking a look at the file.

"What I'm saying is that there's nothing to explain why the company that runs the waste-processing plant has proposed that all the inhabitants within a three-mile radius install special water filters, does it?"

"That could be a precaution. Many companies do that."

"Fair enough. But you don't think there's any harm in me looking into it further, do you? I don't want to get the paper into trouble."

"As long as you don't get people's backs up, I don't see why you shouldn't sleuth away. Now, please, Mel, I've got a client in a few minutes whose file is a mystery to me, okay?"

"You know that this whole plant thing is one of Harlan MacBride's pet projects, right?" he said, rising reluctantly while rubbing his curly blond head and peering at her through thick glasses.

"Yes, which is why I doubt there can be anything fishy going on. He'd be the last person to link his name to anything that wasn't kosher, with an election around the corner."

"You may be right. But you know me," he laughed, picking up his canvas satchel, "once I get an itch, I've got to scratch it—and this one just keeps bothering me. I'll keep you posted," he said, coming over and giving her a quick hug. "And, Mer, thanks for the advice."

"Sure. Anytime." She saw him out the door, then came back to her desk, shaking her head. Harlan had been very keen on promoting the water-processing plant; indeed, he'd been the major force behind getting it privatized and built. He was eager to flash his environmentalist credentials—and the strategy seemed to be working for him in the polls—so it would be too bad if there was something amiss over there. The party couldn't afford for him to stumble. But that wasn't likely. These places had to run a tight ship or the EPA jumped on them like fleas.

She sat down at her desk, eyeing the Jennings file with guilt, and decided there hadn't been any harm in encouraging Mel to look into things. In the meantime, she'd focus on more pressing problems, like the fact Harlan was still dragging his feet about discussing the details of the divorce. Just like a politician, she snorted, thinking that ignoring a problem would make it go away. She recognized the temptation, because she'd once had political ambitions herself. It had taken two kids and a loving lecture from her husband to realize she wasn't Wonder Woman and that a political career simply wasn't in the cards.

Problem was, Harlan still thought of himself as Superman. He thought that he could do the things he'd done to Elm and still keep her by his side. Well, she grinned, good thing she was packing some kryptonite. Because Harlan could use all the stalling tactics and mind games he wanted—in the end, Elm would be free.

21

Johnny waited anxiously at Dublin airport to pick up Nicky for the half-term break. He looked forward to spending the next few days with his son, who since his appendectomy and return to school seemed to have matured considerably.

Once Nicky arrived—wearing some god-awful slouchy outfit that Johnny supposed was the fashion these days—they boarded the chopper and headed home. Nicky was full of questions. How was the Derby, did Johnny have a DVD of the race? Had he seen Elm while in the U.S.? Was Grandma coming over in the summer and could he take his friends Jimmy and Peter with him to the house in St. Barthes in July?

By the time they reached Graney, Johnny had switched fully back into "Dad" mode. He suddenly realized that this was the first time he'd looked forward to Nicky's visit without trepidation, without the usual aura of guilt that had pursued him all these years. Foolishly, he'd somehow believed he didn't have the right to enjoy their son simply because Marie Ange no longer could. And all at once, he realized everything he'd missed.

They spent the next couple of days riding, discussing horseflesh and racing, Johnny imparting as much information as he could. It was only in the evenings, when he sat down in his study, that his thoughts turned to Elm. Sometimes he wished he'd never issued the invitation, while at other times, he wished she would just make up her mind one way or the other. They seemed to spend more and more time on the phone, with no mention of the invitation, conversation remaining on neutral territory.

Only yesterday, Elm had told him about the cotton trader's house she and her father were selling in Savannah, how the broker had conveniently discovered a ghost that had decided the buyer, a small amusing anecdote that he treasured as a part of her everyday life. And he told her about the horses, recounted Blue's ups and downs, a swollen ankle, the decisions about what races he would participate in next. And, of course, Nicky's arrival. They'd shared more on the phone, he realized ruefully, than in person.

Pouring himself a whiskey, he joined Nicky in front of the new flat-screen TV in the den and tried to figure out what the movie was about.

"Look, Dad—" Nicky pointed to the screen "—doesn't that girl look just like Elm?"

"Not really," Johnny countered, eyeing the film star with narrowed eyes. "Elm's eyes are brown, not blue, plus she's taller, and has a much better figure and—"

Nicky turned, laughing. "Dad, why don't you admit that you really like her?"

"I never said I didn't," Johnny replied smoothly.

"Then why don't you see her more often?"

"Well, she has her own life to lead, too, you know."

"That's BS, Dad. If she really wanted to be with you, she would," Nicky said perceptively, turning the knife in the wound. "Why don't you ask her over here?"

"Would you mind if I did?"

"Of course not. It'd be cool. Elm's cool. I like her. Is she married or something?"

"Look, Elm's life is her own business," Johnny responded, half annoyed, half amused at his son's persistence. "Actually, I've already issued the invitation. If she wants to, she'll come, I suppose," he added somewhat morosely, for it was two and a half weeks now since the Derby and nothing had come of his offer.

"If it was me," Nicky responded in a worldly-wise tone, "I'd send her a first-class ticket and just see what happened. But then, that's me," he said with all the nonchalance of his sixteen years.

"You would, would you?" Johnny quirked an eyebrow and laughed. He felt in his old corduroy pants pocket for his pipe, then reached for the tin of tobacco, the idea not entirely unpleasing.

Later that night, after the film was over and Nicky had gone up to bed yawning, he checked the doors and turned out the lights in the great hall. Walking up the wide oak staircase to his bedroom, Johnny had to admit that the idea of sending Elm a ticket had definite appeal. At least that way she'd be obliged to decide one way or the other, he reflected, lips curving as he flipped the visor of a suit of armor on the landing. Not that he wanted to put pressure on her, he reasoned, not at all. She'd obviously had enough of that from that slick bastard she was married to. Still, it might not do any harm to give her a little push in the right direction. And if she sent the damn ticket back and refused, well, so be it. At least they'd all know where they stood, and that had to be better than waking each morning, wondering if today was the day she was finally going to make up her mind.

Elm stood in the corner of the screened porch, utterly absorbed in dabbing a third layer of paint onto the canvas that she'd been working on for some time. For some reason it wasn't cooperating—and the persistent headache she had wasn't helping matters in the least. She stepped away from the painting and tilted her head, unsatisfied. Maybe she should add some more yellow, she reflected, glancing up when Isah walked in.

"Here's a letter for you, Miz Elm, via courier service." She laid the package on the lowboy just inside the drawing room. "Lunch'll be ready in fifteen minutes. There's rice, terrapin soup, okra gumbo an' fried chicken. And I ain't cookin' nuthin' else for that gaggle you got out there, no, ma'am. I've set it up for them downstairs, under the arches on the big tables like when we have the oyster roast. I ain't havin' them eatin' in here like respectable folks, no, ma'am.''

"Isah! That's a terrible thing to say,'' Elm exclaimed, laying down her brush and reaching for a rag and the turpentine. "They're just women down on their luck through no fault of their own.''

"They's white trash, Miz Elm, and should've had more sense than to join up with those nasty husbands of theirs. Don' you make no mistake about it.''

"It's not their fault their husbands beat them, Isah. And I don't care if they're white, green or purple,'' she said patiently. "If they're finding some measure of healing or hope in working our garden, then I'm all for letting them continue.'' She wiped off the paint from her fingers, popped her brushes into the turpentine and reached for the letter as Isah moved back into the kitchen, mumbling about changed ways and what Elm's grandmother would have said, were she still among them to say it.

Elm held up the envelope. Probably something from Meredith that needed signing. Without so much as a glance she slit open the plastic cover and pulled out the inner envelope. Then her breath caught at the sight of a crest followed by sloping engraved letters that read Graney Castle.

She fingered the envelope. It felt thick. Perhaps Johnny had sent her some photos of the Derby, she reasoned, sitting in her favorite wicker rocker. Then she opened the actual envelope and let out a small gasp as she pulled out a sleek British Airways ticket jacket. She stared at it, fingers trembling. Inside was a first-class ticket from New York to Dublin. Her pulse raced. The dates were open. She looked inside the envelope again and pulled out a single sheet of monogrammed paper. The message on it was brief and to the point.

Dear Elm,

I know that by asking you to come here we both risk getting hurt. Just as I know your life is filled with hurdles, letting go of the past isn't easy, but I promise to try. Still, I think we owe it to ourselves to take a whack at it. If you do decide to come, please advise flight number and time of arrival.

Love,
Johnny

Elm sat utterly still, clutching the ticket and the note. She heard the women laughing outside, chattering as they headed to lunch under the arches below, reminding her of all her responsibilities. For a moment she panicked. She couldn't go, couldn't just leave it all again. Could she?

Oh, God, this was all so very difficult. The real issue, she acknowledged, was that she knew she'd fall in love with him if she went. She was probably already halfway there, she admitted—and look where love had gotten her the last time around. She leaned back in the wicker rocker, let out a long breath and stared hard at the ticket.

Why didn't she just admit that she spent the better part of her days and nights thinking about him, waiting for the darn phone to ring, pretending to herself that she was getting on with everyday life when all she was doing was filling time?

She glanced at her watch. It was seven in the morning in Ireland.

Suddenly she rose, holding the ticket and grabbed the phone. She would do it before she could change her mind, before she came up with some perfectly valid excuse not to go. After all, what harm could there be in spending a few days with him? Anyway, she'd never been to Ireland, she reasoned, swallowing hard as she dialed the number and listened to the burr of the double ring on the other end.

"Hello, Graney Castle," a melodic Irish voice replied.

"Good morning," Elm murmured. "Could I speak to Lord Graney, please?"

"If ye hold on a minute, dear, I'll see if I can catch him. He just stepped out to the stables. Or better still, I'll transfer ye, if I can get this new-fangled telephone system His Lordship's installed to work. It's a wee bit difficult to—ah, there we go. Now, if ye get cut off, dear, just phone back and I'll let it ring so they pick up down there. That is, if young Shea's around and not away drinkin' tea and haggling over a horse trade—" the woman's voice cut off. Then there was a click, a buzz and a man whom she presumed must be "young Shea" answered.

"Could I speak to Lord Graney, please?" she asked tentatively, hoping she wasn't calling too early. But if he was already down at the stables, surely it should be all right.

Then Johnny's wonderful deep British voice was on the line and her heart leaped once more.

"Hello, Graney speaking."

"Johnny, hi, it's Elm."

"Elm." Silence followed, as if he knew why she'd phoned and was waiting for her response.

"I—I got your letter. It was very kind of you, I—"

"Yes?"

"Well, I thought perhaps I could fly out next week."

There was a moment's silence and she wondered if he'd suddenly regretted sending the ticket, when at last he spoke.

"You've just made my day," he said in a low, warm voice that allayed all fears. "But couldn't you make it tomorrow?"

She laughed now, tension replaced by warm anticipation and excitement. "Well, I have to pack and leave things set up here, and I—"

"Just teasing, my love. I'll be waiting at Dublin. Make sure you don't change your mind."

"I won't," she whispered, delighted and relieved he'd pushed her out of her indecision. "I'll be there."

"Good. We've a lot of catching up to do."

"What do you mean she's left?" Harlan exploded into the phone as the plane from D.C. began its descent. "Isah, what the hell do you mean she packed up and left?"

"She's gone since yesterday, Mister Harlan. Didn't say where she was going, neither," she added with a touch of satisfaction.

"It's intolerable," Harlan muttered, clenching his fingers and slamming the phone down, furious at how helpless he felt. Didn't the bitch remember that she was supposed to attend the debate on Thursday? How the hell was he going to explain to the reporters that his own wife couldn't be bothered to show up and support him? She couldn't just up and leave whenever she felt like it, he stewed. Obviously, she'd lost all notion of what she owed him.

He glanced at Charles Ensor, seated in the cream leather seat opposite him, intently studying the latest polls. In an hour they'd be landing in Savannah. Harlan let out a long huff.

"Elm playing her games again?" Charles asked without looking up. "That's hitting at a really bad time. Some of these polls are down, Harlan. Looks like some big money's gotten behind your opponent. There's been a bunch of expensive ads against you. We need Elm on board."

"How the fuck can I get her on board when she keeps disappearing on me?" he asked crossly. "God knows where she's jetted to this time. Probably Italy or some other friggin' European wasteland. She's preparing some goddamn exhibition over there. I suppose Gioconda would know."

"Then call her and find out, but get the woman back. By the way, Tyler was on the line a few minutes ago. Wants to see you when you land. Something to do with that municipal-waste project."

"I haven't got time for that right now," Harlan dismissed, accepting a sheaf of papers from one of the aides and signing off on them.

"I think you should find the time." Charles raised his bald head, eyes narrowed. "We need every buck we can muster right now. You keep people like Tyler happy, Harlan, and we win this election. Make no mistake about that." He leaned his shirtsleeved frame forward and lowered his voice.

"The senator's pulled in just about every favor he has out there."

"Well, what else do you suggest I do, approve the legalization of same-sex marriages to rake in some disposable income from the liberal left?"

"Very funny. The only result of that would be half your constituency closing their wallets! Look, the point I'm trying to make is, don't mess with Brock. He's our lifeline right now. Elsa White is creeping up on your heels, buddy. She has great appeal, particularly in the feminist camp, and that's exactly who comes out in force at election time."

"Okay, okay," Harlan answered irritably. He'd had just about enough of being told what and what not to do, of Elm's freakish whims and his suddenly popular political opponent, another bitch he could do without. He stared morosely into the clouds. He simply must find some way to control Elm's movements, at least until after the election.

It was time to get tough.

Two nights later, Harlan walked into the bedroom, discarding his clothes as he went. He was exhausted. All week, he'd been working damage control, but he knew it wouldn't be enough. He needed to remind everyone that he was the only candidate with real experience. Only he could leverage the influence of the Hathaway name to win money and jobs for his constituency.

What he needed was Elm.

He stared, frustrated, at the silver-framed photo of his errant wife resting on the bedside table. He still had no clue where she was. Meredith, who probably knew exactly where she'd gone, was being as damned tight-lipped as was Aunt Frances, and the senator, who'd flown straight from Kentucky to Arizona to spend time with old friends, probably didn't even realize she'd left.

Harlan flicked on the blue-and-white Chinese porcelain bedside lamps and tossed his cell phone on the dresser. *Damn Elm.* She was becoming an increasingly tiresome liability. How he could be expected to go on like this? How could he manage? It simply wasn't fair.

He pulled off his loafers and sat pensively on the long ottoman at the end of the bed. There was no controlling her any longer, that was for sure. He'd finally understood that when he'd found himself sleeping on the sofa in the suite at the Seelbach.

That still galled, especially because now he'd bet good money that there was another man in her life. Seeing how she'd looked at Graney at the Barnstable Brown party had really pissed him off. She had no business doing that, much less mooning over him at the Derby, with reporters everywhere. She was still his wife. Even if they weren't sleeping together, she was still his. Her name, the money, the house, and everything she represented belonged to him. And so it would remain, he vowed.

But that, he realized with a sigh as he stood up, undoing his cuff links and unbuttoning his shirt, was easier said than done. Hadn't she just flown the coop once again, without so much as a by-your-leave? Despite her constant whining about feeling sick, apparently she was well enough to just take off.

He had just thrown his shirt crossly into the dirty clothes basket in the walk-in closet when he stopped dead in his tracks. Her sickness. Ashby. Why, that might be just the thing. He was almost afraid of voicing the thought even within the secrecy of his own mind. What if Elm could be gotten rid of, once and for all? The idea was brilliant, yet so daring it left him dizzy. My God, if that could be brought about, then all his problems would be resolved in one majestic sweep of the wand.

He moved pensively back into the bedroom and finished undressing, dazed, shocked at the sheer boldness of the idea, at its undeniable appeal. The first time Elm was away, an envelope had arrived and he'd found out about her test results, and had realized he knew Ashby from college. When he'd called to speak with him, hadn't the man said something about her being exposed to some sort of toxin? Said that's why she'd been sick?

What was to stop her from getting sick again?

Or getting worse?

There had to be a way to get her to visit Ashby's clinic, as she was supposed to have done before Kentucky. As several ideas multiplied in his fertile imagination, Harlan became increasingly inspired with the creative process. By the time he'd brushed his teeth and climbed into bed he had a well-formed picture in progress. And the consequence of that picture afforded him considerable pleasure.

Switching off the lamps, hands clasped behind his neck, he concentrated fully on his new scheme. It was daring, yet so obvious. And so simple he wondered how he hadn't figured it out sooner. If he managed to pull it off, well, then he'd really be in business. Not only would he enjoy the full benefit of Elm's prestige and status, but he wouldn't be encumbered by her presence. He would retain the senator's support, which he'd worried about in the case of a divorce, and be the sole beneficiary of all the financial benefits, too, he realized suddenly. Switching the lamp back on, he gazed at the well-polished antiques that moments before had annoyed him. Suddenly they took on a new aura. They really were quite lovely, now he came to think about it.

Unable to sleep, Harlan rose and paced about the Aubusson-carpeted bedroom. It was still early days, of course. And first he needed to get her back home, before his plan could be implemented. But he already had Ashby in his back pocket, thanks to the man's cocaine habit. And knowing Elm, she wouldn't stay away from her family too long. After that, it was simply a matter of seeing she physically got to the clinic.

With his usual optimism Harlan grinned, glanced at himself in the cheval mirror and gave himself a thumbs-up. It would work. It had to.

It would, he assured himself, be *made* to work.

With a grin, he picked up the phone and dialed Ashby's number. It was never too soon to set matters in motion.

22

The day before Elm's arrival, Johnny was seriously regretting having issued the invitation. It wasn't that he didn't long to see Elm—he did. Almost desperately, in fact.

But now that it was actually happening, he wasn't sure he wanted her *here*.

The past two days had been all bustle. He'd had Maeve and the girls do a thorough spring cleaning. But in the process, they'd managed to dredge up the very reason why he'd never invited a woman to Graney before. When they'd cleared out the cupboard of the room Elm was going to occupy, they came across a stack of Marie Ange's clothes that had never been disposed of. It had felt like a sucker punch, he remembered.

"What'll I do with these, m'lord?" Maeve had asked in her rich brogue, her permed gray hair bobbing around her weather-beaten cheeks. "They're quite old, of course." She lifted a silk blouse and wrinkled her nose. "All good stuff in its time, but frankly the mites have been at them. Look, there're holes here." She pointed. "Maybe I should just put it all out. It might be better," she added, her understanding gray eyes softening.

Johnny, who had been seated in the library, Remus snoozing at his feet while he went over some of the maintenance bills, gazed at the pile of clothes in shock.

Seeing Marie Ange's clothes, a sudden vision of the last time she'd worn that very blouse, the way her eyes had matched the blue in the silk pattern, left him frozen. He pinched the ridge of his nose. God, this was all becoming so damned complicated. Not that her things should be kept like some withering shrine, but how could he throw them out?

"Just leave them there and I'll take a look at them," he said to Maeve at last. "How's the room coming along?"

"Fine, m'lord. We've had an almighty clean, and my goodness, it was necessary. I don't believe that room's had a good airing out for many a year, m'lord. It was time, believe me."

"Yes. Of course it was." He smiled perfunctorily and Maeve went back to her cleaning.

Putting down the calculator, Johnny moved toward the pile of garments strewn on the ottoman. He picked up the blouse and held it close, wondering if there'd be some lingering scent of his wife. But it smelled only of mothballs. With regret, he laid it gently aside and sifted through the pile of skirts, shirts, dresses and pants, each of them conjuring up images he'd believed were long laid to rest.

What on earth was he thinking, bringing Elm here? How could he have forgotten that the room he was planning to put her in stored Marie Ange's extra clothes? And what was he to do with them? Maeve was right. Most of the articles were either moth-eaten or too old and yellowed to be of use to anyone. Still, the thought of tossing them callously into the trash was unbearable. Perhaps they could just be put away in the attic in an old trunk or something, until he got around to dealing with them.

He was about to call Maeve back and give the order when something stopped him. He glanced thoughtfully at Marie Ange's photograph sitting on the desk. He was about to receive another woman into the castle. Not as a guest, but as someone special, someone for whom he had deep feelings. He eyed the clothes uncomfortably, wishing now that he'd invited Elm to the house in St. Barthes, somewhere that was free of memories, free of ghosts and regret.

But it was too late to retract, he realized, suddenly afraid.

Johnny let out a huff. Leaving the clothes in a pile, he left the library, followed by Remus, and made his way across the great hall and upstairs to the room that in a few hours would house its new occupant. He pushed open the door and stopped in the doorway.

The room had been well aired and the four-poster bed made up with freshly scented linen. Wildflowers poured from Waterford crystal vases. The curtains—those looked a bit shabby—were tied back, letting in the morning sun, its light pooling on the muted pattern of the ancient tapestry rug. The newly polished furniture gleamed and the room looked welcoming and bright, despite the ragged brocade on the arm of the chair and the faded dressing table skirt. Some day he would have to take his mother's advice and call in a decorator, he suspected gloomily. Still, the place was in fairly good shape and he'd warned her, hadn't he? Right from the word go, he'd been quite clear about Graney and the discomforts it offered.

He stood a few more moments, wondering what it would be like to see Elm in this room, to undress her here and make love to her. Then he closed his eyes, banishing the images. There was something wrong about the idea, something that left him uneasy. But neither could he face the thought of taking her into his own bedroom, either. That was where Nicky had been conceived, the bed he and Marie Ange had shared so eagerly. It had been a long time, he realized, since he'd thought about any of that. In fact, the whole thing was all rather hazy now. But it was sacred nevertheless. Nicky might be very upset if he knew his father was sleeping in that particular bed with another woman.

Leaving the clothes to take care of themselves, Johnny closed the door carefully, then marched along the corridor and up the winding turret stairs to his lair, where he promptly buried himself in a pile of paperwork, half hoping Elm would call to say she'd missed her flight and changed her mind.

* * *

She hoped she'd brought suitable attire, Elm reflected, remembering the assortment of garments and open Vuitton suitcases strewn on her bed. It had been hard to know what to pack. Should she take elegant, smart and evening, or just casual? Johnny had been vague when she'd asked him what she should bring to Ireland, saying anything would do, a typical male comment and of little help. In the end, she'd opted for a little of each.

Now as the plane landed at Dublin airport, she could hardly contain her excitement. She felt so…free, as if mustering the courage to take this trip had been a test of how far she'd come since learning that her marriage was at an end. She hoped Johnny would never realize how difficult the decision to travel to Ireland had been, not when he'd been so sincere in his desire to be with her, so generous in his offer to let her come to his home and see his world. He'd taken the first big step, the one they both knew might lead to a deeper relationship or end up in tears. She owed it to him to let down her own guard, to prove to herself that what they'd experienced together on the mountain was worth taking a chance on.

She saw his tall, dark figure immediately in the arrival hall and her heart leaped. This was it, she realized. No going back, no last-minute qualms. Then Johnny waved, smiled and moved toward her, and all she could do was stand still and remind herself to breathe.

"Hi." She clutched her handbag and her raincoat and smiled brightly, trying to look at ease.

"Hello. Welcome to Ireland." He dropped a light kiss on her cheek and took her tote bag. "You don't mind doing the rest of the trip by helicopter, do you?"

"Of course not."

"Have a good trip?" he inquired as they walked through the airport.

"Great, thanks."

"Good."

She smiled, masking her disappointment at his rather formal greeting. But of course, they were in public and on his home turf, she reasoned. She could hardly expect the man to throw himself about her neck.

A few minutes later they were walking across the tarmac toward a chopper that glimmered in the morning sunlight. Johnny helped her in and gave the pilot the go-ahead. Soon Elm was gazing down, enchanted by the vista, the lush green fields spreading out below, the occasional fortress, the small villages with whitewashed cottages and winding roads that looked as if they led to never-never land. She let out a sigh of pleasure and took a sidelong look at Johnny. He turned and grinned at her, then looked away. He remained strangely quiet until some fifteen minutes later, when he pointed out the window.

"There it is," he said as they circled Graney Castle and Elm gazed down, enthralled by the medieval fortress below, the Graney flag billowing from its ramparts. Seen from the air it looked absolutely enormous…and rather foreboding. She let out a sigh of anticipation, certainly, and joy at finally being here, but also of apprehension at just what she was getting herself into.

They landed safely on a lawn beyond the castle gates and two young boys came hurrying up to help with the luggage. Johnny and Elm jumped out and the pilot saluted, keeping the engine running.

"It's always fun to fly in. Approaching Graney from the air gives you a better impression of the layout of the place," he remarked as they walked toward the ancient stone ramparts and the chopper took off.

"It's perfectly wonderful," Elm exclaimed, banishing any unease.

Soon they were inside the castle, crossing the great hall, and she was being introduced to Maeve, dressed in her formal housekeeper's outfit of gray skirt, white blouse and cardigan.

Then they mounted the stairs, and after showing Elm her bedroom, Johnny left her to unpack.

* * *

Three days later, cantering with him across lustrous green fields, past peat bogs and grazing sheep munching stolidly under the light spring rain, a gentle west wind blowing in under the old felt hat he had insisted she wear, Elm felt confused and hurt. Since her arrival, Johnny had shown none of the loving affection he'd demonstrated in both Switzerland and Kentucky. It was as though he was a completely different person.

He was still a charming, amusing, perfect host always seeing to her needs. But he was distant and reserved, too, making no attempt at physical contact except when he occasionally took her hand or patted her arm. As for making love to her…well, he hadn't so much as mentioned it, let alone made any moves.

And Elm felt sadly bewildered, his manner leaving her oddly disconcerted. Not that she'd come here looking for a week of constant sex, she thought, feeling herself blush, but that quiet sense of intimacy they'd shared, those moments of mutual discovery, yes, she'd fully expected that—indeed, had believed that was what this week together was all about. Obviously, she couldn't have been further from the truth, she reflected as the horses trotted sedately back toward the castle, visible through the mist. It looked like a remnant of another world.

His world, she reminded herself. A world he clearly wasn't prepared to share. A world she was beginning to regret having entered. Why had he asked her here—even sending her the damn airplane ticket!—if his intention was to treat her like a visitor he was obliged to entertain? She felt ill at ease, unsure of why she was here. Was she a lover, companion or merely a friend? she wondered, annoyance turning slowly into anger. What right did he have to invite her here, make her believe they could make a fresh beginning together, only to treat her like a stranger? Had she suddenly turned unattractive? Had she grown a beard or something?

As they passed the last fence and headed toward the stables, despite her inner turmoil, Elm couldn't fail to appreciate the beauty of the scene. Under different circumstances, it would have been a lovely ride over the moors, under soft, warm spring rain. But here she was, trotting next to the man she'd begun to believe she loved and realizing that she knew not the first thing about him. While he was being so excruciatingly polite she thought she would scream.

Crossly, Elm pulled the old felt hat down farther on her head as the rain increased and followed him into the stables. There they dismounted and Shea came hurrying out of a stall to take the reins.

"She's in good shape," Johnny commented, patting the mare's neck. "Needs regular exercise, though. I'll be taking her out again tomorrow."

"To be sure, m'lord. That'll be fine," Shea agreed in his rich brogue and looped the reins of Elm's mount. "She's a fine lass, she is."

Elm smiled in agreement, thanked him and joined Johnny out in the cobbled courtyard. With its striking center fountain, it was almost French in nature, and she wondered which of the many Graneys she'd been introduced to through the portraits in the gallery had come up with this attractive idea. Perhaps it was one of the wives. She'd seen some fascinating faces, and she wondered what life here was like back then, how those men and women had lived, whether they had been happy or sad or merely indifferent.

Happy, she decided as she fell into step next to Johnny. There was definitely a warm, contented, cheerful energy here, despite the mist and the antiquity of the place and Johnny's sudden lapse into stiff reserve. The castle did not possess that musty, creepy, uncanny feeling she'd sometimes come across in ancient homes. The atmosphere, she decided, sending him a sideward glance, belied the attitude of its owner.

She smothered a sigh. From the moment she'd stepped on to the plane, Elm had been sure this was to be a special week, one that she would cherish, regardless of what the future brought. Now she was beginning to regret every second of it and was seriously considering packing her bags and leaving. She had not, after all, flown all the way across the Atlantic for this. But to give up so easily didn't feel right, either. One thing she was certain of, she decided as they made their way indoors to the cloakroom, either they cleared the air or she'd burst. She would not, she decided, let him maneuver her as she had been maneuvered all these years. And, frankly, that was what it felt like.

Elm marched up the stairs, her anger fanned to a sizzling heat.

"Is something the matter?" Johnny asked blandly once they'd reached the library. Tea awaited them on a large, richly laden tray, set on the leather ottoman before the huge stone fireplace.

"Actually," she said, turning to face him head-on, "there is."

"I'm dreadfully sorry," he replied, frowning and standing straight as a poker by the fire. Very much the lord of the manor, Elm thought, casting him an angry glance. "May I ask what's wrong?"

"Look, Johnny, I shouldn't have to tell you what's wrong," she responded, irritated. "I think you know that yourself." She stood behind the sofa and clasped her hands. She was damned if she was going to feel embarrassed.

"I'm afraid I've no idea," he replied blankly. "Has someone upset you? Is something not to your liking?"

"Yes, something is very much not to my liking." She sent him a brittle smile, arching her brows. "And no, no one has said anything at all. Not one word. Which, in fact, is precisely what's wrong." She slammed both hands on the back of the sofa. "Johnny, I'm sincerely beginning to wonder why you bothered to invite me here in the first place. To show me your horses? To give me a guided tour of your castle?

"In fact," she continued deliberately, "I've been asking

myself just why you went to the trouble of sending me a ticket to join you here, in your home, and furthermore to suggest—unless I read your letter wrong—that what we enjoyed together in the mountain was worth putting to the test, when all you've done since I arrived is avoid me, stick yourself up in that turret with your paperwork—'' she pointed upward ''—or give me Irish history lessons, in which I'm not in the least bit interested.'' She stopped, chest heaving, eyes bright with unshed tears.

''I'm so sorry you feel this way—'' he murmured, taken aback.

''Oh, shut up.'' Elm controlled the desire to slap him. ''What do you take me for? A fool? How dare you bring me here, then treat me in this manner? Was it to test yourself? See whether or not you're finally over your marriage and ready to go forward? Or how well you handle yourself with a woman in your own home? Well, I'm not an experiment. I suppose that now that you've inspected me here, you've decided I don't quite suit. But of course,'' she continued witheringly, ''being the perfect gentleman and host that you are, you would never, ever dream of being so impolite as to tell me the truth, now would you?''

''Elm, this is absurd. I—''

''There's nothing absurd about it,'' she flung, controlling her tears with difficulty. ''You had no right to invite me to come here when you're still all tied up inside dealing with your own ghosts. Why not admit that you just can't move on? That your memories have become a security blanket you're unable to let go? Well, so be it. I'm very sorry if that's the case. But I'm not sticking around while you take the time to sort yourself out.'' She let out a long, ragged breath and dragged shaky fingers through her hair as she composed herself. ''Thanks for the stay—Ireland's lovely— but I didn't come for the weather. I came to be with you. But you're hiding behind a wall, and you won't come out. Your ancestors may have sat around, meek as mice, patiently doing their tapestries until the lord of the manor graciously deigned to honor them with his favors, but I have better things to do with my time than await your bidding. I'm probably just too brash and too American to understand this aristocratic reserve, but I've seen enough of it to know I don't like it, and I'm not putting up with it anymore.''

"Elm, please, I—''

"Don't say anything.'' She lifted her hand to ward him off as he reached for her. "I'll be leaving tomorrow morning. If you would be so kind as to order me a car, I'd be grateful.'' She spun on her heel.

"Elm, this is ridiculous.''

"Yeah? To you, it may seem so. In the meantime, do me a favor and order that car. And you know what?'' She tossed her long blond hair back rebelliously, her anger fuelled. "Order it right away, please. If I leave now, I can reach Dublin in time for an evening flight. I think the sooner I depart, the better it'll be for both of us.''

Slamming the door behind her, she ran up the huge oak stairs, along the corridor, past the empty suits of armor and into her room, where she promptly threw herself on the bed and howled.

23

Standing alone in the library, Johnny stared at the door that was still shaking from Elm's remarkably forceful slam. His first reaction was to follow her upstairs, but something stopped him. He turned and faced the fire, gazing into the flames, and rested his foot thoughtfully on the bronze fireguard, recalling her every word. She was right, he concluded savagely, bringing his fist down on the mantelpiece, nearly upsetting the carriage clock.

He'd no right to bring her here, into his home, when he wasn't one hundred percent certain that he was ready to move on, to leave the past behind him and look toward the future. God, when Maeve brought him Marie Ange's clothes the other day, hadn't he been incapable of doing what needed to be done? No, he'd escaped, allowed them to be packed away in a trunk and sent up to the attic in another pathetic attempt to avoid the truth. Why didn't he just face the fact that Marie Ange was gone? His guilt wasn't going to bring her back, and he needed to forgive himself and move on.

Looking up, Johnny eyed his reflection in the heavy gilt mirror above the fireplace. Had he lived all these years in denial? Was he so afraid of facing the past? What was stopping him from taking what life offered, and living?

Fists clenched, knuckles white and eyes closed, he fought

his inner demons, those beautiful yet painful memories distorted by time and imagination that still had the power to haunt him. Surely he'd suffered enough. And what about Marie Ange? Would she have wanted him to live trapped in time, tied to a long-gone past? He thought suddenly of her laughing blue eyes, her carefree spirit and joyous nature, and realized she would never have wanted him to enshrine her memory. For that was what he'd done all these years—set her up as a sort of protective symbol, an excuse to not face another relationship, too afraid to risk the pain of loss once more.

God, he was nothing but a damn coward, he realized, staring at himself in the mirror. He'd always pretended it was to spare Nicky distress, the pain of seeing someone replace his mother. He'd even persuaded himself he was trying to protect others, as though coming into contact with him would automatically imply a disastrous end. The real truth, he reflected savagely, was that he'd been running from the horrors of his past.

And Lord, he thought, shading a shaking hand over his eyes, how he wanted to stop running.

So what was he really afraid of? Was it just the apprehension of reliving a similar horror? Of knowing love, then experiencing the anguish of having it wrenched so completely from him, leaving a void that nothing could fill? Was that what was stopping him from running up those stairs and telling Elm that what he most wanted was her presence, here in his home? That having her at Graney both frightened and enchanted him? That what was really bothering him was knowing that if he did what he so desperately wanted to do—take her in his arms and love her as never before—that he would have stepped across a line that he could never retreat behind again?

Slowly he turned and walked over to the long mullioned windows behind the large mahogany desk that had been his grandfather's and gazed out, past the thick stone walls that had withstood so many enemies, past the lawn and out to the green fields stretching beyond. For the past fourteen years, he'd assumed Graney Castle would be enough. But now he recognized that his home was incomplete…because he was.

Nicky and he lived here like two bachelors. There was no feminine presence in the place. Having Elm here over the past few days had shown him—quite glaringly—all that was lacking. Did he want to go on living in the shadows, caring only for his horses or the next race, never loving another person or being loved in return? Swallowing, he glanced now at the door, realizing he had to choose. He could walk up those stairs and tell Elm that he needed her more than he could begin to describe. Admit that he craved her presence here, her voice, her scent, her gorgeous hair on his pillow, her body under his. Or, he could lose that chance forever.

For a moment he stood, the silence disturbed only by a fallen log crackling in the grate and Remus's soft snoring and the tumultuous feelings roiling within. There was a choice to be made, right here and now, or it would be too late. If he didn't do something, didn't face himself immediately, Elm would walk out of his life forever. He would close that immense door behind her and perhaps lose the greatest gift he'd ever been offered.

Dragging his hand savagely through his hair, Johnny swore. What a bloody fool he'd been. What a bloody, brainless fool.

Then, in a few quick paces he crossed the library, pulled the door open and, taking the stairs two at a time, mounted the wide staircase. He would not let her go. Whatever the cost, whatever the risks, he would not let her leave without telling her just how much he—

Loved her.

Stopping dead in his tracks, he stared down the corridor. Now, wait a minute. He mustn't let things get out of hand, either. He had feelings, very strong, wonderful feelings churning inside, but… Was that what he was so terribly afraid of? Admitting that he loved her and the possibility that she just might not be ready for all he had to give?

Well, too bad, he thought, half grinning. Now it was too late. Even if he wanted to, he couldn't step back behind the line he'd already unconsciously crossed. His face broke into a broad smile as he walked toward Elm's room with new determination. He felt light-headed, as though a yoke weighing him down for too long had all at once been lifted.

After a tempestuous bout of tears, Elm had risen, rubbed her eyes, blown her nose and thrown her suitcase crossly on the bed. She, who all her life had been meticulously neat and tidy, blindly grabbed silk, cotton and cashmere, tossing her clothes indiscriminately into the case, not giving a damn if they were crushed or tore. All she wanted was out of here, away from this place, from this terrible pain. And she hated Johnny Graney with a passion, she decided, throwing a lifetime of measured feelings and rational responses to the wind. He'd had no right to bring her here under false pretenses, implying that he was ready to give their relationship a chance, then treat her like some—some—formal guest with whom he'd had no closeness, nothing. Why, she could hardly relate him to the man who'd loved her so passionately, so completely, on the mountain or the man who had stared into her eyes with such longing and understanding in Louisville.

She slammed the top of the suitcase down, squeezed in a protruding sweater and the toe of a rebellious shoe, and pulled the zippers closed.

Time to get out of here, she reflected, drawing herself up. She was desperate now to wipe the dust of this place off her feet, to get back to her life—the one she never should have left in the first place. She had priorities, didn't she? What the hell had gotten into her to make her come running as soon as he beckoned? She should have had more self-respect. Well, she'd learned her lesson, she fumed, grabbing her jacket from the hanger and realizing that she'd forgotten to pack her makeup. She just hoped Johnny had ordered the damn car as she'd asked and that she could get the hell out of Dodge. It was bad enough that she'd have to compose herself sufficiently to say goodbye without flying at him and bringing her hand across his odiously handsome cheek. Never before had she experienced such raging, unbridled anger.

Then a knock echoed on the door and she froze.

"Yes?" she called, staring at it woodenly. If he dared to enter, she would not be responsible for her actions.

"May I come in?"

"No, you may not. Is the car ordered?" She planted her hands on her hips. The nerve of the man, the sheer nerve. She supposed now he wanted to smooth things over in his polite, British, well-bred manner. Well, guess what? She'd had a lifetime of being well-bred and hiding her feelings. Enough was enough.

When the door opened and he stepped inside the room, anyway, Elm glared at him. "How dare you come in here? Get out. All I asked was that you order the car. Surely that was sufficiently clear?"

"We need to talk. I've made a terrible mistake."

"Oh, really? What a shame."

"Elm, please." He held up his hand. "You have every right to be angry, every right. All I can ask is that you hear me out."

"Why should I?"

"Because…" He threw up his hands, then let them drop. "No reason," he admitted, jaw tightening. "There is absolutely no earthly reason why you should listen to what I have to say. Still, I'd like you to all the same." He lifted his eyes to hers, pleading with her to take this one last step.

"Did you order the car?" she countered, turning toward the window.

"No. I won't until you've heard me out."

"In other words, you're blackmailing me."

"Not at all. If you don't wish to hear what I have to say, then I'll go and call one immediately. But please, Elm, give me one more chance. I don't deserve it, I've been a fool and an idiot, I know, but I need to explain some things."

"What's so important now that you couldn't have told me before?" she replied, keeping her back turned.

"That you're right. All of what you said downstairs was one hundred percent true."

"So you're not ready to let go of the past?"

"I wasn't. I think in the last fifteen minutes or so, I've finally had a reality check. All at once everything became so clear to me."

"Well, hip-hip hooray." She sent a withering glance over her shoulder. "I'm ready to go now."

"Please don't be cynical," he pleaded. "I mean every word I'm saying to you. Yes, I was still tied to Marie Ange, to her ghost, to everything I thought—wanted—to believe she still meant to me. It was only when you stormed from the library that I was able to see clearly, understand that I've been hiding from the truth. My life has moved on. I just wasn't willing to acknowledge it. I'm so scared of hurting someone else by—" He dropped his hands, shook his head.

"Johnny—" she turned to face him "—you're hurting me right now. You've hurt me more during the past three days than Harlan did in twelve years of marriage."

"I know. I'm so sorry. But please don't leave. Elm, I never meant to hurt you. Quite the opposite. I thought if I showed you just how much I truly care that I would be harming you more. I desperately want you here, in my life. I can't begin to tell you just how much."

He was moving toward her now, unable to stay still, needing to feel her close to him.

"Don't you dare touch me," she said angrily, backing until she was cornered against the flowered wallpaper. "It's over. I don't want to talk to you or see you ever again, is that understood? Let me—" She caught her breath as he reached out, his eyes never leaving hers, and touched her cheek.

"Don't," she exploded, but her voice was cracking. "Just go away and leave me alone. Haven't you humiliated me enough as it is?" She made as though to push him off, slapped both her palms against his chest.

"Elm, my darling Elm, I'm so sorry, I didn't mean to humiliate or hurt you, I—"

"Well, you did. And that's just fine. At least this way we know exactly where we stand."

He stood over her now, gazing down into her eyes with that same intense expression she'd learned to know and love so well. For a moment her heart flinched. Then anger reasserted itself and she pushed hard. "Stop it," she hurled, "stop trying to play whatever game it is you play with women, and leave me be."

"I'm not playing games." His arms came about her, fighting her resistance, forcing her body close until she was crushed in his arms. Then, as she was about to protest, yell at him to leave her alone, his mouth came down on hers, replacing words with passion.

Elm's head reeled. She struggled but knew that already she'd lost the battle. As his lips moved over hers, his hands squeezed her to him and she felt the hard response of his body grinding into her, her own body flaring to life.

He half dragged her to the bed. She heard her suitcase tumbling to the floor as they fell onto the covers. Then they struggled, not with each other, but with buttons and zippers and all the other bits of apparel keeping them apart.

Desperation pushed him, the intense, primeval need to enter her, possess her, make her his. He kissed her shoulders, heard her sigh, and felt a rush of victory, sheer male triumph spearing through him as he feasted on her breasts then moved on down, hands seeking the sinuous, hauntingly familiar curves of her slim body.

Then, with one sharp thrust he entered her, caught her gasp as he plunged deep within her, felt the hot damp heat of her encircling him. He couldn't have pulled back now even had he wanted to. He was too far gone for that, too far beyond the realm of his own desires to do anything more than give way to the savage need—too long denied—to love her, a feverish delight laced with glorious anguish, a primitive need to possess entirely. And know that at last he was home.

Elm surrendered and allowed her body to follow his in a marvelous, enchanting rhythm, each thrust bringing her closer to the peak, to the exhilarating fulfillment she'd known only with him, that made her feel whole.

And together they rose in a never-ending spiral, riding wave upon wave, reaching farther and farther, until at last their eyes met and together they drowned in a sea of completion, bodies saturated and spent, entwined in a tangle of covers and contentment.

Five days later Elm stood on the lawn, Johnny's arm wrapped around her, as they watched the chopper approach. Their quarrel seemed a lifetime away, so much had transpired since, a new level of intimacy and closeness acquired that had nothing and everything to do with their lovemaking afterward. The answer, she realized, swallowing, had been his sudden and real understanding, his true desire to let down the barriers he'd erected so long ago and take a risk. And she loved him for it. For seeking the courage and taking the step, one she realized, looking up at him as the chopper prepared to land, that couldn't have been easy.

Neither was leaving.

In five days, she felt as though she'd been here five months. So much had been said, shared, given and taken. There had been no actual plan or commitment set for the future, but a tacit understanding reigned that required no words, merely the awareness that a future together, whenever that future might be, was a fact they both desired, accepted and mutually rejoiced in.

"Better get going," Johnny remarked above the whir of the engines as the chopper waited several feet away. "Promise you'll ring me as soon as you reach Savannah?"

"Of course," she replied, grateful for his strong arms as he steadied her against a sudden gust of wind.

"I won't rest till I know you're back safely," he shouted above the noise of the engine.

"Don't worry, it's just a quick stopover in Atlanta, then back on home." She smiled as he picked up her case and her bag, thinking how wonderful it was to suddenly know such caring, such concern on her behalf. Then, ducking, they hurried to the chopper. The pilot took her bags and she turned, flinging her arms around his neck. "I'm going to miss you so much," she whispered in his ear.

"Me, too, my darling, you have no idea."

They held each other tight, eyes closed, for several seconds. Then Johnny dropped a firm kiss on her lips and took her hand to help her climb in.

Elm's last view of Graney Castle was of Johnny waving and blowing kisses, Remus next to him and Maeve at the window of the turret, waving a feather duster.

When the castle was nothing more than a speck in the distance, she settled back, trying to sort through the riotous tumult of thoughts and emotions, attempting to put into perspective all that had transpired since her arrival here eight days earlier.

She had come to Graney filled with anxious expectations, had suffered disappointment, rage and humiliation. Then in the next breath it had all changed, turned right around, transformed into the most precious time of her life.

Elm let out a little sigh of contentment. She was sad at having to leave, but happy in the knowledge that soon—very soon—they would surely be together again. Then, once her own hurdles were behind her, they could begin to look toward the future, toward all that had been said in each touch and each look—a tacit bond forged between them that, she hoped, would last forever.

Part IV

24

The decision to see Ashby, to fit the visit into her schedule on her return flight from New York, made sense, Elm decided. For although she'd felt perfectly well during the stay in Ireland, the fact remained that she'd been feeling nauseous on and off just before the trip. The sooner she found out the cause of the annoying ailment and remedied it, the better.

Now, seated comfortably in Ashby's waiting room—which looked more like a stylish penthouse library than a medical clinic—Elm was pleased that the staff had gone out of its way to accommodate her tight schedule. They'd managed to fit her in during her layover in Atlanta, and had promised to help her get a car back to the airport in time for her flight to Savannah.

As she waited to see the doctor, Elm continued to do what she'd done for the whole of her flight across the Atlantic: daydream about the latter half of her trip to Ireland, the glorious, blissful days shared with Johnny once he'd finally faced the gremlins of his past. She experienced a rush of satisfaction and happiness, certain that their relationship—for she could finally admit to herself that they had one—now had a chance to flourish. Gazing blindly past the large ikebana flower arrangement and magazines gracing the table in the center of the room, she allowed herself to wonder what a future with Johnny might be like.

She sighed, flipped a page of the magazine she was pretending to read. This was something she hadn't experienced before—being an equal partner in the relationship, being cherished and cocooned but also respected as her own person. Clearly, it wasn't just Johnny whose inner demons were being overcome. Little by little over the past few days, Elm had learned what it was like to be free of the fear that she somehow didn't measure up. For Johnny had treated her with respect as well as affection—and this attitude was obviously just an ingrained part of his being. What a rare gift he was turning out to be.

She flipped another page and gazed through it, seeing instead Graney Castle, Johnny and that new unguarded expression in his eyes that meant so much to her. But she realized, with a rueful smile, those walls would have to be permanently surmounted for this to work.

And there was still the election to get through and then the final dissolution of her marriage, she remembered, wishing it were otherwise—but even that didn't seem nearly as daunting anymore. She felt as though Johnny's love underlined and assured the new being she was gradually becoming. She'd truly changed, she realized with pride, transformed herself from a tentative, almost sheltered woman into one who was self-confident and independent, sure of her actions and desires, and replete with a delicious sensation of inner security and peace she'd never known before. That Johnny could love and accept this new woman served as a confirmation of how far she'd come. Nothing, simply nothing could come between her and the wonderful new sense of awareness that was hers.

"Mrs. MacBride, Dr. Ashby will see you now." The receptionist smiled.

"Thank you." Elm rose and followed the young woman along the corridor, covered in cream carpet. She glanced at the attractive watercolors gracing the walls, enjoyed the soft background of classical music. Today, she thought with a smile, she was prepared to like everything. Even the hassle of taking another blood sample seemed insignificant when so much was right with her world.

The receptionist turned the brass handle of a white, double-paneled door and Elm stepped inside.

"Mrs. MacBride." Doctor Ashby rose, stepped out from behind his large mahogany desk and shook her hand. He was a good-looking man, tallish, with brown hair graying at the temples. He was even-featured and gray-eyed, and had the kind of physique that went well with his profession, gave one confidence, she reflected.

"I'm very pleased you've finally come in, Mrs. Mac-Bride." The doctor settled behind his desk while Elm sat opposite. "I really must get more samples from you. The first ones were…well, a little concerning." He frowned, looking over the file. "Shall we get on with that right away? Then we can chat afterward." He smiled professionally. "The technicians will run your tests immediately so that we can compare the results to the first lot."

"Fine." Elm smiled and rising, followed him next door to a small exam room, where she lay down and extended her arm. The nurse entered, saying hello as she prepared the syringe, and Elm turned away. She didn't like watching the needle enter her arm.

A few minutes later they were done. She pulled down the sleeve of her silk sweater, climbed to her feet and returned with Ashby to his office. She was surprised he'd decided to stay by her side; most doctors would have left her alone with the nurse. She found that reassuring.

"Now, Mrs. MacBride, it will just take a short while to run the tests. If you wait here, Lucy can fetch you a coffee."

"Oh, don't bother, I'm fine, thanks. I've been drinking coffees all the way across the Atlantic."

"You were traveling?"

"Yes." She would have elaborated and told him she'd just returned from Ireland, but then realized she'd feel like a truant; Ashby had been needling her to come in for some time now. Leaving Elm comfortably seated with a stack of magazines at her side, the doctor excused himself to oversee the progress of her blood tests.

Elm looked up when Dr. Ashby returned, surprised to see his expression was unusually grave. She experienced a twinge of anxiety as he sat down again behind his desk, put on his glasses and appeared to be comparing the present results with the past ones. Was her blood sugar too low, or her cholesterol too high?

"Is something the matter, Doctor?" she finally asked, breaking the silence.

"Mrs. MacBride, I'm afraid there is." Ashby looked up, laid down his glasses and sent her a penetrating gaze across the desk. "I hate to be the bearer of bad tidings, my dear, but I have to warn you that these results confirm my initial misgivings."

"But what's wrong?" Elm sat on the edge of her chair, legs tightly crossed, fiddling nervously with the clasp of her purse.

"I thought it must be impossible," he murmured, glancing again at the sheaf of papers before him, "but I'm afraid this second batch of results mirror the first."

"Mirror what?" she asked, barely able to contain her impatience.

"Well, I can't actually substantiate this, it's not a confirmed diagnosis, you understand. Your condition is extremely rare. In fact, in my twenty-year career, I've only had two other patients who exhibited the same symptoms and blood profile."

"What are you trying to say, Doctor?" Elm asked, trying to contain a rising feeling of hysteria. "Please speak plainly."

"It would appear—and of course, I can't confirm this without further testing—that you have a highly evolved strain of an uncommon degenerative disease of the nervous system, Mrs. MacBride. It's barely known in this country, and I'm possibly the only doctor in the nation who's even encountered it in a clinical setting. In my experience, if not treated immediately and radically, I'm afraid—'' He looked straight at her, eyes filled with concern.

"Afraid of what?" she urged.

"That it could be fatal," he responded quietly.

"Fatal?" she echoed, sure she couldn't have heard correctly. This couldn't be happening. "What do you mean, a degenerative disease? What is it called?"

"We know very little about it. I must ask you to enter the clinic immediately for further testing so that we can—hopefully—arrest the evolution of the illness."

"Hopefully?" Elm repeated blankly.

"Yes. You're lucky Dr. Philips sent you here, since I've seen two similar cases in my care."

"And—and what happened to them?" she asked, dreading the answer.

He paused. "I'm afraid they didn't survive."

Elm swallowed a gasp and reeled. This man was telling her she might die.

"But of course, they were diagnosed at a much later stage," he continued quickly. "Your case is different. I have great hope that if we begin treatment immediately, there is a very high chance we can cure you."

"But I feel fine," Elm protested. "I haven't experienced any of the symptoms again. In fact, I've never felt better, I—"

"Unfortunately, this can be a treacherous disease. You may have been feeling better, but your actual condition has been deteriorating. If I compare the results taken in November with these—" he lifted the file and frowned "—there's a substantial difference, Mrs. MacBride, and I'm sad to say it's not for the better."

"Oh, my God." Elm clenched her hands, still unable to assimilate what he was saying. She wanted to tell him to shut up, to stop lying, that there was absolutely nothing wrong with her, that she was finally in love and that made her invincible. Instead she smothered her gnawing fear. "What...what do you suggest, Doctor?" She felt as though a noose was encircling her neck, a trap door closing behind her. This was unreal, couldn't be happening. Not to her, not now. Not when she finally was waking up to life, had tasted her first measure of true happiness.

"I must strongly recommend you to enter the clinic immediately. If we don't waste any more time, we may be able to stop the disease's progression. I can't guarantee anything, I'm afraid, but I can assure you that you'll be in the best possible hands. My staff is outstanding and our clinic is considered one of the finest in the country. Much of what we do here is experimental, of course—it has to be, because we're often working with conditions for which there are no known cures. Our treatments range from traditional medicine to homeopathy, osteopathy, acupuncture and other non-Western disciplines. Over the years I've pursued knowledge and treatment modalities wherever I could—and as a result, I've developed quite a range of cures," he finished proudly.

"Oh, yes, I'm sure. It's just…how can I enter the clinic immediately? I need to go home, I have so much to do, I—"

"Mrs. MacBride," Dr Ashby interrupted and getting up, leaned against the desk close to her and took her hand. "I know this has come as a terrible shock to you. If only you'd come in sooner, when I asked you to, we would have had a better chance at nipping this thing in the bud. Time is still on our side. But only just. I can't help you if you won't allow me to. I'll need your full cooperation. And that means trusting my judgment implicitly, Mrs. MacBride, believing in what we're about to undertake." He looked at her intently, increased the pressure on her fingers. "And right away. Not tomorrow or the day after. We must begin at once."

Elm nodded numbly. Her mouth was dry. She couldn't swallow and an icy chill ran down her spine. He was right, of course. If she indeed was so very ill, then of course she must take his advice and begin the treatment immediately. Oh, God. She thought suddenly of Johnny, of her father, of Aunt Frances, of Gio and Meredith, and a knot rose in her throat. She wanted to rage, to slam her fist into something. Instead she battled back the hot, rebellious tears charging to the surface. How could she tell Johnny? How could she break the news to him? It wasn't fair, wasn't right.

She finally managed to swallow. "I—I guess I'd better make some calls," she said, barely recognizing her own tremulous voice.

"I wouldn't worry about that right now, Mrs. MacBride. We'll be happy to contact your family on your behalf. First we must get you settled in your room. Is your suitcase with you?"

"Just my hand luggage. The rest went straight through to Savannah."

"We can provide anything you might need. I'll see that one of our best rooms is made ready for you." Ashby squeezed her hand and returned behind the desk, where he lifted the phone and spoke into it.

Elm sat motionless. Her head spun. How could this have happened? Why hadn't she known, felt something? Didn't people have intuition when they became terminally ill, know deep inside that something was wrong? And where was God? Where was that God she'd heard so damn much about all her life? The all-forgiving, generous being so dedicated to her well-being? Where the hell was he right now? Certainly not anywhere close. He had abandoned her in her hour of need. She controlled herself with difficulty, battled the urge to get the hell out of this clinic and run back to Johnny's healing arms.

The next few minutes went by in a haze as she followed the nurse out of Ashby's office and through the building to the clinic next door, where they checked her in. Another nurse came and helped her up to an elegant room. The nurse wanted to help her undress—as though she were incapable of doing so herself—but she refused. She was not ill, not an invalid.

Yet.

Then she turned and stared at the hospital bed and instantly recoiled from it. She didn't want to get in it, didn't want to be ill, didn't want to die.

She felt suddenly dizzy and clutched the rail. *My God.* It

was coming back. The symptoms were beginning again, the dizziness, the weakness; soon the nausea would follow. She swayed on the balls of her feet, then collapsed onto the bed as the nurse came back in the room.

"I need to give you this injection, Mrs. MacBride."

"What is it?" Elm asked weakly. She wanted to call Johnny but didn't know if she could face it right now, needed a few minutes on her own to calm down. She eyed the needle with misgiving. This was all so crazy, all happening so fast.

"It's just a mild sedative before we set up your IV to deliver the first dose of antidotes. I don't know if Dr. Ashby told you anything about the medication you'll be taking?"

"No, he didn't."

"Oh, well, I'm sure he'll be up in a little. Now, if you'll allow me." She lifted the needle and smiled. "This won't hurt."

Elm lay back and closed her eyes reluctantly, felt the tiny nip of the needle in her arm. A few seconds later her head began to swim and the room spun. She tried to speak, to protest, tell the woman she didn't want to sleep, that she needed to speak to Johnny, that—

Then her eyes closed and there was only darkness.

"Good job," Harlan exclaimed, his face bursting into a wide grin. Finally the tables had turned and luck was smiling his way. About time, too. This was working out much better than even he could have dreamed of. Elm was already in the clinic, sedated and isolated and undergoing treatment. He leaned back and let out a contented sigh. It just proved that all good things came to him in the end. "I'll be over there tomorrow morning," he said, cradling the phone next to his shoulder. "Make sure you keep her knocked out. I want no contact with the outside, understood?"

"Are you sure you want to go through with this, Harlan?" Ashby asked uneasily. "You can't possibly have thought through all the ramifications. I don't think this is such a good idea. You could damage your career—"

"Trust me. I know what I'm doing. And you won't regret it. What was the estimate you gave for the new wing of the clinic? Seven million?"

"Yes," Ashby answered irritably. "But just remember that prolonged ingestion of this stuff can have long-term effects, such as tachycardia and liver damage—and that's if she's lucky. This isn't something that can be used indefinitely."

"Don't worry, it won't get to that. I just need your help until the primary. After that, we'll be fine."

"Okay," he agreed reluctantly, "but if anything goes wrong, I want my name kept out of it."

"Fine. No problem. I'll be visiting regularly, we'll discuss it."

"And we're going to do this on my schedule," Ashby insisted. "We can't move too fast or there'll be questions."

"Don't worry about a thing. Oh, and by the way, you'll be receiving a check for part of the amount for the new wing by the end of the week. As for the rest, we'll see how well you do."

Ashby set down the phone and leaned back, trying to ignore the fact that what he was doing went against everything he believed in. If they weren't careful, well… He'd need to balance the mix in the drip just enough to make her convincingly ill without causing any irreversible damage. He didn't like it, though, not one little bit. Not that MacBride had left him a choice, he thought bitterly. Still…he leaned his chin thoughtfully on his palm and visualized the new wing he'd long dreamed of. He already had architects working on the plans. Plus, if he kept Mrs. MacBride as sedated as she was now, then she wouldn't feel as much discomfort from the side effects of the treatment. Yes, he decided, glad he'd thought of it; that was the ethical thing to do.

Harlan put down the phone and rubbed his hands gleefully. He wasn't loath to letting the process build up, or keeping Ashby in the dark about his real plans; the more time it took, the longer he'd have to prepare the electorate for his next role. When was that interview he had on FOX? Marcy would know. It was the perfect place to start hinting at something. Not too much, just enough to get public opinion intrigued.

And of course, the lobby of the clinic might prove a perfect platform for a press conference. He could already see himself, haggard and distraught, giving daily briefs on Elm's deteriorating health.

It was a glorious vision.

He stood up, eyed the cabinet, and then thought better of it. He didn't need anything to give him a high today—he already felt on top of the world.

He wandered to the French doors and stepped out into the small garden that Elm had laid out so beautifully. He would keep it all the same, like a sort of shrine. He could imagine people coming here to the house—*his* house—glancing sadly at the beautiful silver-framed pictures of her placed strategically throughout. He would entertain. Not lavishly at first, of course; in fact, right after her death he'd need to tone things down for a while, just do his duty, get through the first few months and lead the sober existence of a grieving widower. But little by little, he'd be encouraged. His friends—even the senator—would insist that he put an end to the grieving, that he leave the past behind him and look toward a new future. His electorate deserved no less.

And little by little he'd agree, give in to their insistence. There would be intimate dinner parties where slowly he would open up to his friends about her, how much he missed her, what an empty life it was without her.

No one would guess that he considered her death to be the day of his liberation.

He sighed with satisfaction. Finally it had begun. He'd reached the turning point. From now on it would be a smooth run from here to the Senate—for, of course, Hathaway would retire after Elm's death—and then on to the White House.

Harlan straightened up. The first thing he had to do was call Judge Wetherspoon, tell him in confidence that Elm was gravely ill, but please not to tell anyone. That would ensure the rumor got about.

"Ha!" He let out a harsh laugh and smacked his thigh. It was brilliance. Sheer, fucking brilliance.

On that happy note Harlan turned back inside and set about composing himself for the upcoming meeting with his father-in-law. He'd have to break the sad news to the family. It would be a challenge to act all upset when he was beside himself with joy. But he could do it. That was one of his great gifts—the ability to be a reflection of the emotion around him. Elm's family would be devastated by her illness, and thus, in their company, he would intuitively absorb their grief and project it back at them.

He was like Clinton in that way, he reflected proudly. He'd feel their pain—even though he'd be joyful inside.

"In the hospital?" Frances, sitting in the Queen Anne chair in the corner of her brother's drawing room, frowned at Harlan and lowered her reading glasses.

"What's wrong with her?" the senator asked anxiously. "I know she had those tests run back in the fall, but I thought she'd recovered in Switzerland, that all that was over and done with."

"Unfortunately not, sir. Elm underwent a new set of tests at the clinic in Atlanta today." Harlan looked grave and his hand shook as he spoke. "I'm afraid it's—it's rather more serious than we thought, sir."

"What do you mean? What's wrong with her?" George Hathaway faced his son-in-law anxiously. "Tell me what's going on, Harlan. I need the truth."

"Well, sir, from what I could gather from the doctor, it might be a rare degenerative disease that attacks the central nervous system."

"What?"

"A degenerative disease?" Frances chipped in, needlework poised on her knee, eyes narrowed.

"Yes."

"My poor little girl," the senator muttered, pacing the

living room. "We'd better get to Atlanta right away. This is dreadful, simply dreadful." He looked pale and drawn, as though he had aged ten years in the past few minutes. "You did the right thing to come here at once, Harlan. What else did the doctor say? I want his number. I'll call him right away."

"I understand your desire to speak with him, sir, but Dr. Ashby feels it's best that he communicate with me, and I can deliver the information to you and the family. That way, he can spend his time focusing on Elm's treatment. As for visiting her, he said she needs to be kept very quiet for the first few days. No visitors, complete rest. Of course, I told him I was coming over there, regardless of what he said. After all, Elm's my wife." He straightened his shoulders, looked up defiantly.

"Your determination reflects well on you, Harlan," the senator replied, settling heavily into his favorite chair, "but if the doctor feels it would be better to leave her be, then we should respect his judgment."

"He's agreed to give me a few minutes tomorrow morning. Dr. Ashby understands that I'm desperate to check in on her. I'm just so grateful Elm's in the best possible hands."

"Who is this Ashby?" Frances asked. "I've never heard of him."

"His clinic has a worldwide reputation," Harlan responded patiently.

"But has she been to see someone else? Are they getting a second opinion? After all, if it's so serious, there should be a team of specialists on board," Frances argued.

Trust the old bitch to try to put a spoke in his wheel. But instead of allowing his anger to show, he shook his head sadly and threw up his hands. "I don't know any more than you do, Aunt Frances. But Ashby, thank God, is the top man in the country. This has been such a shock, so unexpected. I'm as flummoxed as you. Hopefully I'll be able to tell you more tomorrow, have a better idea of all that's going on. But I'm sure if there's anyone or anything that can be brought in to help Elm, Dr. Ashby will be the first to recommend it.''

"Quite right," the senator agreed. "I'll call Jim Halibut in Washington and get him to tell me who the best people are. He'll know about this disease, I'm sure. I'll have him call this Ashby fellow and get a full report."

"Don't you think we should wait and see how Elm reacts to the treatment first?" Harlan said, his tone persuasive. "Let's give the man a chance. After all, in a few days she may be feeling much better and we would have bothered Dr. Halibut for nothing."

"Well, I suppose we could wait a couple of days," the senator agreed reluctantly, "but no more. If this—" he waved his hand "—this degenerative nerve thing is really serious, then the sooner she's in the best hands, the better."

"Oh, she's in the best hands, all right, sir. The first thing I did was to research Ashby, and the consensus is that he's one of the top neurologists in the country. People come from all over for treatments in his experimental clinic." Harlan regretted the word the moment he'd spoken.

"Experimental?" The senator frowned, his bushy eyebrows coming together over the ridge of his patrician nose. "I don't want my daughter being used as a guinea pig."

"No, sir, that would be outrageous. But apparently Ashby's renowned for his extraordinary contributions in his field."

"I see. Well, that's good. Very good. Isn't it, Frances?" George Hathaway turned to his sister for reassurance.

"Hmm. I would imagine it must be," she said guardedly.

What was the old bitch getting at? Harlan wondered, eyeing her dolefully. She was one of the few people who'd proved utterly impervious to his charm and it annoyed him to no end. She was also Elm's confidant and had made it clear she didn't trust him. He'd be willing to bet that she knew exactly where Elm had been hiding this past week. Well, no use in turning over old stones. Right now Elm was exactly where he wanted her, and if he had his way, she wouldn't be leaving there anytime soon.

He glanced at his watch. "I have to be going, sir. I'll fly into Atlanta first thing in the morning and keep you posted."

"Very well, Harlan. But don't you think I'd better come along, make sure she's all right?"

"No, Dr. Ashby was very clear on that. Elm needs absolute rest and quiet. Trust me, sir, I'll do everything I have to to make sure Elm is taken care of as she should be," Harlan reassured him.

The beautiful part of that last phrase, he reflected as he walked out the door, was its truth.

He would make sure Elm got exactly what she deserved.

His exhilaration and excitement was such that it took a moment to remember to let his shoulders droop and walk head bowed until he got into the car, certain that dearest Aunt Fran was watching him from behind the living room curtains.

She didn't realize whom she was messing with, he reflected with a surge of satisfaction. If she weren't careful, he just might teach her a lesson, too.

Why hadn't she phoned? Johnny wondered, nervously pouring himself a nightcap from one of the Waterford decanters on the silver tray on the lowboy next to the library's empty fireplace. Surely she should have arrived in Savannah by now? Perhaps the flight had been delayed, or she couldn't get a connection.

He shrugged and sat down on the well-worn sofa where he'd enjoyed such delightful evenings with Elm, watching old movies and sharing quiet confidences. He eyed the room despondently. The place felt so empty without her, as though an essential part of it was missing. He sipped the whiskey slowly and absently kneaded Remus's neck. Perhaps he could rearrange his schedule and pop over to the States to see her before the big English races began. Frankly, he didn't know how long he was going to last out. After all, it was only hours since she'd left and he missed her like the devil.

He took a brief glance at the day's papers, then, draining

his glass, decided to go to bed. She had probably decided it was too late to call and would ring tomorrow once she'd settled back at the plantation. He was sure there must be a perfectly reasonable explanation for her silence. But as he walked slowly up the stairs with Remus, he couldn't subdue his growing anxiety.

Now, stop it, he commanded himself. He must put an immediate end to this paranoia, this conviction that something dreadful would happen to her simply because she was out of his sight. Just because Marie Ange had suffered a horrible fate didn't mean that every woman who crossed his path was subject to the same, he reasoned while he undressed and got ready for bed. Then he picked up the phone once just to check that it was working properly. Getting into bed, he read for a while, taking in little of the book. Several hours passed before he finally managed to let go the niggling unease troubling him and get to sleep.

"Mom, come and look," Zach, Meredith's nine-year-old son, called out. "It's Uncle Harlan on TV."

"Oh? So what's new," she muttered, popping a last nibble of toast into her mouth and moving from the kitchen into the den. "Are you two ready for school? Mick, where's your backpack?"

"Mom, look, it's that *FOX & Friends* show you sometimes watch."

Meredith stopped in front of the television, her eyes suddenly narrowed. It was Harlan, all right, but God, he looked awful. Frankly, knowing how meticulous he was about his appearance, she was surprised he'd gone before the cameras looking so pale and haggard.

"Mom, I can't find my sneaker," Mick complained, dragging the pair on the floor.

"Shush, let me listen."

"But I can't find—"

"Will you please be quiet?" Meredith picked up the remote control and upped the volume.

"It's been a terrible shock to all of us, of course," Harlan was saying, "but we know she's getting the best care possible. No, I'm afraid we don't know how things will progress," he said, answering the newscaster's question with a sad shake of his head, "or when she'll be out of here. At this stage it's in God's hands."

Meredith listened, frowning, as the commentator closed out the interview, explaining that they'd been talking with Harlan MacBride, the popular young congressman from Savannah, who would soon be introducing a bill proposing increased federal funding for research into rare diseases. Congressman MacBride's wife, the commentator recapped, had recently been diagnosed with a rare and possibly fatal neurological illness.

"What the hell is going on?" Meredith exclaimed, grabbing the kids' stuff. "Come on, guys, I have to run to the office early. I'll drop you off on the way."

"But my sneaker—"

"Wear the blue ones, Mick, but please hurry," Meredith begged, already punching in numbers on her cell phone while snatching up lunch boxes.

Half an hour later, she was sitting in Senator Hathaway's living room, where Frances, the senator and Doc Philips were assembled.

"Just what did those blood tests show, Doc?" Meredith asked, worried, while accepting Beau's offer of coffee.

"Well, frankly, the blood work was hard to interpret. Besides low potassium and sodium levels, the results showed unexpected electrolyte imbalances that were inconsistent with Elm's level of fitness and health. Given her other symptoms—the loss of balance, the occasional nausea and muscle weakness—I thought there might be neurological indications, which is why I sent her results to Ashby in the first place. He has a great reputation."

"But if she's so sick, why did the symptoms take so long to reemerge?" Meredith questioned. "I mean, it doesn't make sense. She was fine in Switzerland, fine in Ireland—she sounded great."

"Ireland?" The senator looked at her, surprised. "Elm was in Ireland?"

"Uh, only for a short visit," she said hurriedly, meeting Aunt Frances's eyes and quickly changing the subject. "When I spoke with her a couple of days ago, she'd never sounded better," Meredith finished. "I tried to call her this morning after I spoke with you, but her phone was off and they wouldn't put me through to her room. Something about not receiving any calls."

"Well, she probably needs the rest right now. These things can come on in a hurry and be fairly debilitating, I guess," Doc Philips said, shaking his head. "She must have been in some kind of remission. Also, Ashby hinted this morning that Elm has been rather irresponsible—said she'd put off getting the second set of tests, despite his warnings that she needed to come in. A pity. I asked him to copy me on all the results. I expect I'll have them in the next day or so."

"Excellent. That way we can send them to Halibut immediately and get his take," the senator agreed, pacing the floor, his face worried. "I don't know what to do. Harlan was here last night. He told me—and so did Ashby, by the way—that the clinic isn't allowing Elm any visitors. They believe total peace and quiet will speed her recovery. But I don't know. I want to see my daughter," he complained, eyeing Meredith. "I want to know exactly what's going on."

"Me, too." Meredith hesitated, then decided to say what was on her mind. "Did you see Harlan on a talk show, Uncle George? I thought it was absurd—him discussing Elm's illness in such a public forum. She would hate it if she thought everyone knew she was sick. She's very private about these things."

"Talk show? No, when was that?" the senator asked, taken aback.

"Oh, about an hour ago. It was on FOX. I was quite surprised. He seemed very distraught, almost as though—" She cut herself off, caught Aunt Frances's eye and held it.

Neither of them liked Harlan. This latest episode—using Elm's illness to benefit his own ends—was a typical example of why. But the last thing needed right now was more fuel on the fire.

"Harlan was on FOX?" The senator stopped in front of Meredith. "He should have alerted me."

"Yes, on the morning show. He was explaining about Elm's absence, that she was ill."

"I see." The senator looked over her head out into the courtyard, where a cast-iron dolphin fountain spouted next to the lily pond. Meredith read the conflict in his eyes and heard him sigh, his natural desire to preserve Elm's privacy battling with the indisputable truth: that her illness provided excellent exposure for Harlan. She watched him turn, his white linen suit immaculately starched and pressed, his bow tie straight as a chloroformed butterfly, and felt slightly sick.

"I feel strongly about this, Uncle George. I'm a close friend of the family, besides being Elm's attorney. I think we should have the right to see her, even it's only for a short visit."

"Perhaps we should take the doctor's advice, just for the moment," Frances said finally. Meredith watched the older woman carefully, and could tell she wasn't altogether happy about the decision, had weighed her words before replying.

"Okay," she answered reluctantly. "If it's in Elm's best interest to spend a few days without being disturbed, then so be it." But God, it seemed so damned inappropriate that Harlan, the one person Elm was farthest from right now, should have access to her merely because he was still legally her spouse.

"Right." The senator nodded. "We'll be in touch, Merry Bell. Let's give it forty-eight hours before we make any decisions and take it from there."

"Okay." Meredith let out a resigned sigh. "I need to get going. I have to be in court in half an hour." She rose, crossed the room and dropped a kiss on Aunt Frances's soft white cheek. "I'll give you a call later," she murmured, out of the senator's hearing.

Frances silently acquiesced.

"Goodbye, Uncle George. I just hope Elm will be fine and we'll discover this is nothing but a scare. Don't hesitate to phone me if there's anything I can do to help. And, please, let me know what your doctor friend at Bethesda says about those results. I've got this gut feeling those are going to be important."

"As soon as they arrive, I'll do just that." He gripped her shoulder and smiled. "You're a good girl, Merry, but stop worrying. I'm sure Elm's going to pull out of this. My best to Tom and the boys." Then he walked her out across the marble hall and Beau opened the front door.

"Good day, Miss Meredith." His old face crinkled into a frown. "How's Miss Elm, ma'am?"

"She'll be fine, Beau. Not to worry. You take good care of the folks here, won't you?" She smiled and hurried down the steps and out to her car.

As she got in, her cell phone beeped. It was Mel. She frowned, trying to guess at what he might want. Oh, yes, that article he wanted to run on the Mogachee processing plant. He was worried that the paper might get sued.

Reaching to turn the key in the ignition, her hand stilled. Something wasn't right. At what level, she didn't quite know yet. Mel had gathered information about a disturbing rise in hospital admissions among people living in a roughly three-mile perimeter around the plant. Oleander Creek was part of that area, she realized. It seemed far-fetched, but could it be in some way related? Could something at Oleander have made Elm sick?

She wondered if she should mention it to Harlan, suggest he run some soil tests. She'd try to reach him later today. That was, if she could tear him away from the cameras long enough, she thought with disgust. Her feelings about her candidate were increasingly mixed. She might deplore his morals concerning women and his treatment of women, but she still believed he was the best man for the job, and had confidence in much of his platform. But there was something about him... Still, all politicians had quirks and Harlan's

probably weren't any stranger than anyone else's. Her issue
here was with Elm, not with Harlan's political agenda.
Though that agenda might come under fire, if it turned out
there was something untoward at the plant.

Placing Harlan on the backburner, Meredith steered the
car into the morning traffic and concentrated on the upcoming court case, knowing there was little use in worrying
when there was nothing she could do right now.

25

Another two days passed but still there was no news of Elm's condition except the same reports: that she needed to be kept completely quiet.

Meredith set her elbows on the desk and rested her head against her hands, beyond frustrated by the entire situation. Although she'd reluctantly agreed to the doctor's orders that they not visit the clinic, she was increasingly surprised that she hadn't heard from Elm.

That just wasn't like her.

Elm was always conscientious about checking in, keeping tabs on her various projects, especially the ladies at Oleander Creek. That there'd been no word at all was disturbing, and she couldn't shake an increasing sense of unease.

Her talk with Aunt Frances the day before had done nothing to alleviate her anxiety. They both resented Harlan for using the situation to promote his own agenda—he certainly was taking full advantage of the publicity it was affording him. He'd sent out a press release, informing all and sundry that he was dropping everything to run to his sick wife's side. And he seemed to be everywhere—on the nightly news, on the cable shows, in the paper. Meredith was disgusted. How could he use his wife's illness to promote his candidacy? It was revolting. Uncle George had been circumspect, of course, issuing a simple statement asking the press to respect the family's privacy; Harlan, on the other hand, was prostituting it.

When yet another twenty-four hours passed without news, Meredith decided it was time to take matters into her own hands. She called directory assistance, found Dr. Ashby's number, and phoned him herself.

After identifying herself as Elm's lawyer, she immediately asked him for a clarification of his "no visitors" policy.

"Mrs. MacBride is undergoing a difficult treatment right now," the doctor explained, his tone firm and officious. "It would be inadvisable and too tiring for her to be disturbed. The agitation—"

"Doctor," she interrupted, trying to keep the irritation from her voice, "unless my client is unconscious, I see no reason why she can't receive visits from her family, even if it's only for five minutes. They're very concerned about her. We all are. Surely you understand?"

"Of course. But I really must do what I believe is best for my patient, and that is complete rest and seclusion."

"This is ridiculous," Meredith exploded. "We don't even know what's really wrong with her. I've checked the major medical journals and haven't been able to locate any information—indeed, even a single reference—about the illness you claim she has."

"Precisely, Mrs. Hunter. Mrs. MacBride has a very rare disorder. I happen to be one of the very few specialists who even have any experience with it. You'll simply have to trust me when I say I know what's best here."

"I appreciate your expertise, Dr. Ashby, but surely you understand my concern. That's why we're eager to have a second opinion. I believe Senator Hathaway has requested that you forward Elm's test results to a specialist in the Neurosciences Department at Bethesda Navy Medical Center. Have you sent them?"

"As soon as we've finished reviewing the latest tests, we'll get them out to him. Now, I'm afraid I really must run." She heard a click and the line went dead.

Meredith stared at the receiver and then hung up, feeling

that Dr. Ashby was stonewalling—though for what earthly reason, she couldn't guess. Harlan had told them that although Elm was very weak, tired and unable to talk much, she was on the mend.

But his word just wasn't good enough.

What surprised her most was that Uncle George seemed so meek and accepting of the fact that he couldn't visit Elm, as though Harlan and Ashby's dictums were the damn law!

Well, she'd had it. Her gut told her something wasn't right and she refused to be put off any longer. Today was Monday. She glanced at her calendar. She had no court proceedings tomorrow. She could board the first flight to Atlanta and be back before the kids got home. She wondered a moment if she should tell the senator of her plans, then decided he'd only share the information with Harlan—and she was starting to wonder if he was the last man she should trust to have Elm's best interests at heart.

Knowing there was nothing else she could do for now, Meredith rolled up her sleeves and got on with the pile of work on her desk, juggled phone calls and clients, trying to get as much out of the way to allow for her absence tomorrow. It was just before her lunch break when the phone rang.

"Who is it, Ally?"

"It's some guy with a British accent. Claims he's Lord Graney. Do you think it's a joke?"

"Oh, my God, no, put him straight on through," Meredith exclaimed, recognizing the name and wondering how Elm's beau had found her number.

"Hello?" A well-bred, modulated voice reached her down the line.

"Hi, this is Meredith Hunter."

"Yes, I'm sorry to disturb you. Allow me to introduce myself. I'm Johnny Graney, a friend of Elm Hathaway's."

"Yes. I know."

"Ah…" There was a moment's hesitation. "Look, I'm dreadfully sorry to bother you, but I haven't heard from Elm in more than four days and, frankly, I'm worried about her."

"I see." Meredith wondered if she was betraying the

Hathaways in any way by telling him what was going on. Still, Elm obviously thought the world of this man and he sounded so polite and worried. "I'm afraid Elm's been sick."

"What do you mean? What's wrong with her?" he asked, immediately concerned.

"Well, that's just the thing. She's in a private clinic in Atlanta. According to her doctor she's suffering from an illness that no one in the medical profession seems to know much about."

"What?" She could hear the disbelief in his voice.

"I know it sounds strange. For the last couple of months, Elm's been experiencing the same mild bouts of nausea and weakness she had last fall—nothing terribly serious, but enough to have some blood tests run. The symptoms had disappeared by the time she went to Gstaad, and from what I gather, she must have felt fine in Ireland, because this is clearly a surprise to you. Anyway, on her way back from visiting you, she stopped at the clinic for a second round of tests and they just kept her there."

"I remember her mentioning the appointment. It sounded very routine. Excuse me, but this is all very odd. What is supposed to be wrong with her, did you say?"

"As I said, they think it's a degenerative disease, but they're not certain."

"I see." There was a moment's silence. "Look, Meredith—you don't mind me calling you that—"

"Of course not."

"Right. I'm sorry to interfere in something you probably consider to be none of my business, but I've been deeply worried about her. I just have this…this odd sense that something isn't right. Have you been able to see her in this hospital?"

"Well, no," Meredith said carefully. "Dr. Ashby, the head of the clinic, doesn't want her to see anyone. He says she's too tired, that it will harm her. That she needs to remain isolated." Meredith doodled on a pad, realizing as she repeated Ashby's strictures to Johnny that they sounded increasingly far-fetched. "But I can't believe seeing me or her family for five minutes could impede her recovery," she continued, deciding to be frank. "Plus, Harlan—that's her soon-to-be ex—seems to be camping with the press in the clinic lobby and milking Elm's illness for all it's worth," she added bitterly, glad to be able to vent her anger.

"I don't like the sound of that at all," he agreed. "Is there nothing you can do?"

"Well, I've decided to go to Atlanta tomorrow and force my way in there. After all, I'm her attorney. If I'm physically present, I don't see how Ashby can stop me from seeing Elm."

"Please go. Oh, God. I hope and pray she's all right."

He sounded so concerned that Meredith's tone softened.

"Why don't I phone you after I've seen her?"

"If she's well enough, please tell her to call me. I don't understand why she hasn't done so."

"I have the nasty feeling they've denied her access to a phone," she said grimly, "which is one of the reasons I want to see her in person."

"This husband of hers—MacBride. You don't think he could be up to something, do you?"

"Up to something?" She frowned.

"I don't quite know. I…it's just that he's so clearly annoyed that she's going to leave him. He came all the way to Gstaad to try to persuade her to change her mind. Elm told me he keeps pestering her. You don't think that he would be capable of, well, harming her in any way, do you?"

"Harlan?" Meredith thought for a second, then dismissed the idea. "No, he's just a lot of hot air."

"Hmm. Well, keep me posted, will you? I can't believe I'm stuck here at Graney when she might need me."

"Don't worry. I'll call as soon as I have news." She proceeded to jot down several numbers where he could be reached, then hung up.

She sat for a while, drumming her desk with her pen, and thinking about the call. Frankly, Johnny's doubts resonated with her own sense that things didn't really add up. But she hoped everything would be clearer tomorrow, after she'd had a chance to speak with Elm.

It was eleven by the time the taxi pulled up in front of Dr. Ashby's Atlanta clinic. The place looked more like a private mansion than a hospital, Meredith thought cynically. From what she'd been able to discover, Ashby had a high-end clientele who'd pay any price for his services. He also was known for utilizing experimental treatments that most hospitals wouldn't touch with a ten-foot pole. Not that she'd heard anything bad about the man—he was extremely well regarded in the medical community—but clearly the liability risks involved in using untested techniques made it easier to operate out of a private clinic, where he could better control the treatments and outcomes.

She'd bet it also meant he could keep more of the reimbursement revenue for himself.

Stepping inside the clean, contemporary interior, its walls lined with modern art, Meredith decided Ashby must be doing something right—the place had to have cost him a fortune in decorator's fees. She moved toward the sleek reception desk and laid down her briefcase.

"Good morning," she said brightly to the well-groomed receptionist. "I'm Meredith Hunter. I'm here to visit Elm Hathaway MacBride."

The receptionist checked her flat-panel computer monitor and frowned. "I'm afraid your name's not on the authorized list. If you'll just wait one moment please, Ms. Hunter." The woman lifted a phone and murmured something indistinguishable. Meredith watched her closely.

"If you'll please take a seat, ma'am, Dr. Ashby will be out in a few minutes."

"There's no need to disturb the doctor. I merely want to see my friend and client."

"I'm afraid the doctor's notes are quite explicit that no one is to see Mrs. MacBride without his permission. She isn't receiving visitors."

"So I've heard," Meredith responded dryly.

Taking a seat in one of the black leather armchairs opposite the reception desk, Meredith drummed her fingers impatiently on the arm. She had no intention of being fobbed off.

Several minutes later, a tallish, handsome man in a white coat appeared. He smiled at her and stretched out a large hand. "Hello. I'm Abe Ashby."

"Hi, Meredith Hunter. I'm here to see my client, Elm MacBride."

"I'm afraid that won't be possible, Ms. Hunter. I thought I'd made that quite clear when we spoke."

"Why not? I believe you informed Senator Hathaway that she'd soon be better and able to have visitors."

"Yes, well, of course that is what we hoped," he said, his eyes not meeting hers. "Unfortunately, that will be a matter of weeks, not days. Despite what you may have heard to the contrary, I'm not a miracle worker." He laughed deprecatingly.

"Doctor…" Meredith's voice turned hard. "Perhaps it'll save us both time and trouble if I make it clear to you that I have no intention of leaving here without seeing my client. She has a right to see me, as I have a right and an obligation to see her."

"I really can't allow—"

"Doctor, would you prefer that I return with a court order?"

Ashby started visibly, then held up his hands. "Please, now, don't be ridiculous. Of course if you insist, I won't stop you from looking in on her. But please, you'll have to be very quiet. No agitation. Anything, the slightest upheaval, could upset her very delicate health."

"Very well," Meredith replied, wondering if she was right to insist. What if Elm had a setback? She'd never forgive herself. No, she decided, stiffening her shoulders as she lifted her briefcase and followed the doctor to the elevator, she owed it to Elm to make sure she wanted to be here.

"Dr. Ashby?" A young intern hurried down the corridor.

"There's an emergency in room C. Mrs. DuPont. They want you there at once."

"Oh, my goodness. Well—"

Meredith watched as Ashby glanced anxiously at her, then at the intern, as though undecided. She frowned. What was the man so darned apprehensive about?

"Don't worry about me, Doctor, what room is Mrs. Mac-Bride in?"

"I should really have someone accompany you—"

"Please, go to your emergency, I'll be fine." She smiled sweetly. "The room?"

"It's 4-D."

Meredith watched him hurry off down the corridor, wondering at his obvious reluctance. Well, at least she would get to see Elm alone.

On the fourth floor she hurried down the corridor, following the arrows that indicated the room numbers, found the right door and quickly knocked. There was no response. Quietly she opened the door and peeked inside.

Elm lay pale and still on a large but luxurious hospital bed set in the corner beneath a bank of monitors. She had an IV in her arm. At the unexpected sound, she turned her head with effort toward the door. "Meredith?" she called weakly. "Is that really you?" She struggled to sit up, seeming instantly agitated. "Oh, Mer, thank God you're here. Why did you take so long? I've been desperate to reach you but they won't allow me any phones. I—"

She fell back against the pillow, apparently exhausted by the effort of speech. Meredith rushed to her side, shocked at how pale and gaunt she looked. She touched Elm's arm; the skin felt flaky and dry. Then she noticed that Elm's hair, usually so full and perfectly groomed, looked lank and lusterless. And her eyes... Lord, she seemed to be struggling to focus them; the pupils were dilated.

Swallowing a surge of panic, Meredith grabbed another pillow and propped it beneath Elm's head, helping her to sit up once more.

Elm stared at Meredith, sightlessly at first, then with a

renewed look of urgency. "It's awful, Mer, I can't believe this is happening to me." The words tumbled out in a torrent. "Instead of getting better, I'm worse. I can't believe I may die," she whispered, plucking the sheet.

"Die?" Meredith asked, genuinely shocked. "What nonsense is this? Now, tell me what's going on here." She looked over her shoulder. "They won't give us much time."

"It's true," Elm whispered, agitated. "Dr. Ashby told me. Look at me! I'm getting worse by the hour. It's so horrible...." Her head sank and tears seeped down her cheeks.

"Honey, don't believe it," Meredith insisted, not knowing what to think. "Surely they must be wrong. Has Harlan been in to see you?"

"Yes. No. I don't know. They come in and stand there and whisper, him and Ashby. Otherwise, no one but the nurses has been in. Mer, please," Elm begged, her voice straining, "lend me your phone. I have to call Johnny. He hasn't heard from me since I left Ireland. He must be so worried." She tried to wipe the tears from her cheeks. "God, I feel so weak I can hardly lift my arm."

"Actually, he called me yesterday. Here." Meredith sat on the edge of the bed, found a tissue and gently swabbed Elm's face. Then she took the phone out of her pocket. "What's the number," she said, eyes trained on the door. "Shit, the battery's really low. I should have charged it before coming in."

Elm repeated the number and Meredith dialed, then held the phone to her. Elm took it, propping it against the pillow with effort.

"Johnny? Oh, my God." Tears came rushing down at the sound of his voice. "I'm, look, I'm in the hospital, I can't— Oh, God, I don't know how to tell you—"

"I know, darling, I know all about it. I talked to Meredith yesterday. I'm coming out at once. I—"

Elm's sobs came faster and Meredith grabbed the phone.

"Hi, it's Meredith. My battery is about to run out."

"Is she all right?"

She shot a quick glance at her friend, catching her breath

as she noticed a large, angry rash on Elm's right arm where her sleeve had fallen back. "Honestly, no."

"Can you tell me what's happening?"

"Not right now," Meredith muttered, worried at Elm's pallor as she lay prostrate on the pillows.

"Please, call me back as soon as you can talk. I won't budge. I have to know what's going on."

"Certainly," Meredith agreed, thinking again that this was a man whose voice instantly inspired trust.

She rang off and slipped the cell phone back in her pocket. "Elm, honey, tell me everything—what they've said, what they do, why you're here. I can't seem to get a straight explanation from anyone, especially Ashby. And you're not sure if Harlan has been in to see you?"

Elm seemed to find it an effort to speak. "He has. But he just looks at me in this weird way, then leaves. I tried to talk to him and he just says, "Shush, you'll be fine," and then whispers things to Ashby. Oh, God, Mer, I... Will you explain everything to Johnny? I feel terrible that I can't speak to him properly. It's just that I can't bear the thought of him suffering because of me. Please, Mer," she urged, grabbing her friend's arm, "he mustn't know how bad this is. You see, he's already lost someone he loves, and it affected his whole life and I can't make him go through all that again," she said, greatly distressed.

"But, Elm, this is ridiculous," Meredith exploded. "You are not going to die," she insisted, praying she was right. "Your father wants to have your blood work sent to Bethesda Navy Medical. He's just waiting for Ashby to get him the results."

"What good will that do? Dr. Ashby says his treatment is the only one that has a chance of curing me. And I believe him."

"Right. Well, that remains to be seen," Meredith muttered cryptically, stroking Elm's hand. There was no disputing Elm was seriously ill. So why was Harlan, who had been seen every day shuttling in and out of the clinic, giving impromptu press conferences on the clinic steps, lying to the family about Elm's prognosis? Why had he been claiming she was getting better when that clearly wasn't the case? Surely he knew that the senator would prefer the truth, no matter how painful?

It just didn't make sense. Unless, Meredith realized with a jolt of alarm, Harlan thought the truth would bring them all running to Atlanta to see what could be done. Instead, by keeping everyone at bay, he was able to keep Elm under his complete control. And now, listening to her friend's anxious ramblings, she wondered if Johnny was right and something underhanded was going on here. God, it was all so confusing, she thought, running a hand through her hair. Surely Harlan wouldn't harm Elm? She had no idea what was happening in this place, but she didn't like it one little bit. She glanced at Elm, then at her phone. Why hadn't she charged the damn battery? Then she could have left her phone with Elm. But uncharged, it would be no use to her. She sighed. Something must be done. And fast.

Johnny paced the ancient library with the portable phone in his hand, unable to stay seated, Meredith's words and Elm's distress still echoing in his ears. It wasn't possible that one moment she'd been here with him fit as a fiddle, and next thing she was lying ill with some disorder nobody had ever heard of. It just didn't ring true.

Once Meredith called him back, he'd phone the travel agent immediately and make reservations to leave tomorrow. He didn't care that he had no legal rights, no status at all in Elm's life; he wanted to be with her, whatever the consequences. Maybe his presence could somehow shield her from whatever threats he sensed might be taking place behind the scenes. And maybe, he thought bitterly, he was just fooling himself, refusing to believe that he was once again going to lose the woman that he loved. He groaned. Elm had sounded so upset and distraught, not like herself at all.

He stared out of the long windows over the lawn, absently watching Conway, the keeper, let the pointers loose in the field beyond. The past few days had been hell, and all at once he felt exhausted. Since Elm's departure he'd experienced worry, anger, jealousy and everything in between. Thank God he'd at last heard the sound of her voice. At least he knew she was alive and, if not well, able to talk. Still, she'd been too weak to go on, too upset. Now he willed the phone to ring, for Meredith to tell him what was really going on.

The next five minutes felt like hours. For a while he stared blindly at the rain drumming the windows, then turned and stopped in front of the fireplace before pacing the room again.

At last the phone rang and he answered immediately, shoulders drooping and irritation soaring when he heard the wrong voice on the line. "Oh, Mrs. Doherty, yes, Maeve's in, but I'm afraid she can't talk right now," he said, curbing his frustration. "I'm waiting for a long-distance call from America."

"Would that be your mother, then? How are the family doing, m'lord?"

"Fine, thanks. Now, I'm afraid I really must hang up."

"Yes, of course. Now, you give her ladyship my best when you speak to her, won't you?"

"Of course. Goodbye, Mrs. Doherty," Johnny barked and hung up. The frustration and worry would kill him if he didn't hear something soon.

At last the phone rang again.

"Sorry I took so long." Meredith's voice came down the line.

"How is she? She sounded awful. I'm going mad here."

"Not good, I'm afraid. Sorry about my phone battery. I should have charged it before leaving home, then I could have left her my phone. I hate her being incommunicado."

"Never mind. Just tell me what's going on. And please don't sugarcoat it, Meredith, I need to know exactly what's happening."

"Frankly, I was shocked—" Meredith hesitated a moment. She didn't know this man, but something told her to trust him. On the other hand, Elm clearly wanted to spare him any pain. From the desperation in his voice, it seemed obvious that he loved her. She considered the facts, and then made a split-second decision.

"Hello? Can you hear me?"

"Yes, I'm sorry. Look, the doctor seems to think she has some rare degenerative nervous disease that might be fatal."

"Good God," Johnny whispered, the news hitting like a physical blow.

"She looks…very sick. But—"

"What is it? Tell me?"

"I'm beginning to think your suspicions might be valid. Something doesn't gel. Harlan seems entirely too comfortable with the fact that she's ill. Indeed, I think he's downright pleased, if his preening over his rising poll numbers is anything to go by. And when he's been in to see her, Elm says he spends most of his time whispering with Ashby and treating her like she's already half dead. Of course, knowing Harlan, all he's really interested in is the publicity this is all causing. And, I find it impossible to believe he would actually do Elm any harm."

"Hmm."

"Second, I practically had to break in there today, and as I suspected, Elm hasn't been allowed to make any calls. I wasn't there ten minutes before Ashby appeared and hustled me out again."

"I see. I know this is going to sound far-fetched," Johnny said slowly, "but you don't think her husband could have orchestrated this whole thing to get publicity for his campaign? To prove that he and Elm are still together, and to show himself in a good light?"

Meredith hesitated. It seemed impossible. But after what she'd witnessed today, she wondered. "I don't think so," she said doubtfully. "What kind of monster would let someone believe she was dying just to win himself a few extra votes? Anyway, that would be a criminal offence and require the collaboration of the medical staff. Besides, she's definitely genuinely sick."

"Hmm. It's probably just a crazy notion of mine."

"Maybe. Maybe not," she said suddenly, an uneasy fear rising in her gut as she remembered Mel's discoveries. "Look, I can't say any more right now, but I'll do some investigating and keep you posted."

"For God's sake, do. Here, take my cell number. I'm getting on the next plane to Atlanta."

"Are you sure that's a good idea?" Meredith hesitated, hating to tell him that he might not be welcome.

"Look, I don't plan to make a nuisance of myself. I'm very aware that this is a tricky situation, to say the least. But I can't stay here, climbing the walls, when Elm may need me."

"Okay." She admired his attitude. It said a lot for the man. "Where will I be able to find you?"

"The Ritz-Carlton Buckhead."

"Fine." She jotted down his cell number. "Any news, and I'll be in touch with you right away. In the meantime, you can contact me at this number." She gave him hers, then hung up and walked despondently toward the flight departure lounge, determined to call Mel as soon as she reached Savannah.

Elm's mind wandered restlessly. Most of the time she floated in a haze, in an ephemeral world that was not quite real. And each time she began to feel better—when the haze cleared a little and she remembered what the doctor had said and why she was here—something beeped over her bed and someone would come and soothe her, telling her not to become agitated. They would fiddle with the drip next to her bed and she'd be off again, back in that strange, blurred, undefined miasma where it was impossible to linger on any specific thought for any length of time.

Occasionally she mustered the strength to ask questions of the nurse, but no one responded except in soft monotones, telling her to rest, not to worry, to just lie back and relax, that soon she'd be feeling better.

And all she could do was cooperate, fall back against the pillows, exhausted from even the smallest effort, trying to capture images of Johnny, hold on to them for dear life. But even that was hard.

She didn't have any clear sense of how long she'd been here, just knew that each day she felt worse, until even the slightest effort became virtually impossible and an overwhelming sense of lethargy overwhelmed her. Where was everyone? she wondered. Where was Daddy? Why hadn't he come? Didn't he love her anymore? And Johnny, where was Johnny? Why hadn't he called?

But these were fleeting, transient thoughts, fruit of a moment's lucidity that came and went as fast as the medication was popped back into the IV. Mostly she dreamed of Oleander, saw her own face looking out from the beds of flowers, her fingers stretching alongside the thick roots of the ancient live oak tree, her hair rippling over and through the grass toward the river. She was of the earth and in it, and as she watched old Ely come ever closer with his shovel, she knew that he meant to turn up the bed and bury her under the generations of rich black soil.

26

Plastering a wistful smile on his handsome countenance, Harlan worked the church hall, patting backs, kissing babies, and all the while asking himself what he was still doing at pancake prayer breakfasts, chatting with small-fry contributors who brought in ten, fifty or a hundred bucks at most to his campaign. His time would be much better spent courting the big donors in D.C. or Atlanta, people who grasped what he could do for them and for the country.

Of course, he reminded himself, even the poorest person still had a vote, which was the only reason he'd agreed when Ensor had insisted he come to the Sweet Jesus Hallelujah Sunshine Hall this morning. But in the future, he decided, he'd delegate this stuff to his chief of staff; a man could only eat so many pancakes before he was turned off them for life.

Still, he reflected, listening attentively to another constituent's complaints regarding the local school bus service and promising to look into it, it wouldn't do to get too far ahead of himself. Every candidate, from George Washington to the present, had had to pay his dues at places like this. Heck, when John Kennedy had been on the primary trail back in the spring of 1960, he made a point of visiting the hillbilly backcountry of West Virginia where no other candidate would go, and it had been a turning point in his campaign;

it was also where the future president learned that some people in America still worshipped snakes. The smile still in place, Harlan decided he'd worship snakes, too, if it got him to the White House.

Harlan gave himself a mental pat on the back for remembering that the hoi polloi were people, too, and surveyed the room. Now that things were under control, with Elm in a holding pattern, where she could be kept while she was still of use to him, there wasn't as much to worry about. Elm's illness had given a great boost to his campaign. He was getting more national press and daily TV coverage than any other candidate in the race. It was a real stroke of genius, one he could thank himself for. And now he'd even shaken Brock off his back. In fact, the man was downright thrilled with all the positive press.

The one niggling worry—not that he was losing any sleep over it—was the news from one of his people that a reporter, citing the Freedom of Information Act, had been submitting requests to the Southeast office of the EPA for documents related to the Mogachee plant. Apparently the man was also digging into how the plant had been financed. Stretching his hand out for the umpteenth time and accepting yet another offer of prayers for his wife, Harlan made a mental note to contact the reporter, lay on the charm, throw him off the scent and get that small but potentially dangerous detail taken care of.

On the return flight to Savannah, Meredith couldn't get the image of Elm's haggard face out of her mind—those beautiful eyes filled with fear and desperation and an implicit plea that she do something to save her. Again she reviewed all the facts, unable to dismiss Johnny's words. Surely it was impossible that Harlan could be contriving some kind of scam that involved Elm's health? Absolutely impossible, she reassured herself. A professional of Ashby's caliber would have no reason to fall in with Harlan's plans, in the extremely unlikely event that he had managed to make Elm take ill, which of course was ridiculous and— *God, Mere-*

dith, get a grip! She must stop letting her imagination run away with her and keep her mind focused on the facts.

But her growing suspicions, however absurd, remained and the knowledge that she *must* do something at once was a terrifying responsibility.

Once they touched down and she left the airport, Meredith grabbed her car from the parking lot and made her way back into town on I-16. Thank God Tom was picking up the kids, for she was too overwhelmed and shaken to deal with them right now. Plus, she needed to go into the office for a little, sort through her mail and review tomorrow's schedule. On the way into the city, she plugged her phone into the cigarette lighter and checked her phone messages. There were three from Mel, asking her to call him right away. What did he want now? she wondered. *Shit.* She didn't have his number on her mobile.

Once inside her office, Meredith dropped her purse on the spare chair and sat down behind her desk, ignoring the stacks of unexamined files. She flipped through the pile of messages that Ally had left her, returned a couple of important calls from clients, then finally got around to Mel.

"Hi, Mel. You called. What can I do for you?" She glanced at her watch impatiently. It was almost six and she had the PTA meeting at eight. Still, the uneasy thought couldn't be dismissed.

"I need to meet with you as soon as possible."

"Why?"

"What we talked about the other day. I don't want to discuss it over the phone," he answered mysteriously.

"Look, Mel, this had better be good, because I have a packed schedule." She flipped through her agenda, Johnny's words gnawing at her. "How about tomorrow afternoon at four?"

"Okay. Fine."

"This had better be worth it."

"It is."

"Good. Then I'm glad you're coming in. But make it the two-minute pitch, okay? I'm squeezing you in between clients.'' At least that way he'd know she couldn't give him more than ten. Mel was a sweetheart, but inclined to dramatize. She was already letting her imagination get the better of her. If there was something new on the waste plant, she wanted it clear-cut. Mel was inclined to believe that behind every political act lay a hidden agenda. Still, coupled with the uneasy feeling that had grown ten-fold since leaving the clinic, she was not about to dismiss any leads.

By seven she was out of the office and on her way. Just time to drop by the house, she figured, and have a quick bite before picking up Tom and heading to the meeting. She made a mental note to check in with Johnny Graney tomorrow, see if he'd found a flight. She smiled, remembering the determination in his voice. There was something about that man that inspired confidence. And the fact that he was coming just for Elm, regardless of the situation, of any hassle and possible embarrassment, well, that spoke volumes for him.

Overtaking an elderly lady in an ancient Buick, Meredith turned into her street, remembering the medication list she'd removed from the chart at the end of Elm's bed, now safely stowed in her purse. Swiping it hadn't been exactly ethical. Why, she wondered, questioning her motives, had she been so certain that Ashby would refuse to give her a copy? In fact, what the hell was she doing stealing reports and sneaking them into her purse when she could simply ask for them?

With a huff, Meredith drove into her driveway and tried to calm down before seeing her family. Tomorrow she'd drop the meds list by the senator's office so that he could fax it up to Bethesda. Maybe then things would become clearer.

As she closed the car door, she wondered again if she wasn't being paranoid. Just because Ashby gave her the creeps didn't mean he wasn't giving Elm the best possible care. And Harlan, for all his faults, wouldn't have dreamed up something as crazy as doping his wife of twelve years in order to win a few votes. She felt suddenly ashamed. After all, Harlan was one of *them,* not some weirdo from God knows where. Not to mention that such a scheme would require the doctor's help, and there was no reason why someone of Ashby's reputation would lend himself to any dishonest practice. She must not let her prejudice for the way Harlan had behaved toward Elm in the Jennifer affair blind her. Her responsibility here was to do whatever she could to help Elm get better. Becoming her husband's enemy without cause certainly wouldn't help her friend.

Two minutes later, she entered her house and was assailed by plaintive cries for help with homework and demands for food. The familiar chaos left her little room to think of anything beyond her family's needs and the PTA meeting she dearly wished she could skip.

"Thirty-five million in public funds was set aside to build that plant with the understanding that once it was up and running, responsibility for all operating costs would be assumed by the private company that had won the contract." Mel Bamburger paused, looking at Meredith to make sure she was following him. She nodded. "Right, so on the surface, everything looks fine. The company submitted documents showing that the full allocation of funds was used, and now the plant's paying its own way, kicking out a respectable profit that the company's splitting with the county. But as far as I can tell from the construction records," Mel insisted earnestly, "only twenty million was spent to build the thing. That means not only was the Mogachee plant done on the cheap—perhaps dangerously so—but also that $15 million in public funds has disappeared. Now, what I would like to know, is where did all that money go?"

"But that's a huge discrepancy, Mel. I can't believe someone wouldn't have discovered this before now. There must be a perfectly logical justification."

"Actually, one of the subcontractors admitted to me that he had some serious reservations about how things were being done and sent a letter to Congressman MacBride's office—even followed it up with a personal visit. But it doesn't look like Harlan MacBride took the matter any further. My bet is that he buried the guy's letter in the ol' circular file.''

"That's absurd, Mel. I'm sure there must be a reasonable explanation," Meredith murmured, glancing at the clock but unable to escape the growing unease.

"Possibly you're right. But then why won't MacBride's office give me a clear-cut answer? And get this. The waste plant is supposed to meet all EPA regulations, right?''

"Well, of course it's EPA-approved," Meredith responded, drumming her fingers on her knee.

"Actually, that's not entirely clear. I suspect that the area where the plant's builders skimped was in installing critical environmental protections," he said triumphantly. "Remember how MacBride was such a vocal backer of privatizing the municipal-waste processing plant, claiming it would save the county money and increase efficiency?''

"Yes. It was based on his assurances that the county commissioners fast-tracked the licensing process." She looked across at him, beginning to sense the connection, unease turning to dread at all the possible implications.

"Right. Which meant the plant never had to submit its proposed environmental safeguards for review. Once the plant was built, it appears Congressman MacBride got them a two-year waiver on EPA inspections—which he was able to do because he chairs the House subcommittee on Environment and Hazardous Materials. Now that the waiver period is almost up, he's quietly trying to get it renewed— indefinitely. Problem is," he continued, pausing for dramatic effect, "as we know, people living near the plant are getting sick.

"Oh, my God." Meredith gripped the arms of her chair and stared at him.

"Here's a list. I checked with the local hospital and the records show that several folk, all living within a three-mile radius of the plant, have checked in with nausea, sickness, flaky skin, dehydration and—''

"Let me see that." Meredith grabbed the sheet from him, skimming over it rapidly, her pulse beating faster. "My

God,'' she whispered, remembering Elm's lank hair and flaking hands, ''this is too much of a coincidence.''

''Just what I said. I checked with the families and—''

The phone on her desk rang. ''Excuse me, Mel, I have to take this call.'' Meredith lifted the receiver while Mel, brow creased, studied the information before him.

''Sure, put her through. Hi, Jane,'' she said impatiently. ''What can I do for you?''

''Oh, Meredith,'' Jane sobbed.

''What's wrong?'' Meredith asked, suddenly anxious. Jane MacGregor was heading up the Oleander garden project in Elm's absence.

''I need to find Elm immediately. I don't care if she's in Antarctica, something dreadful has happened.''

''For Christ's sake, tell me what's wrong.''

''It's Julie,'' she said, voice cracking.

''Julie Grayson?''

''Yes.''

''What about her? I thought she'd made a real turnaround.''

''Oh she has—had,'' Jane sobbed. ''That's what makes this so much worse. Oh, my God, it's awful.''

''What's awful?'' Meredith asked, thoroughly confused.

''Meredith, Julie died an hour ago.''

''What?'' She jumped to her feet, toppling her chair. ''How? What happened?''

''They rushed her to the hospital last night. She hadn't being feeling well for several days. By the time they got her in she could hardly breathe. She was staggering about blindly and was severely dehydrated. It was horrible. And her skin. Oh, my God, you should have seen her skin, it was covered with this dreadful rash. She didn't look like the same woman. Her hair was all lank and thin and falling out and—I'm sorry, but I'm so shocked.''

''Take your time,'' Meredith soothed while raising a finger, indicating for Mel to wait.

''I told her to go see the doctor about two weeks ago,'' Jane continued, the words gushing forth, ''but she wouldn't, she insisted on working in the garden, spent most of her days knee-deep in the dirt. Then yesterday evening, old Ely found her lying among the flower beds and rushed her to Memorial. Oh, Meredith, I don't know what to do, this is so terrible. Poor Julie. I have to tell Elm,'' Jane wailed.

''Now, Jane, stay calm and don't budge. Did they say what she had?''

''They talked about the possibility of some sort of allergic reaction—''

''Stay right where you are. I'll cancel all my appointments and meet you at the hospital right away. Promise you won't move? I'm on my way.'' She slammed the phone down and grabbed her purse. ''You'd better come with me, Mel,'' she said tightly, ''you may actually be on to something. But you have to promise me—swear it—that not one word of this goes in the paper until I get to the bottom of it, do you understand?''

''Scout's honor.'' Mel grabbed his canvas bag and threw his documents inside it. Slinging the bag over his shoulders, he followed Meredith hurriedly out the door into the reception area, where she was already giving Ally instructions.

Mel was alive with pent-up excitement. This was going to be his big break, the lucky strike he'd been waiting for.

As he raced after Meredith, he pumped his fist in the air. Goodbye *Savannah Morning News,* he exulted, hello *New York Times.*

Elm awoke groggy, sensed a cloud of depression hovering and tried to ward it off by escaping back into sleep. She held on tight to the remnants of her dream. Johnny, smiling at her by the fireplace at Graney, horses galloping across emerald moors, rain falling softly, lots of tinkling laughter. But reality gradually intruded, and with it an anguished sense of inevitability as she recalled where she was and why she was here.

Opening her eyes slowly to the stark light of the impersonal clinic room, Elm turned, shivering, and glanced at the clock on the bedside table. It was five minutes after eleven.

But of what day, what month? She'd lost track of how long she'd been here. Why was it so late? Surely they woke you early in hospital. Why hadn't the nurse been in with her injection? That at least helped her relax, sent her off again into a half-baked state where nothing was too clear and life in this bed became bearable.

Part of her protested.

She shouldn't want to be in a half-baked state. It wasn't right. She should be fighting—after all, there was so much to live for now.

She raised her hand, tried to shove herself up in the bed, but the effort exhausted her and she collapsed among the pillows. Good God, was she really too weak to even sit up? Was this the end approaching? Could it really be true that her life was draining away?

For a while she lay completely still and her thoughts drifted back to Johnny. She visualized his eyes smiling at her, those gentle, tender eyes bathed with warmth. God, how she wished she'd told him that she loved him. Now it was probably too late. Her family hadn't come to see her. Or had they and she'd just forgotten? She must ask the nurse when she came in. Surely they wanted to see her. And Johnny, why couldn't he be here? She desperately needed him.

Her eyes closed and she drifted off again. But this time her dreams were agitated. She tossed and moaned.

When the nurse entered the room and tried to shake her awake, Elm dreamed that death itself had come to claim her.

Meredith slowly replaced the receiver, digesting the latest information that Mel had dug up on the Mogachee plant. So Tyler Brock had once owned the land on which the plant was built. She shivered. Based on Mel's review of real estate values in the area, it appeared the plant's owners had paid a significantly inflated price for the land. Looks like Mr. Brock hit the jackpot with that one, she thought, remembering, horrified, that Harlan had handpicked the project's site-selection committee.

This news, added to the other details they'd compiled,

including the indisputable fact that several residents around the plant had been hospitalized with symptoms that sounded disturbingly similar to Elm's, formed a clear and daunting picture, one she still had difficulty accepting but that was ever sharper. Particularly now that Julie, who'd spent so much time at Oleander, was dead, and that no one at Harlan's office was ever available to give an explanation regarding the missing funds. But, as she'd told Mel, right now that wasn't a priority. What her horror-struck mind was trying to piece together was why Harlan had been so keen to approve the plant, had lobbied hard for it, and had gone to great trouble to promise that it would be one of the safest municipal-waste processing projects in the country. And she'd believed him. Been proud of the fact. Upheld his candidacy adamantly because she'd bought his arguments, even backed them staunchly. She shifted uneasily. There was no denying that Tyler Brock was one of Harlan's biggest donors. Could Harlan really have sold his soul to the devil? she wondered, sitting back and biting her lip.

My God. Apart from all the implications it had for Elm and her illness, this could be disastrous for the party as well. Meredith let out a groan and closed her eyes. Had they all been blind all these years? She'd met Brock only a couple of times. She knew that he lived in a multimillion-dollar mansion on Skidaway Island, and that Harlan had been sucking up to him for years. But that wasn't unusual—most politicians were obsessed with fund-raising and cultivated a cadre of high-net-worth individuals, so she'd never thought much of the connection. Still, it all seemed too pat to be mere coincidence.

A thousand different thoughts careered like a hailstorm through her agitated mind. She glanced at her watch. Johnny Graney was due in on the twelve o'clock flight from New York, where he'd spent a couple days, apparently arranging for his well-connected brother to do some digging into Harlan's activities, and she'd promised to meet him to tell him all she knew before he headed for Atlanta. Perhaps he'd have gathered some more information. She didn't know whether she sought it or dreaded it. She picked up her purse and thought about Elm, about Johnny going to the clinic. She doubted he'd be able to get in to see her; with all the press coverage, the security around the clinic was even tighter than before. Was that another of Harlan's ruses? she wondered.

As she drove out to the airport, Meredith dissected all she'd learned over again, reasoning that perhaps Elm's illness was coincidental. After all, with all the traveling she'd been doing, Elm hadn't been working on the project at the plantation for some time. But Julie's symptoms had sounded so similar. An idea occurred to her as she changed gears and she swallowed, wondering if she could pull it off.

What if she persuaded the coroner to do an autopsy on Julie's body? Then, if the results tallied with Elm's blood work, well…though how she could arrange that without raising a stink, she wasn't sure. She would have to deal with the matter very discreetly. She'd already asked the senator's permission to have soil samples taken at the plantation and he'd granted it immediately, too shaken by Julie's death to question Meredith about her motives. With any luck, she'd have the soil test results by this afternoon. Maybe they would provide an explanation. Not that she expected anything spectacular. This morning, Harlan's office had verified that the plant had just recently received full EPA approval. Surely he couldn't lie about something as serious as this? Be that brazen?

Suddenly aware that she had almost reached the airport, Meredith paid attention and turned into the parking lot. Despite everything they'd uncovered, she must keep her head and her focus rational. Truth was, the only concrete fact she possessed was that Elm was very sick and not getting any better. The rest was still conjecture.

Harlan reread the newspaper article, eyes narrowed. The fucking reporter hadn't said it outright, but he knew that the next thing would be an exposé linking the woman's death

at Oleander Creek with the Mogachee plant. In fact, he was
actually rather surprised that the annoying journalist hadn't
already made the connection. Well, he wasn't going to wonder why, he'd just thank his lucky stars there was still time
to do damage control. He hoped Tyler Brock—who was
mercifully away on business—wouldn't get a whiff of this.

What a damn nuisance that the woman had decided to die
on their property. It was typical that Elm should have gotten
him into a tight spot by hiring those battered women for the
project, he reflected, glancing angrily at his watch. Why
couldn't she just get gardeners to do the work, like normal
people did, instead of messing with a bunch of freaks?

He stood by the window a moment and brooded. If there
really were problems at the plant, then he must take immediate action. The woman's death was bound to focus un-
warranted attention on the plantation, the waste plant and,
of course, his own association with both. He stared out at
the garden and wondered if he could dig up anything to use
as leverage. What was that woman's name? He returned to
the desk and glanced back at the paper. *Julie Grayson.* He
leaned over and picked up the phone.

"Marcy, put me through to Jed Framer's office, will
you?" Jed had a nose like a bloodhound—he'd be able to
dig something up, if anything was there.

After giving Jed his assignment, Harlan sat down again
and waited, weighing up different scenarios. What if somebody got curious and decided to have an autopsy done on
the body? Or if they investigated the area, took soil samples
and discovered toxins? It wasn't impossible. He glanced
over at the cabinet, tempted to take a snort, then thought
better of it. Marcy might be coming in any minute with
papers for him to sign. Too risky.

Half an hour later, Harlan had the required information.
Next thing he was on the line to Julie's estranged husband,
Sam Grayson, a convicted felon with a sizable record and a
history of beating up his now-dead wife. Ten minutes and
five grand later, Harlan had convinced the man to request

an immediate cremation of the body. He'd even offered to pay for the costs of a memorial service plus flowers.

He was not turned down.

Johnny had wanted to fly directly into Atlanta to see Elm, but Meredith had insisted it was a waste of time. So, against his will, he had listened and spent the past two days in New York strategizing with Liam and his mother.

"I just can't believe she's so ill," he'd kept repeating. "If she's so sick, surely she would have felt something in Ireland. But she was fine. There was nothing wrong with her at all, she was blooming," he insisted for the hundredth time. "I have this gut feeling that something is up."

"But, honey, I don't see that there's anything we can do," Grace repeated, sending Liam a pained glance. This was too cruel to be true and she only wished the nightmare was over.

"Johnny, I'm sure she's getting the best possible treatment. We're talking big names here—Senator Hathaway is no lightweight. What could possibly be up?" Liam insisted.

"I haven't the faintest idea. Just my gut tells me."

Liam hesitated, then said quietly, "Look, bro, I am more sorry than I can tell you that Elm is sick, as much for you as for her. But I think you've got to accept it."

"I'm afraid your brother's right," Grace sighed, reaching over and squeezing his hand gently. "I'm sure that she'll get better honey, it's only a matter of time."

"Her husband was very against any idea of divorce," Johnny murmured, paying little attention, far away in his own thoughts.

"Well of course he would be. A well-publicized divorce is the last thing a congressman needs on the eve of an election."

"Exactly." Johnny pounced. "Perhaps he decided it was easier to rid himself of Elm rather than go through with it."

"That's impossible, dear, absurd," Grace exclaimed, shocked.

"Not impossible, but certainly very far-fetched." Liam replied firmly. "American politicians just don't go around murdering their wives."

"I know," Johnny muttered sullenly. "I'm just so worried about her.'' He was terrified that Elm's situation was deteriorating instead of improving. ''And whatever you say, I don't like that husband of hers,'' he repeated. ''Thanks for the name of the detective, Liam. I've put him on the case.''

''He's a good man,'' Liam said, moving toward the drinks cabinet and bringing out a decanter of Scotch. ''Still, I think you're pushing it, trying to dig up dirt on MacBride. Seems the guy has a pretty good record.''

''We'll see.''

''Mother, Scotch?''

''Please.''

Johnny nodded his assent from the armchair. ''I'm going down to Savannah tomorrow to meet with her lawyer.''

''Are you sure that's wise, darling?'' Grace accepted the Scotch and soda, her expression pained.

''Mother, I really don't give a damn. At this stage, all I care about is Elm's well-being.''

Liam exchanged a look with Grace and they dropped the subject.

Now, as the plane touched the tarmac in Savannah, the same anger he'd experienced after Marie Ange's capture raged through him. Why her, why him, why them?

He wouldn't—couldn't—let it happen again. With Marie Ange, there'd been a terrible feeling of powerlessness, impotence before the unchangeable. This time, he vowed, he would do everything he could, everything in his power, to save the woman he loved.

Meredith met Johnny for lunch, and she liked him on sight. But as they conversed and ate distractedly, she was still loath to express her niggling doubts about Harlan and the plant, knowing he would pounce on them like a drowning man.

Then at one-thirty her cell phone rang.

''Shoot,'' she told Mel, who had picked up the results of Oleander's soil tests for her.

''I was right, Mer,'' he said, excited, ''they've come up positive for several toxins.''

"Okay," she replied, mind racing, "but that doesn't establish a direct link. We need more. See if you can get a variety of samples from different areas within a radius of the plant. I want tests taken from the farthest perimeters, right up to the plant's front door."

"Okay. I'll do my best."

Meredith tweaked her hair back, glanced at Johnny and listened carefully, all her fears returning. She must be very careful, she realized—the ramifications of all of this could be enormous. But as Mel described the effects of each toxin on the human body, detailing whether and how each could be absorbed, she was chilled.

"Selenium—which the tests have revealed is present in elevated levels around the plantation—can be absorbed both orally and through the skin," Mel continued.

Why hadn't Harlan himself ever ordered these soil tests? she wondered. Maybe she should remind him and gauge his reaction. Jesus, but this was getting complicated—it sure as hell smelled like a cover-up.

"Mel," she said, right before he hung up, "be careful."

She packed the phone into her purse, then, realizing Johnny had heard every word of her conversation, knew she had no choice but to fill him in.

"Look, what I'm about to tell you is highly sensitive information."

"Don't worry, it won't go any further. But there's something dodgy going on, isn't there?" His eyes narrowed and he concentrated. Feeling the intense energy he projected, Meredith felt suddenly glad that he was here. This whole thing was leading them into some very dicey territory, and she suspected Johnny Graney was exactly the kind of man one wanted by one's side when the going got rough.

"I had soil samples taken from the plantation and tested. The results identified toxins in the soil, several of which, with sufficient exposure, can cause symptoms similar to Elm's. One in particular, selenium, can be especially dangerous in high concentrations."

"But Elm hasn't been near the plantation for weeks," he argued.

"I know. But perhaps the effects only surface after an incubating period...." She hesitated.

"Possibly," he agreed, looking dubious.

"Look, normally I hate to presume things, but I have to wonder—"

"If her husband had her admitted to the Atlanta clinic in order to cover up the fact she's sick because of exposure to toxic runoff from the plant he green-lighted?" he interrupted harshly.

"Something like that," she responded warily. "And now, after Julie's death, he must be even more scared. Oh, God." She passed a hand over her eyes. "I hope Elm's okay."

"Well, from what you've told me, she's not. But what bothers me is that apparently she's not getting any better. If her condition were the result of exposure at the plantation, presumably being away from there would alleviate the symptoms. That's not the case here." Johnny stopped, frowned and hesitated.

"Maybe I should call Ashby and ask him what exactly is present in Elm's blood work. He still hasn't sent the results to Bethesda."

"Why not give it a try? Be interesting to see what he says."

"Okay." Meredith nodded, then pressed her select calls button and looked for the number. "Here goes." She punched the button and waited. Several minutes later, after she argued with his receptionist, Ashby was on the line.

"Hi, Meredith Hunter speaking. I've been working on a theory here that I'd like to run by you. Any chance Elm's blood tests showed an exposure to the mineral selenium?"

"Selenium?" he echoed, sounding surprised. "Well, uh, it's a naturally occurring substance, so there's always a chance it's there, but no, I'm almost certain there was nothing like that present in unusual quantities. I'd have to take a look to be perfectly sure. Can you hold a minute?"

"Sure." Meredith covered the mouthpiece. "He's gone to take a look."

"You mean he doesn't know something as serious as that off the bat?" Johnny queried.

"Well, he does have more than one patient, and diagnosing something without absolute confirmation would be opening himself up to a lawsuit. Particularly with me," she grinned.

"I forgot we were in America," he replied, rolling his eyes.

"Yes?" Meredith's brows creased as Ashby came back on the line. "No evidence of selenium, then."

"What made you think there might be selenium?" Ashby asked casually, his voice a little unsteady.

"Oh, nothing, just a hunch."

"I see. Well, I think you're totally off base. It's very rare to exhibit elevated levels of selenium in the blood. I don't see where Elm might have been exposed to it."

"No. Neither do I," she lied. "Thanks, anyway." She hung up and looked at Johnny. "He was worried. I'm sure he was worried, didn't like me asking. I wonder…"

"What?"

"No, nothing. Give me a couple of days to verify some things and I'll tell you."

"Meredith, might I remind you that I'm working with you, not against you?" Johnny said patiently. "If we share our doubts, we may come to some conclusions that just might save Elm's life."

"I know. I'm sorry. Habit." She smiled apologetically. "It's just so risky." She looked at him, thought a moment, then took a deep breath. "I'm investigating something right now, but I can't talk about it—yet."

"Okay. I see I'll have to be patient. Which I'm not," he added darkly. "What about those blood tests, why hasn't Ashby sent them to the senator's doctor yet?"

"Good question. I'll have the senator call and make another request."

"Fine."

Meredith let out a silent breath. She must not let her imagination run away with her. Conjecturing was one thing. But making her conjectures public, even if only to Johnny, was another. More than just Elm was involved here; it was the future of the Georgia Democratic party as a whole. She was a staunch party member who had long backed Harlan's candidacy. Even though she didn't entirely approve of him, she'd always considered him the best man for the job. Mel's revelations were terrifying, not just personally but politically.

"What about some pudding?" Johnny suggested.

"Dessert? No, thanks, just coffee."

Johnny signaled the waitress and ordered. "You know, I can't rid myself of the thought that MacBride is behind all this," he mused, echoing the thoughts Meredith was unwilling to voice. "How can you be sure Harlan isn't trying to get rid of Elm?"

"Look, you asked me that question before, and of course I can't be sure. But why on earth would he want to do that? Elm brings him status and financial support. Not to mention the senator's political base."

"Well, there you have it in a nutshell. After the divorce, he may lose some of that."

"Wait a minute." Meredith leaned forward and looked him straight in the eye. "Are you implying that Harlan might be trying to murder Elm so as *not* to lose his status and financial backing?"

Johnny shrugged. "It's a thought."

"If I were you, I'd keep it that way," she said, shaken. "American politicians are not in the habit of whacking their wives."

"Funny, someone else told me the same thing a couple of days ago."

"You mean you've been expressing this opinion publicly?" Meredith stared at him, horrified.

"No, just to my brother. Who is the soul of discretion," he reassured her.

"Whew! Thank God. But please, there are a number of

issues at stake here. We can't just come out with hypothetical theories accusing one of our most respected congressmen of being a murderer.''

"All right. Point taken." He raised his hands and leaned back.

"Harlan would be incapable of hurting a hair on Elm's head," Meredith asserted, hoping she was right. "The mere thought is horrible."

"Okay, fine, I'm sorry. But between you and me, are you sure that you can entirely exclude the theory?" he asked, holding her gaze.

"It's preposterous," she said, twisting her paper napkin, hating the thoughts that were crowding her brain.

"But not entirely outrageous. You said yourself that he's almost pathologically ambitious."

"Well, sure, he wants to be a POTUS, but that doesn't mean he's willing to murder his spouse to get it."

"POTUS? What on earth is that?"

"Oh, that's the code name the Secret Service used for Clinton—it stands for President of the United States, which is of course what Harlan wants to be. Honestly, I think he sees himself as another Clinton—a charismatic Southern politician who's destined for the White House. He's obsessed with his own image and power. But to go from that to murdering Elm in cold blood—'' She shook her head vigorously. ''No. It's absurd. Has to be.''

"Is it? You've painted a pretty odd profile of the man. I'd say that perhaps it fits. Especially if there was a way to do it without raising suspicion.''

Meredith looked at him, forcing herself to consider his allegations honestly, and felt another chilling shudder run through her. "But wait a minute," she said, logic reasserting itself, "if he was actually poisoning Elm, then Ashby would have to be party to it. That's impossible."

"You told me yourself that he was strangely reluctant to allow you to have any contact with your friend and client. And what about the test results? Why won't he send them? Is he trying to cover something up?''

"Okay." Meredith laid her palms on the table and let out a long breath. "I agree that none of this is straightforward, but we mustn't get carried away. Why would Ashby lend himself to such a scheme? It could ruin him."

Johnny shook his head and shrugged. "I have no idea. Just a feeling. It's the Irish in me," he said with the first smile of the day.

"Suppositions just aren't good enough—particularly if you're alleging murder."

"You're right," he admitted, "but you know, there's something else. Let's imagine the following scenario. Let's suppose that Harlan somehow knew about Elm's exposure to selenium, let's say, as that's what's turned up in the soil tests, and found a way to increase her contact with the mineral, perhaps topically or through some of the experimental medications she's been receiving at Ashby's clinic. He's the only person visiting her, after all. He could actually be poisoning her without anyone else's assistance."

"That is ridiculously far-fetched."

"I don't care how far-fetched it may seem. It's still possible," he insisted eagerly. "Let's go to Atlanta, Meredith. We'll find an excuse to visit Elm and get hold of a sample of whatever is in that drip you said they've got in her arm twenty-four hours a day, any creams she's using, anything. We'll have them tested and take it from there. I've seen examples of this kind of thing with horses. Repeated exposure to certain elements can be thoroughly detrimental—and very hard to detect until it's too late."

"Okay." She nodded. "I'll see if I can rearrange my schedule for tomorrow. But at this point, I think I should go alone. It'll raise too many suspicions if a total stranger shows up on Elm's doorstep." She saw that he was about to protest and held up her hand. "Look, I know you're desperate to see her, but that will have to wait until we've got a plan. Now, I have to go." She swooped up her purse and made to rise. "I'll drop you off at the hotel."

"Thanks." Johnny signaled for the bill. "Of course, if the results of your additional soil tests turn out to be positive, we've got an obligation to go the authorities with this." He looked up and their eyes met.

"Look, you know nothing about the soil tests, okay? Or anything else, for that matter. God, you could get me into some serious shit, Graney."

"This is already serious shit, Meredith," he said grimly, "and you know it, even if you won't admit it. But we'll face this together. I am not about to let Elm suffer or be hurt by anyone," he vowed, holding the door for her. "I don't give a damn who gets hurt along the way."

27

Elm's despair had reached new heights. Defying the doctor's orders, she'd stumbled out of bed and, barely able to stand, somehow managed to reach the bathroom sink. She stared in the mirror, horrified. Could this be the same woman who had entered the clinic? Her face looked pale, like parchment. Her eyes were hollow, like an old woman's, and her hair—what had happened to her hair? she wondered, passing her trembling fingers through it while steadying herself with her other hand, appalled to feel it falling out. She muffled a sob, forced herself not to retch and stumbled back to the bed, where she sank into the pillows and depression.

This truly was the end.

Thank God Johnny hadn't come. Nobody should have to see her in this awful, diminished state. She would tell Ashby that she didn't want any visitors. Harlan had been in, she remembered that. He'd been very nice, very solicitous, very kind. But she didn't care if he saw her like this. She was suspicious of him, of why he was here, of all the things that occasionally floated through her hazy mind and that somehow didn't gel.

Something wasn't right.

She felt desperately uneasy. For herself, for her father. If Harlan was up to no good, what would happen when she was gone? She'd have to remember to ask Ashby to arrange a meeting with Meredith so that she could make sure the divorce was finalized, so that even if she were dead, her father would not be linked to Harlan in any way.

She became quite agitated as this train of thought progressed. She called the nurse, clung to her arm, insisted she must see Meredith, that she needed her phone. The nurse soothed her, promised that she would tell Dr. Ashby, that everything would be taken care of.

Finally, Elm calmed down and fell asleep. She didn't even feel the needle pricking anymore.

Meredith sat in her office and studied all the information she and Mel had gathered. She'd written it all out, put it in order, and now was trying desperately to find some sort of pattern. Problem was, a lot of it just didn't make sense.

Tyler Brock. How did he fit into the puzzle? From what she could ascertain he had some pretty creepy connections in Miami. His corporation, Brock International, seemed to have its fingers in lots of businesses, none of them remotely related to municipal-waste processing. So what was his involvement with the plant, other than selling them the land it was sitting on? Harlan had exerted a lot of pressure on local authorities to rubber-stamp Brock's election to the plant's oversight board. Could the waste plant somehow be a front for other operations, something much more sinister?

And Harlan. What was his agenda here? Despite her reluctance to admit it, she was almost certain now that there was much more to his involvement with Tyler Brock than just fund-raising. The assorted companies under the Brock International umbrella had all made significant contributions to Harlan's campaign. But a little digging by Mel had revealed that Harlan's Leadership PAC—ostensibly set up to help fund other candidates' campaigns, but that was clearly a ploy to help him gain clout among his colleagues and position himself for a leadership job—was one of the best-funded PACS in the entire Congress, with more money than even the Senate Majority Leader's. Many of the contributions had come from out-of-state entities—and the question was, why? Harlan was a promising politician, yes, but by no means a figure of national importance, despite his own delusions. What sort of political favors were being traded for that level of monetary support? Did Brock and the other major contributors expect some sort of reciprocity, a payback?

The third factor in all this was the unexplained symptoms plaguing residents in the area around the waste-processing plant. Despite Mel's article, no one seemed to be questioning the cause of the uptake in hospital admissions. And while Julie's unfortunate death had presented a chance to get some real answers, Meredith's attempt to have the body autopsied had hit a wall when she'd learned that Julie's estranged husband had had her cremated within days of her death. From Harlan's standpoint, that sure was convenient, she decided darkly.

Perhaps she was just being paranoid. But remembering a small piece in the paper about how Congressman MacBride had graciously visited the grieving family, she couldn't help wondering if he'd somehow had a hand in arranging for the body's quick disposal.

She ran her fingers through her hair, disappointed that avenue was closed to her now. Still, with Johnny's help, she'd figure something out. He'd been in Savannah now for two days. She had to admire his patience, knowing he was frantic to see Elm. They'd both agreed, however, that he shouldn't make his presence known until they'd developed a plan. Working day and night, they'd been trying to piece together every scrap of information, fear mounting as they did so. Yesterday, at his urging, she'd returned to Atlanta and, after another discussion with Ashby, had insisted on visiting Elm.

What she saw had left her bereft of speech. Elm was withering before her eyes, a shadow of the woman she'd seen only days earlier. It had taken all her ingenuity to get Ashby to leave them alone for a few minutes, insisting she had private matters to discuss with her client. Elm had drifted in and out of consciousness but seemed aware of her presence.

As soon as the door closed behind Ashby, Meredith had locked it, then carefully removed the tube from the drip and poured some of the contents into a small plastic vial, which she'd slipped into her handbag. Then hastily she'd reattached the tube. By the time Ashby returned, she was ready to leave, agreeing with him that Elm was simply too tired to follow what she was saying and that she would return another day. Although she noticed that Ashby seemed calmer when she adopted a posture of distraught friend rather than determined attorney, he made a point of warning her that this would be the last time he'd let her see Elm on her own; he didn't think his patient was tolerating the visits well.

Meredith had wanted to protest, but she could tell he wasn't going to back down. The man looked decidedly worried. He was haggard and his eyes kept shifting back and forth, as though he was afraid of something. Harlan, she'd noted, was nowhere in sight, but that was likely because he was back on the campaign trail, vacuuming up as many votes as he could.

Now she sat at her desk with all the information spread in neat piles before her, waiting for Mel to bring her the results of the drip content and for Johnny to arrive. She glanced at her watch. They should be here shortly.

A few minutes later Ally rang through, announcing both men simultaneously.

"Come on in," Meredith beckoned.

"Good morning." Johnny smiled briefly, shook hands with Mel, and they sat down.

"Here. I didn't open it," Mel said expectantly, handing her the envelope with the results.

Meredith handled it with care and growing unease. The information inside this envelope could determine so much, she realized, her hand shaking slightly as she slit open the side.

Then, as she unfolded the single page and her eyes pored over the words, she caught her breath. Her expression grim, she passed the letter silently to Johnny. His eyes skimmed the paper.

"What does it say?" Mel asked impatiently.

"Here, take a look," Johnny said bitterly, handing it to him.

"My God. We were right. According to this lab technician's report, Elm's IV fluid contains dangerously high levels of selenium. She's being poisoned," he muttered, horrified. "I told you that bastard MacBride was up to no good." He handed the paper back to Johnny, who scanned over it once more.

"This says the EPA's reference dose for selenium is .005 milligrams per kilogram body weight per day," Johnny noted, "and that a fatal exposure level would be around 240 milligrams." He sat up suddenly. "My God," he exclaimed, doing some quick calculations, "at the present dosage and drip rate, it might take only five or six more days for the selenium in Elm's blood to reach a lethal concentration level—and we don't know what her baseline is. A good amount might already be present."

"What?" Meredith grabbed the paper from him and stared at it. "Good Lord, you're right."

"Time to call in the cops," Mel said decisively.

"We can't do that," Meredith jumped in. "We're just presuming that Harlan's behind all this. How can we be sure? We have no proof." Meredith leaned back, her legal mind at work. "Let's presume for a moment that he actually has nothing to do with this, that for whatever reason, Ashby is performing this sick experiment on his own. I'm not saying MacBride's a choir boy—" she waved her hand "—but until we have proof, we can't very well make accusations that will destroy his career; he'll sue us for libel."

"Who cares about his reputation?" Johnny said angrily. "We're talking about Elm's life."

"Johnny, believe me, I'm on her side. I'm just arguing that going to the police now will only slow us down. They'll demand proof that we don't have, and then they'll drag their heels on the resulting investigation because they'll know their butts are on the line if they make a misstep."

"But what about these test results?" Mel asked. "Isn't this enough evidence to get something started?"

"Unfortunately, we can't be sure. Let's remember, I acquired the sample without getting a release from the clinic or Ashby's permission. The cops would probably reject our sample as inadmissible and solicit a warrant from a judge so they could go get their own. All that will take up valuable time that Ashby—if he's guilty—could use to tamper with the contents of the IV. It's time that Elm just doesn't have, I'm afraid."

"You're right," Johnny broke in. "At this point, it doesn't matter who's doping the drip with selenium—what matters is getting Elm out of there. The hard proof can follow later."

"Well, if you think that's for the best," Mel said tentatively. "But, jeez, wouldn't you guys just love to open your paper tomorrow morning and see MacBride's ugly mug staring out from beneath a big fat headline? The story would be huge."

"We owe this to you, Mel, and you'll get your story in the end, don't worry. But we can't afford a scandal right now. If Harlan really is using Elm's illness for political advantage, then pressure might just push him over the edge, make him decide the safest course is to finish her off. Our first and only priority at this point is to save Elm, get her out of that clinic ASAP. The problem is," Meredith groaned, "I don't have a clue how we're going to do it. Ashby has everything under tight control. No one comes or goes without him clearing it first."

"Well, we've got to find a way, "Johnny said, voice raw, "or they're going to keep feeding her that poison until she's dead, and then Ashby will just sweep it all under the rug, falsify the death certificate and destroy the evidence."

"I agree, there's no time to waste." Meredith shoved on her glasses and flipped through her notes. "But Harlan's not going to sign her release, that's for sure," she said bitterly.

"Wait a minute." Johnny laid his hand on the desk and leaned forward, staring hard at Meredith. "If Elm is in a sufficiently coherent state, couldn't she sign herself out?"

"Technically, yes." Meredith laid down her pen and a slow grin covered her face. "That's brilliant, Graney. Of course. Why didn't I think of that? She can sign her own release form and there is absolutely nothing Ashby or anyone could do about it," she finished, excited. "The trouble is when to do it," she continued thoughtfully. "We'd have to find a moment when Harlan isn't there to prevent us. If he gets wind of this, he'll try to have her declared unfit."

"He sent a press release to the paper this morning saying that he was heading back to D.C. tonight to present that new bill he's been pushing," Mel chipped in. "I'll use that as a pretence to set up an interview with him—in fact, I'll arrange to interview him up there. You know how he never misses an opportunity for press coverage."

"Boy, do I," Meredith concurred bitterly.

"Then let's go to Atlanta today," Johnny broke in. "We have no idea what state Elm's in."

"That's impossible. I have to set up the interview."

"Then get on with it." Meredith clapped her hands together and rose. "Let's get cracking. Mel, you call Harlan's office and get that set up. Afternoon's probably easier to organize than the morning. Make sure he misses any connections out of D.C. Oh, and see if you can find out if he still has the use of Tyler Brock's plane, okay?"

"Sure thing." Mel jumped up. "Nice meeting you," he said to Johnny. "Good luck."

"To you, too. And many thanks. Your help has been invaluable." The two men shook hands and Mel headed for the door, pulling out his cell phone as he went.

Meredith returned to her desk. "Now," she said briskly, "there are so many details to cover. We need to think how we can set up the actual exit from the clinic, what transport we'll use and where to take her. She'll need to be hospitalized immediately."

"I've been thinking about that. Transport isn't a problem.

I'll have my brother, Liam, send the company jet to Atlanta. We can have a nurse and doctor on board. We'll fly her straight to New York. My mother's on the board at Columbia, she can arrange for a private hospital room and the proper specialists.''

"Yes, but what about the departure from the clinic?" Meredith mused. "Everything will need to run very smoothly.''

"We'll hire a private ambulance that can use the back entrance. I presume there must be a special dock for delivering patients?''

"Yes. Around the back. I noticed that. Good idea. You really think of everything, don't you?" She smiled at him across the desk, liking him more and more, appreciating his clear, efficient thought process. "I wonder if we shouldn't tell the senator what's going on," she added, frowning suddenly. "Elm's his daughter, after all. Plus, he could pull a lot of weight.''

"In due course," Johnny said firmly. "Right now, it's far too risky. If we're going to do this right, then the fewer people who are in on this, the better. We can't go in there with the stated intention of getting her to sign release papers, or Ashby will refuse us admission. We have to handle things so that they don't know what's going on until the last possible minute. Otherwise, Harlan—or whomever—just might finish her off before we get that chance to see her." He swallowed and went suddenly pale again.

"Sounds like we're going to need a diversion," Meredith observed.

"But what? I know—I had a call from Gioconda yesterday. She's worried to death about Elm and is arriving in New York this afternoon. I'll tell Liam to bring her down to Atlanta with him. She's got an admirably devious mind— maybe she'll help us come up with something." He dragged his hand through his hair. "My God. Twenty-four hours seems an awfully long way away.''

"I know," Meredith replied softly, "but we must be sensible, make sure all our ducks are in a row before we head in there. Otherwise we might mess up and then it'll be too late.''

"Right." He nodded absently. "I'll call Liam and arrange for the jet and the medical staff to be readied while we think of a cover."

"Good. I think we should try to visit in the late morning or early afternoon when Ashby's tied up with patients. Although, they know me now at reception, so it may be difficult for me to get access to her room—Ashby's already told me I won't be allowed to see her without him. The other big if," she remarked pensively, laying down her pen, "is how Elm is going to receive this. She's very sick, Johnny, not at all herself, and if she's being persuaded that this is the only treatment for her illness, she may not want to give up on it. God knows what Ashby and Harlan have put into her head.''

"You have a point. But I'm sure that if I can get to her, she'll listen to me."

"But that's just the problem," Meredith argued. "If they balk at letting me in, there's zero chance that they'll admit a complete stranger."

"Well, we'll just have to figure something out between now and tomorrow, won't we?" Johnny answered with an optimism he was far from feeling. "I'd better be on my way, I've got a lot of calls to make." He rose, carefully pushed the chair back into position, then smiled. "Thanks, Meredith, for trusting me.''

"Thanks for coming." She came out from behind her desk and they shook hands warmly. "Hang in there, Johnny. By this time tomorrow, we'll have her out of there."

"God willing," he murmured, squeezing her hand, eyes meeting hers for a brief moment before he turned and walked out the door.

Only a few more days and he'd be home free, Harlan reflected, hanging up the phone, thrilled with the Cayman bank's confirmation that funds had been wired into his offshore account. Brock was pleased with all the publicity engendered by Elm's illness—it had been worth several points in the polls. Of course, the man had no idea what the final outcome would be, Harlan noted, knowing it would come as quite a surprise.

The blue telephone on his desk rang and he picked up. "Yes?"

"It's that reporter again, Harlan," Marcy whined. "He's called asking for this, that and the other, wanting to know things about the waste plant and the budget. But now he sounds real nice. He wants to interview you tomorrow in D.C. for a special insert the paper is running in next Sunday's issue. He says he's sorry it's such short notice, but his editor couldn't decide which personality to choose and they finally settled on you. A two-page spread, center page."

"Really?" Harlan smiled, gratified. "Tell him he can come over to my congressional office tomorrow around eleven."

"Will do."

There would be many more interview opportunities, Harlan reflected, grinning broadly, and not just with Podunk papers like the *Savannah Morning News*. In fact, just last week, he'd met Bob Woodward, the powerful political reporter for the *Washington Post*, at a Georgetown cocktail party. Their contact had been brief, but Harlan knew he'd made an impression. He made a mental note to have Marcy put Woodward on his weekly fax blast—get him following his career. Maybe he could give him an exclusive when Elm died?

Things were definitely looking up, he decided, and by next Sunday, Ashby had assured him, things would be very rosy indeed. Elm was deteriorating by the day and couldn't last much longer. In fact, this reporter's piece—Mel something or other—would be perfect. America would wake up Sunday morning, read the article over breakfast and say, "Oh, my God, that's the poor congressman who just lost his wife. What a shame. Look honey, such a good-looking young couple."

Harlan heaved a satisfied sigh, savoring the image just a

moment longer, then went back to work. He reviewed the morning's messages, noting with dismay that the senator had called again. He was getting to be something of a problem. Although Ashby swore that he'd sent Hathaway's friend in D.C. a false set of blood samples that wouldn't raise any suspicion, Harlan wasn't completely comfortable. George Hathaway hadn't gotten where he was by being an idiot— and Harlan didn't trust Ashby not to screw things up. The sooner this all was over, the better.

Senator Hathaway sat quietly, trying to suppress a vague sense of unease. Harlan had assured him Elm's treatment was progressing well, but he was still deeply concerned that he hadn't been able to see his little girl. Ever since the news of her illness, he'd found it hard to think of his daughter as a grown woman, could only see her as the small, lonely child who'd lost her mother at such a tragically young age. He'd brought her up alone, with only the help of his sister, Frances—thank God she'd been there to show him the ropes. And luckily, Elm herself had been such a fiercely strong little thing. Still, he knew he hadn't been the world's best father. He had allowed other competing interests, he was ashamed to admit, to become more important than his family in Savannah. Now he wanted to make it up to her, wanted desperately to wrap her in his arms, whisper that everything would be all right, assure her that the monsters in the closet didn't exist.

Only problem was, now he wasn't so sure—about the monsters not existing, that is. Since learning of her illness, he'd had terrible dreams of dark shadows haunting his daughter's steps. He could never see into the shadows, discover what was threatening her, but the presence there seemed arrogant and angry, even evil, and it left him, a man who'd never been scared in his life, feeling totally helpless. His sweet child needed him and he could do nothing.

He heard a noise in the living room, jolted nervously at the sound, then remembered Frances was waiting for him there. He shook off the sense of disquiet and climbed to his feet, sternly reminding himself that he was a United States senator and not susceptible to such nonsense.

"Any news about Elm, George?" Frances asked, plying her petit point and eyeing him over the top of her reading glasses as he entered the room.

"Not much," he said gruffly. "Harlan says she's doing better, but she's still not well enough for visitors—not even a phone call."

"Oh. That's a little concerning, isn't it? You know, I think we should insist on seeing her. I don't feel comfortable not having access to her."

"I know, but if it's for the best, then we shouldn't interfere with Ashby's policy. Harlan's seen her and he says she sends her love. That's reassuring."

Frances pursed her lips but refrained from voicing her opinion. "I find it strange that she can't even receive a phone call."

"Might get her agitated," he responded, sitting down in the armchair opposite. "I don't think we should question the experts. Is Beau serving tea?"

Knowing it was useless to argue with her brother once he'd gotten a bee in his bonnet about something, Frances let out a deep sigh and gave up. But she was unhappy with the situation. She would talk to Meredith tomorrow, she decided, and if George wouldn't take any action himself, she'd take measures of her own to visit her niece.

That was one of the few rewards of living to her advanced age, she realized. People practically expected you to be an interfering, cynical old coot.

And she fully intended to live up to the stereotype.

28

"**B**ut, ma'am," the flustered receptionist insisted, "I can assure you that we have no reservation in the name of Countess Mancini."

"*Impossibile,*" Gioconda countered autocratically. She stood, elegantly clad in a lemon Chanel suit and black high heels, a huge black crocodile purse positioned on the reception desk. The receptionist couldn't help but stare at the immense diamonds dripping from the countess's fingers and neck.

"But I—"

"My secretary called from Florence yesterday. I was promised the best suite in this establishment. I wish to start my cure immediately. I have a slight rash and was assured Dr. Ashby was the only physician to see. Look," Gioconda insisted, drawing up her sleeve and extending her elegant unscathed forearm. "It's loathsome," she said, shuddering.

"I'm afraid I can't see a thing," the girl replied apologetically.

"That's because it's of nervous origin, you fool," Gioconda replied scathingly. "Where is the director of this place? I wish to speak to him immediately. Tell him the Contessa Gioconda Mancini is waiting and does not like to be delayed." She spun on her heel and addressed the chauffeur, laden with a battery of Louis Vuitton suitcases. "You may put those over there. I'm afraid there seems to be a stupid misunderstanding here, so you'll just have to wait to carry them upstairs.''

''Yes, ma'am.'' Johnny relinquished the cases, setting them on the floor, careful to keep the cap over his eyes, then went to stand by the window. My God, this just might work. Gio was certainly putting on quite a performance.

After a hurried phone call, the receptionist disappeared behind a white lacquered door. Several minutes later, she reappeared with a tall, good-looking man in a white coat whom, he presumed, must be Ashby. Johnny mastered the longing to take two steps across the room and slam his fist into the man's face, forcing himself to listen carefully to the conversation.

''Ah, *dottore*,'' Gio purred, handing him her fingers as a queen would to a vassal. ''I'm sure there must be some mistake. Your girl has told me the reservation I made with your clinic to treat this very annoying nervous rash is not in your books. I find it unbelievable that such a mistake could take place, since I was assured at the highest levels that your clinic is the very best. I have flown all the way from Italy, I am tired and I wish to be installed in my suite immediately. I intend to put myself completely in your hands,'' she added, flapping her long dark lashes, ''and simply will not countenance any one else's care.''

Ashby looked flustered. ''I'm terribly sorry, um, Contessa, that you've been inconvenienced, but—''

''And of course,'' Gioconda interrupted, making a grand, sweeping gesture with her hand, ''money is no object. I presume you'll accept cash for your services? My health is priceless to me.''

Ashby's expression changed, becoming instantly solicitous, Johnny noted cynically. Then the doctor frowned at the receptionist. ''I'm sure there must be a mistake. Perhaps it was Patricia who took your reservation. She's off today. I'll be sure to discipline her for the oversight when she returns.''

Johnny watched the receptionist's eyes open wide in blank

amazement and smiled inwardly. There was no Patricia and the ruse was working. *Bravo, Gio.*

"We'll have you installed in the Tara suite immediately, Contessa," Ashby said, taking Gio's arm.

"What floor is that on?" she demanded.

"The second."

"Oh, but I hate being too low." She sniffed derisively. "My nose is very sensitive to smells, and I do not wish to be so close to the odors of the street. I wish to be on the highest floor."

"That would be the fourth."

"Perfect. Please see to it."

"Yes, of course." He smiled nervously, and Johnny heard him murmuring to the receptionist about moving Mrs. Whitburn's reservation while Gioconda drummed her scarlet nails impatiently on the reception desk.

"Well?" she asked, "is that finally settled?"

"Of course, Contessa. I'll take you up personally."

"Good. You," she said, turning in Johnny's direction, "may follow us up with the bags. Make two trips. I don't want you dropping anything." She turned and bestowed her most gracious smile upon Ashby. "These people can be so careless, can't they? Now, *dottore*," she said languorously, laying a hand delicately on his arm, "I must tell you all about my dreadful ailment." She accompanied the doctor down the corridor and on toward the elevator and embarked on a long soliloquy of her ills.

Johnny heaved two of the bags, winked meaningfully at the receptionist and whispered, "Keep an eye on those for me, will you? She'll have me hung, drawn and quartered if I lose anything." The girl nodded and giggled, watching as the convoy made its way to the elevator.

When the doors opened on the fourth floor, Ashby ushered Gioconda down the corridor, murmuring sympathetically as she explained how her skin simply couldn't tolerate jewelry that wasn't platinum or twenty-four-carat gold. Johnny, following behind with the luggage, felt his pulse beat faster as they passed the room Meredith had identified as Elm's.

Then Ashby stopped two doors down.

"I hope you'll be comfortable, Contessa, it's our most luxurious suite." He sent Gioconda a charming, ingratiating smile. Still, the man looked somewhat strained, Johnny reflected, placing the suitcases inside the door. He watched as Gioconda, continuing her bravura performance, entered the room, stood in the center of it for a minute looking critically about her and then nodded her haughty approval.

"It will do. I can always have my decorator fly in to touch things up if it proves necessary to make a longer stay," she said condescendingly. "Not that I expect to be here too long, dear *dottore*." She looked meltingly at Ashby, who, Johnny noted, was having a hard time keeping his eyes off Gio's admittedly impressive breasts. "I am sure you are nothing like that imbecile I visited in Switzerland who couldn't cure a hangnail, much less a mysterious and unpredictable condition such as mine. I know you will rid me of this odious illness in no time." After wiggling her fingers at Ashby, she turned and addressed Johnny.

"You. Put my bags over here," she ordered, pointing to the bed. "And please don't dawdle, I don't have all day and there are the rest of my things to be brought up."

"Yes, ma'am." Johnny hastily placed the bags where she directed, then disappeared from the room while Gioconda continued enumerating a lengthy list of amazingly diverse symptoms. He just hoped she'd be able to keep it up.

Carefully Johnny eyed the corridor and, seeing it empty, hurried down it. Without hesitation, he opened the door to Elm's room. Shutting it quickly and silently behind him, he turned, stopping dead in his tracks. He gazed, horrified, at the pale figure lying motionless in the bed.

For a ghastly moment, he thought she was dead.

Then, pulling himself together, aware that he had little time to spare before his absence would be noted, he approached the bed, pulling the release forms Meredith had drafted from the jacket pocket where he'd concealed them.

Meredith, he remembered grimly, had spent most of the trip from Savannah reminding him that Elm might not sign them.

She looked so tiny, he reflected, heart aching, as though she'd shrunk to half her size. Moving toward the bed, he stood over her, dying to touch her, afraid of scaring her. Then, carefully, he reached out his trembling fingers and gently caressed her brow.

"Elm, my darling," he whispered, taking her emaciated white hand in his and lifting it to his lips, unable to believe he was actually here with her, touching her at last. But he had to be quick. He had only a few minutes to accomplish the task and get the bags up to Gio before they executed the second stage of their plan.

"Johnny?" Her voice was faint and her eyes opened slowly, disbelieving. "Is that really you?"

"Yes, my darling, it's me."

"Oh, Johnny," she whispered, the ghost of a smile lighting up her hollow face, "you came after all."

"Of course I came, my love. You didn't think I'd leave you here all on your own, did you?" he said in a low voice, hoping they couldn't be heard in the corridor. "I've come to get you out of here."

"But I can't leave." She clung to his hand and shook her head sadly. "You see," she whispered, "this is my only chance. Oh, Johnny." She stared at him now, her sunken eyes filled with unshed tears, "I'm so sorry, so terribly sorry, I never meant for this to happen to you, I never thought—I don't want to die and leave you. I have to stay and try to get well." Her voice cracked and the tears trickled down her dehydrated, colorless cheeks.

"Darling, you must trust me," Johnny insisted urgently, wiping her cheeks with his thumb in a tender gesture. "We have to get you out of here. I can't explain everything right now, but there are things going on that make it essential that you sign these papers and leave with me immediately."

"But don't you see," she murmured through her tears, becoming agitated, "this is my only chance of survival. I can't leave, I simply can't. Dr Ashby's the only doctor who can cure me. I think I'm feeling a little better than I was before, and I can drink today and—"

"Elm, please, just trust me," Johnny begged, gazing down at her, suddenly beset by doubt. What if they were wrong and he didn't manage to save her? What if she died and he failed her?

For a moment he closed his eyes. He simply had to take that risk, make her put her life in his hands whatever the consequences. "Look, I can't explain it all now, it would take too long," he said finally, "but I think you know how much I love you, even if I've never told you outright before. Elm, you have to believe me," he insisted, squeezing her hand tight, "I would never do anything to harm you."

Their eyes met and held in a long gaze.

"I want to do whatever will make me better," she said finally.

"Then sign these and everything will be okay," he urged with renewed insistence. "Trust me. You'll die if you stay here." He looked for something to write on, picked up a magazine from the bed table and uncapped the pen he'd brought. "Here. I'll help you sit." He leaned forward and cradled her back, astonished at the bones pressing through her skin, then propped her up with pillows. Elm grasped the pen, her hand barely able to hold it.

"But what are they?" she queried, eyes blurry. "I can't read."

"They're release forms."

"Release forms? Why would I sign release forms?" she asked feebly.

"Because you have to get out of here."

"But, I—"

"Trust me, darling. Sign here." He guided her hand to the proper place on the page.

"Are you sure this is the right thing to do?" Elm hesitated, the pen shaking in her weak fingers.

"Absolutely." He looked straight into her eyes once more and held them in his gaze. "Just trust me, Elm. I promise you'll be fine."

At that moment, despite her reluctance, despite logic that dictated she should stay, Elm knew there was only one option—to trust Johnny, to put her life into the hands of the man she loved. Slowly she scratched her name on the page, then fell back against the pillows, exhausted but also aware of a sudden rush of peace. He had come, hadn't he? He was somehow miraculously here beside her, had never let her down. Now, even if she died, she realized suddenly, she would do so in his arms.

Lifting the completed papers, Johnny let out a sigh of relief and slipped them back underneath his jacket.

"Now, darling, you're going to have to trust me a little longer, I'm afraid." He smiled gently down at her. "I'm going to have to leave you for a few minutes."

Elm reached her hand out anxiously. "Don't go. Please."

"Darling, I have to. But I'll be back in a little, I promise. If anyone comes in, don't tell them anything about this, okay?"

"Okay." Her hand fell limply on the coverlet and she closed her eyes.

"Darling, please don't worry, I'll be back in about fifteen minutes."

Elm merely nodded, opened her eyes a few moments, and then closed them again as though she was too tired to do more.

Reluctantly Johnny slipped back into the empty corridor and headed for the elevator. He pressed the button, praying that Ashby wouldn't come out of Gio's room and wonder where he'd been all this time. When the elevator arrived, he stepped back inside and returned to the lobby. With a grin at the receptionist, he picked up the rest of the bags and placed them inside the elevator.

"Is she staying?" she asked in a hushed tone.

"Seems like it," he replied with shrug. "You know what these rich Euros are like. Crazy." He grinned, touching his temple as the doors closed. On the fourth floor, as he approached the room, he could hear Gio rambling on dramatically.

"I've brought the rest of your bags, ma'am," he said as he reached the doorway of the room.

"Well, thank goodness for that! Where on earth did you get to? *Mamma mia,* it is increasingly difficult to come by decent staff nowadays, isn't it?" She sent the overwhelmed Ashby a look that included him as one of her set. "But *dottore,* I've been holding you back with all my complaints," she gushed. "I'm so dreadfully sorry. Please feel free to go. I still have to pay off this incompetent creature," she added in an undertone that, despite the tension he was experiencing, made Johnny hide a smile.

"Well, Contessa, if you don't mind, I should be on my way. There are many patients to see, although of course, none," he said obsequiously, "as important as you."

"Of course," Gio agreed. "But I'll be fine now," she said, waving him out. "A rest will do me good."

"I'll have the nurse come by in a little while to run some diagnostic tests."

"Not for at least an hour, if you please," she said imperiously. "I still have to deal with this unpacking and getting settled in."

"Of course, Contessa, I'll see that you're not disturbed."

When Ashby finally left, Gio flopped in the armchair and groaned. "*Madonna mia,* I don't know how I held out. I thought you were never coming back. Did she sign them?"

"Yes. Thank God. I have the papers here. Are you set?"

"Of course." Gio stood up briskly and straightened her suit. "Shall we go?"

"I'll check the corridor." Johnny peeped out and, seeing that it was once again empty, beckoned to Gio. "Come on, the coast is clear. Now, let's hope our ambulance driver, Liam, managed to place the gurney in the service elevator, as we arranged."

"He'd better have," Gio said darkly.

Johnny found the service corridor and, sure enough, the gurney was waiting in the elevator. On it was a male nurse's scrubs. After removing his jacket and stowing the release forms safely in his pants pocket, he quickly slipped the scrubs over his chauffeur's uniform and tossed the black jacket in an adjacent laundry bin and handed Gio a doctor's white coat to slip on.

Then Gio rushed to Elm's door while he wheeled the gurney after her at a slower pace. "Don't be shocked when you see her, she doesn't look well at all," he murmured anxiously, touching Gio's arm as she was about to turn the door handle.

"I know."

They looked at each other, then Johnny nodded. "Okay, let's do it."

She nodded back and they entered the room. With a gasp, Gio rushed to the bed.

"Elm, *cara,* it's me, I'm here."

"Gio?" Elm opened her eyes, amazed. "Why, I didn't know that—"

"Shh…" Gio leaned over and kissed Elm's shrunken cheek, hiding her alarm at her friend's appearance. "We'll have you out of here in a second."

"But—"

"Darling." Johnny approached the bed after leaving the release papers in an easily visible place on the desk. Elm was far too weak to move by herself, so after carefully removing her IV, Gio held the gurney still as he carefully lifted Elm from her bed.

"Johnny," she whispered, "what's happening, why are you both here? And in those clothes?" She seemed confused, but he could read the relief in her eyes as he lowered her to the gurney.

"Once we're out of here, we'll explain everything," he responded, dropping a kiss on her tired brow. "Now, just relax and let us do the work, will you? I promise you'll be fine, my darling. Just hang in there."

Elm smiled weakly and closed her eyes, too tired, now that she'd made the decision, to do more than let them take charge.

Gio opened the door and looked both ways down the corridor.

"The coast's clear. *Andiamo,*" she beckoned.

Together they rolled the gurney toward the service corridor, not too fast in case someone appeared and it looked suspicious. Gio pressed the elevator call button. "Come on, *presto*," she hissed under her breath.

It took several nerve-racking minutes for the service elevator to arrive. When the doors finally opened up, there were two people inside. Johnny gritted his teeth and moved the gurney inside. The two nurses paid little attention to them and went on chatting.

The door opened onto the ground floor, and the two nurses got out. Several agonizing seconds passed before the doors closed once again. When they finally reached the basement, Johnny swiftly pushed the gurney out down the back corridor to the ambulance dock, with Gio, tottering in her high heels, in tow.

"My God, this can't be happening," Ashby muttered, staring horrified at Elm's empty bed. He had told Harlan it was too damn dangerous, that something was bound to happen.

And now it had.

He'd come to Elm's room, only to find it empty. Then he'd run to the Contessa's room, a dreadful suspicion forming in his mind. Her room was empty, too. The suitcases were still closed on the bed where she'd left them. He'd rushed back to Elm's room, trying to suppress his panic. Now his eyes fell upon a small stack of papers lying on the desk. He rushed forward, heart racing.

"Oh, Jesus," he muttered hoarsely.

Then, turning on his heel, Ashby rushed out of the room and, not waiting for the elevator, raced down the stairs to his office. Slamming the door shut, he hurried to the desk and picked up the phone, his fingers barely able to press the right numbers.

Oh, Christ, he was screwed.

Once they reached the wide doors of the ambulance dock, Johnny pushed Elm through.

"Is she okay?" Gio asked, rushing to keep up.

"She bein' moved?" the woman in charge asked, checking her list. "What's her name?"

"MacBride. Elm MacBride.

"I don't remember Dr. Ashby mentioning her." She frowned.

"The order just came through. She's being transferred," Johnny replied indifferently. "Call Ashby if you like." He held his breath while the woman wavered.

"Nah, that should be okay." She smiled and waved them through. Still holding his breath, Johnny exchanged a relieved glance with Gio as he wheeled Elm as quickly as he could toward the ambulance where Liam stood waiting by the open door. A few minutes later they were heading out of the compound, sirens blazing.

"We did it!" Gio exclaimed. "Johnny, you were *magnifico.*"

"If anyone was great, it was you, my dear. You have obviously missed your calling. Julia Roberts has nothing on you," he retorted, pulling off the hospital greens and reaching for Elm's hand.

"At this rate, we should make it to the airport in ten," Liam remarked, enjoying the way cars and trucks veered out of his way at the sound of the siren. "I could get used to this."

"Just drive," Gio said censoriously, pulling off her hospital coat.

"I thought that was what I was doing."

"*Caro,* please, let's make sure we arrive there alive."

"You fool, you fucking idiot. How could you let her go, you moron? You said she was too ill to move, that she was about to die. So how's she signing herself out of the goddamn clinic?" Harlan spoke in a low voice, for he wasn't alone on the flight. Two senators, friends of George Hathaway, were accompanying him to Savannah.

"There's nothing I could do. A patient has a right to sign

him or herself out at any given time if they are coherent enough to do so. How could I know that the other woman was taking me for a ride?''

"What other woman?" Harlan barked.

"This gorgeous Italian countess, with the most amazing bre—''

"Shit, shit, shit! It's that bitch, Gioconda."

"Yes, that was her name," Ashby said eagerly.

"I know, I know. What the hell is she doing in the States?" he muttered. "Never mind. You're still an idiot. You *said* that Elm was incapable of—''

"I never said she was unconscious or incoherent, I said her situation was deteriorating fast."

"Well, obviously not fast enough. You've just got to get her back, damn it." Harlan glanced around the plane at the two senators seated opposite each other, sipping Scotch in their shirtsleeves, while he stood at the other end of the aircraft near the galley. "I don't think I need to tell you that we can't let her escape from our hands. I simply have to know where she is, ASAP."

"I'm sorry," Ashby said, sounding distraught, "I tried to stop them, I really tried, but it was too late. By the time I got to the ambulance dock they were gone."

"What do you want, a medal? You should have locked her in her room, seen to it that she was supervised at all times."

"That's ridiculous and you know it." Ashby's voice was rising to a hysterical crescendo. "I've done everything you asked, tried my best, but I can't go on, I can't, you'll ruin me, I—''

Harlan hung up and stood, clenching and unclenching his fingers, trying to master the overwhelming rush of fury he was experiencing. How had this happened? How could Gioconda have known? She wasn't even... Of course. *Meredith.* He should have been more careful. But he hadn't thought of Meredith as a threat. Apparently he should have. *Bitch.* Clearly, she'd been the one who'd prepared the release forms. Which prompted another question—just how much did Meredith know?

For a moment he considered eliminating her, too—and maybe Gio and also that man who'd helped, whoever he was. Then reality hit. It was too risky, he recognized, shoving his hand into the pocket of his Brooks Brothers chinos.

"Hey, Harlan, stop all those calls and come join us." Tom Willer, a portly man in his mid-sixties who chaired the Senate's all-powerful finance committee, raised his glass and beckoned.

Plastering on his usual smile, Harlan joined them and accepted a Scotch. "Make it a double," he murmured as the older man poured. "It's been a long day." He loosened his tie and flopped into the wide cream leather seat, trying to determine how he might regain control of a rapidly deteriorating situation.

Then he remembered that reporter and his mood worsened. He didn't like the way the man had kept asking questions at the end of the interview. It troubled him. There was something about the guy, about the way he nosed around the subject of the waste plant, that stunk of scandal. *Shit.* It was only at the end of the interview that he'd put two and two together. This was the same guy who had written that article the other day. He really must look into what was happening over there. He'd probably staved off the reporter long enough to turn the situation to his advantage. Still, if people were being hospitalized with similar symptoms, something would have to be done fast.

Like changing his position on the whole project.

By the time the plane landed in Savannah, Harlan had recovered something of his usual punch. He would visit his constituents, promise to have a thorough investigation into the matter, come up with solutions and excuses for any failures, maybe even promise some compensation if it came to that. Tyler Brock would just have to cough up the necessary funds, he decided confidently.

But then, as he walked through the airport, he saw Brock, dressed in a smart silk suit, standing in front of Starbucks and evidently awaiting Harlan's arrival. His new surge of confidence faded and for the first time in recollection Harlan experienced a wave of doubt. It lasted only seconds before he moved consciously away from it, relegating it to the nether regions of his mind, then waved jauntily, introducing the two senators.

That would impress Tyler.

But he could see that the man wanted a word with him alone. Sending the others on ahead to the car, he stood in the arrival area and waited for what Brock had to say.

"I hear that little lady of yours is on the road again. Checked out of the clinic earlier this afternoon. You know why?" Brock's expression boded ill.

"We're transferring her to another clinic," Harlan lied blandly. His tie felt suddenly tight and a cold sweat broke out under his shirt. How the hell did Brock know?

"Really? And where might that be? Look, Harlan, don't fuck with me." Brock leaned closer. "I know damn well that there was a scene after she left. Someone heard the doctor on the phone and I'd be willing to bet he was talking with you. What the fuck is going on?"

"Nothing, I tell you, nothing. Look, I have to go." He glanced at his watch. "Why don't we lunch together tomorrow and we can talk all this over calmly? There's nothing to worry about," he said, flashing what he hoped was a reassuring smile.

Reluctantly Tyler fell back. "Okay, but you make sure you're there. I have a lot to talk to you about. Some crazy reporter came knocking at my door the other afternoon. Seems they know that I'm the silent partner in the Mogachee plant. Now, how the fuck did that get out, I wonder?" His tone was menacing.

"I haven't the faintest idea," Harlan replied truthfully. Then he said goodbye and walked out to the waiting car, determined to keep up his self-confident appearance. Somehow he didn't feel quite as invincible as he had a half hour earlier. Never mind, a sniff of coke would help remedy that problem, he realized thankfully.

Climbing into the back of the car, he changed his mood, disguising his worries and joking with his companions all the way to their hotel. Then, as the car dropped them off and headed toward the town house, his shoulders slumped and he closed his eyes. His first priority was to find Meredith and discover where Elm was. It was a nuisance that things hadn't worked out according to plan. In fact it was damned inconvenient and left him with very few options.

He'd had no intention of dirtying his own hands with this. After all, it was always better to have others take care of unpleasant business, because then they could take the fall if things went wrong. But now, he recognized, the greater risk was in not finishing the job and since he could no longer trust that worthless Ashby, he'd probably have to do it himself. He certainly didn't want to hurt Elm in any way. The mere thought left him uncomfortable and distressed. The other solution had seemed so simple, so wonderfully distant and humane.

Still, it was her own fault, he reminded himself. If she'd stayed put at the clinic, none of this would be happening. Now, he decided grimly, she'd have to face the consequences of her misjudgment.

29

"Okay," Tyler asked bluntly as they sat down at the restaurant table, "so where is your wife?"

"You know, I'm beginning to wonder just why you're so damned interested in her whereabouts. My wife is none of your business," Harlan muttered crossly, unfolding his napkin and taking a look around the other tables; no one here worth talking to, he noted.

Tyler looked at him coldly. "I don't appreciate the tone, MacBride. After all the money I've given you, I think I've earned the right to a little more respect. Besides, I have my reasons," Tyler answered sullenly. "And so does my partner in Miami, Juan Ramirez."

"Juan Ramirez? Your partner?" Harlan raised a brow, the name causing him to forget the jab he'd been about to administer. "You never told me you had a partner." Harlan felt shock ripples running up his spine. Juan Ramirez. He might as well have said Pablo Escobar.

"Why should I mention it? It's not your business. But it will be unless you get your wife back. Fast." He sent Harlan a dark look and let the news sink in.

"I don't see what my wife's presence or absence has to do with either of you," Harlan answered belligerently, adopting an offended air. Picking up the menu, he gave it a cursory glance, trying to remain nonchalant. But damn.

Could it be true about Ramirez? He'd never thought of Brock's partners as anything but other American business-men. In fact, he hadn't thought about Brock's partners at all.

"Stop kidding yourself, MacBride. I play in the big leagues. Where the fuck do you think the bucks come from, hey, buddy? From real estate or some goddamned waste plant? Or the trash I'm pickin' up in Jersey?" Brock gave a harsh bark of a laugh and leaned back, his pink-shirted belly flopping over the gold buckle of his Gucci belt. "You didn't really believe all this was lily white, did ya now?"

"I still don't know what that has to do with Elm." Harlan lowered his voice, seeing the waiter hovering. "Why don't we order, then we can have some privacy."

"Okay, what the hell. Gimme a steak and fries," he muttered at the waiter, slapping the menu shut with a bang. "Oh, and a Bud."

"Sure will, sir. Comin' right up. And you, Congressman, what can I get you, sir?"

For the first time in his political career, Harlan wished he were a little less recognizable. But he smiled, glanced at the waiter's name tag and pointed to the first item his finger hit on the menu. "I'll have this please, Joe. Maybe you could see that we aren't bothered? We're having a business lunch. And I'll take a cold beer as well." He grinned conspiratorially and the waiter nodded.

"Of course, Congressman, it'll be my pleasure." He picked up the menus and hurried over to the bar to put in the drink orders.

Tyler Brock leaned back and studied Harlan with an insolent air. "You know, MacBride, for someone as smart as you, you sure can be dumb," Tyler said, grabbing a roll from the breadbasket.

"Is that so? In what way?" Harlan raised an offended brow and looked at him down his elegant nose. The sleaze-ball better not think he could treat him like shit. He knew how to handle himself.

"You never realized why your wife is so important to us, did you?" the other man queried in comic amazement.

"Us?"

"Yes, MacBride, *us,*" he leered. "That's me and my buddies Down South. We want you married—or widowed, we don't care which—to that beautiful, snotty bitch."

"Don't talk like that about my wife."

"I'll talk any fucking way I want about your wife and anyone else I choose. She's the only thing that's kept our little association here going."

Harlan felt his collar tighten and his anger rise. "I think you'd better explain yourself, Brock. I'm afraid I don't get your meaning."

"Don't you, now?" Brock muttered, and leaned across the table, poking a finger at Harlan. "Well, let me paint you a picture, buddy. You listen up and you listen good. What fucking use would a second-rate, small-time congressman from Georgia be if he weren't married to that rich bitch, and if her old man weren't your father-in-law? Answer that."

"Excuse me?" Harlan froze and a choking anger took hold. "Surely even someone like you," he said, eyeing Brock with distaste, "must realize all I represent personally, that I'm the only one who has the balls to get the job done, the only one who can—" His face had paled and his breath was short.

"Aw, shut the fuck up, MacBride. Nobody's indispensable." Brock laughed scathingly. "There's tons of guys like you, all believing they can walk on water, thinking that someday they'll hit the big time, make it to the top, all racing around with mega egos because somebody's puffed 'em up to make 'em believe they're some big deal." He leaned across the table, his face inches from Harlan's. "The only thing that makes you worth my time is the Hathaway connection. No one would believe anything George Hathaway is involved with could be anything but aboveboard, and, fortunately for you, his luster extends to his son-in-law. You're our insurance policy against the authorities looking too closely at what we do. And if old man Hathaway manages to get you into the White House, well then, that's fine with us, too, because we're gonna be there with you, enjoying the ride.

"So get this straight," he continued, jabbing his index finger in Harlan's direction once more, "without the Hathaways, you're history, bud. And if little Elm goes, you go. I suggest you figure something out, and fast. I want her back in the saddle doing her thing. Is that clear? And don't you try to fool me with bullshit. Right now you have no fucking idea where she is. Probably screwing around with that Irish fella, the guy who won the Derby. She sure looked taken with him in the winner's circle," he jeered. "And you know what? Cancel that steak. I'm getting the fuck out of here. Just make sure you get this sorted out in twenty-four hours, or it'll be both our asses on the line."

As Brock started to rise, Harlan happened to catch the slight look of anxiety in his eyes. The man didn't want to show it, Harlan realized, but he was scared. Despite the bitter shock of his revelations, Brock's fear gave him the fuel he needed to regroup. "Wait a minute," he barked in a commanding tone. "You're not the only one with a say here. Sit down."

Brock was so surprised at Harlan's demand that, amazingly, he did as he was told.

"Now, you listen up," Harlan said, voice low and eyes narrowing. "My wife has been very sick. And do you know why?"

"Not a fucking clue."

"Let me enlighten you. She got sick because of toxic runoff from your waste plant—you know, the one you like to pretend you're not involved with? Apparently other members of the community are getting sick, too. One woman on my wife's gardening project even died. Aside from the fact that the IRS is bound to be interested in your little shell games, I know some lawyers who wouldn't hesitate to bring charges of criminal negligence against you. So if I were you, I'd stop your empty threats, Brock, because I won't hesitate to make that knowledge public and put your face on the six o'clock news."

"Don't try to smart-ass me, MacBride. I know what kind of weasel you are, and if you think I didn't prepare for something like this, you're a worse moron than I thought. I have you down on tape, buddy, taking wads of cash and checks. Believe me, it ain't pretty. Particularly in an election year. Isn't there a hefty jail sentence for politicians who accept kickbacks?"

Keeping his expression neutral, Harlan battled the sudden urge to slam his fist into Brock's grinning piglike face. He could not, he reminded himself rigidly, afford to lose his control in such a public place.

He had to think fast.

As Brock rose once more, eyeing him with disdain, he looked up, tried to appear chastened. "Sorry you won't stay for lunch," he remarked in an ingratiating tone. "I'll have news for you by tomorrow."

"Ah, that's better." Brock's face broke into a cynical smile. "I see you got the message, MacBride. Bravo." He patted him condescendingly on the shoulder and made his way out between the tables.

Harlan watched him, following Brock's squat figure until it disappeared out the door, his mind racing. This was bad. He had no idea where Elm had disappeared to, or even where to start looking for her. Maybe the senator would be able to help track her down, but, strangely, he'd been having a hard time getting him on the phone. It felt like he was getting the runaround, although of course that couldn't be true.

Jesus, he couldn't believe Ashby had fucked things up so royally. He'd have to be dealt with, he decided coldly. The last time they'd spoken, Ashby had sounded like he was on the verge of a nervous breakdown. He had little doubt that if the man lost it, he'd try to take him down, too.

He sat quietly, controlling his shaking fingers while he sipped the beer and tried to figure out exactly where things had begun to fall apart. Everything seemed to be closing in around him: Brock and his insulting revelations, Elm's mysterious disappearance, the senator's sudden chill, Ashby's total collapse, the waste plant, the sick constituents, the nosy reporter. Christ, there was just too much to handle.

He'd have to take things one step at a time, he reminded himself, striving for a sense of control, and right now priority number one was getting Brock off his back.

After another few sips of beer a plan began to emerge. Brock had mentioned Juan Ramirez. The man was a big drug lord that nobody—not even the FBI—had been able to touch. A real smooth operator—and very dangerous. But what if... As the thought grew, Harlan's face broke into a smile. What if he planted a few ideas in Ramirez's head? Not an easy task, getting in to see a man like that, but nothing was impossible. And if he could arrange a meeting, reveal certain things to Ramirez that showed Brock in a different light, who knew what might happen?

The question was, how to reach him? He had tighter security than the president of the United States.

And not the kind you messed with.

Twenty-four hours later, Harlan had flown to Miami and was being shown into the vast living room of Ramirez's pink-and-white-stucco Mediterranean villa on Star Island by two dark-suited security guards who'd frisked him on arrival. He stepped warily inside the huge room, noting the panoramic windows overlooking the bay and Miami Beach. He couldn't quite believe he'd pulled this off, that he was actually here, but frankly he didn't have much choice. It was eat Brock or be lunched upon, as he saw it.

He moved toward a massive couch and looked about him. The room was surprisingly tasteful, modern white sofas strategically placed in groups, potted palms gracing the alcoves between the arched French doors, and attractive kilim and Oriental rugs lay strewn on the terracotta-tiled floor. He'd expected something more in the style of Brock's place— glitzy marble and bad Louis XV—but this place held a different aura; the aura of money, real money that's gotten past the initial stages and has acquired some class, he realized. This was a far more subtle game than he was used to playing. He would be dealing with a subtle man, too, despite the frisking and the show of side arms at the front gate, he observed thoughtfully.

He'd already thought long and hard about what might set a guy like Ramirez against one of his right-hand men. And the answer had come to him in the night, like a revelation. Betrayal, of course. That was it, in a nutshell.

So when, several minutes later, Juan Ramirez appeared from under one of the limestone arches surrounding the terrace, Harlan stood a little straighter, checked his tie and mentally rehearsed his speech.

Ramirez was of medium height, bronzed, gray-haired and wearing well-cut pants and a white polo shirt. He carried himself with authority, and Harlan respected that. Power of any kind always impressed him.

"You caught me just before my golf game, Mr. Mac-Bride, please sit down." They shook hands and Harlan accepted a seat on one of the couches. "Now, what can I do for you?" Ramirez asked, sitting opposite, arm thrown casually over the back of the sofa. There was little to be read in the dark, hooded eyes. Well, thought Harlan, taking a deep breath, time to start sowing the seeds.

Harlan left the house an hour later and headed toward the airport. He had an hour to catch his flight to Grand Cayman. Boy, did he need the break, a few days to regroup and get a game plan going for the next phase. He was satisfied that his instincts had been dead-on and that he'd accomplished his goal of convincing Ramirez of Brock's treachery. It had been surprisingly easy to persuade the man that Brock planned to make Ramirez the fall guy for their import firm in Fort Lauderdale, which was at present under federal investigation. Ramirez had covered well, but Harlan could tell that the hints about the feds' intentions had shocked and infuriated him. Stumbling on that particular piece of information had proved another stroke of good luck, like so many that came his way.

Harlan congratulated himself as he drove back onto the

MacArthur Causeway, experiencing an almost sexual rush of satisfaction. He'd proved himself in the past hour, demonstrated that Brock's scathing words were little more than the ravings of a jealous man, and established once again that he was possessed of qualities that were unique. His gifts, he reminded himself, must be guided toward their true destiny: that of leading the nation. But in the meantime, he'd put them to spectacular use. Brock, he reflected gleefully, would have a lot of explaining to do.

What had proved even more satisfactory was Ramirez's obvious desire to retain Harlan's political influence and connections. He had made that gratifyingly plain, urging him to stay in touch. It was encouraging, Harlan reflected, to know that one was now dealing not with a mere subordinate, but with the head of the organization.

Elated, he headed west toward the airport, fingering the generous contribution that Ramirez had pressed him to take. Okay, it was laundered money, but he'd been through all that before, and let's face it, those scruples Elm had so admired in their youth had long since been blunted. What he'd once thought of as shocking now seemed commonplace—even necessary. And that, he argued, was for a very simple reason: his ultimate objective was what really mattered. The rest—the ways and means, all the sacrifices and risks he was now obliged to take—were insignificant in the bigger scheme of things.

His euphoria lasted throughout the journey to Miami International, and even through the takeoff. But once the plane was well on its way to Grand Cayman, Harlan recalled the problem that had triggered his journey to Miami.

Elm still hadn't been located.

A cloud shadowed his mood and he suddenly resented her deeply. Once again, she was the problem. He sighed and stared down at the ocean waves. He simply must find her and neutralize the threat she posed, once and for all. He could not afford to have her continuously jeopardizing all his good work.

He sat back and catching sight of the flight attendant,

ordered another Scotch on the rocks. He had no doubt he'd win a third term. As Elm's widowed husband and with the support of his father-in-law, it was a given. But added to that was the new, reassuring knowledge that Ramirez's funds would be filling his coffers.

He would, he reflected, a slow grin covering his face, have his cake and eat it, too.

Meredith turned from the window of Grace Graney's resplendent penthouse overlooking Central Park and took a deep breath. "Uncle George, I'm afraid what we have to tell you is...well, it's not pleasant," Meredith said, shifting uncomfortably under the senator's piercing gaze. He'd just flown up from D.C. and spent a half hour with Elm, who, though considerably better, was still weak. Johnny and Meredith had agreed that the shock of knowing Harlan was trying to kill her would be too much to take right now, so Elm was still under the impression they'd simply removed her from Ashby's clinic because they'd learned of a better cure for her illness at Columbia. And because the treatment had miraculously worked, she'd accepted their explanation, too amazed and happy at being alive to question it. Neither had Meredith informed her of Julie's death. All that, she felt, could wait until her friend was strong and well again.

But Uncle George was a different matter. Too much hung in the offing for him not to know the truth. And perhaps it was about time he found out exactly what his beloved protégé had become, before he was sucked under, too.

Meredith sighed and glanced at Johnny, standing to the side of the mantel of the fine marble fireplace, wishing she wasn't the one to have to do the telling. But they'd agreed it was better this way. After all, Johnny barely knew the senator and Meredith was not only Elm's friend and attorney, but also a trusted family confidant.

"Well, Merry Bell, all I can say is that I'm mighty relieved to know Elm is better. And it's all thanks to you," he said, smiling at Johnny approvingly. "I look forward to seeing your mother again and thanking her personally for all she's done for my little girl, having her to stay here and all," he added. "I can't think what Ashby was up to. For a doctor of such repute, he certainly didn't do much for Elm. Appalling. Once all this is over, I'll have a thorough investigation of that clinic of his." He shook his head, brows creased. "Right now I'm just happy you were able to use your mother's influence at Columbia, Graney, and that they knew exactly what they were doing."

"Uh, yes. But I'm afraid it isn't quite that simple, Uncle George." Meredith took another deep breath.

"What do you mean?" George Hathaway asked, startled.

"Well, this whole matter of Elm's illness wasn't exactly what it appeared."

"I don't care what it was, what matters is she's cured now, right?" He looked suddenly worried. Meredith realized that he'd aged noticeably over the past few weeks.

"Of course," she said quickly. "This has nothing to do with Elm's actual state of health—she's much better, and she'll go on being fine. The thing is, Uncle George, she wasn't really sick at all, or at least not in the way you think. She was being poisoned."

"I beg your pardon?"

"Exactly what I'm saying. There's no weird illness. Elm was suffering from selenium poisoning."

"Now, wait a minute." George Hathaway rose and turned toward Johnny. "This is absurd. Who in heaven's name would want to poison my daughter?" He threw his hands up and let out a laugh. "That's ridiculous."

"I'm afraid not, sir." Johnny looked very serious as he moved into the middle of the room. "Here, take a look at this." He handed the senator a copy of the reports they'd gathered.

"Elm's symptoms last year were caused by excessive selenium exposure at the plantation, Uncle George."

"Selenium?" He frowned. "But that's a recommended mineral. I take some myself."

"In the right dosage it is. But when the body absorbs

excessive amounts, the resulting toxicity causes all sorts of debilitating symptoms.''

"I don't understand, this is crazy."

"Perhaps I'd better start at the beginning," Meredith said. "Why don't you both sit down and I'll tell you exactly what happened."

"I think you'd better," the senator agreed in a stentorian tone while lowering himself onto the nearest chair. "Neither of you is making any sense."

The two men sat in armchairs opposite Meredith on the deep couch and the senator frowned attentively.

"Uncle George, I don't know how to break this to you nicely, so I'll shoot from the hip. Harlan arranged for Dr. Ashby to poison Elm."

"What?" the senator exclaimed, sitting ramrod straight, a look of shock on his face. "Meredith, have you completely lost your mind?"

"Unfortunately not. We think that once Harlan realized Elm truly intended to divorce him, he decided he had to act."

"But this is crazy, unbelievable, absurd."

"I know it seems that way, but it isn't." She leaned forward and clasped her hands. "You know yourself how ambitious he is."

"Well, of course he's ambitious. Anyone'd need to be ambitious to get where he's going. What has that to do with Elm?"

"The only place he's going is straight to jail," Johnny interrupted dryly.

"Would you kindly explain this clearly," the senator continued, irritated.

"You remember last fall, when Elm began having those symptoms?"

"Of course I remember."

"She went to see Doc Philips—"

"Who sent her to Ashby and so on." He waved his hand. "I know all about that. Get to the point, Merry. You've made a serious allegation, substantiate it."

"I know, but this is important. Elm left for Switzerland before the results of the blood work were available. Over there, she felt so much better she thought no more about it. Then when she came back and was working on the garden project at Oleander, she began feeling a little sick again. That's when she remembered to call Ashby, who told her the first results were inconclusive and that she'd have to come to Atlanta for another test."

"And?"

"Well, after a little while—"

"Why didn't she go at once?"

"Because she felt better again. You see, the minute she stopped working in the garden, the symptoms left her."

"Still, why didn't she go right away?"

"Because she was in Ireland with me," Johnny said, his eyes meeting the senator's dead-on.

"With you? What was she doing in Ireland with you?"

"Senator, this is probably not the right moment to tell you, but I plan to marry Elm when all this is over."

George Hathaway sat silently, staring at him. "But that's outrageous," he said at last.

"I don't see why. I know this must come as a bit of a shock to you, but I love your daughter very much."

"So all the time poor Harlan was trying to woo her back, she was with you—and in Switzerland, too, I suppose."

"Yes."

"Please, gentlemen, let's not go off on a tangent here," Meredith begged hastily. "I would like to finish my story, then you'll understand the rest, Uncle George."

"Very well, but I find Elm's behavior—and yours, for that matter—" he threw at Johnny "—reprehensible."

Johnny bristled and opened his mouth to give what Meredith knew would be a pithy rebuttal. "Would you please both listen to what I have to tell you?" she interjected.

"Very well," the senator replied grimly. "Go ahead."

"As I was saying, Elm left for Ireland, where she spent a week at Graney Castle." She ignored the fulminating look the senator sent Johnny and forged ahead. "On her return journey she stopped over in Atlanta and went to the clinic to have the new blood tests Ashby had requested. We believe Harlan wanted Ashby to keep Elm at the clinic where he could control her, so Ashby told her the results confirmed his earlier fears, that she was suffering from some rare nervous disease, and that the only way to zap it was for her to enter the clinic immediately. He then proceeded to poison her through her IV line with increasingly large doses of selenium—the same mineral that had already been introduced into her system through exposure to the soil at Oleander Creek."

"But that's preposterous. Selenium at Oleander? How'd it get there?"

"Toxic runoff from the Mogachee waste plant, Harlan's pet project."

The senator blanched. "Oh, my God, that's terrible. But surely it's impossible. The plant is EPA-approved. And even if what you say about Harlan's motives is true—and I'm not saying I believe you—why would someone of Ashby's repute agree to do such a thing? He must know the state'll pull his license."

"Because Harlan was blackmailing him," Johnny supplied.

"But how? Why?" The senator looked at them both, perplexed.

"I asked my brother Liam to do a little checking into Ashby's background. Apparently Ashby has—or rather, had—a drug problem. It seems Harlan knew about it. They were in college together many years ago. We believe that Harlan must have discovered Ashby's connection to Elm and decided to use it to his advantage."

"Harlan," Meredith said dryly, "has a tendency to accumulate information he thinks might prove useful."

"The phone records," Johnny continued, "reveal that there were several calls between Ashby and Harlan while Elm was in Switzerland."

"Phone records?" the senator questioned with a raised brow.

"Liam again," Johnny admitted.

"Resourceful man," Hathaway murmured, face pale.

"My bet is that Harlan told Ashby to sit on the results. After all, he knew it would look bad if word got out about toxic waste leaking from the plant. Meredith had an environmental agency run tests on soil samples from the plantation, and from ever-closer rings around the plant, and the selenium level—not to mention those of other dangerous substances—is off the charts."

"Harlan would have wanted to run damage control," Meredith explained, "keep news of the toxins from getting to the press, so he arranged for Ashby to persuade Elm to enter the clinic on the pretense of having a rare disease needing to be treated."

"That's monstrous! But where's the proof? And how do you get from a simple cover-up to murder?"

"While we don't know all the particulars, Uncle George, it's quite clear Harlan made the decision to withhold the information about her selenium exposure from Elm. It's equally clear that once Elm was in Ashby's clinic, her health declined precipitously. And then, of course, there are the chemical tests we had run on a sample from Elm's IV fluids. They show she was being given megadoses of selenium."

"But the blood profile I sent Granby—"

"Was fabricated." Johnny said bluntly.

"But this is madness. Why didn't Ashby just come to me when Harlan threatened him?"

"Because apart from being blackmailed, he was also being promised substantial funding for a new wing of his clinic," Johnny chipped in. "We've tied some deposits that were made into Ashby's account to an offshore bank in the Cayman Islands. I'd bet good money the account that wired the funds belongs to Harlan."

The senator shook his head, his face ashen. "I find it hard to believe that Harlan would do such a thing. His whole future is at stake."

"Uncle George, Harlan's future is history," Meredith said softly. She leaned across and touched his arm. "He's been fooling us all along. He never loved Elm. Oh, maybe right at the beginning he had feelings for her, but they were all linked to your power and where he saw himself going because of your patronage. But then he fell in with Tyler Brock. Mel Bamburger at the *Savannah Morning News* has unearthed some pretty damaging information about their real relationship.

"It appears Harlan started cultivating Brock early in his first term. Pretty soon he was being entrusted with money. Big money, by Harlan's standards, and I guess it seemed ridiculous not to do the man a few favors, and buy what he envisaged was his freedom from you."

"But he never could have made his way alone, surely he must have seen that? Harlan's bright and charismatic. I've treated him like my own son, I..." The senator shook his head once more. "This is unbelievable."

"But true," Johnny confirmed, his voice very serious. "Senator, I'm dreadfully sorry about this. I realize your son-in-law's future meant a lot to you. But have you thought about what poor Elm must have been going through all these years?"

"I thought she was happy. She seemed happy, didn't she, Merry?" he asked, sending a supplicating glance at Meredith.

"*Seemed* is the operative word, Uncle George. Elm has always done her best to make sure those around her weren't affected by what she saw as her own failures. She took the blame, she felt responsible. And you can bet your bottom dollar Harlan did his best to make her feel that way. Then slowly she began to rebel, to go her own way. First she discovered her painting talent, then her love affair with Oleander—I think they became her escape valves. What Harlan never expected was that when he became careless about his philandering and she found out about his affair with Jennifer Ball, she'd be strong enough to hold him accountable."

"So there *was* an affair."

"Of course there was. And several others that have since

come to light. He thought Elm would just be a good Southern wife and turn her eyes the other way."

George Hathaway hesitated. Part of him, the part that loved his daughter, was revolted. The other part, the cynical politician that was having a hard time assimilating all this information, felt perhaps that was what she should have done for all these problems to have been avoided, was to turn the other cheek.

Sensing his hesitation, Johnny rose and stood once more by the mantelpiece, unable to hide his feelings. "Elm has suffered unduly in this marriage, sir. Surely you wouldn't have expected her to go along with it, be a party to her husband's deceit?"

"No, of course not. Still, perhaps if she'd been more understanding, things might have turned out differently."

"Differently? You mean he might have had her drowned instead of poisoned?" Johnny barked.

"What I don't understand is why he wanted to kill her in the first place."

"Because he was scared the divorce would undermine his campaign," Meredith cut in, sending Johnny a reproving glance. "Think, Uncle George. As your son-in-law—your *widowed* son-in-law, rather—he would have had not only your considerable support, but also the sympathy of the electorate. Imagine all those voters lauding Harlan as the bereaved young widower struggling to do his duty despite his grief. I'm sure he envisioned himself as the star in some sort of sick D.C. melodrama. It makes me ill just to think of it."

The senator sat up straighter, thinking of Harlan's flair for the dramatic, his love of the limelight—and his utter abhorrence of negative publicity. "You're right," he breathed, his head swimming. He stood up and began pacing the room angrily. "I'll nail him for this," he said, eyes gleaming with new determination. He stopped, stared at Meredith and spoke suddenly, as though hit by a flash of realization. "This is all my fault. I should have seen through his game, understood what he was up to. Instead I let myself be flattered and cajoled, and Elm suffered the consequences. My God, how blind I've been. Even when she was in the clinic, I couldn't help admiring how he handled those TV interviews. It makes me wonder whether I'm not crazy, too." He bowed his head, pinched the bridge of his nose and stared sadly at the floor. "I guess I'm as much to blame for Harlan as he is for himself. Lord, what a terrible, terrible error in judgment I've made all these years."

He stood for a moment by the window, looking out over the New York high-rises, staring far away, into the past, facing his shattered hopes and the realization that he'd placed his own blind ambition ahead of his daughter's welfare. Suddenly he felt very old, and very tired. Then something inside him clicked. *Damn it, Hathaway, don't let it all be about you again. Think of your daughter for once. Do what you need to do.*

Straightening his shoulders, he raised his head. He would get the bastard, whatever it cost him in personal humiliation. His first reaction, to engineer a huge cover-up, wasn't worthy of him—or his daughter. Turning from the window, he faced the room. Meredith, who'd been watching him sadly, thinking he looked utterly defeated, saw instead the old drive in his eyes that she knew so well—the formidable, unbending, determined will that had made George Hathaway such a legend in the Senate.

"We've got to go out and get him. Where is the bastard?" he asked in a level voice. "I don't care how much publicity this gets, we've got to get him before he does more harm."

"Don't worry, sir. My brother's got some pretty highly placed friends at the FBI, and it seems they've had their eye on him for a while. The association with Brock did not go unnoticed. The thing is, they want to hold off awhile— they're trying to hook a much bigger fish."

"Well, I've got a few connections in D.C. myself, and what I want is to get Harlan off the streets," the senator repeated. "I'm going to call up the director and make sure he knows where his priorities should be. Do they even know where Harlan is?" he queried angrily.

"No one knows. Right now he seems to have fallen off

the planet. Elm's safe here—we've been careful to cover our tracks—but it's only a matter of time before he starts looking for her. The way I see it, in his present predicament, he has two ways to play it. Either he can pretend he's thrilled that she's back to normal, admit he was wrong about the treatment, pretend to be innocent and blame the whole thing on Brock, or…he's going to try to finish her off himself.''

"But that's impossible," Hathaway blustered. "How could he do that?"

"I can think of several ways," Johnny said tightly, "but as long as I'm alive, he's not getting a bloody chance to put any of them into practice."

"Good God, this is terrible," the senator muttered once more, passing a hand over his brow. "I'd better see what needs to be done. I'll have to talk to the leadership of the House at once, warn them of what's going on. The party's going to have a real mess on their hands, Merry."

"Aren't you more concerned about your daughter than the damn party?" Johnny could not help saying. After all Elm had gone through for her father's sake, the senator still put politics first. "Aren't you aware that your daughter has suffered years of humiliation, undermining herself, because of some perverse sense of duty to you?"

"Yes, young man, I am," the senator replied quietly, looking him straight in the eye. "In the past half hour I've learned a lot of things I was unaware of, and you have every right to feel angry," he said heavily, "particularly if you love my daughter as you say you do. I have a lot of righting to do. If I still can. But I also have a duty to the party and to my country. I put this man in the position he occupies, got others to place their faith in him, and their trust. It is as important that I right the public wrong I've committed as it is that I right my relationship with my daughter. Elm, I know, would be the first to agree."

"As a matter of fact, Daddy, you're right. I do."

Nobody had noticed her standing in the doorway, dressed now in black slacks and a pretty silk blouse. They turned as one and Johnny rushed forward.

"It's okay," she assured him, letting him take her arm and guide her into the room. "Of course, it's a terrible shock to learn my husband was trying to kill me, but strangely— and I can't believe I'm saying this—I'm not surprised. When I was at the clinic, I was aware of this need to do everything in my power to keep Harlan away from my family. And I guess, deep down, I never really believed the rare nervous disease theory. I tried, but somehow it all seemed so unreal. What I don't comprehend," she said, eyeing Johnny and Meredith severely, "is why you've kept this information from me."

"Darling," Johnny took her hand and gazed down at her, his concern evident. "You've been dreadfully ill. We didn't think that you were well enough to handle it. You've had a difficult enough time getting better without being told your husband was the one who made you sick."

"You underestimate me if you think I can't handle the truth," Elm said, drawing her hand away and facing her father. "Daddy, I'm sorry this has turned out so badly. I know all the hopes you had, all that you've invested in Harlan."

"Elm, honey, the only person that should be sorry here is me. I should've realized who he was, what he was scheming. I feel deeply ashamed that my ambition has put your life at risk."

Elm moved toward her father and opened her arms. "Oh, Daddy."

"Elm, darling. I love you more than anything in the world," he said hoarsely, hugging her tight. "I've been so blind, too taken up with politics to see the truth staring me in the face. I dread to think what your mother would say if she were alive."

Johnny stepped forward. "Sir, I never had the pleasure of meeting your wife, but if she was anything like your daughter," he said softly, eyes glistening as he looked at Elm, "I'd bet she'd tell you to let go of your demons, make peace with the past, and most important, allow yourself to believe in a better future."

Elm turned to Johnny, smiling through her tears, then looked back at her father. "Oh, Daddy, he's right. Just let it go. It's all over now." Elm sank into his arms and they held each other.

"Can you ever forgive me, Elm?"

"Of course I forgive you, Daddy," she said, drawing away, her hands on his shoulders. "But in the future, please just let me be myself."

"I swear I will."

"Anyway, you're not the only one to blame," she countered, squeezing his hand. "If I'd insisted when I knew I was right, instead of always shying away, and not worn such blinkers where Harlan was concerned, none of this would have happened." She turned back to Johnny and smiled sadly. "I guess what I need to do now is tie up all the loose ends. Does anyone know where Harlan is?"

"On the run, I think," Meredith said. "He was last seen boarding a plane to Miami. But they'll catch up with him. He can't get far."

"That's true. I feel almost sorry for him," Elm murmured. "He must be a very sick man to have gotten to this point."

"That's very generous of you, darling," Johnny muttered dryly, looking down at her. "I'm afraid I view the situation rather differently." He slipped a protective arm around her shoulders.

"Well, at least it explains a lot of his behavior. You know, it's strange, but I don't feel so bad about the marriage now. He stopped being the Harlan I married years ago. Now I just have to bring closure to all this."

"Of course you must," he replied tenderly.

"What I'm saying," she continued, drawing herself up and addressing everyone, "is that I need to go back to Savannah."

"But you can't. You're still too unwell. You can't go take a trip now, that's ridiculous," Johnny countered.

"Actually, I'm feeling much better. This rest these past

few days has done me a world of good, and the more I do, the sooner I'll be right as rain.''

"Yes, but you still can't travel.''

"Why on earth not? I asked the doctor and he said he was amazed at how quickly I was recovering.''

"Maybe, but that doesn't mean—''

"Johnny, darling, I have to. It's the only way to put the past to bed, the only way I'll be able to move on. I want to get it over with as soon as possible,'' she insisted stubbornly.

"Fine,'' he said, defeated, "then I'll come with you.''

"Right,'' the senator agreed, nodding and seeking Meredith's support. "We'll all come with you.''

"No, no, please, you don't understand.'' Elm disengaged herself and stepped back beside the French doors that opened out onto the terrace, determined to make her point. "This is something I must do on my own. I need to go back to Savannah by myself, pack and close up the house, put it on the market. It's the only way I'll be able to bring real closure to this chapter of my life. And I *need* to do it on my own,'' she insisted quietly.

"But that's absurd, Elm. Graney's right.'' The senator's voice took on a censorious tone. "You must be sensible.''

"Daddy—'' Elm closed her eyes "—I've been sensible my whole life. Can't I, just this once, do it my way?'' she asked, opening her eyes again, her smile sweet but firm and her tone leaving no doubt of her intentions. "It's not as if Harlan is there, or will be any time soon. The last place he'll show up is Savannah. Harlan's strongest instinct is self-preservation. For all we know, he's fled to South America with some of Brock's pals.''

"Maybe,'' Meredith agreed doubtfully.

Elm looked suddenly sad. "It's terrible this has happened. He really did have the makings of a great politician. But I think that if he turns up anywhere, it'll be in D.C. He's addicted to the air of power there. In fact, his favorite pastime is to sit on that bench in Lafayette Park that faces the White House, and imagine the day he'll move in. It's pathetic and compulsive.''

"Christ, Elm, don't feel too sorry for him. Next you'll be blaming yourself for what happened."

"Oh, no, Mer. No way. Not anymore." Elm shook her head decisively. "I won't lose my perspective."

"Well, why don't we fly back together? Then you can go to the house and do whatever you have to do, and we'll be nearby if you need us," the senator compromised in a persuasive tone.

"Good idea," Meredith chipped in. "But are you sure you're well enough, Elm? Hadn't we better get the doctor's okay before you travel?" She looked at her friend critically.

"She's right," Johnny said, grabbing at this last straw. "You're much better, but I don't feel comfortable with you going on your own. Your father's right."

"Okay, I'll fly back with Daddy. But will you please all stop trying to baby me?" Elm exclaimed, exasperated. "All I want to do is take care of business. Don't you see that that will make me feel so much better? And I need to go to Oleander and see how the girls are doing with the project. I need to make a clean break, and I need to do it on my own."

Johnny and Meredith's eyes met. Like it or not, they were going to have to tell her about Julie and the events at Oleander Creek.

"Okay, have it your way." Meredith smiled at her, glad she'd conceded to fly with the senator. Then she sent Johnny a reassuring glance. She would tell Elm about Julie when they were by themselves and the time was right. Enough had been said for one day.

30

Tycoon's Body Discovered In Bay, the headline read.

Oh, my God.

Harlan experienced a sudden chill as he unfolded the newspaper and read further. "Tyler Brock, multimillionaire and real estate tycoon, was discovered floating in the bay in front of his expansive Skidaway mansion early yesterday morning...."

Shit! He hadn't actually intended for Ramirez to murder Brock, just keep him quiet. He swallowed, his mouth dry. These guys were no lightweights.

Wiping a film of sweat from his brow, he read the rest of the article, shock fading as the implications sank in. Actually, it wasn't such a bad thing, and what he really felt, now he came to think of it, was relief. Ramirez's method was pretty radical, but it sure solved his own problem very neatly. Brock was no longer a threat, and since dead men didn't talk, their past association would remain a secret. Still, the arbitrary manner in which his death had occurred left him uneasy.

Trying to block out the image of Brock's bloated body bobbing in the water, Harlan pored over the rest of the three-day-old copy of the *Savannah Morning News* that he'd asked the local newsagent to procure. Turning a page, he stopped short. What was this? "Questions Abound at the Mogachee

Plant.'' Pulse racing, he quickly skimmed through the article. Nothing too damaging to him personally, he decided, relieved, just hints about shoddy construction compromising the plant's efficiency. But it was obvious someone was digging. And digging fast.

It was probably that young reporter whom he'd given the interview to. Perhaps it was just an effort by the liberals to tarnish his record. Problem was, he reflected bitterly, if they dug any deeper and found out the truth, well, they just might get somewhere with it.

Harlan stared out across the pristine stone terrace to the smooth blue ocean beyond, his eyes resting on a yacht moving slowly on the horizon. He could not let this happen. Could not let anything damage all the plans he'd so carefully contrived. Taking a long sip of whiskey, he thought hard and rationalized. Perhaps this was just a flash in the pan. He really mustn't let things like this get him in a sweat. They happened all the time. Par for the course, really. Still, what if they found out about the surplus construction funds that had trickled to his Cayman account? Or that he'd finally secured the EPA's approval by means he'd rather not think about right now? That was less easily explained.

Stop it, he ordered himself. That was ridiculous. He was panicking for no reason. Folding the paper, he threw it on top of the unread stack on the deck chair beside him, then leaned back and turned his face up to catch a tan. He'd let the dust settle. By the time he got back, something else would have popped up to capture the public's attention. It was a good thing he'd decided to work in a little R and R this week, because it looked like he'd need all his resources to deal with these tentative—as he liked to think of them—allegations. And to deal with Elm, as well, he reflected, still bothered that he hadn't been able to locate her.

No, he decided firmly, feeling the sun seep in, he wasn't about to let it worry him. He knew how to handle her better than anyone. He'd always fixed things, and there was no reason why this little storm wouldn't blow over, just as all the others had. It was part of being in the game. He just had to ride it out. Still, it bothered him that the private detective he'd discreetly hired still hadn't located Elm—or Gioconda, for that matter. Perhaps they'd both run off back to Europe. Oh, well. At least that would keep things quiet for the moment and avoid involving the senator.

Maybe she was already dead, he thought suddenly. But no. That wasn't possible. He would have seen something in the news or heard of it on TV. He would catch up with her, of course, but right now he was more concerned with shutting up Ashby. He could not afford to have him blabbering.

Punching in the number on his mobile, he rang the clinic and asked for the doctor.

"Harlan, is that you? I've been so damn worried. Where the hell are you?" Ashby's voice sounded tremulous.

"I'm traveling," he snapped. "Now, tell me, how about Elm? You said you'd put out feelers. Any idea where they might have taken her? Where she might be?"

"None, I'm afraid. I've kept a very low profile," he added, "just told the family she'd signed herself out and hadn't advised me of her whereabouts. I said I was worried about her. Still, Harlan, if they've put her in another hospital, and I reckon they must have, it's all bound to come out. Frankly, I'm terrified. I don't know what to do, I—"

"Don't worry. Once they realize the diagnosis is bullshit, they'll trace her selenium levels to the waste plant and become obsessed with that. They'll forget all about you."

"Perhaps. Yes. You're probably right. But we've got to come up with a logical alibi in case, get our stories straight. I've canceled my patients for the next few days. I'll come meet you and we could straighten this out. Where are you?" Ashby insisted, eyeing the FBI agent planted 24/7 outside his window.

"As I told you, I'm traveling. No fixed spot. I'll be back soon," Harlan replied vaguely.

Ashby smothered his disappointment. It would have helped his cause to no end if he could have handed Harlan to the feds on a platter. He'd cut a deal with them and he wasn't about to screw it up. Fuck Harlan. Served him right for blackmailing him in the first place, forcing him to compromise his career. It would be a miracle if he wasn't ruined as it was.

"When do you think you'll be back in Savannah?" he asked, hopeful that Harlan might let drop some hint of his whereabouts.

"Not sure yet. But if there's any news of Elm, call me immediately, okay?"

"Okay. I will."

Harlan hung up and stared once more across the white balustrade of the terrace and out into the Caribbean. Where was she? he wondered, brows creasing. Surely Meredith must be behind this disappearing act. And what about the senator? Did he know anything yet? Suspect that Harlan was in any way involved in his daughter's plight?

No. He shook his head. No way. No one would imagine he could be linked to her ill health. That, he realized, a grin covering his bronzed face, was the beauty of it all. Now he must play it by ear. If Elm was better—which might be the case, if she wasn't being poisoned any longer—then, heck, he'd go back and pretend to be delighted at her recovery, pick up where they'd left off. Still, the prospect of being rid of her, once and for all, and having an unimpeded ride from here onward was enormously tempting, despite the inconvenience it would inevitably cause. It really was a pity Ashby hadn't finished the job in time. Oh, well. Either way, he reckoned, taking a long sip of his cocktail, there would be no end of publicity. And now that Brock was out of the picture, he'd be able to launch an "investigation" into the plant, then profess shock and horror that his constituents had been duped and endangered. Not only would it burnish his image as a defender of the little people, but he'd also be able to earn brownie points with the Sierra Club, which had an impressive record of mobilizing its members on election day.

He climbed to his feet, set his empty glass on the stack of newspapers, smoothed his fine white linen shirt and decided it was time for a dip in the pool. An efficient busboy came with a fresh drink, placed a warm towel on the beach chair and, as an afterthought, cleared away the stack of papers.

Which was just as well, because had Harlan bothered to look at the front page of yesterday's paper, he would have felt decidedly less chipper.

Little by little, Elm's strength was returning, and the recent nightmare receding. She tried not to think too much about all that had occurred, realizing now, as she lay in the vast four-poster of the charming bedroom where she'd slept with Harlan for so many years, that she must look ahead, not back. She'd be foolish to dwell upon a past that had brought her so much unhappiness when her future—a life with Johnny—was so very bright.

Still, it wasn't easy to just pretend the events of the last few weeks hadn't taken place. The news of Julie's death had come as a terrible shock, and realizing it had been caused by Harlan's pet project that he'd defended so passionately, and that she herself had blindly believed in, had filled her with guilt.

Sinking back against the pillows, she acknowledged that maybe she wasn't quite ready for the enormous task of clearing out and closing up the house. Despite her rapid recovery and her determination to prove to Johnny and her family that she was fine and could cope on her own, she was still recovering her strength. Still, it had to be done, and the sooner she brought closure to this chapter of her life, the better.

She gazed about the room, remembering her excitement when her father had given her the house as a wedding gift, all her hopes and the thrill she'd experienced at decorating her own home. Now, sipping the tea that Isah, who'd come in from the plantation to help her pack, had brought up on her mother's hand-painted wooden tray, she contemplated each detail of the room that years ago she'd gone to such trouble to create. The precious antiques bequeathed to her by her mother. The exquisite silk wallpaper, reproduced for her in England from an early twentieth-century design created for her great-grandmother, featuring some of the flora from Oleander Creek—irises, Cherokee roses, water lilies, dogwood and willows. Her canopy bed, which had been in the family for several generations, hung with yards of antique European lace. The overall effect was of a genteel and serene Southern retreat, one of the many secret niches she'd created for herself so that she'd have somewhere to escape to.

It hadn't proved much of a refuge, she realized. But then, how could she have known that the most dangerous threat to her world would be the man who'd slept in this bed beside her? Elm set down the dainty Wedgwood cup and tried to digest that the man she'd been married to for so long had actually attempted to murder her in cold blood. It still seemed an almost impossible concept to pair with reality, as though she were viewing the scene of someone else's life through a pair of unfocused binoculars.

She felt a strange sense of detachment. Despite her disgust, she felt pity for the cowardly, corruptible, contemptible being for whom power and position had become so paramount. Harlan had set himself on a demanding path and become so obsessed with the final destination that he'd lost sight of why he'd ever started the journey. Worse, she thought sadly, the voyage had apparently cost him his soul.

Even if she was inclined to help him—and the hell she'd endured at his hands had dried up any lingering sense of obligation—Elm knew that Harlan was beyond saving. Once the FBI found him, as they'd assured her was inevitable, his whole world would be ruthlessly stripped from him. The dissolution of their marriage was the least of his concerns.

How strange that the final chapter of life, as he knew it, should coincide with the start of a new beginning for her.

She placed the tray to one side of the lace coverlet and turned her thoughts to the man who'd, quite literally, given her back her life. She smiled. Johnny had stuck by her side, never leaving her even for a moment. At the hospital in New York, he'd slept on the uncomfortable sofa night after night, waiting patiently next to her while she made her slow recovery, gently steadying her through the initial shock, that incredible, wonderful yet almost unbelievable realization that she was going to live. Surprisingly, the knowledge had not translated into immediate delight. Instead, she'd experienced a profound sense of relief and thankfulness, followed by the quiet certainty that she must not waste this second chance.

She thought also of her faithful, trustworthy friends, Meredith and Gioconda. The latter had flown back to Europe only a few days after her escapade in Atlanta, once she knew Elm was safe. The thought of Gioconda posing as an eccentric Italian patient to dupe Ashby made her laugh out loud. Then, pushing back the covers, she glanced at the clock, knowing it was time to get up and get on with the packing. She sat up on the edge of the high bed, pulled on her Edwardian lace robe bought years ago at an antique store in London, and slipped on her matching slippers. The faster she finished up here, the sooner she'd be back in Johnny's arms.

Not that she had any notion of what the future held in store for them. She loved Johnny, without a doubt. But was she ready to enmesh herself in his life? Settle with him at Graney Castle? Take on a new set of responsibilities that included a sixteen-year-old?

She rose and walked to the window, peeped out at the rain falling onto the heavy foliage below, and acknowledged that before she committed to anything she must be absolutely certain. She was not prepared to give up her new independence. Neither, she reflected, her mouth curving into a smile, had Johnny ever asked her to. He hadn't even mentioned the word *marriage,* now she came to think of it, although it seemed implied.

She was grateful Johnny had never overwhelmed her with plans for the future that she wasn't yet ready for. It was one of the things she most loved and appreciated about him, she realized. He was simply there, a permanent tower of strength that she could lean on whenever she needed to.

He seemed to understand that the work of recovery had to be her burden alone, especially in those moments of overwhelming sadness when, tears shimmering in her eyes, she thought of poor Julie, who had not been as lucky as her. Or when she realized all the harm Harlan had committed—and that she'd unwittingly blinded herself to—moments of self-accusation when she wondered why she hadn't opened her eyes wide enough to see things she might have helped avoid. She caught herself, then leaned her brow against the cool windowpane and smiled. There was little use packing up the house, she reminded herself, if she was going to carry it symbolically on her back like a tortoise.

Time to take charge, she reflected, turning and gazing at the many photographs, some dating back to her great-grandparents' time, some of her mother and father, others of Harlan and herself. Moving toward the high mahogany chest of drawers, she looked at her wedding picture, at the beautiful young couple walking out of Christ Church under an archway of roses, as distantly as though it were someone else's life. Lifting the frame and wrapping it in tissue paper, she placed it carefully in the bottom of one of the open cartons on the floor with no regrets.

She was profoundly thankful that Johnny had given her this time alone. He wasn't hurt or upset by her need for solitude, but seemed to completely understand, able to accept her for whom and what she was. It was the kind of unconditional acceptance she'd always longed for from her father.

Who, she recalled, was coming over for dinner tonight. She placed another photograph in the box and glanced at the pretty ormolu clock above the mantel of the fireplace. He'd be here at eight o'clock.

Elm felt strangely ambiguous about the senator right now. All her life she'd loved him, adored him unreservedly. But now she'd opened her eyes and could see his flaws as a man and a politician. Of course, he would always be her dad, that wonderful pillar of wisdom she cherished and respected. Still, she had to face the truth about him, too—that his own obsessions were in some measure responsible for what Harlan had become.

Facing her father's imperfections was a necessary part of her growing up, she recognized, though it was hard to reconcile the two beings within the man she loved. A gnawing pain persisted, a silent nostalgia for the perfect image she'd held so blindly all her life. It was hard to admit that her dad was as human as the next man.

But now, she realized, taking a stack of old letters out of the top drawer of the chest, she could acknowledge his flaws without the trauma that, in the past, would have existed with the recognition of her father's weaknesses. Now she was able to look reality in the face with a certain detachment, and evaluate, without judging, her father's qualities and failings.

Her near-death experience had given her a new and enlightened perspective on life. She knew now that she would never again make compromises for the sake of avoiding conflict. Life—hers and everything around her—was simply too precious, too important, too short not to be treasured. She looked about her now with a fresh ability to see detail, to listen with new emphasis to the surrounding sounds, each musical note, each inflection in a voice, catching the subtle undertones that before had gone unnoticed. She smelled scents intensely, captured the slightest aroma with an acute new awareness.

Even her tactile sense had changed. Textures, surfaces, the touch of a hand all registered now; soft, velvety, electric, tense, hard, rough, smooth, cold or hot. Every nuance of sensation was increased one-thousand-fold for having looked death in the eye.

Occasionally she wondered if these sensations would remain concentrated or if, with the passage of time, they would fade. She hoped not. Hoped that this new sensitivity would remain with her always, and felt privileged for the strange gift that in its infinite wisdom life had offered her.

Realizing she must dress, Elm opened her closet and studied the array of clothes, some old, some new, some that needed to be discarded. She smiled. These, too, had taken on new meaning. Suddenly what she wore had become important, because she wanted her outer self to be the reflection of the inner.

With this in mind, she selected a simple cream Valentino sheath, realizing what she wanted from her father was exactly that: simplicity. Straightforwardness. No hidden agendas, no ulterior motives. Was it too much, she wondered, slipping on the dress, to expect change from a man of his age and background, one so used to unconsciously manipulating and maneuvering others?

She sighed and smiled, turning to the dressing table to pick up the hairbrush. Perhaps it was. But nevertheless, they needed to set the foundations of their new relationship. Of course, they would discuss Harlan. That was inevitable, for her husband had betrayed them both. But then they'd have to reestablish the father-daughter bond that Harlan had helped to distort.

Leaving the room, she moved across the landing and made her way downstairs, her mind still filled with thoughts of Harlan. Was he hiding out, or totally unaware of the tightly meshed net closing rapidly about him? Knowing him and how oblivious he could be when he didn't want to face the truth, the latter might very well be true.

It would be awful when it all came down, she reflected, entering the living room with a sigh, but at least it would be over.

31

What was she doing here at home? he wondered, rubbing his eyes and trying to think straight. Wasn't she supposed to be dead? Could this be her ghost, coming back to haunt him?

Harlan stood rigidly outside the drawing room and took a better look, then remembered that, no, in the end that particular plan—killing her—hadn't worked out. His mind felt fogged, and as he tried to focus, he wondered if he shouldn't have taken that last snort of cocaine. But he'd been listening to that ridiculous radio talk show on the way back from the airport and he'd been so infuriated by the things people were saying about him that coke had seemed the only thing capable of calming him down.

The callers had been full of angry accusations, responding to reports that he'd misappropriated public funds earmarked for an inner city playground. They were mad, not to mention ungrateful, considering all he'd done to help those folks, he thought bitterly. Besides, they were wrong, weren't they?

He did remember vaguely that there'd been a budget shortfall on his last big fund-raiser. He always prided himself on putting on a good show—no way was he going to serve the same cheap crap that most politicians dished up at their events.

A memory scratched through the fog.

Oh, yeah, the caterer's bill had been outrageous. Well, it wasn't his fault if they'd grossly overcharged, and after all, the money had had to come from somewhere. Anyway, didn't these folks realize the money was far better spent on getting him re-elected?

With effort, he reminded himself that he was home now and that he'd fix things—this and the other nasty surprises he'd seen in the morning papers.

As he watched Elm, he realized in an abstract manner how beautiful she looked, with the evening shadows and the lamplight playing on her hair, her graceful figure moving about the room in that cool, elegant way she had. Watching from just outside the French door, he experienced a moment's nostalgia. Perhaps it was better she hadn't died. Perhaps she was an asset after all. He smiled. Elm's continuing support would do so much to silence his critics. Sighing, he watched as Elm plumped one of the brocade cushions on the couch then poured herself a glass of white wine.

As Harlan breathed in the scents of early evening, the air fresh after the day's storms, the jasmine and the camellias exhaling their perfume as they opened their petals to the night, a sudden wave of peace swept over him. All at once he felt young again, experienced that same wonderful wave of anticipation he'd felt when he'd first married Elm and came to this house, a time when the future had spread out before him like a wonderful endless highway waiting to be traveled.

For a brief moment he envisioned a new world, unfettered by Brock's demands and financed by Ramirez's money, where he could run things to his liking. Then suddenly the spell broke, his eyes narrowed, and he looked past Elm, who was crouching next to a pile of tissue paper. All at once his eyes focused upon a number of large cartons littering the floor. His brows creased and he straightened up and leaned against the wall, blinking, realizing that something was wrong; the room didn't look the same.

His pulse quickened as he noted a dull empty space on the wall above the fireplace. Where were the Hogarth prints, the ones that had graced that particular spot for as long as he could recall. He swept his angry gaze over the lowboy, shocked to see that his collection of silver mugs was gone. In fact, he realized, a mix of dread and anger creeping over him, the room was practically bare except for the furniture. Why, he wondered, his outrage growing, was she changing his house around? How did she have the gall to return here, looking the picture of health, and empty *his* home of its prized treasures, when she was supposed to be dead or, at the very least, dying?

Following Elm as she moved toward the small mahogany bookcase that held a number of leather-bound first-edition books, Harlan watched, stunned, as she removed them in little piles, stopping a moment to glance at some of the covers before stacking them neatly on the floor.

Something inside him jolted and he could wait no longer. A sudden unprecedented need to protect his home from being summarily dismantled overwhelmed him, and in one swift movement he stepped inside the French door.

"Just what, exactly, do you think you're doing?" he asked imperiously.

Elm spun around. The books she'd been holding clattered to the floor and her face froze in horrified astonishment. "Harlan," she murmured after a few seconds of strained silence. "What on earth are you doing here?"

"Good question. I might ask the same of you. What are you doing here? Aren't you supposed to be sick? In the hospital?"

"Not anymore," she said, quickly recovering her poise. How had he gotten in? she wondered, only to realize she hadn't thought to change the locks. He must have been spying on her. She shivered, remembering that she was alone in the house, her thoughts tripping over one another in quick succession. What was he doing in Savannah? Surely he couldn't be unaware of all that had happened? Why was he spying on her?

Hiding the rush of fear that his presence wrought, Elm

stood tall. "So. What brought you back here, Harlan? You've been away." She glanced at the books littered around her as though casually observing the mess, then bent down, pulse racing, and made as though to pick them up.

"I'm home, Elm."

"Home?" she repeated dully, looking up.

"And glad to see you're back," he added, the automatic smile breaking on his handsome face. This was perfect, he realized suddenly. Ashby had screwed up, but there wasn't the same need to get rid of her anymore. Killing her was the best option in the long run, but since she'd apparently come to her senses and had returned home to him, he could deal with that. Life would simply go on as it always had. The smile broadened as he walked farther into the room in an authoritative manner and waved a hand about the room. "What is this? A major spring cleaning?"

"No, not exactly," she said warily, rising and laying the books on the table. "I'm packing up the house."

"Packing up the house? What for?"

"Because I'm going to sell it." She faced him now as he crossed the room toward her.

"But you can't do that, Elm. Surely you realize that?" he said in a matter-of-fact tone. "I know you've been sick, dear, and maybe you're a little confused," he continued, his tone turning solicitous, "but you can't pack up our house, our home. That's ridiculous, you know it is."

"Harlan, this is not our home any longer," she said, regaining her composure, her voice ringing clearly across the room. He'd stopped next to the couch, staring at more empty spaces on the walls where the paint was lighter than the rest.

"What happened to my Turner?" he asked, ignoring her and pointing to the empty patch above the half-moon table.

"The Hathaway Turner is packed and will be loaned to a local museum."

"You have no right to remove my things without first seeking permission, Elm, you know that," he said severely. "This is out of line."

"I don't think so," she remarked coolly, turning her back

on him and continuing to remove books from the bookcase, determined to steady her shaking hands. She wished her father would arrive early or that Annie and Isah, who'd gone to their Tuesday church social, would return unexpectedly.

"And why is that?" he asked, his tone conversational.

"Because we're getting divorced, Harlan. In case you didn't remember, I already initiated the proceedings."

"Elm, we both know that's unreasonable. Of course you're not going to divorce me."

"Why? Because you'd prefer to be rid of me once and for all, is that it?" she cried, unable to restrain herself. She stood straight and faced him, eyes glittering. "It's over, Harlan, this whole damn farce is finally at an end. You should have done the job properly or not at all."

Harlan waved his hand dismissively, as though that were of little importance. "Elm, please try and reason like an adult. You're so childish. Just think what a divorce would do to my ratings. I have not spent all this time and money on the campaign for you to ruin it."

"You would rather have killed me than see your ratings go down, is that right?"

"Don't be theatrical," he countered. "That's all over now. Water under the bridge. You're back home and we can pick up where we left off. Don't worry, we'll get Annie to tidy all this tomorrow." He made a sweeping gesture. "It'll be different now that I'm back in charge."

"In what way?" she retorted, eyes glittering dangerously, fear replaced by cold, icy anger and a strange sense of detachment. She moved to the mantelpiece and leaned against it. This was the first time, she realized, amazed, that she had viewed her husband objectively. Surely by now he must know his career was at an end, that the show was over. Yet he clung to his image, like a rambling dictator who in the face of defeat still blusters on, fervently justifying every action, however dishonest, harmful, criminal or mad. If it weren't so utterly grotesque, she realized sadly, it would be funny.

He was laughing now, raising his hands and gesturing

with the same mannerisms he used to persuade his public to bend to his will.

"We'll need to have a small, elegant party—just the best people—and prove to everyone that the rumors were false," he was saying, stepping forward, stretching his hand toward her, his face breaking into its most dazzling smile. "No one needs to know that you let me down. You just put everything back where it belongs, like a good girl, and we'll start all over, no problem."

"Harlan," Elm said quietly, caught between alarm and exasperation, "what do I have to do to make you understand that no matter what you say or do, I am never, ever going to live with you again?" She stopped, breathed deeply, then continued. "Harlan, when I said it's over, I wasn't just referring to our marriage," she said, gaining courage from the pathetic figure grinning so confidently at her. Could he possibly be completely unaware that his face was all over the news, or that the party was scrambling to find a new candidate to replace him?

All at once, Elm knew she had to tell him the truth.

"Harlan, you need to listen to me," she said earnestly. "This is important. It's over. You can forget all your dreams of re-election, of going to the White House and becoming president. You're finished, Harlan, sunk. The only place you'll be going to is prison. You can't come back here. They know everything."

"What do you mean?" He took a step forward.

"Oh, don't pretend," she cried. "I'm trying to help you, explain to you that they know you were covering for Brock, taking kickbacks, that you're involved with some dangerous drug lord in Miami, that the waste plant isn't safe and that you used your influence to get it EPA-approved, and—" She stopped, hesitated.

"Yes, go on." He raised his brows.

"That you blackmailed Ashby into trying to poison me," she ended hoarsely. "Harlan, they know everything. The game's up." She watched, half afraid of him, half sorry for him as he stood staring blankly at her, the grin still plastered

on his face, his eyes wide and unblinking. "Harlan, did you
hear what I said?"

"Yes, I heard you." He looked at her, his lips twitching
now as the words finally sank in, echoing eerily through this
vacant room. He'd always felt so good in this room that
emphasized better than all else just who he was and what
he'd become. It was emptied suddenly of its aura, of the
trappings that had polished his image, and he was faced now
with a blank stage that Elm seemed to believe he was no
longer capable of filling. He looked at her. She was lying,
of course. Had to be lying. They were all lying. After all,
he was going to be president one day, surely everyone knew
that?

But as he stared about, he was overwhelmed by a sudden
despondency. The room seemed so different, so dead, so
unreal. The dazzle was suddenly gone, as though the foot-
lights had dulled and the magic been destroyed. For a long,
fearful moment Harlan wavered, wondered, asked himself
the unutterable question: could she be telling the truth?

Of course not. That was impossible. The role he'd been
dreaming of for a lifetime was still within reach. Had to be
within reach.

Wasn't it?

For a split second, doubt overwhelmed him and he stood,
feeling suddenly vulnerable, his hands dropping to his sides.
"What do you think I should do?" he asked in a small
voice, sounding like a bewildered child. "What should I do,
Elm?"

Elm let out a sigh of relief and reached for the portable
phone. Thank God, he'd at last come to his senses. "Do the
right thing and hand yourself over to the feds," she said
quietly. "Maybe if you cooperate, you can still cut a deal.
I'll ring 911 and advise the police. It's the only decent thing
to do, Harlan."

"What on earth are you talking about?" He took a quick
step toward her, brows creased.

"Like I said, I'll call the police."   ·

Before she could react, he took several hasty steps across the room and stood before her, eyes glittering. "You're just saying all this to scare me, aren't you? To try to stop me from dealing with you. You want me to abandon my home, to be free of me. But I won't. I won't go anywhere without you. You're mine, Elm, just as this house is mine, and these pictures and books and paintings and silver are mine." He waved his hand, encompassing the room and then gripped her shoulder. "All this is a part of who I am, of what the electorate expects of me. How can you be so selfish? So utterly fucking selfish?" He gazed into her eyes with real anguish.

"Harlan, won't you please try to understand what I'm telling you?" she begged. "You don't have an electorate, not anymore," she said, her voice belying her fear as he loomed closer and she could smell his aftershave, feel his body heat. She willed herself not to cringe at the strength of his well-worked-out body, not a foot away. She felt for the buttons on the phone, but he closed in on her.

Then, yanking the phone from her hand, he stepped back and in one quick movement drew a gun from his pocket.

"Elm, I don't believe a single word of what you're saying," he hissed, sending the phone hurtling across the room. "My electorate loves me, and unlike you, they're faithful." He brought the gun level with her chest.

"Harlan, please believe me," she whispered, voice hoarse, eyes pinned on the revolver aimed directly at her heart. "The only option you've got is to hand yourself in."

"No way. I won't do anything so absurd." His voice sounded petulant now. "I refuse to go. All these years I've been toyed with and manipulated by you and your father. Well, I've had enough. Now *I'm* the boss. And I have money, you know, lots of money, more money than even you ever dreamed of. Oh, I know it was easy to manipulate me and get me to be your puppet while I didn't have any cash," he continued jeeringly, "but those days are over, baby. Now you'll sing to my tune."

Suddenly he lowered the gun, looked up and blinked, as

if listening to some strange inner voice. "Let's get the fuck out of here. I have a bad feeling." He spun her around, stuck the gun into the small of her back and pushed her toward the open French door. "Come on, move it. Fast."

"Don't, Harlan," she begged, stumbling on the edge of the carpet. "This will only make it worse for you, please listen to me."

"Shut the fuck up and move."

They were almost to the door. Elm looked desperately for something to grab. She was about to scream when she felt Harlan's hand clap over her mouth. It was useless to struggle, dangerous even. He was mad, she realized with sudden clarity, and there was nothing to stop him from pulling the trigger.

He marched her past the fountain, through the garden and out the wrought-iron gate into the side street where a new gleaming red Ferrari stood parked.

"Where did you get that?" she whispered, astonished, as he withdrew his hand slightly.

"Get in and shut up. Don't make a sound or I'll kill you right here." He opened the passenger door.

Trembling, Elm climbed into the low-slung sports car and watched, powerless, as he hastened to the driver's door and climbed in next to her.

"You're crazy, Harlan, please let me go," she begged in a desperate plea as he pocketed the gun and ignited the engine. She gazed frantically about her, but the street was empty.

"Maybe I am crazy, and maybe I'm going to hell, but you're going with me."

"Where are you taking me?" she whispered, hands clasped tightly in her lap as he drove along the street. Even presuming she managed to signal to someone, he'd know what she was doing and might shoot her.

"You'll see. Now, stop worrying," he said, his voice suddenly solicitous once more. "Everything'll be just fine, as long as you cooperate. No need to worry." He patted her knee, flashed her another of his crazy dazzling grins, then turned on the radio. "Ah, I love that," he exclaimed as "Sweet Home Alabama" blasted forth and Harlan sang along with it, his voice jarringly out of tune.

They left the city center with a screech of tires, and Elm's fears increased tenfold when she realized they were headed for I-95. He was planning to take her out of town. She glanced desperately at the car phone. But there was nothing she could do without risking her life. All at once she thought of Johnny, of his strange unease at her coming here to Savannah alone, as though he'd sensed deep down that she was in danger. She closed her eyes tight and suppressed the sudden rush of tears.

If only she'd listened to him, hadn't been so determined to do things her own way.

And now it was too late.

The senator arrived on Elm's doorstep punctually at eight o'clock and rang the doorbell. It echoed through the hall. After several minutes had passed, he frowned and rang again. When that brought no response, his frown deepened and he walked around the side of the house. As he crossed the garden, he noted the gate was open, as were the French doors that led into the living room. He frowned and stepped anxiously inside.

"Elm?"

He stood for a moment, gripped by sudden fear. Glancing at the open boxes, the half-emptied room, he was struck by the silence. He hurried across it and into the hall. Maybe she was still upstairs getting ready. "Elm?" he called up the sweeping staircase. "Honey? Are you there?"

But there was no response. Taking the stairs as fast as he could, the senator rushed to her bedroom and opened the door. But all was quiet, with only the table lamps lit. There was no one there.

George Hathaway stood in the middle of the bedroom, overcome by cold fear. Something was wrong, desperately wrong, and he prayed it was not what he thought.

He walked over to the bed and sank down on it. Oh, God, please not again. He couldn't lose her.

Hand trembling, he reached for the phone and dialed his assistant's cell number in D.C. "Patch me through to the Bureau," he demanded when she came on the line, "I want to speak to the director."

32

"But that's impossible," Agent Conrad Burns insisted, cradling the telephone at his ear while gesturing to his colleague to stand by. "We've been here all evening, watching. Nobody left the house except the maids. No, sir. No, we don't have a full view of the side of the house… I see. I'm sorry, sir. We'll be on to it at once." Conrad slammed the phone down and scowled at Agent Wakefield. "Damn it, Sam, it looks like MacBride got her. Must have gone in through the garden and got her out the same way, with no one the wiser. Fuck. We look like total schmucks."

"I can't believe it," Wakefield muttered.

"Fuck."

"You said it. God knows where he's taken her. I guess he must be in a vehicle. Only way he could have spirited her out of there without anyone realizing. Let's get a chopper on it. Advise the cops in all the precincts. Shit, we don't even know what his damn car looks like. See if they can't spot anything out of the ordinary from the air."

"Pretty hard if we don't know what to tell them to look for."

"Okay, okay, but that's all we've got. And tell them if they do spot him not to get too close or he'll get suspicious. I've no idea what frame of mind this fella's in. He may be dangerous. We'd better bring in a hostage team. Jesus, this would have to be on my watch. Look, call headquarters back while I try to figure out what the hell we're going to do. Fuck, fuck, fuck. Why did this have to happen to me?" Conrad muttered under his breath, pulling out his cell phone as he ran downstairs and across the street to the MacBride mansion where Senator George Hathaway waited for him.

The senator stood ominously at the top of the front steps and Conrad sighed. He was going to have to eat shit. Just his luck.

"Good evening, Senator, I'm real sorry about what's happened."

"Not sorrier than I am, I assure you," the senator bit back. "I was assured my daughter would be safe here, and look what's happened."

"We don't know definitively that her husband kidnapped her," Conrad countered.

"And whom, pray, do you imagine would do such a thing, if not Harlan MacBride?" the senator asked menacingly. "I want her back. Now. Is that understood?"

"Yes, sir. Of course, sir. The problem is, we need to locate MacBride. You wouldn't happen to know what car he'd be driving, would you?"

"He may be driving a red Ferrari. I heard he'd purchased one shortly before last leaving Savannah. That shouldn't be too hard to trace. Now find the son of a bitch and get my daughter."

"Yes, sir, of course, sir. But we also have to be very careful. We don't know the psychological dynamics at work here."

"Cut out the psycho garbage and get to work," George Hathaway demanded.

"Yes, sir. At once, sir."

Conrad turned around and hurried down the steps, glad of the reprieve. People like Hathaway weren't men you messed with. No sir.

"I knew it. I just knew it," Johnny repeated as he laid down the receiver and, face haggard, turned to his mother and Liam.

"What on earth has happened, dear?" Grace asked anxiously, laying her book on the ottoman.

"That was the senator. Elm has disappeared. Hathaway went to Elm's for dinner, but the town house was empty and the French doors to the garden were open. I think it's pretty obvious what happened," he said bitterly. "That bastard sneaked back to Savannah and slipped through the FBI's so-called 'tight mesh.' How could they be so bloody inept?" he said angrily. "I never should have let her go down there by herself. It's my own bloody fault for listening to her—and to you lot," he added, throwing Liam and his mother a furious glance. "All that American nonsense about needing to bring closure to the past and blah, blah, blah. All she needed was to be properly protected from that bastard so that something like this wouldn't happen. Liam, where's the number you wrote down for that FBI agent, the one who was so cocksure and treated us all so damn condescendingly? I've got a couple of things to say to him."

"You think Harlan got in the house and has taken her hostage?" Liam clarified, brow creased.

"Well, what does it seem like to you? That she went off on a bloody picnic? So much for their psychological profiles. What was it that FBI chap said?"

"That Harlan MacBride is the type who gets others to do his dirty work for him."

"Exactly. That he was unlikely to pose a threat on his own. Those were his exact words. That he would, of course, avoid Savannah once he knew the FBI were after him. Well, apparently he doesn't know."

"Not necessarily," Liam said warily. "He might have gotten someone else to lure Elm out of the house. Or maybe she just went down to the store."

"Right before her father arrived?" Johnny sent his brother a withering glance. "Rubbish. I'm sure it was him. Hell, I don't know where your heads were at. Not even her father agreed to try and stop her from packing up her damn house on her own. Here, Liam, give me that number, please."

"Let me speak to them," Liam said, fishing the number out of his breast pocket.

"No. I want to give those idiots a piece of my mind."

"It won't help. We need them on our side. Why don't we concentrate on finding Elm instead of wasting time on re-criminations? The main thing is to get her back."

"God, I can't believe this!" Johnny paced back and forth like a caged leopard, unable to contain his worry, his anger, his own failure to protect her. Why had he let her go to the house when he knew, just knew, that something would go wrong? He should have listened to his gut and made a nuisance of himself, whether she liked it or not.

And where was she right now? In Savannah? At the plantation? They didn't have the first idea where to begin looking.

He sat down suddenly and dropped his head in his hands. This was all too familiar, he realized, overwhelmed by the same panicked fear he'd felt when Marie Ange had been kidnapped. He raised his head and met his mother's eyes as she sat silently opposite, completely aware of what he was going through. Then she stretched out her hand and touched his.

"I know it's little use saying this, darling, but it's going to be all right. Don't get upset. Stay calm and levelheaded. For her sake."

He nodded, squeezed her hand and managed a weak smile.

"I will. Thanks, Mother."

Then he realized Liam was finishing his call.

"Yes, I understand. Call you back in five."

Liam set the receiver down. "I'm afraid you're right, they're pretty sure Harlan's got her and they think he's armed," he said, glancing up at his brother. "A highway cop spotted a red Ferrari heading north on I-95. Apparently Harlan bought one recently. They still don't know his destination."

"Oh well, that's just great, isn't it? Anything else they

want to share with us? Like how they're planning to rescue her?" Johnny's tone was bitter.

"Right now they have to be very careful. They don't want him to suspect that they're on his trail. There's a chopper on the lookout but not too close."

"To hell with that. I'm going."

"You can't. You've no idea how far north they are. We'll have to wait until we get some idea of where they're heading. I'll call them back right now."

For a moment Johnny hesitated. His brother was right. However agonizing, he would have to wait, sit it out until they had a better idea.

But if that bastard harmed a single hair on Elm's head, he'd kill him with his own bare hands.

Just outside Richmond, the car slowed and Elm heard Harlan mutter something about a gas station. She became suddenly conscious of her limbs, stiff from sitting virtually motionless for five long hours, as fearful of the speed Harlan was driving as of him. At one point she'd prayed some cops with a radar gun might pick him up and begin pursuit, that she might be able to make some kind of a sign to them. But clearly, today was not her lucky day.

Another chopper had buzzed overhead and again her hopes had soared. Maybe by now her father had alerted the FBI and they were on the lookout. But then the chopper had disappeared in the opposite direction and her mood slumped once more.

After the first few minutes of driving, Harlan had said little, merely hummed or sung tunelessly along to the country music station that was giving her a throbbing headache. She prayed now that there wouldn't be any news bulletins, anything that might set him off. She still didn't know where they were headed, she realized. Maybe D.C., given their general direction. But she dared not ask, dared not risk angering him, fearful of the unfamiliar, glassy, glittering expression in his eyes, his flushed face and overexcited movements. Oh,

God, she'd escaped from him once; would she be so lucky as to get a second reprieve?

Johnny was never far from her thoughts. She visualized him again and again, warning her not to go to Savannah, that it wasn't safe. Oh, how she wished now that she'd listened to him, not been hell-bent on doing things her own way.

So much for closure. Instead, she'd opened a full can of worms.

"The feds are on his tail," Liam said, covering the mouthpiece with his hand. "The car's still on I-95 and traveling at one hundred and twenty miles an hour. They're betting that MacBride will run out of gas soon and have to stop. He's crossed the Virginia border, so it would seem that he's headed for D.C. They're going to fly a second chopper out from Norfolk for backup. And the New York branch is sending in a team from its Critical Incident Response Group."

"Right." Johnny turned abruptly on his heel, then stopped by the door. "Tell them I'm going with them," he said to his brother. "I think I know where he might be headed. Where do I pick up the chopper?"

Liam spoke on the phone again. "The headquarters is on Broadway between Duane and Worth Streets, south of Canal."

"Fine." Johnny gave a terse nod, then left the penthouse living room, grabbed his jacket and headed toward the elevator. As he pressed the button he felt numb, as though everything that was happening was occurring in a movie—a movie he'd already seen.

But this time, he vowed, remembering Marie Ange, he'd make sure it had a different ending.

Harlan came to a halt before the gas pump in a small strip mall that seemed virtually abandoned except for the station.

There was one other vehicle pumping gas as he took careful stock of the place.

"Don't move," he exhorted Elm, "and don't even think of screaming or crying for help. I have my eye on you." He patted the revolver in his jacket pocket. Then, on second thought, he pulled it out and pointed it straight at her. He relished the feeling of absolute control. "Not one fucking move, understood?"

"I don't believe this." Chad Ward sat in the driver's seat of his old Jeep Cherokee, eyes almost popping out of their sockets. The man in the fancy Italian sports car was waving a gun in the woman's face. His eyes narrowed as he peered excitedly. Even in the sketchy gas-station light, that face was familiar. He thought for a few seconds, then his brain suddenly focussed. MacBride. The congressman from Georgia who was being accused of all sorts of misconduct. He'd seen a report on the nightly news. It had to be him. Hand trembling, Ward felt in the pocket of his jeans for his cell phone, then dialed 911. After speaking with the dispatcher, he hung up, then warily dialed another number.

One minute later he was talking to the newsroom at CNN. "It's MacBride, all right, and I think it's his wife he's holding hostage. My God—" he drew in his breath "—he just turned and saw me staring at him. Oh, Jesus, I'd better get the hell out of here." He quickly gunned the engine, then screeched out of the gas station and back onto the highway, weaving his way into traffic as he talked excitedly on the phone.

The chopper hovered over downtown D.C. and Johnny stared out the window, trying to catch a glimpse of the red Ferrari, which they'd been told was fast approaching on Connecticut Avenue. Thank God his hunch had been right. Elm had mentioned that Lafayette Park was Harlan's favorite place in the capital, and since the park was directly across the street from the White House, that seemed to fit with

Harlan's obsession with the presidency. He'd shared his theory with the feds, and after studying his profile once more, they'd agreed he was probably correct.

Incredibly, the police and the FBI had decided to let Harlan reach his destination. Right now they were clearing out the park, concerned that in his present frame of mind, he might very well begin indiscriminately shooting anyone who got in his way.

Johnny watched angrily as several choppers from different networks swarmed around them, greedy, expectant vultures in the capital's dawn skies. What wouldn't they do for a hot piece of news, he wondered, disgusted, praying that the sight of them would not set Harlan off before they could rescue Elm.

"Hadn't we better get down?" he said into the mouthpiece, pointing toward the ground.

"In a minute, can't rush it," the agent behind him muttered. "The guy's clearly a psychopath. We can't make any moves until they've finished cordoning off the park."

"Yeah," the other agent agreed. "Thank God the president's out of town. Be careful, Jim," he cautioned the pilot, "don't get too close to the restricted area."

"It's a go for Lafayette," the other agent signaled. "We'll need authorization to land on Pennsylvania Avenue."

"No," Senator Hathaway shouted into the phone, his eyes glued to the television. "Don't let them take any action. Let Harlan reach his destination. Remember, he's armed and that's my daughter in there. We can't risk it." He rubbed a hand over his tired eyes. It was nearly 8:00 a.m. and he hadn't slept a wink. Thank God his old friend Howard Maclean's plane had been available and he'd been able to fly into D.C. as soon as they'd determined it was Harlan's probable destination. He concentrated on what the man was saying.

"No, sir. But that will require blocking off half the streets around the White House."

"I don't give a damn what it takes. The president will

back me up on this. Just do it. You've made enough mistakes as it is. Let's try to get this right, shall we?" he growled, turning to Frances, who'd flown up with him. He appreciated the fact that Grace and Liam Graney had rushed to the scene as well and were standing next to him in one of the suites of the distinguished Hay-Adams hotel, conveniently situated on Lafayette Square. "She'll be all right," he muttered, as though trying to convince himself, "she'll be all right."

"Of course she will," Frances replied with a confidence she was far from feeling, then gave a quick glance at Grace Graney, who squeezed her arm reassuringly.

"Liam, dear, everyone's exhausted. Get some of that coffee over there, will you?" Grace sent an imploring look at her son and indicated the silver tray that the hotel staff had provided. Liam, standing rigid in front of the television next to the senator, nodded absently.

"Please, don't worry about me," Frances murmured, throwing Grace an anxious smile. "I couldn't swallow a drop, I'm afraid."

"Johnny was right," Liam muttered almost to himself, "we should have listened to him. She shouldn't have gone there on her own."

"I'm as much to blame as anyone," the senator replied bitterly, eyes turned up toward the ceiling. Then, leaning on the mantel of the ornamental fireplace, he continued, "I thought the feds would manage to do their job right. I was wrong," he said, throwing a dark look at Charlie Malone, the director of the FBI, who was hovering on the phone at the desk on the other side of the enormous suite's living room. "Any news?" he asked as the man hung up.

"We're organizing the evacuation of the park right now. We're fortunate that the early hour means there aren't a lot of tourists yet, but there were some protesters staging a sit-in around one of the statues. By the time MacBride reaches the park—and we expect that's imminent—it'll be surrounded. Two hundred men have already been deployed."

"I don't want any smart-ass mistakes," the senator threw harshly. "Make sure my daughter is safe."

"Yes, sir. We're taking every possible measure."

"Make sure you do. Remember, I chair the committee that determines your damn budget." There was a knock at the door and the senator looked toward it. "Ah, Sam, thanks for coming." The senator reached out and shook hands with the president's chief of staff, who had just walked in.

"Look." Liam pointed at the screen once more and they gazed transfixed as the camera zoomed in on the red Ferrari at the park entrance on Fifteenth and H.

"This is it," said Malone.

An anticipatory hush came over the room as they stared at the slowing vehicle.

"Oh, my God," the senator whispered, blanching. "My baby, my daughter is in that car," he said, almost to himself, "at the mercy of a maniac I helped create."

Frances gripped his arm and closed her eyes. A film of cold sweat covered her brow. She felt short of breath. If only she'd insisted on helping Elm clear out the house, none of this would be happening.

Grace sat down with a bang on the nearest armchair and clutched the arm for dear life, unable to bear the thought of her son going through another loss.

Liam sent up a silent prayer for his brother and Elm's safety and braced himself.

33

Harlan opened the door and pointed the gun at Elm. Slowly she got out of the car, joints aching from the long, terrified hours of sitting and barely changing her position. Her numb legs began to tingle now as her feet touched the pavement.

"Remember, just do as I say and everything will be fine," Harlan muttered, eyes flitting everywhere. "Elm?"

"Yes?" she whispered hoarsely.

"Come on. I want to show you something."

Elm advanced slowly with Harlan close behind her, the pistol hovering at her back, and moved into the park, looking desperately about her. The protestors and the early morning visitors were being herded down the opposite path. A fat woman with a small child clinging to her hand screamed hysterically as a man in a suit—she was sure it must be an FBI agent—hurried her along. Elm swallowed, determined to stay calm as a sudden ray of hope flickered and she felt absolutely certain that Johnny was somewhere close by. She could sense it, knew that she wasn't dreaming, that in all this craziness she intuited his presence nearby.

Then Harlan shoved her in the back with the gun and she stepped mechanically forward, walking toward the statue of Andrew Jackson in the center of the now-empty gardens. Except for some remnants of fast food hastily discarded on a bench and a ragged coat that probably belonged to some homeless inhabitant of the place, there was nothing to indicate that moments earlier the park had held any life.

Elm moved toward the large base of the statue, frightened now of what Harlan might suddenly decide to do to her. In his unbalanced state, he barely resembled the man she'd once known. She glanced at him, then at the White House, shrouded in the misty early morning haze just across Pennsylvania Avenue, and trembled. What would happen when the shoe finally dropped, when he realized that the future he'd dreamed of so consistently, so determinedly, was not to be?

They stood now in the shadow of the equestrian statue. Elm became aware that she was cold, although it was summer. She noted dew on the grass, a sparrow hopping along a nearby path, and shuddered, daring to peek at Harlan, standing at her side. He was in another world, transfixed, staring at the White House. For a moment she thought he might have slackened his grip on the pistol, but it still nudged her. As she peered at him warily, Elm suddenly recalled a piece of Washington trivia that now seemed chillingly significant: this was the only statue in D.C. that didn't face the White House. She shivered once more, tried desperately to control the dizziness that was slowly creeping up on her, and stood perfectly still, trying to distinguish movements around the park's perimeter. The FBI must be here somewhere, she reasoned, trying not to panic. The park was unusually empty, even for this early hour.

"There it is, Elm. Just look at it," Harlan said, suddenly waving the gun at the mansion across the street. "It's just waiting for us. I knew one day we'd make it, I always told you so."

"Yes," she answered, hands trembling, "yes, you did."

"I'm the right man for the job. You know that, Elm, don't you?"

"Yes, I know that," she answered, hearing a buzz of choppers overhead and praying that something would break.

"You know, don't you, that everything I've been trying

to achieve makes total sense?'' His voice turned plaintive, begging for her approval.

"Yes, it all makes sense," she repeated, suddenly spying a sharpshooter behind the trees to her right. Oh, my God. There were several of them, she realized now, trying to stay calm. Were they going to take him out? And there were more up on the roof of the White House. She could distinguish them clearly now. Surely Harlan must see them? But he seemed utterly oblivious to the snipers over on the roof of the presidential mansion, his thoughts far away in a world of his own. Elm knew a moment's desperation. She could tell that their rifles were aimed directly at them. Was it about to end right here, in the supposed Peace Park?

Finally he was back, Harlan realized, relieved, the haze that had formed in front of his eyes over the last few hours slowly fading. He was home. He had finally reached his long-sought-after destination. This was the spot he loved best in all the world, he reflected longingly. He took a loving look at the White House and sighed. He would never tire of this sight, never. Nothing else mattered but this, his true destiny, the place from where finally he would exert his power and be heard, where he would lead the nation and recover some of its lost glory, where all his dreams would at last be realized.

Then all at once he raised his hand, rubbed his eyes and hesitated. He stared for a moment at the gun he was holding, and a slow film of realization descended upon him. He looked at Elm standing rigidly still by his side, her eyes trained on the White House. Then his eyes swooped around the empty park and he frowned. The park was never empty. Something was different, spooky, as though the park were waiting for something to happen. Where were the demonstrators who usually stood in the street in front of the House itself? His brow creased and he shook his head, staring about uncomprehending, and listened. All he could hear was the rumble of a chopper, maybe two, overhead. He paid sudden attention to them. Could it be the president returning from

Camp David, as he would one day? he wondered. A glorious smile ignited his features as he pictured himself climbing out of the chopper onto the South Lawn, snapping his fingers at his dogs—oh yes, he'd definitely acquire a couple of dogs for his presidency—and Elm walking beside him, looking cool and beautiful as he waved to an enchanted crowd before heading to the Rose Garden, followed by his adoring staff, to give a significant speech.

Then, as fast as the image had materialized, it faded and Harlan stared blankly down at his hand again, at the gun it carried. He blinked, suddenly conscious of his rumpled clothes, of Elm's eyes filled with doubt and fear.

Then all at once the past few days flashed before him and he stared straight into her eyes, mesmerized, trying to make sense of all the facts, to grasp what was happening. Elm had been going to die, but she hadn't, and he'd gone back to Savannah and seen her dismantling the house. That wasn't fair. She hadn't the right to do that. He felt a burst of anger as suddenly the Mogachee plant materialized before him, those headlines he'd seen yesterday, accusing him of all sorts of terrible untrue things that none of the reporters understood. Didn't they know that he'd had to do them? That otherwise, nothing would remain the same, that he needed to—

All at once Harlan's lip began to tremble, his legs shook, and he experienced a wave of complete exhaustion. A rush of tears that he was unable to stem choked him—hot, heavy tears that wouldn't stop even though he tried desperately to wipe them off his cheeks.

What was happening? Why didn't anyone understand what he was doing for the nation? Hell, what was stopping him from moving toward the White House, standing there before him invitingly, walking up the steps and being welcomed? Why was he still here standing under a statue in the park, pointing a gun at—

Elm.

He blinked again, looking straight at her, reading the wariness in her eyes, all the fear and hesitation. He sent the gun a bewildered glance, tried to focus again on the White House standing majestically before him, but failed, the events of the past few months flashing before him like a fast-forward movie.

Harlan swallowed. Despair gripped him, and he wished desperately that he'd stashed some coke in his pocket. That would help him think clearly. He began to mutter, took a few steps, first left, then right, then stopped and stared again and shook his head. "No," he whispered as the truth dawned. "No, this can't be." The dream couldn't escape him, not now, not after all he'd done, all he'd strived for.

Then suddenly he stood stock still and knew it was too late. The dream would never come true. It was over.

All at once the mist cleared, the haze lifted and he became acutely aware of all that was occurring around him. There were sharpshooters on the roof of the White House with their rifles aimed at him. He picked up quick, stealthy movements among the trees and realized the park was cordoned off.

So they knew. And it was over.

The realization came as something matter-of-fact, an unbidden consequence. His mind worked quickly. He had two choices. Either he could take Elm hostage again and threaten them with shooting her, perhaps cut a deal with the feds. Or...

Then another image flashed. Harlan saw himself in all his glory. Right now he was probably the center of the nation's attention. It was just a pity that it was so early. Still, every TV network in the country was likely featuring him, here in Lafayette Park, waiting in suspense for what he would do, how he would act. His dream might be over, but at least he could go out with a bang. They'd remember him. Oh, yes, they'd remember him all right. Why, every time his name was mentioned, they'd recall all he'd done, realize their terrible mistake, regret their actions, see what they'd driven him to and how fucking stupid and ignorant they'd all been to underestimate him. They'd think of him and say, "If only MacBride were here to resolve matters, he was our man...."

He shifted his arm.

"No!" Elm screamed as in one swift movement Harlan raised the gun. Taking one last longing look at the object of his dreams, he placed the muzzle to his temple and knew a moment of delirious triumph.

The last thing he heard as he collapsed into Elm's arms at the foot of the statue was her shriek. And in that instant he knew he was right. They were already regretting their mistake.

"Oh, my God." Elm held Harlan in her trembling arms, staring at the gaping wound, at Harlan's face, surprisingly serene despite the horror and the blood gushing onto it and her cream dress. "Oh, my God," she whispered over and over like a mantra, cradling him in her arms, overwhelmed by dismay, relief, horror, guilt as she gazed down at the remains of the man whose life she'd shared for so many years, who had betrayed her in every possible way, yet who'd been her husband.

Somewhere in the distance she heard shouts, sensed people approaching. But all she could do was go on rocking him.

It was several seconds before she realized someone was saying her name. She turned then, looked up and stared at the crowd surrounding her—FBI agents, her father and Aunt Frances, Grace and Liam impatiently breaking the security cordon and hurrying toward her.

Then all at once, she saw Johnny slightly removed from the crowd, watching her intently, and instantly the fog cleared. She looked straight at him, then down at the limp body lying in her arms. She had to let it go, she realized, had to let go of the past and move toward the future.

The crowd around her remained strangely silent as slowly she lowered Harlan's body to the ground. Gazing down at him one last time, she gently closed his eyes. Then someone at her elbow helped her rise.

She stood up and took a deep breath. It was over. Over, once and for all. She raised her eyes and she reached out to Johnny, still standing apart, waiting for her to make the move, not pressing or pushing her, not overwhelming her with his wishes and wants and needs, just waiting, oblivious of the crowd, of everything but her. And suddenly she ran toward him, the crowd parting as she hurled herself into his arms, and finally felt them close about her.

"It's okay, darling, it's all over," Johnny muttered, quelling his emotions as at last her head finally rested on his shoulder and she let go. He gripped her close, determined never to let her know danger ever again, now that she'd made her choice, finally come to him of her own free will. He felt her body quiver as she let out a long, pent-up sigh.

Elm could hear the others, her father and Liam and Grace and Aunt Frances and the police and the FBI, all hovering in the background, waiting expectantly for her to react. But there was nothing she could do about that, nothing she was prepared to do about it. For she knew that all she wanted—would ever want, now and forever—was to stay cocooned in Johnny's embrace and know, truly know, that the past was behind her and the rest of her life was about to begin.

Epilogue

One year later

"Isn't that typical of Gio," Elm exclaimed, laying down the phone. "How anyone can imagine I'd be able to prepare for an art exhibition as well as run this congressional office is beyond me."

"Maybe you'll get around to it sometime," Meredith answered listlessly from the chair on the opposite side of the large desk.

"Maybe. Once I find a candidate to replace me, that is. Mer, won't you even consider it?" Elm asked for the umpteenth time, her voice softening as she looked worriedly at her friend. Meredith had become so thin and worn down since Tom's death. He'd drowned just a few months after Harlan had shot himself, going down with his beloved boat in a freak squall off the Georgia coast. God, she wished there was more she could do to help. But Meredith had held herself together, never letting her grief overtake her, all the while carrying a massive case load at the firm, and making sure she didn't miss a single one of her kids' ball games. Sometimes Elm worried it was all a show, that Mer was running so hard simply because she was afraid to stand still and realize Tom was gone.

"Hello, ladies." Johnny peered around the door, then walked over to kiss his wife firmly on the lips. "You feeling all right, gorgeous?" he asked, a frown creasing his brow.

"Darling, pregnancy is not an illness," Elm pointed out, returning his kiss.

"I'm aware of that. Still, can't be too careful. I had that problem with Lady Be Good a few months ago and it makes me nervous to think—"

"Johnny, I am not a horse," Elm explained patiently as he sat down next to Meredith and squeezed her arm lightly.

"She'll be fine," Meredith agreed, sending her friend a fond smile. "I have to be off, guys. I volunteered to take over a case one of the junior partners couldn't handle, and I'm up to my eyeballs in briefs. Still, for what it's worth, I still think your best bet would be to approach Earl Stacey. He's a candidate that everyone can agree on—plus he's straight as the proverbial arrow."

"That's what my father said," Elm mused, tapping her pen. "Do you think he's up to running?"

"If your father says so, then he must be. The senator knows what he's talking about when it comes to politics. If you and your father throw your support behind Stacey, he'll be a shoo-in."

"I guess you're right. I'll give him a call later today. After everything the constituents have been through in the last couple of years, I owe it to them to leave the district in good hands."

"Does this mean, my lady, that you've finally seen the light and decided that our child will be born at Graney, as is its due?"

"Of course." Elm smiled at Johnny tenderly. "But don't flatter yourself that it was you who persuaded me."

"Why on earth would I think anything as pretentious as that?" he asked, quirking a brow and grinning.

"Because it was Nicky who called and pleaded with me."

"Did he really? Good chap. I must remember to buy him that Vespa he's been harping on about for almost a year. I don't suppose that was part of your conversation?"

"Absolutely not."

"Oh well, just a thought. Must have been having a fit of altruism, I suppose. No accounting for kids, is there?" he said, rising with Meredith as she prepared to leave.

"None at all," Meredith answered, dropping a light kiss on his cheek. "I'll see you two later at the oyster roast."

"That poor girl's not getting any better," Johnny remarked after Meredith had silently closed the office door behind her.

"I know. I'm very worried."

"Give it time. At this point, I'm sure she's still railing against the unfairness of it all. God knows I did. With luck, in a year or so she'll feel better and be able to look toward the future."

"I sure hope so," Elm said with a sigh.

"And now to us, young lady. How long is it going to be before you can hand things over to this Earl Stacey? Brilliant idea, by the way, that should be implemented at once. Can't the governor appoint him to fill your seat or something?"

"I'm impressed," Elm noted admiringly. "Looks like someone's been paying more attention to American politics than I realized."

"Well, with a congresswoman for a wife, I thought I'd better hit the books," he observed wryly.

The title still surprised her. It was amazing to realize how radically her life had changed. On that dark day when she'd learned of Harlan's infidelity, through the yet darker days of illness and upheaval that followed, she'd never dared to dream life could be so wonderful as it was now. After Harlan's death, the party had urged her to take his place on the ballot. She'd done so out of a sense of loyalty to the people her husband had betrayed, never expecting that she'd actually win. And yet on election night, the electorate had turned out in record numbers to elect her.

Now, just more than a year later, she could say with pride that she'd been able to make a difference. She'd chaired a commission that had looked into the improprieties at the Mogachee plant, and had helped author strict new legislation to fix the system that had permitted such egregious environmental oversights. She'd discovered in herself the same passionate political fire that burned in her father—a new bond that they both treasured, and one that had helped immeasurably in bridging the rift wrought by Harlan.

Still, she reflected, leaning across the desk and bringing Johnny's hand to rest on the slight swell of her belly. Amazing as her new life was, it paled before the complete joy she'd found with her husband, and this miracle they'd made between them. It seemed so precious and incredible that after all she'd been through trying to have a baby, this one had come along quite naturally and so unexpectedly. Her work in D.C. was important, of course. But nothing, she vowed, would come before caring for this child and this incredible man.

"I've already put in a call to the governor," she said reassuringly. "We're going to present the idea to the party, although I suspect it'll take a couple of months to get it all sorted out."

"All right," Johnny sighed, "but no longer. By the way, are you aware that Aunt Fran and Mother are already quibbling about which christening dress the baby will wear, the Hathaway or the Graney?"

"Oh, Lord. You're so wonderful to deal with all that for me. I haven't had time to think about anything except keeping this office running."

"And you've done an incredible job," he said tenderly.

"Well, the party leadership hasn't always been thrilled with some of my positions," she laughed. "I think they expected someone more malleable. Still, it's been fun. Daddy says I'm a born politician," she teased. "He wants me to set my sights higher, maybe go after his seat so he can retire."

"I'd rather not get into that," Johnny said darkly, stroking her hand. "His political ambitions for you are the only area we thoroughly disagree upon."

"Don't worry. My only ambition for the future is to be your loving wife and raise a passel of little Graneys and be a great viscountess. That is, for now," she added mischievously.

"What about your painting?" he queried.

"Well, that too, of course." She laughed.

"Well, Madam Congresswoman, now all that's been decided, I vote we go out to lunch, because I'm famished. They're holding our usual table for us at Mrs. Wilkes's, and I want to get there before they run out of those boarding-house biscuits."

Elm rose carefully, secretly amused by her aristocratic husband's newfound love of down-home Southern cooking. The other day, he'd worn an almost comical look of dismay when she'd reminded him that grits, collard greens, corn bread and barbecue ribs were likely too exotic for your average Irish grocery store.

Johnny took her arm and grinned. "Come on, then. Let's get away before your efficient staff discovers some other meeting you need to attend." He paused a moment, gripping her shoulders, suddenly serious. "You don't think you'll get bored just being a mother and a viscountess after all this excitement?" he asked, looking down into her eyes.

"How could I? Remember, I've been waiting for this since I was fifteen."

"Right, I'd forgotten the basketball court episode. You have a point."

She looked up at him and he dropped a light kiss on her lips that lingered and suddenly developed into a much deeper one as he took her in his arms and held her tight.

Two minutes later, Marcy, now Elm's new secretary, opened the door and was most surprised to see Congresswoman Hathaway being held in a tight embrace. For a moment, she didn't recognize Johnny and her worst fears were realized. Then to her relief, she realized that all that business had gone out with the past administration, and quietly closed the door.

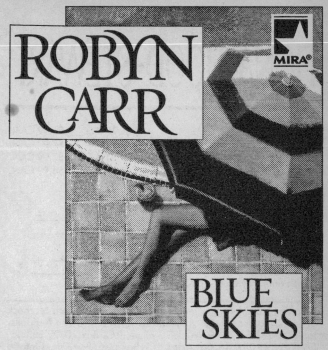

ROBYN CARR

MIRA®

BLUE SKIES

Nikki Burgess, Dixie McPherson and Carlisle Bartlett are three women who could seriously use a break. A fresh start. A shot at success and a chance to shine. Maybe a little romance—the kind that sticks. And some adventure wouldn't hurt.

So when they're presented with the challenge of joining a team starting a new airline in Las Vegas, they don't hesitate. With nothing to lose and everything to gain, these three friends are going in search of their own blue skies.

"Robyn Carr writes books that touch the heart and the funny bone."
—*New York Times* bestselling author
Debbie Macomber

Available in May 2004 wherever paperbacks are sold.

FIONA HOOD-STEWART

66833	THE STOLEN YEARS	___ $5.99 U.S.	___ $6.99 CAN.
66728	SILENT WISHES	___ $6.50 U.S.	___ $7.99 CAN.
66670	THE LOST DREAMS	___ $6.50 U.S.	___ $7.99 CAN.
66606	THE JOURNEY HOME	___ $5.99 U.S.	___ $6.99 CAN.

(limited quantities available)

TOTAL AMOUNT $_____
POSTAGE & HANDLING $_____
($1.00 for one book; 50¢ for each additional)
APPLICABLE TAXES* $_____
<u>TOTAL PAYABLE</u> $_____
(check or money order—please do not send cash)

To order, complete this form and send it, along with a check or money order for the total above, payable to MIRA Books, to: **In the U.S.:** 3010 Walden Avenue, P.O. Box 9077, Buffalo, NY 14269-9077; **In Canada:** P.O. Box 636, Fort Erie, Ontario L2A 5X3.

Name:_____
Address:_____ City:_____
State/Prov.:_____ Zip/Postal Code:_____
Account Number (if applicable):_____
075 CSAS

*New York residents remit applicable sales taxes.
Canadian residents remit applicable GST and provincial taxes.

MIRA®